Hence her care to see that Helen looked especially pretty

THE BISHOP OF COTTONTOWN

A STORY OF THE SOUTHERN COTTON MILLS

—— BY ——

JOHN TROTWOOD MOORE

AUTHOR OF
"A SUMMER HYMNAL," "OLE MISTIS,"
"SONGS AND STORIES FROM TENNESSEE," ETC.

ILLUSTRATED BY THE KINNEYS

"And each in his separate star,
Shall paint the thing as he sees it
For the God of Things As They Are."

Kipling

PHILADELPHIA
THE JOHN C. WINSTON COMPANY

IN MEMORY OF MY MOTHER,

EMILY BILLINGSLEA MOORE,

WHO DIED

DECEMBER 14TH, 1903,

THE FAITH OF THIS BOOK BEING HERS.

CONTENTS

CONTENTS

PART FIFTH — THE LOOM.

CONTENTS

3

PART FIRST — THE BLOOM

THE COTTON BLOSSOM

THE cotton blossom is the only flower that is born in the shuttle of a sunbeam and dies in a loom.

It is the most beautiful flower that grows, and needs only to become rare to be priceless — only to die to be idealized.

For the world worships that which it nopes to attain, and our ideals are those things just out of our reach.

Satiety has ten points and possession is nine of them.

If, in early August, the delicately green leaves of this most aristocratic of all plants, instead of covering acres of Southland shimmering under a throbbing sun, peeped daintily out, from among the well-kept beds of some noble garden, men would flock to see that plant, which, of all plants, looks most like a miniature tree.

A stout-hearted plant,— a tree, dwarfed, but losing not its dignity.

Then, one morning, with the earliest sunrise, and born of it, there emerges from the scalloped sea-shell of the bough an exquisite, pendulous, cream-white blossom, clasping in its center a golden yellow star, pinked with dawn points of light, and, setting high up under its sky of milk-white petals flanked with yellow stars, it seems to the little nestling field-wrens born beneath it to be the miniature arch of daybreak, ere the great eye of the morning star closes.

Later, when the sun rises and the sky above grows pink and purple, it, too, changes its color from pink to purple, copying the sky from zone to zone, from blue to deeper blue, until, at late evening the young nestlings may look up and say, in their bird language: " It is twilight."

What other flower among them can thus copy Nature, the great master?

Under every sky is a sphere, and under this sky picture, when night falls and closes it, a sphere is born. And in that sphere is all of earth.

Its oils and its minerals are there, and one day, becoming too full of richness, it bursts, and throws open a five-roomed granary, stored with richer fabric than ever came from the shuttles of Fez and holding globes of oil such as the olives of Hebron dreamed not of.

And in that fabric is the world clothed.

Oh, little loom of the cotton-plant, poet that can show us the sky, painter that paints it, artisan that reaches out, and, from the skein of a sunbeam, the loom of the air and the white of its own soul, weaves the cloth that clothes the world!

From dawn and darkness building a loom. From sunlight and shadow weaving threads of such fineness that the spider's were ropes of sand and the hoar frost's but clumsy icicles.

Weaving — weaving — weaving them. And the delicately patterned tapestry of ever-changing clouds forming patterns of a fabric, white as the snow of the centuries, determined that since it has to make the garments of men, it will make them unsullied.

Oh, little plant, poet, painter, master-artisan!

It is true to Nature to the last. The summer wanes and the winter comes, and when the cotton sphere bursts, 'tis a ball of snow, but a dazzling white, spidery snow, which warms and does not chill, brings comfort and not care, wealth and the rich warm blood, and not the pinches of poverty.

There are those who cannot hear God's voice unless He speaks to them in the thunders of Sinai, nor see Him unless He flares before them in the bonfires of a burning bush. They grumble because His Messenger came to a tribe in the hill countries of Long Ago. They wish to see the miracle of the dead arising. They see not the miracle of life around them. Death from Life is more strange to them than life from death.

'Tis the silent voice that speaks the loudest. Did Sinai speak louder than this? Hear it:

" I am a bloom, and yet I reflect the sky from the morning's star to the midnight's. I am a flower, yet I show you the heaven from the dawn of its birth to the twilight of its death. I am a boll, and yet a miniature earth stored with silks and satins, oils of the olives, minerals of all lands. And when I am ripe I throw open my five-roomed granary, each fitted to the finger and thumb of the human hand, with a depth between, equalled only by the palm."

O voice of the cotton-plant, do we need to go to oracles or listen for a diviner voice than yours when thus you tell us: Pluck?

PART SECOND — THE BOLL

CHAPTER I

COTTON

THE frost had touched the gums and maples in the Tennessee Valley, and the wood, which lined every hill and mountain side, looked like huge flaming bouquets — large ones, where the thicker wood clustered high on the side of Sand Mountain and stood out in crimson, gold and yellow against the sky,— small ones, where they clustered around the foot hills.

Nature is nothing if not sentimental. She will make bouquets if none be made for her; or, mayhap, she wishes her children to be, and so makes them bouquets herself.

There was that crispness in the air which puts one to wondering if, after all, autumn is not the finest time of the year.

It had been a prosperous year in the Tennessee Valley — that year of 1874. And it had brought a double prosperity, in that, under the leadership of George S. Houston, the white men of the state, after a desperate struggle, had thrown off the political yoke of the negro and the carpetbagger, and once more the Saxon ruled in the land of his birth.

Then was taken a full, long, wholesome, air-filling Anglo-Saxon breath, from the Tennessee Valley to the Gulf. There was a quickening of pulses that had faltered, and heart-beats that had fluttered, dumb and discouraged, now rattled like kettle-drums, to the fight of life.

It meant change — redemption — prosperity. And more: that the white blood which had made Alabama, need not now leave her for a home elsewhere.

It was a year glorious, and to be remembered. One which marks an epoch. One wherein there is an end of the old and a beginning of the new.

The cotton — the second picking — still whitened thousands of acres. There were not hands enough to pick it. The negroes, demoralized for a half score of years by the brief splendor of elevation, and backed, at first, by Federal bayonets and afterwards by sheer force of their own number in elections, had been correspondingly demoralized and shiftless. True to their instinct then, as now, they worked only so long as they needed money. If one day's cotton picking fed a negro for five, he rested the five.

The negro race does not live to lay up for a rainy day.

And so the cotton being neglected, its lengthened and frowseled locks hung from wide open bolls like the locks of a tawdry woman in early morning.

No one wanted it — that is, wanted it bad enough to pick it. For cotton was cheap that fall — very cheap — and picking cotton is a back-bending business. Therefore it hung its frowsy locks from the boll.

And nothing makes so much for frowsiness in the cotton plant, and in woman, as to know they are not wanted.

The gin-houses were yet full, tho' the gin had been

running day and night. That which poured, like pulverized snow, from the mouth of the flues into the pickroom — where the cotton fell before being pressed into bales — scarcely had time to be tramped down and packed off in baskets to the tall, mast-like screws which pressed the bales and bound them with ties, ere the seed cotton came pouring in again from wagon bed and basket.

The gin hummed and sawed and sang and creaked, but it could not devour the seed cotton fast enough from the piles of the incoming fleece.

Those grew lighter and larger all the time.

The eight Tennessee sugar-mules, big and sinewy, hitched to the lever underneath the gin-house at The Gaffs, sweated until they sprinkled in one continual shower the path which they trod around the pivot-beam from morning until night.

Around — around — forever around.

For the levers turned the pivot-beam, and the pivot-beam turned the big shaft-wheel which turned the gin-wheel, and the gin had to go or it seemed as if the valley would be smothered in cotton.

Picked once, the fields still looked like a snowfall in November, if such a thing were possible in a land which scarcely felt a dozen snowfalls in as many years.

Dust! There is no dust like that which comes from a gin-house. It may be tasted in the air. All other dust is gravel compared to the penetrating fineness of that diabolical, burning blight which flies out of the lint, from the thousand teeth of the gin-saws, as diamond dust flies from the file.

It is all penetrating, consumptive-breeding, sickening, stifling, suffocating. It is hot and has a metallic flavor; and it flies from the hot steel teeth of the saws, as pestilence from the hot breath of the swamps.

It is linty, furry, tickling, smothering, searing.

It makes one wonder why, in picturing hell, no priest ever thought of filling it with cotton-gin dust instead of fire.

And it clings there from the Lint to the Loom.

Small wonder that the poor little white slaves, taking up their serfdom at the loom where the negro left off at the lint, die like pigs in a cotton-seed pen.

There was cotton everywhere — in the fields, unpicked; in the gin-houses, unginned. That in the fields would be plowed under next spring, presenting the strange anomaly of plowing under one crop to raise another of the same kind. But it has been done many times in the fertile Valley of the Tennessee.

There is that in the Saxon race that makes it discontented, even with success.

There was cotton everywhere; it lay piled up around the gin-houses and screws and negro-cabins and under the sheds and even under the trees. All of it, which was exposed to the weather, was in bales, weighing each a fourth of a ton and with bulging white spots in their bellies where the coarse cotton baling failed to cover their nakedness.

It was cotton — cotton — cotton. Seed,— ginned,— lint,— baled,— cotton.

The Gaffs was a fine estate of five thousand acres which had been handed down for several generations.

The old home sat in a grove of hickory, oak and elm
trees, on a gentle slope. Ancient sentinels, and they
were there when the first Travis came from North Carolina to the Tennessee Valley and built his first double-
log cabin under the shelter of their arms.

From the porch of The Gaffs,— as the old home was
called — the Tennessee River could be seen two miles
away, its brave swift channel glittering like the flash of
a silver arrow in the dark green wood which bordered it.

Back of the house the mountain ridge rolled; not high
enough to be awful and unapproachable, nor so low as
to breed contempt from a too great familiarity. Not
grand, but the kind one loves to wander over.

CHAPTER II

STRENGTH was written in the face of Richard Travis — the owner of The Gaffs — intellectual, physical, passion-strength, strength of purpose and of doing. Strength, but not moral strength; and hence lacking all of being all-conquering.

He had that kind of strength which made others think as he thought, and do as he would have them do. He saw things clearly, strongly, quickly. His assurance made all things sure. He knew things and was proud of it. He knew himself and other men. And best of all, as he thought, he knew women.

Richard Travis was secretary and treasurer of the Acme Cotton Mills.

To-night he was alone in the old-fashioned but elegant dining-room of the Gaffs. The big log fire of ash and hickory was pleasant, and the blaze, falling in sombre color on the old mahogany side-board which sat opposite the fireplace, on the double ash floor, polished and shining, added a deeper and richer hue to it. From the toes of the dragon on which it rested, to the beak of the hand-carved eagle, spreading his wings over the shield beneath him, carved in the solid mahogany and surrounded by thirteen stars, all was elegance and aristocracy. Even the bold staring eyes of the eagle seemed

18

proud of the age of the sideboard, for had it not been
built when the stars numbered but thirteen? And was
not the eagle rampant then?

The big brass andirons were mounted with the
bronzed heads of wood-nymphs, and these looked saucily
up at the eagle. The three-cornered cupboard, in one
corner of the room, was of cherry, with small diamond-
shaped windows in front, showing within rare old sets
of china and cut glass. The handsome square dining
table matched the side-board, only its dragon feet were
larger and stronger, as if intended to stand up under
more weight, at times.

Everything was ancient and had a pedigree. Even
the Llewellyn setter was old, for he was grizzled around
the muzzle and had deep-set, lusterless eyes, from which
the firelight, as if afraid of their very uncanniness,
darted out as soon as it entered. And he carried his
head to one side when he walked, as old and deaf dogs do.

He lay on a rug before the fire. He had won this
license, for opposite his name on the kennel books were
more field-trials won than by any other dog in Alabama.
And now he dozed and dreamed of them again, with
many twitchings of feet, and cocked, quivering ears,
and rigid tail, as if once more frozen to the covey in
the tall sedge-grass of the old field, with the smell of
frost-bitten Lespedeza, wet with dew, beneath his feet.

Travis stooped and petted the old dog. It was the
one thing of his household he loved most.

"Man or dog — 'tis all the same," he mused as he
watched the dreaming dog —" it is old age's privilege
to dream of what has been done — it is youth's to do."

He stretched himself in his big mahogany chair and glanced down his muscular limbs, and drew his arms together with a snap of quick strength.

Everything at The Gaffs was an open diary of the master's life. It is so in all homes — that which we gather around us, from our books to our bed-clothes, is what we are.

And so the setter on the rug meant that Richard Travis was the best wing-shot in the Tennessee Valley, and that his kennel of Gladstone setters had won more field trials than any other kennel in the South. No man has really hunted who has never shot quail in Alabama over a well-broken setter. All other hunting is butchery compared to the scientific sweetness of this sport.

There was a goodnight, martial, daring crow, ringing from the Hoss-apple tree at the dining-room window. Travis smiled and called out:

"Lights waked you up, eh, Dick? You're a gay Lothario — go back to sleep."

Richard Travis had the original stock — the Irish Greys — which his doughty old grandsire, General Jeremiah Travis, developed to championship honors, and in a memorable main with his friend, General Andrew Jackson, ten years after the New Orleans campaign, he had cleared up the Tennesseans, cock and pocket. It was a big main in which Tennessee, Georgia and Alabama were pitted against each other, and in which the Travis cocks of the Emerald Isle strain, as Old Hickory expressed it, "stood the steel like a stuck she-b'ar, fightin' for her cubs."

General Travis had been an expert at heeling a cock;

and it is said that his skill on that occasion was worth more than the blood of his Greys; for by a peculiar turn of the gaffs,— so slight as to escape the notice of any but an expert — his champion cock had struck the blow which ended the battle. With the money won, he had added four thousand acres to his estate, and afterwards called it The Gaffs.

And a strong, brave man had been General Jeremiah Travis,— pioneer, Indian fighter, Colonel in the Creek war and at New Orleans, and a General in the war with Mexico.

His love for the Union had been that of a brave man who had gone through battles and shed his blood for his country.

The Civil War broke his heart.

In his early days his heart had been in his thoroughbred horses and his fighting cocks, and when he heard that his nephew had died with Crockett and Bowie at the Alamo, he drew himself proudly up and said: "A right brave boy, by the Eternal, and he died as becomes one crossed on an Irish Grey cock."

That had been years before. Now, a new civilization had come on the stage, and where the grandsire had taken to thoroughbreds, Richard Travis, the grandson, took to trotters. In the stalls where once stood the sons of Sir Archie, Boston, and imported Glencoe himself, now were sons of Mambrino Patchin, and George Wilkes and Harold. And a splendid lot they were — sires,— brood mares and colts, in the paddocks of The Gaffs.

Travis took no man's dust in the Tennessee Valley. At county fairs he had a walk-over.

He had inherited The Gaffs from his grandfather, for both his parents died in his infancy, and his two remaining uncles gave their lives in Virginia, early in the war, following the flag of the Confederacy.

One of them had left a son, whom Richard Travis had educated and who had, but the June before, graduated from the State University.

Travis saw but little of him, since each did as he pleased, and it did not please either of them to get into each other's way.

There had been no sympathy between them. There could not be, for they were too much alike in many ways.

There can be no sympathy in selfishness.

All through the summer Harry Travis had spent his time at picnics and dances, and, but for the fact that his cousin now and then missed one of his best horses from the stable, or found his favorite gun put away foul, or his fishing tackle broken, he would not have known that Harry was on the place.

Cook-mother Charity kept the house. Bond and free, she had spent all her life at The Gaffs. Of this she was prouder than to have been house-keeper at Windsor. Her word was law; she was the only mortal who bossed, as she called it, Richard Travis.

Usually, friends from town kept the owner company, and The Gaffs' reputation for hospitality, while generous, was not unnoted for its hilarity.

To-night Richard Travis was lonely. His supper tray had not been removed. He lit a cigar and picked up a book — it was Herbert Spencer, and he was soon interested.

Ten minutes later an octoroon house-girl, with dark Creole eyes, and bright ribbons in her hair, came in to remove the supper dishes. She wore a bright-colored green gown, cut low. As she reached over the table near him he winced at the strong smell of musk, which beauties of her race imagine adds so greatly to their esthetic *status-quo*. She came nearer to him than was necessary, and there was an attempted familiarity in the movement that caused him to curve slightly the corner of his thin, nervous lip, showing beneath his mustache. She kept a half glance on him always. He smoked and read on, until the rank smell of her perfume smote him again through the odor of his cigar, and as he looked up she had busied around so close to him that her exposed neck was within two feet of him bent in seeming innocence over the tray. With a mischievous laugh he reached over and flipped the hot ashes from his cigar upon her neck. She screamed affectedly and danced about shaking off the ashes. Then with feigned maidenly piquancy and many reproachful glances, she went out laughing good humoredly.

He was good natured, and when she was gone he laughed boyishly.

Good nature is one of the virtues of impurity.

Still giggling she set the tray down in the kitchen and told Cook-mother Charity about it. That worthy woman gave her a warning look and said:

"The frisk'ness of this new gen'ration of niggers makes me tired. Better let Marse Dick alone — he's a dan'g'us man with women."

In the dining-room Travis sat quiet and thoughtful.

He was a handsome man, turning forty. His face was strong, clean shaved, except a light mustache, with full sensual lips and an unusually fine brow. It was the brow of intellect — all in front. Behind and above there was no loftiness of ideality or of veneration. His smile was constant, and though slightly cold, was always approachable. His manner was decisive, but clever always, and kind-hearted at times.

Contrary to his habit, he grew reminiscent. He despised this kind of a mood, because, as he said, " It is the weakness of a fool to think about himself." He walked to the window and looked out on the broad fields of The Gaffs in the valley before him. He looked at the handsomely furnished room and thought of the splendid old home. Then he deliberately surveyed himself in the mirror. He smiled:

" ' Survival of the fittest '— yes, Spencer is right — a great — great mind. He is living now, and the world, of course, will not admit his greatness until he is dead. Life, like the bull that would rule the herd, is never ready to admit that other life is great. A poet is always a dead rhymester,— a philosopher, a dead dreamer.

" Let Spencer but die!

" Tush! Why indulge in weak modesty and fool self-depreciation? Even instinct tells me — that very lowest of animal intellectual forces — that I survive because I am stronger than the dead. Providence — God — whatever it is, has nothing to do with it except to start you and let you survive by overcoming. Winds you up and then — devil take the hindmost!

" It is brains — brains — brains that count — brains

first and always. This moral stuff is fit only for those who are too weak to conquer. I have accomplished everything in life I have ever undertaken — everything — and — by brains! Not once have I failed — I have done it by intellect. courage — intuition — the thing in one that speaks.

" Now as to things of the heart,"— he stopped suddenly — he even scowled half humorously. It came over him — his failure there, as one who, sweeping with his knights the pawns of an opponent, suddenly finds himself confronting a queen — and checkmated.

He walked to the window again and looked toward the northern end of the valley. There the gables of an old and somewhat weather-beaten home sat in a group of beech on a rise among the foot-hills.

" Westmoreland "— he said —" how dilapidated it is getting to be! Something must be done there, and Alice — Alice,"— he repeated the name softly — reverently —" I feel — I know it — she — even she shall be mine — after all these years — she shall come to me yet."

He smiled again: " Then I shall have won all around. Fate? Destiny? Tush! It's living and surviving weaker things, such for instance as my cousin Tom."

He smiled satisfactorily. He flecked some cotton lint from his coat sleeve.

" I have had a hard time in the mill to-day. It's a beastly business robbing the poor little half-made-up devils."

He rang for Aunt Charity. She knew what he wished, and soon came in bringing him his cock-tail — his night-cap as she always called it,— only of late he had required several in an evening,— a thing that set the old woman to quarreling with him, for she knew the limit of a gentleman.   And, in truth, she was proud of her cock-tails.   They were made from a recipe given by Andrew Jackson.   For fifty years Cook-mother Charity had made one every night and brought it to " old mars-ter " before he retired.   Now she proudly brought it to his grandson.

" Oh, say Mammy," he said as the old woman started out —" Carpenter will be here directly with his report. Bring another pair of these in — we will want them."

The old woman bristled up.   " To be sure, I'll fix 'em, honey.   He'll not know the difference.   But the licker he gits in his'n will come outen the bottle we keep for the hosses when they have the colic.   The bran' we keep for gem'men would stick in his th'oat."

Travis laughed: " Well — be sure you don't get that horse brand in mine."

CHAPTER III.

JUD CARPENTER.

A N hour afterwards, Travis heard a well-known walk in the hall and opened the door.

He stepped back astonished. He released the knob and gazed half angry, half smiling.

A large dog, brindled and lean, walked complacently and condescendingly in, followed by his master. At a glance, the least imaginative could see that Jud Carpenter, the Whipper-in of the Acme Cotton Mills, and Bonaparte, his dog, were well mated.

The man was large, raw-boned and brindled, and he, also, walked in, complacently and condescendingly.

The dog's ears had been cropped to match his tail, which in his infancy had been reduced to a very few inches. His under jaw protruded slightly — showing the trace of bull in his make-up.

That was the man all over. Besides he had a small, mean, roguish ear.

The dog was cross-eyed —" the only cross-eyed purp in the worl' "— as his master had often proudly proclaimed, and the expression of his face was uncanny.

Jud Carpenter's eastern-eye looked west, and his western-eye looked east, and the rest of the paragraph above fitted him also.

The dog's pedigree, as his master had drawlingly

proclaimed, was " p'yart houn', p'yart bull, p'yart cur, p'yart terrier, an' the rest of him — wal, jes' dog."

Reverse this and it will be Carpenter's: Just dog, with a sprinkling of bull, cur, terrier, and hound.

Before Richard Travis could protest, the dog walked deliberately to the fire-place and sprang savagely on the helpless old setter dreaming on the rug. The older dog expostulated with terrific howls, while Travis turned quickly and kicked off the intruder.

He stood the kicking as quietly as if it were part of the programme in the last act of a melodrama in which he was the villain. He was kicked entirely across the room and his head was driven violently into the half-open door of the side-board. Here it came in contact with one of Cook-mother's freshly baked hams, set aside for the morrow's lunch. Without even a change of countenance — for, in truth, it could not change — without the lifting even of a hair in surprise, the brute seized the ham and settled right where he was, to lunch. And he did it as complacently as he had walked in, and with a satisfied growl which seemed to say that, so far as the villain was concerned, the last act of the melodrama was ending to his entire satisfaction.

Opening a side door, Travis seized him by the stump of a tail and one hind leg — knowing his mouth was too full of ham to bite anything — and threw him, still clutching the ham, bodily into the back yard. Without changing the attitude he found himself in when he hit the ground, the brindled dog went on with his luncheon.

The very check of it set Travis to laughing. He closed the door and said to the man who had followed the dog in: "Carpenter, if I had the nerve of that raw-boned fiend that follows you around, I'd soon own the world."

The man had already taken his seat by the fire as unaffectedly as had the dog. He had entered as boldly and as indifferently and his two deep-set, cat-gray cross-eyes looked around as savagely.

He was a tall, lank fellow, past middle age, with a crop of stiff, red-brown hair, beginning midway of his forehead, so near to an equally shaggy and heavy splotch of eye-brows as to leave scarce a finger's breadth between them.

He was wiry and shrewd-looking, and his two deep-set eyes seemed always like a leopard's,— walking the cage of his face, hunting for some crack to slip through. Furtive, sly, darting, rolling hither and thither, never still, comprehensive, all-seeing, malicious and deadly shrewd. These were the eyes of Jud Carpenter, and they told it all. To this, add again that they looked in contrary directions.

As a man's eye, so is the tenor of his life.

Yet in them, now and then, the twinkle of humor shone. He had a conciliatory way with those beneath him, and he considered all the mill hands in that class. To his superiors he was a frowning, yet daring and even presumptuous underling.

Somewhat better dressed than the Hillites from whom he sprang was this Whipper-in of the Acme Cotton Mills — somewhat better dressed, and with the air of one who had arisen above his surroundings. Yet, withal, the common, low-born, malicious instinct was there

— the instinct which makes one of them hate the man who is better educated, better dressed than he. All told, it might be summed up and said of Jud Carpenter that he had all the instincts of a Hillite and all the arrogance of a manager.

"Nobody understands that dog, Bonaparte, but me," said Carpenter after a while — "he's to dogs what his name-sake was to man. He's the champ'un fighter of the Tennessee Valley, an' the only cross-eyed purp in the worl', as I have often said. Like all gen'uses of course, he's a leetle peculiar — but him and me — we understan's each other."

He pulled out some mill papers and was about to proceed to discuss his business when Travis interrupted:

"Hold on," he said, good humoredly, "after my experience with that cross-eyed genius of a dog, I'll need something to brace me up."

He handed Carpenter a glass and each drank off his cock-tail at a quaff.

Travis settled quickly to business. He took out his mill books, and for an hour the two talked in a low tone and mechanically. The commissary department of the mill was taken up and the entire accounts gone over. Memoranda were made of goods to be ordered. The accounts of families were run over and inspected. It was tedious work, but Travis never flagged and his executive ability was quick and incisive. At last he closed the book with an impatient gesture:

"That's all I'll do to-night," he muttered decisively. "I've other things to talk to you about. But we'll need something first."

He went to the side-board and brought out a decanter of whiskey, two goblets and a bowl of loaf sugar.

He laughed: "Mammy knows nothing about this. Two cock-tails are the limit she sets for me, and so I keep this private bottle."

He made a long-toddy for himself, but Carpenter took his straight. In all of it, his furtive eyes, shining out of the splotch of eye-brows above, glanced inquiringly around and obsequiously followed every movement of his superior.

"Now, Carpenter," said the Secretary after he had settled back in his chair and lit a cigar, handing the box afterwards to the other —" You know me — you and I — must understand each other in all things."

"'Bleeged to be that way," drawled the Whipper-in —" we must wu'ck together. You know me, an' that Jud Carpenter's motto is, 'mum, an' keep movin'.' That's me — that's Jud Carpenter."

Travis laughed: "O, it's nothing that requires so much heavy villain work as the tone of your voice would suggest. We're not in a melodrama. This is the nineteenth century and we're talking business and going to win a thing or two by common sense and business ways, eh?"

Carpenter nodded.

"Well, now, the first is quite matter of fact — just horses. I believe we are going to have the biggest fair this fall we have ever had."

"It's lots talked about," said Carpenter —" 'specially the big race an' purse you've got put up."

Travis grew interested quickly and leaned over excitedly.

"My reputation is at stake — and that of The Gaffs' stable. You see, Carpenter, it's a three-cornered race for three-thousand dollars — each of us, Col. Troup, Flecker and me, have put up a thousand — three heats out of five — the winner takes the stake. Col. Troup, of Lenox, has entered a fast mare of his, and Flecker, of Tennessee, will be there with his gelding. I know Flecker's horse. I could beat him with Lizette and one of her legs tied up. I looked him over last week. Contracted heels and his owner hasn't got horse-sense to know it. It's horse-sense, Carpenter, that counts for success in life as in a race."

Carpenter nodded again.

"But it's different with Col. Troup's entry. Ever been to Lenox?" he asked suddenly.

Carpenter shook his head.

"Don't know anybody there?" asked Travis. "I thought so — just what I want."

He went on indifferently, but Carpenter saw that he was measuring his words and noting their effect upon himself. "They work out over there Tuesdays and Fridays — the fair is only a few weeks off — they will be stepping their best by Friday. Now, go there and say nothing — but just sit around and see how fast Col. Troup's mare can trot."

"That'll be easy," said Carpenter.

"I have no notion of losing my thousand and reputation, too." He bent over to Carpenter and laughed. "All's fair in love and — a horse race. You know it's the 2:25 class, and I've entered Lizette, but Sadie B. is so much like her that no living man who doesn't curry them every day could tell them apart. Sadie B.'s mark is 2:15. Now see if Troup can beat 2:25. Maybe he can't beat 2:15."

Then he laughed ironically.

Carpenter looked at him wonderingly.

It was all he said, but it was enough for Carpenter. Fraud's wink to the fraudulent is an open book. Her nod is the nod of the Painted Thing passing down the highway.

Base-born that he was — low by instinct and inheritance, he had never heard of so brilliant and so gentlemanly a piece of fraud. The consummate boldness of it made Carpenter's eyes twinkle — a gentleman and in a race with gentlemen — who would dare to suspect? It was the boldness of a fine woman, daring to wear a necklace of paste-diamonds.

He sat looking at Travis in silent admiration. Never before had his employer risen to such heights in the eyes of the Whipper-in. He sat back in his chair and chuckled. His furtive eyes danced.

"Nobody but a born gen'us 'ud ever have tho'rt of that," he said —"never seed yo' e'kal — why, the money is your'n, any way you fix it. You can ring in Lizette one heat and Sadie B."——

"There are things to be thought and not talked of," replied Travis quickly. "For a man of your age ar'n't you learning to talk too much out loud? You go and find out what I've asked — I'll do the rest. I'm think-

ing I'll not need Sadie B. Never run a risk, even a
dead sure one, till you're obliged to."

" I'll fetch it next week — trust me for that. But
I hope you will do it — ring in Sadie B. just for the fun
of it. Think of old bay-window Troup trottin' his
mare to death ag'in two fast horses an' never havin'
sense enough to see it."

He looked his employer over — from his neatly turned
foot to the cravat, tied in an up-to-date knot. At that,
even, Travis flushed. " Here," he said —" another
toddy. I'll trust you to bring in your report all right."

Carpenter again took his straight — his eyes had begun to glitter, his face to flush, and he felt more like
talking.

Travis lit another cigar. He puffed and smoked in
silence for a while. The rings of smoke went up incess-
antly. His face had begun to redden, his fingers to
thrill to the tip with pulsing blood. With it went his
final contingency of reserve, and under it he dropped
to the level of the base-born at his side.

Whiskey is the great leveler of life. Drinking it,
all men are, indeed, equal.

" When are you going out to get in more hands for
the mill? " asked Travis after a pause.

" To-morrow — "

" So soon? " asked Travis.

" Yes, you see," said Carpenter, " there's been ha'f a
dozen of the brats died this summer an' fall — scarlet
fever in the mill."

Travis looked at him and smiled.

" An' I've got to git in some mo' right away," he

went on. " Oh, there's plenty of 'em in these hills."
Travis smoked for a few minutes without speaking.

" Carpenter, had you ever thought of Helen Conway
— I mean — of getting Conway's two daughters into
the mill? " He made the correction with a feigned indifference, but the other quickly noticed it. In an instant Carpenter knew.

As a matter of fact the Whipper-in had not thought
of it, but it was easy for him to say what he thought
the other wished him to say.

" Wal, yes," he replied; " that's jes' what I had been
thinkin' of. They've got to come in — 'ristocrats or
no 'ristocrats! When it comes to a question of bread
and meat, pedigree must go to the cellar."

" To the attic, you mean," said Travis—"where their
old clothes are."

Carpenter laughed: " That's it—you all'ers say the
k'rect thing. 'N' as I was sayin' " — he went on —
" it is a ground-hog case with 'em. The Major's drunk
all the time. His farm an' home 'll be sold soon. He's
'bleeged to put 'em in the mill — or the po'-house."

He paused, thinking. Then, " But ain't that Helen
about the pretties' thing you ever seed? " He chuckled.
" You're sly — but I seen you givin' her that airin'
behin' Lizette and Sadie B.— "

" You've nothing to do with that," said Travis
gruffly. " You want a new girl for our drawing-in
machine — the best paying and most profitable place
in the mill — off from the others — in a room by herself — no contact with mill-people — easy job — two
dollars a day — "

"One dollar — you forgit, suh — one dollar's the reg'lar price, sah," interrupted the Whipper-in.

The other turned on him almost fiercely: "Your memory is as weak as your wits — two dollars, I tell you, and don't interrupt me again —"

"To be sho'," said the Whipper-in, meekly —"I did forgit — please excuse me, sah."

"Then, in talking to Conway, you, of course, would draw his attention to the fact that he is to have a nice cottage free of rent — that will come in right handy when he finds himself out in the road — sold out and nowhere to go," he said.

"'N' the commissary," put in Carpenter quietly. "Excuse me, sah, but there's a mighty good bran' of whiskey there, you know!"

Travis smiled good humoredly: "Your wits are returning," he said; "I think you understand."

"I'll see him to-morrow," said Carpenter, rising to go.

"Oh, don't be in a hurry," said Travis.

"Excuse me, sah, but I'm afraid I've bored you stayin' too long."

"Sit down," said the other, peremptorily — "you will need something to help you along the road. Shall we take another?"

So they took yet another drink, and Carpenter went out, calling his dog.

Travis stood in the doorway and watched them go down the driveway. They both staggered lazily along. Travis smiled: "Both drunk — the dog on ham."

As he turned to go in, he reeled slightly himself, but he did not notice it.

When he came back he was restless. He looked at the clock. " Too early for bed," he said. " I'd give a ten if Charley Biggers were here with his little cock-tail laugh to try me a game of poker."

Suddenly he went to the window, and taking a small silver whistle from his pocket he blew it toward the stables. Soon afterwards a well dressed mulatto boy entered.

" How are the horses to-night, Jim? " he asked.

" Fine, sir — all eatin' well an' feelin' good."

" And Coquette — the saddle mare? "

" Like split silk, sir."

" Exercise her to-morrow under the saddle, and Sunday afternoon we will give Miss Alice her first ride on her — she's to be a present for her on her birthday, you know—eh? "

Jim bowed and started out.

" You may fix my bath now — think I'll retire. O Jim! " he called, " see that Antar, the stallion, is securely stalled. You know how dangerous he is."

He was just dozing off when the front door closed with a bang.

Then a metal whip handle thumped heavily on the floor and the jingling of a spur rattled over the hall floor, as Harry Travis boisterously went down the hall, singing tipsily,

> " Oh, Johnny, my dear,
> Just think of your head.

> Just think of your head
> In the morning."

Another door banged so loudly it awakened even the setter. The old dog came to the side of the bed and laid his head affectionately in Travis' palm. The master of The Gaffs stroked his head, saying: "It is strange that I love this old dog so."

CHAPTER IV

FOOD FOR THE FACTORY

THE next morning being Saturday, Carpenter, the Whipper-in, mounted his Texas pony and started out toward the foothills of the mountains.

Upon the pommel of his saddle lay a long single-barreled squirrel gun, for the hills were full of squirrels, and Jud was fond of a tender one, now and then. Behind him, as usual, trotted Bonaparte, his sullen eyes looking for an opportunity to jump on any timid country dog which happened along.

There are two things for which all mills must be prepared — the wear and tear of Time on the machinery — the wear and tear of Death on the frail things who yearly work out their lives before it.

In the fight for life between the machine and the human labor, in the race of life for that which men call success, who cares for the life of one little mill hand? And what is one tot of them from another? And if one die one month and another the next, and another the next and the next, year in and year out, who remembers it save some poverty-hardened, stooped and benumbed creature, surrounded by a scrawny brood calling ever for bread?

The world knows not — cares not — for its tiny life

is but a thread in the warp of the great Drawing-in Machine.

So fearful is the strain upon the nerve and brain and body of the little things, that every year many of them pass away — slowly, surely, quietly — so imperceptibly that the mill people themselves scarcely miss them. And what does it matter? Are there not hundreds of others, born of ignorance and poverty and pain, to take their places?

And the dead ones — unknown, they simply pass into a Greater Unknown. Their places are filled with fresh victims — innocents, whom Passion begets with a caress and Cupidity buys with a curse. Children they are — tots — and why should they know that they are trading — life for death?

It was a bright fall morning, and Jud Carpenter rode toward the mountain a few miles away. They are scarcely mountains — these beautifully wooded hills in the Tennessee Valley, hooded by blue in the day and shrouded in somber at night; but it pleases the people who live within the sweet influence of their shadows to call them mountains.

Jud knew where he was going, and he rode leisurely along, revolving in his mind the plan of his campaign. He needed the recruits for the Acme Mills, and in all his past experience as an employment agent he had never undertaken to bring in a family where as much tact and diplomacy was required as in this case.

It was a dilapidated gate at which he drew rein. There had once been handsome pillars of stone and brick, but these had fallen and the gate had been swung on a convenient locust tree that had sprung up and grown with its usual rapidity from its sheltered nook near the crumbling rock wall. Only one end of the gate was hung; and it lay diagonally across the entrance of what had once been a thousand acres of the finest farm in the Tennessee Valley.

Dismounting, Jud hitched his horse and set his gun beside the tree; and as it was easier to climb over the broken-down fence than to lift the gate around, he stepped over and then shuffled along in his lazy way toward the house.

It was an old farmhouse, now devoid of paint; and the path to it had once been a well-kept gravel walk, lined with cedars; but the box-plants, having felt no pruning shears for years, almost filled, with their fantastically jagged boughs, the narrow path, while the cedars tossed about their broken and dead limbs.

The tall, square pillars in the house, from dado above to where they rested in the brick base below, showed the naked wood, untouched so long by paint that it had grown furzy from rain and snow, and splintery from sun and heat. Its green shutters hung, some of them, on one hinge; and those which could be closed, were shut up close and sombre under the casements

A half dozen hounds came baying and barking around him. As Jud proceeded, others poured out from under the house. All were ribby, and half starved.

Without a moment's hesitation they promptly covered Bonaparte, much to the delight of that genius. Indeed, from the half-satisfied, half malignant snarl which lit up his face as they piled rashly and brainlessly on him,

Jud took it that Bonaparte had trotted all these miles just to breakfast on this remnant of hound on the half-shell.

In a few minutes Bonaparte's terrible, flashing teeth had them flying in every direction.

Jud promptly cuffed him back to the gate and bade him wait there.

On the front portico, his chair half-tilted back, his trousers in his boot legs, and his feet on the balustrade rim, the uprights of which were knocked out here and there, like broken teeth in a comb,— sat a man in a slouch hat, smoking a cob pipe. He was in his shirt sleeves. His face was flushed and red; his eyes were watery, bleared. His head was fine and long — his nose and chin seemed to meet in a sharp point. His face showed that form of despair so common in those whom whiskey has helped to degenerate. He did not smile — he scowled continuously, and his voice had been imprecatory so long that it whined in the same falsetto twang as one of his hounds.

Jud stepped forward and bowed obsequiously.

"How are you to-day, Majah, sah?" he asked while his puckered and wrinkled face tried to smile.

Jud was chameleon. Long experience had taught him to drop instinctively into the mannerism — even the dialect — of those he hoped to cajole. With the well-bred he could speak glibly, and had airs himself. With the illiterate and the low-bred, he could out-Caliban the herd of them.

The man did not take the pipe out of his mouth. He did not even turn his head. Only his two bleared

eyes shot sidewise down to the ground, where ten feet
below him stood the employment agent of the mills,
smiling, smirking, and doing his best to spell out on
the signboard of his unscrupulous face the fact that he
came in peace and good will.

Major Edward Conway scarcely grunted — it might
have been anything from an oath to an eructation.
Then, taking his pipe-stem from between his teeth, and
shifting his tobacco in his mouth,— for he was both
chewing and smoking — he expectorated squarely into
the eyes of a hound which had followed Jud up the
steps, barking and snarling at his heels.

He was a good marksman even with spittle, and the
dog fled, whining.

Then he answered, with an oath, that he was about
as well as the rheumatism and the beastly weather would
permit.

Jud came up uninvited and sat down. The Major
did not even turn his head. The last of a long line of
gentlemen did not waste his manners on one beneath
him socially.

Jud was discreetly silent, and soon the Major began
to tell all of his troubles, but in the tone of one who
was talking to his servant and with many oaths and
much bitterness:

"You see its this damned rheumatism, Carpenter.
Las' night, suh, I had to drink a quart of whiskey befo'
I cu'd go to sleep at all. It came on me soon aftah
I come out of the wah, an' it growed on me like jim'son
weeds in a hog-pen. My appetite's quit on me — two
pints of whiskey an' wild-cherry bark a day, suh, don't

seem to help it at all, suh. I cyant tell whut the devil's
the matter with my stomach.. Nothin' I eat or drink
seems to agree with me but whiskey. If I drink this
malarial water, suh, m'legs an' m'feet begin to swell.
I have to go back to whiskey. Damn me, but I was born
for Kentucky. Why, I've got a forty dollar thirst on
me this very minute. I'm so dry I cu'd kick up a dust
in a hog wallow. Maybe, though, it's this rotten stuff
that cross-roads Jew is sellin' me an' callin' it whiskey.
He's got a mortgage on everything here but the houn's
and the house cat, an' he's tryin' to see if he cyant kill
me with his bug-juice an' save a suit in Chancery.
I'm goin' to sen' off an' see if I cyant git another bran'
of it, suh."

Edward Conway was the type of the Southerner
wrecked financially and morally by the war. His father
and grandfather had owned Millwood, and the present
owner had gone into the war a carefully educated, well
reared youth of twenty. He came out of it alive, it is
true, but, like many another fine youth of both North
and South, addicted to drink.

The brutality of war lies not alone in death — it is
often more fatal, more degenerating, in the life it leaves
behind.

Coming out of the war, Conway found, as did all
others in the Tennessee Valley who sided with the
South, that his home was a wreck. Not a fence, even,
remained — nothing but the old home — shutterless,
plasterless, its roof rotten, its cellar the abode of hogs.

Thousands of others found themselves likewise —
brave hearts — men they proved themselves to be — in

that they built up their homes out of wreck and their country out of chaos.

The man who retrieves his fortune under the protecting arm of law and order is worthy of great praise; but he who does it in the surly, snarling teeth of Disorder itself is worthy of still greater praise.

And the real soldier is not he with his battles and his bravery. All animals will fight — it is instinct. But he who conquers in the great moral battle of peace and good government, overcoming prejudice, ignorance, poverty and even injustice, till he rises to the height of the brave whose deeds do vindicate them — this is the real soldier.

Thousands of Southern soldiers did this, but Edward Conway had not been one of them. For where whiskey sits he holds a scepter whose staff is the body of the Upas tree, and there is no room for the oak of thrift or the wild-flower of sweetness underneath.

From poverty to worse poverty Edward Conway had gone, until now, hopelessly mortgaged, hopelessly besotted, hopelessly soured, he lived the diseased product of weakness, developed through stimulated inactivity.

Nature is inexorable, morally, physically, mentally, and as two generations of atheists will beget a thief, so will two generations of idle rich beget nonentities.

On this particular morning that Jud Carpenter came, things had reached a crisis with Edward Conway. By a decree of the court, the last hope he had of retaining a portion of his family estate had been swept away, and the entire estate was to be advertised for sale, to satisfy a mortgage and judgment. It is true, he had

the two years of redemption under the Alabama law,
but can a drunkard redeem his land when he can not
redeem himself?

And so, partly from despair, and partly from that
instinct which makes even the most sensitive of mortals
wish to pour their secret troubles into another's ear,
partly even from drunken recklessness, Edward Conway
sat on his verandah this morning and poured his troubles
into the designing ear of Jud Carpenter. The refrain
of his woe was that luck — luck — remorseless luck
was against him.

Luck, since the beginning of the world, has been the
cry of him who gambles with destiny. Work is the
watchword of the man who believes in himself.

This thing went because that man had been against
him, and this went because of the faithlessness of another. His health — well, that was God's doing.

Jud was too shrewd to let him know that he thought
whiskey had anything to do with it — and so, very
cautiously did the employment agent proceed.

A child with sunny hair and bright eyes ran across the
yard. She was followed by an old black mammy,
whose anxiety for fear her charge might get her clothes
soiled was plainly evident; from the parlor came the
notes of an old piano, sadly out of tune, and Jud could
hear the fine voice of another daughter singing a love
ballad.

"You've got two mighty pyeart gyrls here," at last
he ventured.

"Of course, they are, suh," snapped their father —
"they are Conways."

" Ever think of it, sah," went on Jud, " that they could make you a livin' in the mill? "

Conway was silent. In truth, he had thought of that very thing. To-day, however, he was nerved and desperate, being more besotted than usual.

" Now, look aheah — its this way," went on Jud — " you're gettin' along in age and you need res'. You've been wuckin' too hard. I tell ycu, Majah, sah, you're dead game — no other man I know of would have stood up under the burdens you've had on yo' shoulders."

The Major drew himself up: " That's a family trait of the Conways, suh."

" Wal, it's time for you to res' awhile. No use to drive a willin' hoss to death. I can get a place for both of the gyrls in the mill, an' aftah the fust month — aftah they learn the job, they can earn enough to support you comf't'bly. Now, we'll give you a nice little cottage — no bother of keepin' up a big run-down place like this — jes' a neat little cottage. Aunt Mariah can keep it in nice fix. The gyrls will be employed and busy an' you can jes' live comf't'bly, an' res'. An' say," he added, slyly —" you can get all the credit at the Company's sto' you want an' I'm thinkin' you'll find a better brand of licker than that you've been samplin'."

Besotted as he was — hardened and discouraged — the proposition came over Conway with a wave of shame. Even through his weakened mind the old instinct of the gentleman asserted itself, and for a moment the sweet refined face of a beautiful dead wife, the delicate beauty of a little daughter, the queenliness of an elder one, all the product of good breeding and rearing, came over him. He sprang to his feet. "What do you mean, suh? My daughters — grand-children of Gen. Leonidas Conway — my daughters work in the mill by the side of that poor trash from the mountains? I'll see you damned first."

He sat down — he bowed his head in his hands. A glinty look came into his eyes.

Jud drew his chair up closer: "But jes' think a minute — you're sold out — you've got no whur to go, you've wuck'd yo'self down tryin' to save the farm. We've all got to wuck these days. The war has changed all the old order of things. We havn't got any mo' slaves."

"We," — repeated Conway, and he looked at the man and laughed.

Jud flushed even through his sallow skin:

"Wal, that's all right," he added. "Listen to me, now, I'm tryin' to save you from trouble. The war changed everything. Your folks got to whur they did by wuckin'. They built up this big estate by economy an' wuck. Now, you mus' do it. You've got the old dead-game Conway breedin' in yo' bones an' you've got the brains, too." He lowered his voice: "It's only for a little while — jes' a year or so — it'll give you a nice little home to live in while you brace up an' pull out of debt an' redeem yo' farm. Here — it is only for a year or so — sign this — givin' you a home, an' start all over in life — sign it right there, only for a little while — a chance to git on yo' feet —."

Conway scarcely knew how it happened that he signed — for Jud quickly changed the subject.

After a while Jud arose to go. As he did so, Lily, the little daughter, came out, and putting her arms around her father's neck, kissed him and said:

" Papa — luncheon is served, and oh, do come on! Mammy and Helen and I are so hungry."

Mammy Maria had followed her and stood deferentially behind the chair. And as Jud went away he thought he saw in the old woman's eyes, as she watched him, a trace of that fine scorn bred of generations of gentleness, but which whiskey had destroyed in the master.

CHAPTER V

A S Jud went out of the dilapidated gate at Millwood, he chuckled to himself. He had, indeed, accomplished something. He had gained a decided advance in the labor circles of the mill. He had broken into the heretofore overpowering prejudice the better class had against the mill, for he held in his possession the paper wherein an aristocrat had signed his two daughters into it. Wouldn't Richard Travis chuckle with him?

In the South social standing is everything.

To have the mill represented by a first family — even if brought to poverty through drunkenness — was an entering wedge.

His next job was easier. A mile farther on, the poor lands of the mountain side began. Up on the slope was a cabin, in the poorest and rockiest portion of it, around the door of which half a dozen cracker children stared at Jud with unfeigned interest as he rode up.

" Light an' look at yer saddle " — came from a typical Hillite within, as Jud stopped.

Jud promptly complied — alighted and looked at his saddle.

A cur — which, despite his breeding, is always a keen

detective of character — followed him, barking at his heels.

This one knew Jud as instinctively and as accurately as he knew a fresh bone from a rank one — by smell. He was also a judge of other dogs and, catching sight of Bonaparte, his anger suddenly fled and he with it.

" Won't you set down an' res' yo' hat? " came invitingly from the doorway.

Jud sat down and rested his hat.

A tall, lank woman, smoking a cob pipe which had grown black with age and Samsonian in strength, came from the next room. She merely ducked her long, sharp nose at Jud and, pretending to be busily engaged around the room, listened closely to all that was said.

Jud told the latest news, spoke of the weather and made many familiar comments as he talked. Then he began to draw out the man and woman. They were poor, child-burdened and dissatisfied. Gradually, carefully, he talked mill and the blessings of it. He drew glorious pictures of the house he would take them to, its conveniences — the opportunities of the town for them all. He took up the case of each of the six children, running from the tot of six to the girl of twenty, and showed what they could earn.

In all it amounted to sixteen dollars a week.

" You sho'ly don't mean it comes to sixteen dollars ev'y week," said the woman, taking the cob pipe out for the first time, long enough to spit and wipe her mouth on the back of her hand. " an' all in silver an' all our'n? " she asked. " Why that thar is mo' money'n we've seed this year. What do you say to tryin' it, Josiah?"

Josiah was willing. "You see," he added, "we needn't stay thar longer'n a year or so. We'll git the money an' then come back an' buy a good piece of land."

Suddenly he stopped and fired this point blank at Jud: "But see heah, Mister-man, is thar any niggers thar? Do we hafter wuck with niggers?"

Jud looked indignant. It was enough.

At the end of an hour the family head had signed for a five years' contract. They would move the next week.

"Cash — think of it — cash ever' week. An' in silver, too," said the woman. "Why, I dunno hardly how it'll feel. I'm afeared it mou't gin me the eetch."

Jud, when he left, had induced their parents to sell five children into slavery for five years.

It meant for life.

And both parents declared when he left that never before had they "seed sech a nice man."

Jud had nearly reached the town when he passed, high up on the level plateau by which the mountain road now ran, the comfortable home of Elder Butts. Peach and apple trees adorned the yard, while bee-hives sat in a corner under the shade of them behind the cottage. The tinkle of a sheep bell told of a flock of sheep nearby. A neatly painted new wagon stood under the shed by the house, and all around was an air of thrift and work.

"Now if I cu'd git that Butts family," he mused, "I'd have something to crow about when I got back to Kingsley to-night. He's got a little farm an' is well

to do an' is thrifty, an' if I cu'd only git that class
started in the mill an' contented to wuck there, it 'ud
open up a new class of people.   There's that Archie B.
— confound him, he cu'd run ten machines at onct and
never know it.   I'd like to sweat that bottled mischief
out of him a year or two.

" Hello ! "

Jud drew his horse up with a jerk.   Above him, with
legs locked, high up around the body of a dead willow,
his seat the stump of a broken bough and fully twenty
feet above the employment agent's head, sat Archie B.,
a freckled-faced lad, with fiery red hair and a world of
fun in his blue eyes.   He was one of the Butts twins and
the very object of the Whipper-in's thoughts.   From
his head to his feet he had on but three garments — a
small, battered, all-wool hat, a coarse cotton shirt, wide
open at the neck, and a pair of jeans pants which came
to his knees.   But in the pockets of his pants were small
samples of everything of wood and field, from shells of
rare bird eggs to a small supply of Gypsy Juice.

His pockets were miniature museums of nature.

No one but a small boy, bent on fun, knows what
Gipsy Juice is.   No adult has ever been able to procure
its formula and no small boy in the South cares, so
long as he can get it.

" The thing that hit does," Archie B. explained to
his timid and pious twin brother, Ozzie B., " is ter make
anything it touches that wears hair git up and git."

Coons, possums, dogs, cats — with now and then a
country horse or mule, hitched to the town rack — with
these, and a small vial of Gypsy Juice, Archie B., as he

expressed it, " had mo' fun to the square inch than ole
Barnum's show ever hilt in all its tents."

Jud stood a moment watching the boy. It was easy
to see what Archie B. was after. In the body of the
dead tree a wood-pecker had chiseled out a round hole.

" Hello, yo'se'f "— finally drawled Jud —" whatcher
doin' up thar? "

" Why, I am goin' to see if this is a wood-pecker's
nes' or a fly-ketcher's."

Bonaparte caught his cue at once and ran to the foot
of the tree barking viciously, daring the tree-climber
to come down. His vicious eyes danced gleefully. He
looked at his master between his snarls as much as to
say: " Well, this is great, to tree the real live son
of the all-conquering man! "

It maddened him, too, to see the supreme indifference
with which the all-conqueror's son treated his presence.

Jud grunted. He prided himself on his bird-lore.
Finally he said: " Wal, any fool could tell you — its
a wood-pecker's nest."

" Yes, that's so and jus' exacly what a fool 'ud say,"
came back from the tree. " But it 'ud be because he is
a fool, tho', an' don't see things as they be. It's a
fly-ketcher's nest, for all that —" he added.

" Teach yo' gran'-mammy how to milk the house cat,"
sneered Jud, while Bonaparte grew furious again with
this added insult. " Don't you know a wood-pecker's
nest when you see it? "

" Yes," said Archie B., " an' I also know a fly-
ketcher will whip a wood-pecker and take his nes' from

him, an' I've come up here to see if it's so with this one."

"Oh," said Jud, surprised, " an' what is it? "

"Jus' as I said — he's whipped the wood-pecker an' tuck his nes'."

"What's a fly-ketcher, Mister Know-It-All? " said Jud.   Then he grinned derisively.

Bonaparte, watching his master, ran around the tree again and squatting on his stump of a tail grinned likewise.

"A fly-ketcher," said Archie B. calmly, " is a sneaking sort of a bird, that ketches flies an' little helpless insects for a — mill, maybe.   Do you know any two-legged fly-ketchers a-doin' that? "

Jud glared at him, and Bonaparte grew so angry that he snapped viciously at the bark of the tree as if he would tear it down.

"What do you mean, you little imp? — what mill? "

"Why his stomach," drawled Archie B., " it's a little differunt from a cotton-mill, but it grinds 'em to death all the same."

Jud looked up again.   He glared at Archie B.

"How do you know that's a fly-ketcher's nest and not a wood-pecker's, then? " he asked, to change the subject.

"That's what I'd like to know, too," said Bonaparte as plainly as his growls and two mean eyes could say it.

"If it's a fly-ketcher's, the nest will be lined with a snake's-skin," said Archie B.   "That's nachrul, ain't it," he added —" the nest of all sech is lined with snake-skins."

Bonaparte, one of whose chief amusements in life was killing snakes, seemed to think this a personal thrust at himself, for he flew around the tree with renewed rage while Archie B., safe on his high perch, made faces at him and laughed.

" I'll bet it ain't that way," said Jud, rattled and discomfited and shifting his long squirrel gun across his saddle. Archie B. replied by carefully thrusting a brown sun-burnt arm into the hole and bringing out a nest. " Now, a wood-pecker's egg," he said, carefully lifting an egg out and then replacing it, " 'ud be pearly white."

" How did you learn all that? " sneered Jud.

" Oh, by keepin' out of a cotton mill an' usin' my eye," said Archie B., winking at Bonaparte.

Bonaparte glared back.

" I'd like to git you into the mill," said Jud. " I'd put you to wuck doin' somethin' that 'ud be worth while."

" Oh, yes, you would for a few years," sneered back Archie B. " Then you'd put me under the groun', where I'd have plenty o' time to res'."

" I'm goin' up there now to see yo' folks an' see if I can't git you into the mill."

" Oh, you are? — Well, don't be in sech a hurry an' look heah at yo' snake-skin fust — didn't I tell you it 'ud be lined with a snake-skin? " And he threw down a last year's snake-skin which Bonaparte proceeded to rend with great fury.

" Now, come under here," went on Archie B. persuasively, " and I'll sho' you they're not pearly white, like a wood-pecker's, but cream-colored with little purple splotches scratched over 'em — like a fly-ketcher's."

Jud rode under and looked up. As he did so Archie B. suddenly turned the nest upside down, that Jud might see the eggs, and as he looked up four eggs shot out before he could duck his head, and caught him squarely between his shaggy eyes. Blinded, smeared with yelk and smarting with his eyes full of fine broken shell, he scrambled from his horse, with many oaths, and began feeling for the little branch of water which ran nearby.

" I'll cut that tree down, but I'll git you and wring yo' neck," he shouted, while Bonaparte endeavored to tear it down with his teeth.

But Archie B. did not wait. Slowly he slid down the tree, while Bonaparte, thunder-struck with joy, waited at the foot, his eyes glaring, his mouth wide open, anticipating the feast on fresh boy meat. Can he be — dare he be — coming down? Right into my jaws, too? The very thought of it stopped his snarls.

Jud's curses filled the air.

Down — down, slid Archie B., both legs locked around the tree, until some ten feet above the dog, and, then tantalizingly, just out of reach, he suddenly tightened his brown brakes of legs, and thrusting his hand in his pocket, pulled out a small rubber ball. Reaching over, he squirted half of its contents over the dog, which still sat snarling, half in fury and half in wonder.

Then something happened. Jud could not see, being down on his knees in the little stream, washing his eyes, but he first heard demoniacal barks proceed from Bonaparte, ending in wailful snorts, howls and whines, beginning at the foot of the tree and echoing in a fast vanishing wail toward home.

Jud got one eye in working order soon enough to see a cloud of sand and dust rolling down the road, from the rear of which only the stub of a tail could be seen, curled spasmodically downward toward the earth.

Jud could scarcely believe his eyes — Bonaparte — the champion dog — running — running like that?

" Whut — whut — whut " — he stammered, " Whut *did he do* to Bonaparte? "

Then he saw Archie B. up the road toward home, rolling in the sand with shouts of laughter.

" If I git my hands on you," yelled Jud, shaking his fist at the boy, " I'll swaller you alive."

" That's what the fly-ketcher said to the butterfly," shouted back Archie B.

It was a half hour before Jud got all the fine eggshell out of his eyes. After that he decided to let the Butts family alone for the present. But as he rode away he was heard to say again:

" Whut — whut — whut *did he do* to Bonaparte? "

Archie B. was still rolling on the ground, and chuckling now and then in fits of laughter, when a determined, motherly looking, fat girl appeared at the doorway of the family cottage. It was his sister, Patsy Butts:

" Maw," she exclaimed, " I wish you'd look at Archie B. I bet he's done sump'in."

There was a parental manner in her way. Her one object in life, evidently, was to watch Archie B.

"You Archie B.," yelled his mother, a sallow little woman òf quick nervous movements, " air you havin' a revulsion down there? What air you been doin' anyway? Now, you git up from there and go see why Ozzie B. don't fetch the cows home."

Archie B. arose and went down the road whistling.

A ground squirrel ran into a pile of rocks. Archie B. turned the rocks about until he found the nest, which he examined critically and with care. He fingered it carefully and patted it back into shape. " Nice little nes'," he said — " that settles it — I thought they lined it with fur." Then he replaced the rocks and arose to go.

A quarter of a mile down the road he stopped and listened.

He heard his brother, Ozzie B., sobbing and weeping.

Ozzie B. was his twin brother — his " after clap " — as Archie B. called him. He was timid, uncertain, pious and given to tears —" bo'hn on a wet Friday "— as Archie B. had often said. He was always the effect of Archie B.'s cause, the illustration of his theorem, the solution of his problem of mischief, the penalty of his misdemeanors.

Presently Ozzie B. came in sight, hatless and driving his cows along, but sobbing in that hiccoughy way which is the final stage of an acute thrashing.

No one saw more quickly than Archie B., and he knew instantly that his brother had met Jud Carpenter, on his way back to the mill.

" He's caught my lickin' ag'in," said Archie B., indignantly — " it's a pity he looks so much like me."

It was true, and Ozzie B. stood and dug one toe into the ground, and sobbed and wiped his eyes on his shirt sleeve, and told how, in spite of his explanations and beseechings, the Whipper-in had met him down the road and thrashed him unmercifully.

" Ozzie B.," said his brother, " you make me tired all over and in spots. I hate for as big a fool as you to look like me. Whyncher run — whyncher dodge him? "

" I — I — wanted ter do my duty," sobbed Ozzie B. " Maw tole me ter drive — drive the cows right up the road —"

Archie B. surveyed him with fine scorn:

" When the Devil's got the road," said Archie B., " decent fo'ks had better take to the wood. I'd fixed him an' his ole dorg, an' now you come along an' spile it all."

He made a cross mark in the road and spat on it. Then he turned with his back to the cross, threw his hat over his head and said slowly: " *Venture pee wee under the bridge! bam — bam — bam!* "

" What's that fur? " asked Ozzie B., as he ceased sobbing. His brother always had something new, and it was always absorbingly interesting to Ozzie B.

" That," said Archie B., solemnly, " I allers say after meetin' a Jonah in the road. The spell is now broke. Jus' watch me fix Jud Carpenter agin. Wanter see me git even with him? Well, come along."

" What'll you do? " asked Ozzie B.

" I'll make that mustang break his neck for the way he treated you, or my name ain't Archie B. Butts —

that's all. *Venture pee wee under the bridge, bam —
bam — bam!* "

"No — oo — no," began Ozzie B., beginning to cry
again — "Don't kill 'im — it'll be cruel."

"Don't wanter see me go an' git even with the man
that's jus' licked you for nuthin'?"

"No — oo — no —" sobbed Ozzie B. "Paw says —
leave — leave — that for — the Lord."

"Tarnashun!"— said Archie B., spitting on the
ground, disgustedly —, "too much relig'un is a dang'us
thing. You've got all of paw's relig'un an' maw's
brains, an' that's 'nuff said."

With this he kicked Ozzie B. soundly and sent him,
still sobbing, up the road.

Then he ran across the wood to head off Jud Carpenter, who he knew had to go around a bend in the road.

There was no bird that Archie B. could not mimic.
He knew every creature of the wood. Every wild thing
of the field and forest was his friend. Slipping into
the underbrush, a hundred yards from the road down
which he knew Jud Carpenter had to ride, he prepared
himself for action.

Drawing a turkey-call from his pocket, he gave the
call of the wild turkey going to roost, as softly as a
violinist tries his instrument to see if it is in tune.

Prut — prut — prut — it rang out clear and distinctly.

"All right,"— he said —"she'll do."

He had not long to wait. Up the road he soon saw
the Whipper-in, riding leisurely along.

Archie B. swelled with anger at sight of the compla-

cent and satisfactory way he rode along. He even
thought he saw a smile — a kind of even-up smile —
light his face.

When opposite his hiding place, Archie B. put his
call to his mouth: *Prut — Prut — P-R-U-T* — it
rang out. Then *Prut — prut!*

Jud Carpenter stopped his horse instantly.

" Turkeys goin' to roost "— he muttered. He listened for the direction.

Prut — Prut — it came out of the bushes on the
right — a hundred yards away under a beech tree.

Jud listened: " Eatin' beech-mast "— he said, and
he slipped off his pony, tied him quietly to the limb of
a sweet-gum tree, and cocking his long gun, slipped
into the wood.

Five minutes later he heard the sound still farther off.
" They're walkin'," muttered Jud —" I mus' head 'em
off." Then he pushed on rapidly into the forest.

Archie B. let him go — then, making a short circuit,
slipped like an Indian through the wood, and came up
to the pony hitched on the road side.

Quietly removing the saddle and blanket, he took two
tough prickly burrs of the sweet-gum and placed one on
each side of the pony's spine, where the saddle would
rest. Then he put the blanket and saddle back, taking
care to place them on very gently and tighten the girth
but lightly.

He shook all over with suppressed mirth as he went
farther into the wood, and lay down on the mossy bank
behind a clay-root to watch the performance.

It was a quarter of an hour before Jud, thoroughly

tired and disgusted, gave up the useless search and came back.

Untying the pony, he threw the bridle rein over its head and vaulted lightly into the saddle.

Archie B. grabbed the clay-root and stuffed his wool hat into his mouth just in time.

"It was worth a dollar," he told Ozzie B. that night, after they had retired to their trundle bed. "The pony squatted fust mighty nigh to the groun'— then he riz a-buckin'. I seed Jud's coat-tail a-turnin' summersets through the air, the saddle and blanket a-followin'. I heard him when he hit the swamp hole on the side of the road *kersplash!* — an' the pony skeered speechless went off tearin' to-ards home. Then I hollered out: '*Go it ole, fly-ketcher — you're as good for tad-poles as you is for bird-eggs* '— an' I lit out through the wood."

Ozzie B. burst out crying: "Oh, Archie B., do you reckin the po' man got hurt?"

Archie B. replied by kicking him in the ribs until he ceased crying.

"Say yo' prayers now and go to sleep. I'll kick you m'se'f, but I'll lick anybody else that does it."

As Ozzie B. dozed off he heard:

"*Venture pee-wee under the bridge — bam — bam —* bam. Oh, Lord, you who made the tar'nal fools of this world, have mussy on 'em!"

CHAPTER VI

THE FLINT AND THE COAL

LOVE is love and there is nothing in all the world like it. Its romance comes but once, and it is the perfume that precedes the ripened fruit of all after life. It is not amenable to any of the laws of reason; nor subject to any law of logic; nor can it be explained by the analogy of anything in heaven or earth. Do not, therefore, try to reason about it. Only love once — and in youth — and be forever silent.

One of the mysteries of love to older ones is that two young people may become engaged and never a word be spoken. Put the girl in a convent, even, and let the boy but walk past, and the thing is done. They look and love, and the understanding is complete. They see and sigh, and read each other's secret thoughts, past and present — each other's hopes, fears.

They sigh and are engaged, and there is perfect understanding.

Time and Romance travel not together. Time must hurry on. Romance would loiter by the way. And so Romance, in her completeness, loves to dwell most where Time, traveling over the mile-tracks of the tropics, which belong by heredity to Alabama — stalks slower than on those strenuous half-mile tracks that spin around the earth in latitudes which grow smaller as they approach the frozen pole.

The sun had reached, in his day's journey, the bald knob of Sunset Peak, and there, behind it, seemed to stop. At least to Helen Conway, born and reared under the brow of Sand Mountain, he seemed every afternoon, when he reached the mountain peak, to linger, in a friendly way, behind it.

And a bold warrior-looking crest it was, helmeted with a stratum of sand-stone, jutting out in visor-shaped fullness about his head, and feathery above with scrub-oak and cedar.

Perhaps it had been a fancy which lingered from childhood; but from the time when Mammy Maria had first told her that the sun went to bed in the valley beyond the mountain until now,— her eighteenth year, — Helen still loved to think it was true, and that behind the face of Sunset Rock he still lingered to undress; and, lingering, it made for her the sweetest and most romantic period of the day.

True to her antebellum ideas, Mammy Maria dressed her two girls every afternoon before dinner. It is also true that she cooked the dinner herself and made their dresses with her own fingers, and that of late years, in the poverty of her drunken master, she had little to dress them with and less to cook.

But the resources of the old woman seemed wonderful — to the people round about,— for never were two girls more gorgeously gowned than Helen and Lily. It was humorous, it was pathetic — the way it was done.

From old bureau drawers and cedar chests, stored

5

away in the attic and unused rooms of Millwood, where she herself had carefully put them in days long gone — days of plenty and thrift — she brought forth rich gowns of another age, and made them over for Helen and Lily.

"Now, this gown was Miss Clara's," she would say as she took out a bundle of satin and old lace. She looked at it fondly — often with tears in her honest black eyes. "Lor', how well I disremember the night she fust wore it — the night of the ball we give to Jineral Jackson when he first come to see old Marster. This flowered silk with pol'naize she wore at the Guvnor's ball and the black velvet with cut steel I've seed her wearin' at many an' many a dinner here in this very house."

And so the old woman would go over all her treasures. Then, in a few days the gossipy and astounded neighbors would behold Helen and Lily, dressed, each, in a gown of white brocaded satin, with a dinner gown of black velvet, and for Sunday, old point lace, with petticoats of finest hand-made Irish linen and silk stockings — all modernized with matchless deft and skill.

"I guess my gals will shine as long as the old chist lasts," she would say, "an' I ain't started on 'em yet. I'm a-savin' some for their weddin', bless Gord, if I ever sees a man fitten for 'em."

It was an hour yet before dinner, and Aunt Maria had dressed Helen, this Saturday afternoon, with great care — for after a little frost, each day and night in Alabama becomes warmer and warmer until the next frost.

Mammy Maria knew things by intuition, and hence

her care to see that Helen looked especially pretty to-day.

There was no sun save where he streamed his ribbon rays from behind Sunset Rock, and threw them in pearl and ivory fan handles — white and gold and emerald, across the mackerel sky beyond.

Helen's silk skirt fitted her well, and one of those beautiful old ribbons, flowered in broad leaf and blossoms, wound twice around her slender waist and fell in broad streamers nearly to the ground. The bodice was cut V-shaped at the throat — the corsage being taken from one of her grandmother's made in 1822, and around her neck was a long chain of pure gold beads.

She was a type of Southern beauty obtained only after years of gentle dames and good breeding.

Her face was pure and fine, rather expressionless at her age, with a straight nose and rich fine lips. Her heavy hair was coiled gracefully about her head and fell in a longer coil, almost to her shoulders. She was tall with a sloping, angular form, the flat outlines of which were not yet filled with that fullness that time would soon add.

Her waist was well turned, her shoulders broad and slightly rounded, with that fullness of chest and breast which Nature, in her hour of generosity, gives only to the queenly woman. The curves of her sloping neck were perfect and carried not a wave-line of grossness. It was as unsensual as a swan's.

Her gown, low cut, showed slight bony shoulders of classic turn and whiteness, waiting only for time to ripen them to perfection; and the long curved lines which

ran up to where the deep braid of her rich brown hair
fell over them, together with the big joints of her arms
and the long, fine profile of her face were forerunners of
a beauty that is strong — like that of the thoroughbred
brood mare after a year's run on blue-grass.

Her eyes were her only weakness. They were deep
and hazel, and given to drooping too readily with that
feigned modesty wherein vanity clothes boldness. Down
in their depths, also, shone that bright, penetrating
spark of a taper by which Folly lights, in woman, the
lamp of ambition.

Her forehead was high — her whole bearing the unconscious one of a born lady.

Romance — girlish, idealized romance — was her's
to-day. A good intentioned, but thoughtless romance
— and therefore a weak one. And worse still, one
which, coupled with ambition, might be led to ruin.

Down through the tangled box-planted walks she
strolled, swinging her dainty hat of straw and old lace
in her hand; on through the small gate that bound the
first yard, then through the shaded lawn, unkept now
and rank with weeds, but still holding the old trees
which, in other days, looked down over the well kept
lawn of grass beneath. Now gaunt hogs had rooted it
up and the weeds had taken it, and the limbs of the old
trees, falling, had been permitted to lie as they fell.

The first fence was down. She walked across the road
and took a path leading through a cottonfield, which,
protected on all sides by the wood, and being on the
elevated plateau on which the residence stood, had escaped the severer frosts.

And so she stopped and stood amid it, waist high.

The very act of her stopping showed the romance of her nature.

She had seen the fields of cotton all her life, but she could never pass through one in bloom and in fruit — the white and purple blossoms, mingled with the green of the leaves and all banked over billows of snowy lint, — that she did not stop, thrilled with the same childhood feeling that came with the first reading of the Arabian Nights.

She had seen the field when it was first plowed, in the spring, and the small furrows were thrown up by the little turning shovels. Then, down the entire length of the ridge the cotton-planter had followed, its two little wheels straddling the row, while the small bull-tongue in front opened the shallow furrow for the linty, furry, white seeds to fall in and be covered immediately by the mold-board behind. She had seen it spring up from one end of the ridge to the other, like peas, then chopped out by the hoe, the plants left standing, each the width of the hoe apart. Then she had watched it all summer, growing under the Southern sun, throwing out limb above limb of beautiful delicate leaves, drawing their life and sustenance more from the air and sunshine above than from the dark soil beneath. Drawing it from the air and sunshine above, and therefore cotton, silken, snowy cotton — with the warmth of the sun in the skein of its sheen and the purity of heaven in the fleece of its fold.

Child of the air and the sky and sun; therefore,

cotton — and not corn, which draws its life from the clay and mud and decay which comes from below.

She had seen the first cream-white bloom come.

She had found it one sweet day in July, early in the morning, on the tip end of the eldest branch of the cotton stalk nearest the ground. It hung like the flower of the cream-white, pendulous abutilon, with pollen of yellow stars beaded in dew and throwing off a rich, delicate, aromatic odor, smelt nowhere on earth save in a cottonfield, damp with early dew and warmed by the rays of the rising sun. Cream-white it was in the morning, but when she had visited it again at nightfall, it hung purple in the twilight.

Then had she plucked it.

Through the hot month of July she had watched the boll grow and expand, until in August the lowest and oldest one next to the ground burst, and shone through the pale green leaves like the image of a star reflected in waters of green. And every morning new cream-white blooms formed to the very top, only to turn purple by twilight, while beneath, climbing higher and higher as the days went by and the cool nights came, star above star of cotton arose and stood twinkling in its sky of green and purple, above the dank manger where, in early spring, the little child-seed had lain.

To-day, touched by the great frost, the last purple bloom in the very tip-top seemed to look up yearningly and plead with the sun for one more day of life; that it, too, might add in time its snowy tribute to the bank of white which rolled entirely across the field, one big billow of cotton.

And in the midst of it the girl stood dreaming and wondering.

She plucked a purple blossom and pinned it to her breast. Then, with a deep sigh of saddened longing — that this should be the last — she walked on, daintily lifting her gown to avoid the damp stars of cotton, now fast gathering the night dew.

Across the field, a vine of wild grape ran over the top of two small hackberry trees, forming a natural umbrella-shaped arbor above two big moss-covered boulders which cropped out of the ground beneath, making two natural rustic seats. On one of these she sat down. Above her head glowed the impenetrable leaves of the grape-vine and the hackberry, and through them all hung the small purple bunches of wild grapes, waiting for the frost of affliction to convert into sugar the acid of their souls.

She was in plain view of Millwood, not a quarter of a mile away, and in the glow of the blazing red sunset, shining through its broken shutters and windows, she could see Mammy Maria busy about their dinner.

She looked up the road anxiously — then, with an impatient gesture she took the cotton bloom from her bosom and began to pluck the petals apart, one by one, saying aloud:

> " One, I love — two, I love —
> Three, I love, I say.
> Four, I love with all my heart,
> And five, I cast away —"

She stopped short and sighed —" O, pshaw! that was Harry; why did I name it for him? "

Again she looked impatiently up the road and then went on:

> " Six, he loves, seven, she loves,
>   Eight, both love —"

She turned quickly. She heard the gallop of a saddle horse coming. The rider sprang off, tied his horse and sat on the rock by her side.

She appeared not to notice him, and her piqued face was turned away petulantly.

It was a handsome boyish face that looked at her for a moment mischievously. Then he seized and kissed her despite her struggles.

For this she boxed his ears soundly and sat off on another rock.

" Harry Travis, you can't kiss me every time you want to, no matter if we are engaged."

It was a strong and rather a masculine voice, and it grated on one slightly, being scarcely expected from so beautiful a face. In it was power, self-will, ambition — but no tenderness nor that voice, soft and low, which " is an excellent thing in woman."

He laughed banteringly.

" Did you ever hear that love is not love if it is a minute late? Just see how long I have waited here for you? "

She sat down by his side and looked fondly up into his face, flushed with exercise and smiling half cynically.

It was the same smile seen so often on the face of Richard Travis.

" Oh, say," he said, dolefully, " but don't start the hubby-come-to-taw-business on me until we are married. I was late because I had to steal the Gov'ner's new mare — isn't she a beauty? "

" Oh, say," he went on, " but that is a good one — he has bought her for somebody he is stuck on — can't say who — and I heard him tell Jim not to let anybody get on her back.

" Well "— he laughed —" she certainly has a fine back. I stole her out and galloped right straight here.

" You ought to own her "— he went on flippantly — pinching playfully at the lobe of her ear —" her name is Coquette."

Then he tried to kiss her again.

" Harry! " she said, pulling away —" don't now — Mammy Maria said I was never to — let you kiss me."

" Oh," he said with some iciness —" Listen to her an' you will die an old maid. Besides, I am not engaged to Mammy Maria."

" Do you think I am a coquette? " she asked, sitting down by him again.

" Worst I ever saw — I said to Nellie just now — I mean —" he stopped and laughed.

She looked at him, pained.

" Then you've stopped to see Nellie, and that is why you are late? I do not care what she says — I am true to you, Harry — because — because I love you."

He was feigning anger, and tapping his boot with his riding whip:

"Well — kiss me yourself then — show me that Mammy Maria does not boss my wife."

She laughed and kissed him. He received it with indifference and some haughtiness.

Then his good nature returned and they sat and talked, watching the sunset.

"Don't you think my dress is pretty?" she asked after a while, with a becoming toss of her head.

"Why, I hadn't noticed it — stunning — stunning. If there is a queen on earth it is you"— he added.

She flushed under the praise and was silent.

"Harry"— she said after a while, "I hate to trouble you now, but I am so worried about things at home."

He looked up half frowning.

"You know I have always told you I could not marry you now. I would not burden you with Papa."

"Why, yes," he answered mechanically, "we're both young and can wait. You see, really, Pet — you know I am dependent at present on the Gov'nor an'—"

"I understand all that," she said quickly —"but "—

"A long engagement will only test our love," he broke in with a show of dignity.

"You do not understand," she went on. "Things have got so bad at home that I must earn something."

He frowned and tapped his foot impatiently. She sat up closer to him and put her hand on his. He did not move nor even return the pressure.

"And so, Harry — if — if to help papa — and Millwood is sold — and I can get a good place in the mill —

one off by myself — what they call drawer-in — at good
wages,— and, if only for a little while I'd work there —
to help out, you know — what would you think? "

He sprang up from his seat and dropped her hand.

" Good God, Helen Conway, are you crazy? " he said
brutally —" why, I'd never speak to you again. Me?
A Travis? — and marry a mill girl? "

The color went out of her face. She looked in her
shame and sorrow toward the sunset, where a cloud, but
ten minutes before, had stood all rosy and purple with
the flush of the sunbeams behind it.

Now the beams were gone, and it hung white and
bloodless.

In the crisis of our lives such trifles as these flash over
us. In the greatness of other things — often turning
points in our life — Nature sometimes points it all with
a metaphor.

For Nature is the one great metaphor.

Helen knew that she and the cloud were now one.

But she was not a coward, and with her heart nerved
and looking him calmly in the face, she talked on and
told him of the wretched condition of affairs at Millwood. And as she talked, the setting sun played over
her own cheeks, touching them with a halo of such exquisite colors that even the unpoetic soul of Harry
Travis was touched by the beauty of it all.

And to any one but Harry Travis the proper solution would have been plain. Not that he said it or even
meant it — for she was too proud a spirit even to have
thought of it — there is much that a man should know
instinctively that a woman should never know at all.

Harry surprised himself by the patience with which he listened to her. In him, as in his cousin — his pattern — ran a vein of tact when the crisis demanded, through and between the stratum of bold sensuousness and selfishness which made up the basis of his character.

And so as he listened, in the meanness and meagreness of his soul, he kept thinking, " I will let her down easy — no need for a scene."

It was narrow and little, but it was all that could come into the soul of his narrowness.

For we cannot think beyond our fountain head, nor can we even dream beyond the souls of the two things who gave us birth. There are men born in this age of ripeness, born with an alphabet in their mouths and reared in the regal ways of learning, who can neither read nor write. And yet had Shakespeare been born without a language, he would have carved his thoughts as pictures on the trees.

Harry Travis was born as so many others are — not only without a language, but without a soul within him upon which a picture might be drawn.

And so it kept running in his mind, quietly, cold-bloodedly, tactfully down the narrow, crooked, slum-alleys of his mind: " I will — I will drop her — now ! " She ceased — there were tears in her eyes and her face was blanched whiter even than the cloud.

He arose quickly and glanced at the setting sun: " Oh, say, but I must get the Gov'nor's mare back. Jim will miss her at feeding time."

There was a laugh on his lips and his foot was already in the stirrup. " Sorry to be in such a hurry just now,

too — because there is so much I want to say to you on
that subject — awful sorry — but the Gov'nor will raise
Cain if he knows what I've done.   I'll just write you a
long letter to-night — and I'll be over, maybe, soon —
ta — ta — but this mare, confound her — see how she
cuts up — so sorry I can't stay longer — but I'll write
— to-night."

He threw her a kiss as he rode off.

She sat dazed, numbed, with the shallowness of it
all — the shale of sham which did not even conceal the
base sub-stratum of deceit below.

Nothing like it had ever come into her life before.

She dropped down behind the rock, but instead of
tears there came steel.   In it all she could only say with
her lips white, a defiant poise of her splendid head, and
with a flash of the eyes which came with the Conway
aroused: " Oh, and I kissed him — and — and — I
loved him ! "

She sat on the rock again and looked at the sunset.
She was too hurt now to go home — she wished to be
alone.

She was a strong girl — mentally — and with a deep
nature ; but she was proud, and so she sat and crushed it
in her pride and strength, though to do it shook her as
the leaves were now being shaken by the breeze which
had sprung up at sunset.

She thought she could conquer — that she had conquered — then, as the breeze died away, and the leaves
hung still and limp again, her pride went with the breeze
and she fell again on her knees by the big rock, fell and

buried her face there in the cool moss and cried: " Oh, and I loved that thing! "

Ten minutes later she sat pale and smiling. The Conway pride had conquered, but it was a dangerous conquest, for steel and tears had mingled to make it.

In her despair she even plucked another cotton bloom from her bosom as if trying to force herself to be happy again in saying:

> " One, I love — two, I love,
> Three, I love, I say —"

But this only hurt her, because she remembered that when she had said it before she had had an idol which now lay shattered, as the petals of the cotton-blossom which she had plucked and thrown away.

Then the breeze sprang up again and with it, borne on it, came the click — click — click of a hammer taping a rock. It was a small gladey valley through which a gulley ran. Boulders cropped out here and there, and haws, red and white elms, and sassafras grew and shaded it.

Down in the gulch, not a hundred yards from her, she saw a pair of broad shoulders overtopped by a rusty summer hat — the worse for a full season's wear. Around the shoulders was strung a leathern satchel, and she could see that the person beneath the hat was closely inspecting the rocks he chipped off and put into the satchel. Then his hammer rang out again.

She sat and watched him and listened to the tap of his hammer half sadly — half amused. Harry Travis had crushed her as she had never been crushed before in her life, and the pride in a woman which endureth a fall is not to be trifled with afterwards.

She grew calmer — even quiet. The old spirit returned. She knew that she had never been as beautiful in her life, as now — just now — in the halo of the sunset shining on her hair and reflected in the rare old gown she wore.

The person with the leathern satchel was oblivious of everything but his work. The old straw hat bobbed energetically — the big shoulders nodded steadily beneath it. She watched him silently a few minutes and then she called out pleasantly:

"You do seem to be very busy, Clay!"

He stopped and looked up. Then he took off his hat and, awkwardly bowing, wiped his brow, broad, calm and self-reliant, and a deliberate smile spread over his face. Everything he did was deliberate. The smile began in the large friendly mouth and spread in kindred waves upward until it flashed out from his kindly blue eyes, through the heavy double-lens glasses that covered them.

Without a word he picked up the last rock he had broken off and put it into his satchel. Very deliberate, too, was his walk up the hill toward the grape arbor, mopping his brow as he came along — a brow big and full of cause and effect and of quiet deductions and deliberate conclusions. His coat was seedy, his trousers bagged at the knees, his shoes were old, and there were patches on them, but his collar and linen were white and very much starched, and his awkward, shambling gait was honest to the last footfall. A world of depth and soul was in his strong, fine face, lit up now with an honest, humble smile, but, at rest, full of quiet dignity.

He shuffled along and sat down in a big brotherly way by the girl's side.

She sat still, looking at him with a half amused smile on her lips.

He smiled back at her abstractedly. She could see that he had not yet really seen her. He was looking thoughtfully across at the hill beyond:

" It puzzles me," he said in a fine, mellow voice, " why I should find this rotten limestone cropping out here. Now, in the blue limestone of the Niagara period I was as sure of finding it as I am —"

" Of not finding me at all," — it came queenly, haughtily from her.

He turned, and the thick lenses of his glasses were focused on her — a radiant, superb being. Then there were swept away all his abstractions and deductions, and in their place a real smile — a lover's smile of satisfaction looking on the paradise of his dreams.

" You know I have always worshiped you," he said simply and reverently.

She moved up in a sisterly way to him and looked into his face.

" Clay — Clay — but you must not — I have told you — I am engaged."

He did not appear to hear her. Already his mind was away off in the hills where his eyes were. He went on: " Now, over there I struck a stratum of rotten limestone — it's a curious thing. I traced that vein of coal from Walker County — clear through the carboniferous period, and it is bound to crop out somewhere in this altitude — bound to do it."

"Now it's just this way," he said, taking her hand without being conscious of it and counting off the periods with her fingers. "Here is the carboniferous, the sub-carboniferous —" She jerked her hand away with what would have been an amused laugh except that in a half conscious way she remembered that Harry had held her hand but half an hour ago; and it ended in a frigid shaft feathered with a smile — the arrow which came from the bow of her pretty mouth.

He came to himself with a boyish laugh and a blush that made Helen look at him again and watch it roll down his cheek and neck, under the fine white skin there.

Then he looked at her closely again — the romantic face, the coil of brown hair, the old gown of rich silk, the old-fashioned corsage and the rich old gold necklace around her throat.

"If there's a queen on earth — it's you," he said simply.

He reddened again, and to divert it felt in his satchel and took out a rock. Then he looked across at the hills again:

"If I do trace up that vein of coal and the iron which is needed with it — when I do — for I know it is here as well as Leverrier knew that Neptune was in our planetary system by the attraction exerted — when I do —"

He looked at her again. He could not say the words.

6

Real love has ideas, but never words. It feels, but cannot speak. That which comes out of the mouth, being words, is ever a poor substitute for that which comes from the heart and is spirit.

"Clay," she said, "you keep forgetting. I say I — I am — was —" She stopped confused.

He looked hurt for a moment and smiled in his frank way: "I know it is here," he said holding up a bit of coal —"here, by the million tons, and it is mine by right of birth and education and breeding. It is my heritage to find it. One day Alabama steel will outrank Pittsburg's. Oh, to put my name there as the discoverer!"

"Then you "— he turned and said it fondly — reverently — " you should be mine by right of — of love."

She sighed.

"Clay — I am sorry for you. I can never love you that way. You have told me that, since — oh, since I can remember, and I have always told you — you know we are cousins, anyway — second cousins." She shook her head.

"Under the heart of the flinty hill lies the coal," he said simply.

But she did not understand him. She had looked down and seen Harry's foot-track on the moss.

And so they sat until the first star arose and shimmered through the blue mist which lay around the far off purpling hill tops. Then there was the clang of a dinner bell.

"It is Mammy Maria," she said —"I must go. No

— you must not walk home with me. I'd rather be
alone."

She did not intend it, but it was brutal to have said it
that way — to the sensitive heart it went to. He looked
hurt for a moment and then tried to smile in a weak
way. Then he raised his hat gallantly, turned and went
off down the gulch.

Helen stood looking for the last time on the pretty
arbor. Here she had lost her heart — her life. She
fell on the moss again and kissed the stone. Then she
walked home — in tears.

CHAPTER VII

IT is good for the world now and then to go back
to first principles in religion. It would be better
for it never to get away from them; but, since it
has that way of doing — of breeding away and breaking away from the innate good — it is well that a man
should be born in any age with the faith of Abraham.

It matters not from what source such a man may
spring. And he need have no known pedigree at all,
except an honest ancestry behind him.

Such a man was Hilliard Watts, the Cottontown
preacher.

Sprung from the common people of the South, he
was a most uncommon man, in that he had an absolute
faith in God and His justice, and an absolute belief that
some redeeming goodness lay in every human being,
however depraved he may seem to the world. And so
firm was his faith, so simple his religion — so contrary
to the worldliness of the religion of his day,— that the
very practice of it made him an uncommon man.

As the overseer of General Jeremiah Travis's large
estate before the war, he proved by his success that even
slaves work better for kindness. Of infinite good sense,
but little education, he had a mind that went to the
heart of things, and years ago the fame of his homely

84

but pithy sayings stuck in the community. In connec-
tion with kindness to his negroes one of his sayings was,
" Oh, kindness can't be classified — it takes in the whole
world or nothin'."

When General Travis got into dire financial straits
once, he sent for his overseer, and advised with him as
to the expediency of giving up. The overseer, who
knew the world and its ways with all the good judgment
of his nature, dryly remarked: " That'll never do.
Never let the world know you've quit; an' let the under-
taker that buries you be the fust man to find out you're
busted."

General Travis laughed, and that season one of his
horses won the Tennessee Valley Futurity, worth thirty-
thousand dollars — and the splendid estate was again
free from debt.

There was not a negro on the place who **did** not love
the overseer, not one who did not carry that love to the
extent of doing his best to please him. He had never
been known to punish one, and yet the work done by the
Travis hands was proverbial.

Among his duties as overseer, the entire charge of the
Westmore stable of thoroughbreds fell to his care. This
was as much from love as choice, for never was a man
born with more innate love of all dumb creatures than
the preacher-overseer.

" I've allers contended that a man could love God an'
raise horses, too," he would say; and it was ludicrous
to see him when he went off to the races, filling the
tent trunk with religious tracts, which, after the races,
he would distribute to all who would read them. And

when night came he would regularly hold prayers in his
tent—prayer-meetings in which his auditors were touts,.
stable-boys and gamblers. And woe to the stable-boy
who uttered an oath in his presence or dared to strike
or maltreat any of his horses !

He preached constantly against gambling on the
races. " That's the Devil's end of it," he would say —
" The Almighty lets us raise good horses as a benefit
to mankind, an' the best one wins the purse. It was the
Devil's idea that turned 'em into gambling machines."

No one ever doubted the honesty of his races. When
the Travis horses ran, the racing world knew they ran
for blood.

Physically, he had been an athlete — a giant, and
unconscious of his strength. Incidentally, he had taken
to wrestling when a boy, and as a man his fame as a
wrestler was coincident with the Tennessee Valley. It
was a manly sport which gave him great pleasure, just
as would the physical development of one of his race
horses. Had he lived in the early days of Greece, he
would have won in the Olympian wrestling match.

There was in Hilliard Watts a trait which is one of the
most pronounced of his type of folks,— a sturdy, honest
humor. Humor, but of the Cromwell type — and
withal, a kind that went with praying and fighting.
Possessed, naturally, of a strong mind of great good
sense, he had learned to read and write by studying the
Bible — the only book he had ever read through and
through and which he seemed to know by heart. He
was earnest and honest in all things, but in his earnestness and strong fight for right living there was the twin-

kle of humor. Life, with him, was a serious fight, but ever through the smoke of its battle there gleamed the bright sun of a kindly humor.

The overseer's home was a double log hut on the side of the mountain. His plantation, he called it,— for having been General Travis's overseer, he could not imagine any farm being less than a plantation.

It consisted of forty acres of flinty land on the mountain side —" too po' to sprout cow-peas," as his old wife would always add —" but hits pow'ful for blackberries, an' if we can just live till blackberry time comes we can take keer ourselves."

Mrs. Watts had not a lazy bone in her body. Her religion was work: " Hit's nature's remedy," she would add —" wuck and five draps o' turpentine if you're feelin' po'ly."

She despised her husband's ways and thought little of his religion. Her tongue was frightful — her temper worse. Her mission on earth — aside from work — work — work — was to see that too much peace and good will did not abide long in the same place.

Elder Butts, the Hard-Shell preacher, used to say: " She can go to the full of the moon mighty nigh every month 'thout raisin' a row, if hard pressed for time an' she thinks everybody else around her is miser'ble. But if things look too peaceful and happy, she'll raise sand in the last quarter or bust. The Bishop's a good man, but if he ever gits to heaven, the bigges' diamon' in his crown'll be because he's lived with that old 'oman an'· ain't committed murder. I don't believe in law suits, but if he ain't got a damage case agin the preacher that married him, then I'm wrong."

But no one ever heard the old man use harsher language in speaking of her than to remark that she was " a female Jineral — that's what Tabitha is."

Perhaps she was, and but for her the Bishop and his household had starved long ago.

" Furagin' is her strong point "— he would always add —" she'd made Albert Sydney Johnston a great chief of commissary."

And there was not an herb of any value that Mrs. Watts did not know all about. Any fair day she might be seen on the mountain side plucking edibles. Ginseng was her money crop, and every spring she would daily go into the mountain forests and come back with enough of its roots to help them out in the winter's pinch.

" Now, if anybody'll study Nature," she would say, " they'll see she never cal'c'lated to fetch us here 'ithout makin' 'lowance fur to feed us. The fus' thing that comes up is dandelions — an' I don't want to stick my tooth in anything that's better than dandelion greens biled with hog-jowl. I like a biled dinner any way. Sas'fras tea comes mighty handy with dandelions in the spring, an' them two'll carry us through April. Then comes wild lettice an' tansy-tea — that's fur May. Blackberries is good fur June an' the jam'll take us through winter if Bullrun and Appomattox ain' too healthy. In the summer we can live on garden truck, an' in the fall there is wild reddishes an' water-cresses an' spatterdock, an' nuts an' pertatoes come in mighty

handy fur winter wuck. Why, I was born wuckin'—
when I was a gal I cooked, washed and done house-work
for a family of ten, an' then had time to spin ten hanks
o' yarn a day."

"Now there's the old man — he's too lazy to wuck —
he's like all parsons, he'd rather preach aroun' all his
life on a promise of heaven than to wuck on earth for
cash!"

"How did I ever come to marry Hilliard Watts?
Wal, he wa'n't that triflin' when I married him. He
didn't have so much religiun then. But I've allers
noticed a man's heredity for no-countness craps out
after he's married. Lookin' back now I reckin' I married him jes' to res' myself. When I'm wuckin' an' git
tired, I watches Hilliard doin' nothin' awhile an' it hopes
me pow'ful."

"He gits so busy at it an' seems so contented an'
happy."

Besides his wife there were five grandchildren in his
family — children of the old man's son by his second
wife. "Their father tuck after his stepmother," he
would explain regretfully, "an' wucked hisself to death
in the cotton factory. The dust an' lint give him con-
sumption. He was the only man I ever seed that tuck
after his stepmother"— he added sadly.

An old soldier never gets over the war. It has left a
nervous shock in his make-up — a memory in all his
after life which takes precedence over all other
things. The old man had the naming of the grand-
children, and he named them after the battles of the
Civil war. Bullrun and Seven Days were the boys.

Atlanta, Appomattox and Shiloh were the girls. His apology for Shiloh was: " You see I thout I'd name the last one Appomattox.   Then came a little one befo' her mammy died, so weak an' pitiful I named her Shi-loh."

It was the boast of their grandmother — that these children — even little Shiloh — aged seven — worked from ten to twelve hours every day in the cotton factory, rising before day and working often into the night, with forty minutes at noon for lunch.

They had not had a holiday since Christmas, and on the last anniversary of that day they had worked until ten o'clock, making up for lost time.   Their pay was twenty-five cents a day — except Shiloh, who received fifteen.

" But I'll soon be worth mo', pap," she would say as she crawled up into the old man's lap — her usual place when she had eaten her supper and wanted to rest. " An you know what I'm gwine do with my other nickel every day?   I'm gwine give it to the po' people of Indy an' China you preaches about."

And thus she would prattle — too young to know that, through the cupidity of white men, in this — the land of freedom and progress — she — this blue-eyed, white-skinned child of the Saxon race, was making the same wages as the Indian sepoy and the Chinese coolie.

It was Saturday night and after the old man had put Shiloh to bed, he mounted his horse and rode across the mountain to Westmoreland.

" Oh," said the old lady —" he's gwine over to Miss Alice's to git his Sunday School less'n.   An' I'd like to know what good Sunday school less'ns 'll do any body. If folks'd git in the habit of wuckin' mo' an' prayin' less, the worl'ud be better off, an' they'd really have somethin' to be thankful fur when Sunday comes, 'stid of livin' frum han' to mouth an' trustin' in some unknown God to cram feed in you' crops."

Hardened by poverty, work, and misfortune, she was the soul of pessimism.

CHAPTER VIII

FROM The Gaffs to Westmoreland, the home of Alice Westmore, was barely two miles up the level white pike.

Jim sat in the buggy at The Gaffs holding the horses while Richard Travis, having eaten his supper, was lighting a cigar and drawing on his overcoat, preparatory to riding over to Westmoreland.

The trotters stood at the door tossing their heads and eager to be off. They were cherry bays and so much alike that even Jim sometimes got them mixed. They were clean-limbed and racy looking, with flanks well drawn up, but with a broad bunch of powerful muscles which rolled from hip to back, making a sturdy back for the splendid full tails which almost touched the ground. In front they stood up straight, deep-chested, with clean bony heads, large luminous eyes and long slender ears, tapering into a point as velvety and soft as the tendril-bud on the tip of a Virginia creeper.

They stood shifting the bits nervously. The night air was cool and they wanted to go.

Travis came out and sprang from the porch to the buggy seat with the quick, sure footing of an athlete. Jim sat on the offside and passed him the lines just as he sang cheerily out:

" Heigh-ho — my honies — go ! "

The two mares bounded away so quickly and keenly that the near mare struck her quarters and jumped up into the air, running. Her off mate settled to work, trotting as steadily as a bolting Caribou, but pulling viciously.

Travis twisted the near bit with a deft turn of his left wrist, and as the two mares settled to their strides there was but one stroke from their shoes, so evenly and in unison did they trot. Down the level road they flew, Travis sitting gracefully upright and holding the lines in that sure, yet careless way which comes to the expert driver with power in his arms.

" How many times must I tell you, Jim," he said at last rather gruffly —" never to bring them out, even for the road, without their boots? Didn't you see Lizette grab her quarters and fly up just now? "

Jim was duly penitent.

Travis let them out a link. They flew down a soft, cool graveled stretch. He drew them in at the sound of an ominous click. It came from Sadie B.

" Sadie B.'s forging again. Didn't I tell you to have the blacksmith move her hind shoes back a little? "

" I did, sir," said Jim.

" You've got no weight on her front feet, then," said Travis critically.

" Not to-night, sir — I took off the two ounces thinking you'd not speed them to-night, sir."

" You never know when I'm going to speed them. The night is as good as the day when I want a tonic."

They had reached the big stone posts which marked

the boundary of Westmoreland. A little farther on the mares wheeled into the gate, for it was open and lay, half on the ground, hanging by one hinge. It had not been painted for years. The driveway, too, had been neglected. The old home, beautiful even in its decay, sat in a fine beech grove on the slope of a hill. A wide veranda, with marble flag-stones as a base, ran across the front. Eight Corinthian pillars sentineled it, resting on a marble base which seemed to spring up out of the flag-stones themselves, and towering to the projecting entablature above.

On one side an ell could be seen, covered with ivy. On the other the roof of a hot-house, with the glass broken out.

It touched even Richard Travis — this decay. He had known the place in the days of its glory before its proprietor, Colonel Theodore Westmore, broken by the war, in spirit and in pocket, had sent a bullet into his brain and ended the bitter fight with debt. Since then, no one but the widow and her daughter knew what the fight had been, for Clay Westmore, the brother, was but a boy and in college at the time. He had graduated only a few months before, and was now at home, wrapped up, as Richard Travis had heard, in what to him was a visionary scheme of some sort for discovering a large area of coal and iron thereabouts. He had heard, too, that the young man had taken hold of what had been left, and that often he had been seen following the plough himself.

Travis drove through the driveway — then he pulled

up the mares very gently, got out and felt of their flanks.

"Take them to the barn and rub them off," he said, "while you wait. And for a half hour bandage their hind legs — I don't want any wind puffs from road work."

He started into the house. Then he turned and said: "Be here at the door, Jim, by ten o'clock, sharp. I shall make another call after this. Mind you now, ten o'clock, sharp."

At the library he knocked and walked in.

Mrs. Westmore sat by the fire. She was a small, daintily-made woman, and beautiful even at fifty-five. She had keen, black eyes and nervous, flighty ways. A smile, half cynical, half inviting, lit up continuously her face.

"Richard?" she said, rising and taking his hand.

"Cousin Alethea — I thought you were Alice and I was going to surprise her."

Mrs. Westmore laughed her metallic little laugh. It was habit. She intended it to be reassuring, but too much of it made one nervous. It was the laugh without the soul in it — the eye open and lighted, but dead. It was a Damascus blade falling from the stricken arm to the stone pavement and not against the ringing steel of an opponent.

"You will guess, of course, where she is," she said after they were seated.

"No?" from Travis.

"Getting their Sunday School lesson — she, Uncle Bisco, and the Bishop."

Travis frowned and gave a nervous twitch of his shoulders as he turned around to find himself a chair.

" No one knows just how we feel towards Uncle Bisco and his wife," went on Mrs. Westmore in half apology —" she has been with us so long and is now so old and helpless since they were freed; their children have all left them — gone — no one knows where.   And so Uncle Bisco and Aunt Charity are as helpless as babes, and but for Alice they would suffer greatly."

A sudden impulse seized Travis: " Let us go and peep in on them. We shall have a good joke on Her Majesty."

Mrs. Westmore laughed, and they slipped quietly out to Uncle Bisco's cabin.   Down a shrubbery-lined walk they went — then through the woods across a field.   It was a long walk, but the path was firm and good, and the moon lit it up.   They came to the little cabin at last, in the edge of another wood.   Then they slipped around and peeped in the window.

A small kerosene lamp sat on a table lighting up a room scrupulously clean.

Uncle Bisco was very old.   His head was, in truth, a cotton plant full open.   His face was intelligent, grave — such a face as Howard Weeden only could draw from memory.   He had finished his supper, and from the remnants left on the plate it was plain that Alice Westmore had prepared for the old man dainties which she, herself, could not afford to indulge in.

By him sat his old wife, and on the other side of the fireplace was the old overseer, his head also white, his face strong and thoughtful.   He was clean shaven, save a patch of short white chin-whiskers, and his big straight nose had a slight hook of shrewdness in it.

Alice Westmore was reading the chapter — her voice added to it an hundred fold: "Let not your heart be troubled. . . . Ye believe in God, believe also in me. . . . In my Father's house are many mansions . . . !"

The lamplight fell on her hair. It was brown where the light flashed over it, and lay in rippling waves around her temples in a splendid coil down the arch of her neck, and shining in strong contrast through the gauzy dark sheen of her black gown. But where the light fell, there was that suspicion of red which the last faint tendril a dying sunbeam throws out in a parting clutch at the bosom of a cloud.

It gave one a feeling of the benediction of twilight.

And when she looked up, her eyes were the blessings poured out — luminous, helpful, uplifting, restful,— certain of life and immortality, full of all that which one sees not, when awake, but only when in the borderland of sleep, and memory, unleashed, tracks back on the trail of sweet days which once were.

They spake indeed always thus: "Let not your heart be troubled. . . . Peace, be still."

Her face did not seem to be a separate thing — apart — as with most women. For there are women whose hair is one thing and whose face is another. The hair is beautiful, pure, refined. The face beautiful, merely. The hair decorous, quiet, unadorned and debauched not by powder and paint, stands aloof as Desdemona, Ophelia or Rosalind. The face, brazen, with a sharp-

7

tongued, vulgar queen of a thing in its center, on a throne, surrounded by perfumed nymphs, under the sensual glare of two rose-colored lamps, sits and holds a Du Barry court.

They are neighbors, but not friends, and they live in the same sphere, held together only by the law of gravity which holds to one spot of earth the rose and the ragwort. And the hair, like the rose, in all the purity of its own rich sweetness, all the naturalness of its soul, sits and looks down upon the face as a queen would over the painted yellow thing thrust by the law of life into her presence.

But the face of Alice Westmore was companion to her hair. The firelight fell on it; and while the glow from the lamp fell on her hair in sweet twilight shadows of good night, the rosy, purple beams of the cheerful firelight lit up her face with the sweet glory of a perpetual good morning.

Travis stood looking at her forgetful of all else. His lips were firmly set, as of a strong mind looking on its life-dream, the quarry of his hunter-soul all but in his grasp. Flashes of hope and little twists of fear were there; then, as he looked again, she raised, half timidly, her face as a Madonna asking for a blessing; and around his, crept in the smile which told of hope long deferred.

Selfish, impure, ambitious, forceful and masterful as he was, he stood hopeless and hungry-hearted before this pure woman. She had been the dream of his life — all times — always — since he could remember.

To own her — to win her!

As he looked up, the hardness of his face attracted even Mrs. Westmore, smiling by his side at the scene before her. She looked up at Travis, but when she saw his face the smile went out of hers. It changed to fear.

All the other passions in his face had settled into one cruel cynical smile around his mouth — a smile of winning or of death.

For the first time in her life she feared Richard Travis.

" I must go now," said Alice Westmore to the old men —" but I'll sing you a verse or two."

The overseer leaned back in his chair. Uncle Bisco stooped forward, his chin resting on his hickory staff.

And then like the clear notes of a spring, dripping drop by drop with a lengthening cadence into the covered pool of a rock-lined basin, came a simple Sunday School song the two old men loved so well.

There were tears in the old negro's eyes when she had finished. Then he sobbed like a child.

Alice Westmore arose to go.

" Now, Bishop —" she smiled at the overseer — " don't keep Uncle Bisco up all night talking about the war, and if you don't come by the house and chat with mamma and me awhile, we'll be jealous."

The overseer looked up: " Miss Alice — I'm an ole man an' we ole men all dream dreams when night comes. Moods come over us and, look where we will, it all leads back to the sweet paths of the past. To-day — all day — my mind has been on "— he stopped, afraid to pronounce the word and hunting around in the scanty lexicon of his mind for some phase of speech, some word even that might not awaken in Alice Westmore memories of the past.

Richard Travis had an intuition of things as naturally as an eagle has the homing instinct, however high in air and beyond all earth's boundaries he flies. In this instance Mrs. Westmore also had it, for she looked up quickly at the man beside her. All the other emotions had vanished from his face save the one appealing look which said: " Come, let us go — we have heard enough."

Then they slipped back into the house.

Alice Westmore had stopped, smiling back from the doorway.

" On what, Bishop? " she finally asked.

He shook his head. " Jus' the dream of an ole man," he said. " Don't bother about us two ole men. I'll be 'long presently."

" Bisco," said the old preacher after a while, " come mighty nigh makin' a break then — but I've been thinkin' of Cap'n Tom all day. I can't throw it off."

Bisco shook his head solemnly. " So have I — so have I. The older I gits, the mo' I miss Marse Tom."

" I don't like the way things are goin'— in yonder "— and the preacher nodded his head toward the house.

Uncle Bisco looked cautiously around to see that no one was near: " He's doin' his bes'— the only thing is whether she can forgit Marse Tom."

" Bisco, it ain't human nature for her to stan' up agin all that's brought to bear on her. Cap'n Tom is dead. Love is only human at las', an' like all else that's human it mus' fade away if it ain't fed. It's been ten years an' mo'— sence — Cap'n Tom's light went out."

"The last day of November —'64—" said Uncle Bisco, "I was thar an' seed it. It was at the Franklin fight."

"An' Dick Travis has loved her from his youth," went on the overseer, "an' he loves her now, an' he's a masterful man."

"So is the Devil," whispered Uncle Bisco, "an didn't he battle with the angels of the Lord an' mighty nigh hurled 'em from the crystal battlements."

"Bisco, I know him — I've knowed him from youth. He's a conjurin' man — a man who does things — he'll win her — he'll marry her yet. She'll not love him as she did Cap'n Tom. No — she'll never love again. But life is one thing an' love is another, an' it ain't often they meet in the same person. Youth mus' live even if it don't love, an' the law of nature is the law of life."

"I'm afeered so," said the old negro, shaking his head, "I'm afeered it'll be that way — but — I'd ruther see her die to-night."

"If God lets it be," said the preacher, "Bisco, if God lets it be —" he said excitedly, "if he'll let Cap'n Tom die an' suffer the martyrdom he suffered for conscience sake an' be robbed, as he was robbed, of his home, an' of his love — if God'll do that, then all I can say is, that after a long life walkin' with God, it'll be the fus' time I've ever knowed Him to let the wrong win out in the end. An' that ain't the kind of God I'm lookin' fur."

" Do you say that, Marse Hillyard? " asked the old negro quickly — his eyes taking on the light of hope as one who, weak, comes under the influence of a stronger mind. " Marse Hillyard, do you believe it? Praise God."

" Bisco — I'm — I'm ashamed — why should I doubt Him — He's told me a thousand truths an' never a lie."

" Praise God," replied the old man softly.

And so the two old men talked on, and their talk was of Captain Tom. No wonder when the old preacher mounted his horse to go back to his little cabin, all of his thoughts were of Captain Tom. No wonder Uncle Bisco, who had raised him, went to bed and dreamed of Captain Tom — dreamed and saw again the bloody Franklin fight.

CHAPTER IX

A MUTUAL UNDERSTANDING

IN the library, Travis and Mrs. Westmore sat for some time in silence. Travis, as usual, smoked, in his thoughtful way watching the firelight which flickered now and then, half lighting up the room. It was plain that both were thinking of a subject that neither wished to be the first to bring up.

"I have been wanting all day to ask you about the mortgage," she said to him, finally.

"Oh," said Travis, indifferently enough —"that's all right. I arranged it at the bank to-day."

"I am so much obliged to you; it has been so on my mind," said his companion. "We women are such poor financiers, I wonder how you men ever have patience to bother with us. Did you get Mr. Shipton to carry it at the bank for another year?"

"Why — I — you see, Cousin Alethea — Shipton's a close dog — and the most unaccommodating fellow that ever lived when it comes to money. And so — er — well — the truth is — is — I had to act quickly and for what I thought was your interest."

Mrs. Westmore looked up quickly, and Travis saw the pained look in her face. "So I bought it in myself," he went on, carelessly flecking his cigar ashes into the fire. "I just had the judgment and sale transferred to me — to accommodate you — Cousin Alethea — you understand that — entirely for you. I hate to see you bothered this way — I'll carry it as long as you wish."

She thanked him again, more with her eyes than her voice. Then there crept over her face that look of trouble and sorrow, unlike any Travis had ever seen there. Once seen on any human face it is always remembered, for it is the same, the world over, upon its millions and millions — that deadened look of trouble which carries with it the knowledge that the spot called home is lost forever.

There are many shifting photographs from the camera called sorrow, pictured on the delicate plate of the human soul or focused in the face. There is the crushed look when Death takes the loved one, the hardened look when an ideal is shattered, the look of dismay from wrecked hopes and the cynical look from wrecked happiness — but none of these is the numbed and dumb look of despair which confronts humanity when the home is gone.

It runs not alone through the man family, but every other animal as well, from the broken-hearted bird which sits on the nearby limb, and sees the wreck of her home by the ravages of a night-prowling marauder, to the squalidest of human beings, turning their backs forever on the mud-hut that had once sheltered them.

To Mrs. Westmore it was a keen grief. Here had she come as a bride — here had she lived since — here had been born her two children — here occurred the great sorrow of her life.

And the sacredest memory, at last, of life, lies not in

the handclasp of a coming joy, but in the footfall of a vanishing sorrow.

Westmoreland meant everything to Mrs. Westmore — the pride of birth, of social standing, the ties of mother-hood, the very altar of her life. And it was her hus-band's name and her own family. It meant she was not of common clay, nor unknown, nor without influence. It was bound around and woven into her life, and part of her very existence.

Home in the South means more than it does anywhere else on earth; for local self-government — wherever the principle came from — finds its very altar there. States-right is nothing but the home idea, stretched over the state and bounded by certain lines. The peculiar in-stitutions of the South made every home a castle, a town, a government, a kingdom in itself, in which the real ruler is a queen.

Ask the first negro or child met in the road, whose home is this, or that, and one would think the entire Southland was widowed.

From the day she had entered it as a bride, Westmore-land, throughout the County, had been known as the home of Mrs. Westmore.

She was proud of it. She loved it with that love which had come down through a long line of cavaliers loving their castles.

And now she knew it must go, as well as that, sooner or later, Death itself must come.

She knew Richard Travis, and she knew that, if from his life were snatched the chance of making Alice Westmore his wife he would sell the place as cold-bloodedly as Shipton would.

Travis sat smoking, but reading her. He spelled her thoughts as easily as if they had been written on her forehead, for he was a man who spelled.   He smoked calmly and indifferently, but the one question of his heart — the winning of Alice,— surged in his breast and it said: " Now is the time — now — buy her — the mother.   This is the one thing which is her price."

He looked at Mrs. Westmore again.   He scanned her closely, from her foot to the dainty head of beautiful, half-grey hair.   He could read her as an open book — her veneration of all Westmoreland things — her vanity — her pride of home and name and position; the overpowering independence of that vanity which made her hold up her head in company, just as in the former days, tho' to do it she must work, scrub, pinch, ay, even go hungry.

He knew it all and he knew it better than she guessed — that it had actually come to a question of food with them; that her son was a geological dreamer, just out of college, and that Alice's meagre salary at the rundown female college where she taught music was all that stood between them and poverty of the bitterest kind.

For there is no poverty like the tyranny of that which sits on the erstwhile throne of plenty.

He glanced around the room — the hall — the home — in his mind's eye — and wondered how she did it — how she managed that poverty should leave no trace of itself in the home, the well furnished and elegant old

home, from its shining, polished furniture and old silver
to the oiled floor of oak and ash.

Could he buy her — bribe her, win her to work for
him? He started to speak and say: "Cousin Alethea,
may not all this be stopped, this debt and poverty and
make-believe — this suffering of pride, transfixed by the
spears of poverty? Let you and me arrange it, and all
so satisfactorily. I have loved Alice all my life."

There is the fool in every one of us. And that is what
the fool in Richard Travis wished him to say. What
he did say was:

"Oh, it was nothing but purely business on my part
— purely business. I had the money and was looking for
a good investment. I was glad to find it. There are
a hundred acres and the house left. And by the way,
Cousin Alethea, I just added five-hundred dollars more
to the principal,— thought, perhaps, you'd need it, you
know? You'll find it to your credit at Shipton's bank."

He smoked on as if he thought it was nothing. As a
business fact he knew the place was already mortgaged
for all it was worth.

"Oh, how can we ever thank you enough?"

Travis glanced at her when she spoke. He flushed
when he heard her place a slight accent on the *we*. She
glanced at him and then looked into the fire. But in
their glances which met, they both saw that the other
knew and understood.

"And by the way, Cousin Alethea," said Travis after
a while, "of course it is not necessary to let Alice know
anything of this business. It will only worry her un-
necessarily."

"Of course not," said Mrs. Westmore.

CHAPTER X

A STAR AND A SATELLITE

AN hour later Mrs. Westmore had gone to her room
and Alice had been singing his favorite songs.
Her singing always had a peculiar influence
over Richard Travis — a moral influence, which, perhaps, was the secret of its power; and all influence which
is permanent is moral. There was in it for him an uplifting force that he never experienced save in her presence and under the influence of her songs.

He was a brilliant man and he knew that if he won
Alice Westmore it must be done on a high plane.
Women were his playthings — he had won them by the
score and flung them away when won. But all his life
— even when a boy — he had dreamed of finally winning
Alice Westmore and settling down.

Like all men who were impure, he made the mistake
of thinking that one day, when he wished, he could be
pure.

Such a man may marry, but it is a thing of conven-
ience, a matter in which he selects some woman, who
he knows will not be his mistress, to become his house-
keeper.

And thus she plods along in life, differing eventually
only from his mistress in that she is the mother of his
children.

In all Richard's longings, too, for Alice Westmore, there was an unconscious cause. He did not know it because he could not know.

Sooner or later love, which is loose, surfeits and sours. It is then that it turns instinctively to the pure, as the Jews, straying from their true God and meeting the chastisement of the sword of Babylon, turned in their anguish to the city of their King.

Nature is inexorable, and love has its laws as fixed as those which hold the stars in their course. And woe to the man or woman who transgresses! He who, ere it is ripe, deflowers the bud of blossoming love in wantonness and waste, in after years will watch and wait and water it with tears, in vain, for that bloom will never come.

She came over by the fire. Her face was flushed; her beautiful sad eyes lighted with excitement.

"Do you remember the first time I ever heard you sing, Alice?"

His voice was earnest and full of pathos, for him.

"Was it not when father dressed me as a gypsy girl and I rode my pony over to The Gaffs and sang from horseback for your grandfather?"

He nodded: "I thought you were the prettiest thing I ever saw, and I have thought so ever since. That's when I fell in love with you."

"I remember quite distinctly what you did," she said. "You were a big boy and you came up behind my pony and jumped on, frightening us dreadfully."

"Tried to kiss you, didn't I?"

She laughed: "That was ever a chronic endeavor of your youth."

How pretty she looked. Had it been any other woman he would have reached over and taken her hand.

" Overpower her, master her, make her love you by force of arms "— his inner voice said.

He turned to the musing woman beside him and mechanically reached out his hand. Hers lay on the arm of her chair. The next instant he would have dropped his upon it and held it there. But as he made the motion her eyes looked up into his, so passion-free and holy that his own arm fell by his side.

But the little wave of passion in him only stirred him to his depths. Ere she knew it or could stop him he was telling her the story of his love for her. Poetry,— romance,— and with it the strength of saying,— fell from his lips as naturally as snow from the clouds. He went into the history of old loves — how, of all loves they are the greatest — of Jacob who served his fourteen years for Rachel, of the love of Petrarch, of Dante.

" Do you know Browning's most beautiful poem? " he asked at last. His voice was tenderly mellow:

" All that I know of a certain star
    Is, it can throw (like the angled spar)
    Now a dart of red, now a dart of blue;
    Till my friends have said they would fain see, too,
    My star that dartles the red and the blue!
    Then it stops like a bird; like a flower, hangs furled:
    They must solace themselves with the Saturn above it.
    What matter to me if their star is a world?
    Mine has opened its soul to me; therefore I love it."

" Alice," he said, drawing his chair closer to her, " I
know I have no such life to offer as you would bring
to me. The best we men can do is to do the best we can.
We are saved only because there is one woman we can
look to always as our star. There is much of our past
that we all might wish to change, but change, like work,
is the law of life, and we must not always dream."

Quietly he had dropped his hand upon hers. Her
own eyes were far off — they were dreaming. So deep
was her dream that she had not noticed it. Passion
practised, as he was, the torch of her hand thrilled him
as with wine; and as with wine was he daring.

" I know where your thoughts have been," he went on.

She looked up with a start and her hand slipped from
under his into her lap. It was a simple movement and
involuntary — like that of the little brown quail when
she slips from the sedge-grass into the tangled depths of
the blossoming wild blackberry bushes at the far off flash
of a sharp-shinned hawk-wing, up in the blue. Nor
could she say whether she saw it, or whether it was merely
a shadow, an instinctive signal from the innocent courts
of the sky to the brood-children of her innocence below.

But he saw it and said quickly, changing with it the
subject: " At least were — but all that has passed. I
need you, Alice," he went on passionately —" in my life,
in my work. My home is there, waiting! It has been
waiting all these years for you — its mistress — the only
mistress it shall ever have. Your mother "— Alice
looked at him surprised.

" Your mother — you,— perhaps, had not thought
of that — your mother needs the rest and the care we

could give her.   Our lives are not always our own," he
went on gravely —" oftentimes it belongs partly to
others — for their happiness."

He felt that he was striking a winning chord.

"You can love me if you would say so," he said,
bending low over her.

This time, when his hand fell on hers, she did not
move.   Surprised, he looked into her eyes.   There were
tears there.

Travis knew when he had gone far enough.   Reverently he kissed her hand as he said:

"Never mind — in your own time, Alice.   I can
wait — I have waited long.   Twenty years," he added,
patiently, even sweetly, " and if need be, I'll wait twenty
more."

"I'll go now," he said, after a moment.

She looked at him gratefully, and arose.   "One moment, Richard," she said —" but you were speaking of
mother, and knowing your zeal for her I was afraid
you might — might — the mortgage has been troubling
her."

"Oh, no — no "— he broke in quickly —" I did nothing — absolutely nothing — though I wanted to for
your sake."

"I'm so glad," she said —" we will manage somehow.   I am so sensitive about such things."

"I'll come to-morrow afternoon and bring your
mare."

She smiled, surprised.

"Yes, your mare — I happened on her quite unexpectedly in Tennessee.   I have bought her for you —

she is elegant, and I wish you to ride her often. I have given Jim orders that no one but you shall ride her. If it is a pretty day to-morrow I shall be around in the afternoon, and we will ride down to the bluffs five miles away to see the sunset."

The trotters were at the door. He took her hand as he said good-bye, and held it while he added:

" Maybe you'd better forget all I said to-night — be patient with me — remember how long I have waited."

He was off and sprang into the buggy, elated. Never before had she let him hold her hand even for a moment. He felt, he knew, that he would win her.

He turned the horses and drove off.

From Westmoreland Travis drove straight toward the town. The trotters, keen and full of play, flew along, tossing their queenly heads in the very exuberance of life.

At The Gaffs, he drew rein: "Now, Jim, I'll be back at midnight. You sleep light until I come in, and have their bedding dry and blankets ready."

He tossed the boy a dollar as he drove off.

Up the road toward the town he drove, finally slackening his trotters' speed as he came into the more thickly settled part of the outskirts. Sand Mountain loomed high in the faint moonlight, and at its base, in the outposts of the town, arose the smokestack of the cotton mills.

Around it lay Cottontown.

Slowly he brought the nettled trotters down to a walk. Quietly he turned them into a shaded lane, overhung with forest trees, near which a cottage, one of the many

8

belonging to the mill, stood in the shadow of the forest.

Stopping his horses in the shadow, he drew out his watch and pressed the stem. It struck eleven.

He drew up the buggy-top and taking the little silver whistle from his pocket, gave a low whistle.

It was ten minutes later before the side door of the cottage opened softly and a girl came noiselessly out. She slipped out, following the shadow line of the trees until she came up to the buggy. Then she threw the shawl from off her face and head and stood smiling up at Travis. It had been a pretty face, but now it was pinched by overwork and there was the mingling both of sadness and gladness in her eyes. But at sight of Travis she blushed joyfully, and deeper still when he held out his hand and drew her into the buggy and up to the seat beside him.

" Maggie "—was all he whispered. Then he kissed her passionately on her lips. " I am glad I came," he went on, as he put one arm around her and drew her to him —" you're flushed and the ride will do you good."

She was satisfied to let her head lie on his shoulder.

" They are beauties "— she said after a while, as the trotters' thrilling, quick step brought the blood tingling to her veins.

" Beauties for the beauty," said Travis, kissing her again. Her brown hair was in his face and the perfume of it went through him like the whistling flash of the first wild doe he had killed in his first boyish hunt and which he never forgot.

" You do love me," she said at last, looking up into his face, where her head rested. She could not move because his arm held her girlish form to him with an over-powering clasp.

"Why?" he asked, kissing her again and in sheer passionate excess holding his lips on hers until she could not speak, but only look love with her eyes. When she could, she sighed and said:

"Because, you could not make me so happy if you didn't."

He relaxed his arm to control the trotters, which were going too fast down the road. She sat up by his side and went on.

"Do you know I have thought lots about what you said last Saturday night?"

"Why, what?" he asked.

She looked pained that he had forgotten.

"About — about — our bein' married to each other — even — even — if — if — there's no preacher. You know — that true love makes marriages, and not a cere-mony — and — and — that the heart is the priest to all of us, you know!"

Travis said nothing. He had forgotten all about it.

"One thing I wrote down in my little book when I got back home an' memorized it — Oh, you can say such beautiful things."

He seized her and kissed her again.

"I am so happy with you — always —" she laughed.

He drove toward the shaded trees down by the river.

"I want you to see how the setting moonlight looks on the river," he said. "There is nothing in all nature like it. It floats like a crescent above, falling into the arms of its companion below. All nature is love and never fails to paint a love scene in preference to all others, if permitted. How else can you account for it making two lover moons fall into each other's arms," he laughed.

She looked at him enraptured. It was the tribute which mediocrity pays to genius.

Presently they passed by Westmoreland, and from Alice's window a light shone far out into the golden tinged leaves of the beeches near.

Travis glanced up at it. Then at the pretty mill-girl by his side:

" A star and — a satellite!"— he smiled to himself.

CHAPTER XI

IT was growing late when the old preacher left Westmoreland and rode leisurely back toward the cabin
on Sand Mountain. The horse he was riding — a
dilapidated roan — was old and blind, but fox-trotted
along with the easy assurance of having often travelled
the same road.

The bridle rested on the pommel of the saddle. The
old man's head was bent in deep thought, and the roan,
his head also down and half dreaming, jogged into the
dark shadows which formed a wooded gulch, leading into
the valley and from thence into the river.

There is in us an unnameable spiritual quality which,
from lack of a more specific name, we call mental telepathy. Some day we shall know more about it, just as
some day we shall know what unknown force it is which
draws the needle to the pole.

It is the border land of the spiritual — a touch of it,
given, to let us know there is more and in great abun-
dance in the country to which we ultimately shall go,—
a glimpse of the kingdom which is to be.

To-night, this influence was on the old man. The
theme of his thoughts was, Captain Tom. Somehow he
felt that even then Captain Tom was near him. How —
where — why — he could not tell. He merely felt it.

117

And so the very shadows of the trees grew uncanny to him as he rode by them and the slight wind among them mourned *Captain Tom — Captain Tom*.

It was a desolate place in the narrow mountain road and scarcely could the old man see the white sand which wound in and through it, and then out again on the opposite side into the clearing beyond the scraggy side of Sand Mountain. But the horse knew every foot of the way, and though it was always night with him, instinct had taught him a sure footing.

Suddenly the rider was awakened from his reverie by the old horse stopping so suddenly as almost to unseat him. With a snort the roan had stopped and had thrown up his head, quivering with fear, while with his nose he was trying to smell out the queer thing which stood in his path.

The moon broke out from behind a cloud at the same moment, and there, in the middle of the road, not ten yards from him, stood a heavily built, rugged, black-bearded man in a ragged slouched hat and pointing a heavy revolver at the rider's head.

"Hands up, Hilliard Watts!"

The old man looked quietly into the muzzle of the revolver and said, with a laugh:

"This ain't 'zactly my benediction time, Jack Bracken, an' I've no notion of h'istin' my arms an' axin' a blessin' over you an' that old pistol. Put it up an' tell me what you want," he said more softly.

"Well, you do know me," said the man, coming forward and thrusting his pistol into its case. "I wa'nt sho' it was you," he said, "and I wa'nt sho' you'd kno'

me if it was.   In my business I have to be mighty keerful," he added with a slight laugh.

He came up to the saddle-skirt and held out his hand,
half hesitatingly, as he spoke.

The Bishop — as every one knew him — glanced into
the face before him and saw something which touched
him quickly.   It was grief-stricken, and sorrow sat in
the fierce eyes, and in the shadows of the dark face.   And
through it all, a pleading, beseeching appeal for sympathy ran as he half doubtingly held out his hand.

" Why,— yes —, I'll take it, Jack, robber that you
are," said the old man cheerily.   " You may not be as
bad as they say, an' no man is worse than his heart.   But
what in the worl' do you want to hold up as po' a man
as me — an' if I do say it, yo' frien' when you was a
boy? "

" I know," said the other —" I know.   I don't want
yo' money, even if you had it.   I want you.   You've
come as a God-send.   I — I couldn't bury him till you'd
said somethin'."

His voice choked — he shook with a suppressed sob.

The bishop slid off his horse: " What is it, Jack?
You hain't kilt anybody, have you? "

" No — no "— said   the   other —" its   little — little
Jack — he's dead."

The Bishop looked at him inquiringly.   He had never
before heard of little Jack.

" I — I dunno', Jack," he said.   " You'll have to tell
me all.   I hain't seed you sence you started in your robber career after the war — sence I buried yo' father,"
he added.   "An' a fine, brave man he was, Jack — a

fine, brave man — an' I've wondered how sech a man's son could ever do as you've done."

"Come," said the other —" I'll tell you.   Come, an' say a prayer over little Jack fust.   You must do it "— he said almost fiercely —" I won't bury him without a prayer — him that was an angel an' all I had on earth. Hitch yo' hoss just outer the road, in the thicket, an' follow me."

The Bishop did as he was told, and Jack Bracken led the way down a rocky gulch under the shaggy sides of Sand Mountain, furzed with scraggy trees and thick with underbrush and weeds.

It was a tortuous path and one in which the old man himself, knowing, as he thought he did, every foot of the country around, could easily have been lost.   Above, through the trees, the moon shone dimly, and no path could be seen under foot.   But Jack Bracken slouched heavily along, in a wabbling, awkward gait, never once looking back to see if his companion followed.

For a half mile they went through what the Bishop had always thought was an almost impenetrable cattle trail.   At last they wound around a curve on the densely wooded side of the mountain, beyond which lay the broad river breathing out frosty mist and vapor from its sleeping bosom.

Following a dry gulch until it ended abruptly at the river's bluff, around the mouth of which great loose rocks lay as they had been washed by the waters of many centuries, and bushes grew about, the path terminated abruptly.   It overlooked the river romantically, with a natural rock gallery in front.

Jack Bracken stopped and sat down on one of the rocks. From underneath he drew forth a lantern and prepared to light it. " This is my home," he said laconically.

The Bishop looked around: " Well, Jack, but this is part of my own leetle forty-acre farm. Why, thar's my cabin up yander. We've wound in an' aroun' the back of my place down by the river! I never seed this hole befo'."

" I knew it was yo's," said the outlaw quietly. " That's why I come here. Many a Sunday night I've slipped up to the little church winder an' heard you preach — me an' po' little Jack. Oh, he loved to hear the Bible read an' he never forgot nothin' you ever said. He knowed all about Joseph an' Moses an' Jesus, an' last night when he died o' that croup befo' I c'ud get him help or anything, he wanted you, an' he said he was goin' to the lan' where you said Jesus was —"

He broke down — he could not say it.

Stepping into the mouth of the cave, he struck a match, when out of sight of the entrance way, and stepping from stone to stone he guided the Bishop down some twenty feet, following the channel the water had cut on its way underground to the river. Here another opening entered into the dry channel, and into it he stepped.

It was a nicely turned cave — a natural room,— arched above with beautiful white lime-rock, the stalactites hanging in pointed clusters, their starry points twinkling above like stars in a winter sky. Underneath, the soft sand made a clean, warm floor, and the entire

cave was so beautiful that the old man could do nothing
but look and admire, as the light fell on stalagmite and
ghostly columns and white sanded floors.

" Beautiful," he said —" Jack, you cudn't he'p gettin' relig'un here."

" Little Jack loved 'em," said the outlaw.   " He'd lay
here ev'y night befo' he'd go to sleep an' look up an'
call it his heaven; an' he said that big column thar was
the great white throne, an' them big things up yander
with wings was angels.   He had all them other columns
named for the fellers you preached about — Moses an'
Aaron an' Joseph an' all of 'em, an' that kind o' double
one lookin' like a woman holding her child, he called
Mary an' little Jesus."

" He's gone to a prettier heaven than this," said the
Bishop looking down on the little figure, with face as
pale and white as any of the columns around him, neatly
dressed and wrapped, save his face, in an old oil cloth
and lying on the little bed that sat in a corner.

The old man sat down very tenderly by the little dead
boy and, pulling out a testament from his pocket, read
to the outlaw, whose whole soul was centered in all he
said, the comforting chapter which Miss Alice had that
night read to the old negro: " *Let not your hearts be
troubled.   . . .*"

He explained as he read, and told the father how
little Jack was now in one of the many mansions and far
better off than living in a cave, the child of an outlaw,
for the Bishop did not mince his words.   He dwelt on
it, that God had taken the little boy for love of him,
and to give him a better home and perhaps as a means

of changing the father, and when he said the last prayer over the dead child asking for forgiveness for the father's sins, that he might meet the little one in heaven, the heart of the outlaw burst with grief and repentance within him.

He fell at the old man's feet, on his knees — he laid his big shaggy head in the Bishop's lap and wept as he had never wept before.

" There can't be — you don't mean," he said —" that there is forgiveness for me — that I can so live that I'll see little Jack again! "

" That's just what I mean, Jack," said the old man —" here it all is — here — in a book that never lies, an' all vouched for by Him who could walk in here to-night and lay His sweet hands on little Jack an' tell him to rise an' laugh agin, an' he'd do it. You turn about now an' see if it ain't so — an' that you'll be better an' happier."

" But — my God, man — you don't know — you don't understan'. I've robbed, I've killed. Men have gone down befo' my bullets like sheep. They was shootin' at me, too — but I shot best. I'm a murderer."

The old Bishop looked at him calmly.

" So was Moses and David," he replied —" men after God's own heart. An' so was many another that's now called a saint, from old Hickory Jackson up."

" But I'm a robber — a thief "— began Jack Bracken.

" We all steal," said the old man sadly shaking his head —" it's human nature. There's a thief in every trade, an' every idle hand is a robber, an' every idle tongue is a thief an' a liar. We all steal. But there's somethin' of God an' divinity in all of us, an' in spite of our shortcomin' it'll bring us back at last to our Father's home if we'll give it a chance. God's Book can't lie, an' it says: "*Tho' your sins be as scarlet they shall be white as snow!*" . . . an' then agin, *shall have life everlasting!*"

"Life everlastin'," repeated the outlaw. "Do you believe that? Oh, if it was only so! To live always up there an' with little Jack. How do you know it ain't lyin'? — Its too gran' to be so. How do you know it ain't lyin', I say? Hilliard Watts, are you handin' it out to me straight about this here Jesus Christ?" he cried bitterly.

"Well, it's this way, Jack," said the old man, "jes' this away an' plain as the nose on yo' face: Now here's me, ain' it? Well, you know I won't lie to you. You believe me, don't you?"

The outlaw nodded.

"Why?" asked the Bishop.

"Because you ain't never lied to me," said the other. "You've allers told me the truth about the things I know to be so."

"But now, suppose," said the old man, "I'd tell you about somethin' you had never seed — that, for instance, sence you've been an outcast from society an' a livin' in this cave, I've seed men talk to each other a hundred miles apart, with nothin' but a wire betwix' 'em."

"That's mighty hard to believe," said the outlaw grimly.

"But I've seed it done," said the Bishop.

" Do you mean it? " asked the other.

" As I live, I have," said the Bishop.

" Then it's so," said Jack.

" Now that's faith, Jack — an' common sense, too. We know what'll be the earthly end of the liar, an' the thief, an' the murderer, an' him that's impure — because we see 'em come to thar end all the time. It don't lie when it tells you the good are happy, an' the hones' are elevated an' the mem'ry of the just shall not perish, because them things we see come so. Now, if after tellin' you all that, that's true, it axes you to believe when it says there is another life — a spiritual life, which we can't conceive of, an' there we shall live forever, can't you believe that, too, sence it ain't never lied about what you can see, by your own senses? Why ever' star that shines, an' ever' beam of sunlight fallin' on the earth, an' ever' beat of yo' own heart by some force that we know not of, all of them is mo' wonderful than the telegraph, an' the livin' agin of the spirit ain't any mo' wonderful than the law that holds the stars in their places. You'll see little Jack agin as sho' as God lives an' holds the worl' in His hand."

The outlaw sat mute and motionless, and a great light of joy swept over his face.

" By God's help I'll do it "— and he bowed his head in prayer — the first he had uttered since he was a boy.

It was wonderful to see the happy and reconciled change when he arose and tenderly lifted the dead child in his arms. His face was transformed with a peace the old man had never seen before in any human being.

Strong men are always strong — in crime — in sin.

When they reform it is the reformation of strength. Such a change came over Jack Bracken, the outlaw.

He carried his dead child to the next room: " I've got his grave already chiseled out of the rocks. I'll bury him here — right under the columns he called Mary and little Jesus, that he loved to talk of so much."

" It's fitten "— said the old man tenderly — " it's fitten an' beautiful. The fust burial we know of in the Bible is where Abraham bought the cave of Machpelah for to bury Sarah, his wife. And as Abraham bought it of Ephron, the Hittite, and offered it to Abraham for to bury his dead out of his sight, so I give this cave to you, Jack Bracken, forever to be the restin' place of little Jack."

And so, tenderly and with many kisses did they bury little Jack, sinless and innocent, deep in the pure white rock, covered as he was with purity and looking ever upwards toward the statue above, wherein Nature's chisel had carved out a Madonna and her child.

CHAPTER XII

JACK BRACKEN was comfortably fixed in his underground home. There was every comfort for living. It was warm in winter and cool in summer, and in another apartment adjoining his living room was what he called a kitchen in which a spring of pure water, trickling down from rock to rock, formed in a natural basin of whitest rock below.

" Jack," said the old man, "won't you tell me about yo'self an' how you ever got down to this? I knowed you as a boy, up to the time you went into the army, an' if I do say it to yo' face, you were a brave hon'rble boy that never forgot a frien' nor —"

" A foe," put in Jack quickly. " Bishop, if I cu'd only forgive my foes — that's been the ruin of me."

" The old man was thoughtful a while: " Jack, that's a terrible thing in the human heart — unforgiveness. It's to life what a drought is to Nature — an' it spiles mo' people than any other weakness. But that don't make yo' no wuss than the rest of us, nor does robbery nor even murder. So there's a chance for you yet, Jack — a mighty fine chance, too, sence yo' heart is changed."

" Many a time, Jack, many a time when the paper 'ud be full of yo' holdin' up a train or shootin' a shar'ff, or robbin' or killin', I'd tell 'em what a good

127

boy you had been, brave an' game but revengeful when aroused. I'd tell 'em how you dared the bullets of our own men, after the battle of Shiloh, to cut down an' carry off a measley little Yankee they'd hung up as a spy 'cause he had onct saved yo' father's life. You shot two of our boys then, Jack."

"They was a shootin' me, too," he said quietly. "I caught two bullets savin' that Yankee. But he was no spy; he was caught in a Yankee uniform an'— an' he saved my father, as you said — that settled it with me."

"It turned our boys agin you, Jack."

"Yes, an' the Yankees were agin me already — that made all the worl' agin me, an' it's been agin me ever since — they made me an outlaw."

The old man softened: "How was it, Jack? I knowed you was driven to it."

"They shot my father — waylaid and killed him — some home-made Yankee bush-whackers that infested these hills — as you know."

The Bishop nodded. "I know — I know — it was awful. ' But vengeance is mine — I will repay '— saith the Lord."

"Well, I was young, an' my father — you know how I loved him. Befo' I c'ud get home they had burned our house, killed my sick mother from exposure and insulted my sisters."

"Jack," said the old man hotly — "a home-made Yankee is a 'bomination to the Lord. He's a twin brother to the Copperhead up north."

"My little brother — they might have spared him," went on the outlaw —"they might have spared him.

He tried to defen' his mother an' sisters an' they shot him down in col' blood."

" ' Vengeance is mine,' saith the Lord," replied the old man sadly.

" Well, I acted as His agent that time,"— his eyes were hot with a bright glitter. " I put on their uniform an' went after 'em. I j'ined 'em — the devils! An' they had a nigger sarjent an' ten of their twenty-seven was niggers, wearin' a Yankee uniform. I j'ined 'em — yes,— for wasn't I the agent of the Lord?" He laughed bitterly. " An' didn't He say: ' He that killeth with the sword must be killed with the sword.' One by one they come up missin', till I had killed all but seven. These got panicky — followed by an unknown doom an' they c'udn't see it, for it come like a thief at midnight an' agin like a pesterlence it wasted 'em at noonday. They separated — they tried to fly — they hid — but I followed 'em 'an I got all but one. He fled to California."

" It was awful, Jack — awful — God he'p you."

" Then a price was put on my head. I was Jack Bracken, the spy and the outlaw. I was not to be captured, but shot and hung. Then I cut down that Yankee an' you all turned agin me. I was hunted and hounded. I shot — they shot. I killed an' they tried to. I was shot down three times. I've got bullets in me now.

" After the war I tried to surrender. I wanted to quit and live a decent life. But no, they put a bigger price on my head. I came home like other soldiers an' went to tillin' my farm. They ran me away — they hunted an' hounded me. Civilization turned ag'in me. Society was my foe. I was up ag'in the fust law of Nature. It is the law of the survival — the wild beast that, cowered, fights for his life. Society turned on me — I turned on Society."

" But there was one thing that happen'd that put the steel in me wuss than all. All through them times was one star I loved and hoped for. I was to marry her when the war closed. She an' her sister — the pretty one — they lived up yander on the mountain side. The pretty one died. But when I lost faith in Margaret Adams, I lost it in mankind. I'd ruther a seen her dead. It staggered me — killed the soul in me — to think that an angel like her could fall an' be false."

" I don't blame you," said the old man. " I've never understood it yet."

" I was to marry Margaret. I love her yet," he added simply. " When I found she was false I went out — and — well, you know the rest."

He took a turn around the room, picked up one of little Jack's shoes, and cried over it.

" So I married his mother — little Jack's mother, a mountain lass that hid me and befriended me. She died when the boy was born. His granny kep' him while I was on my raids — nobody knowed it was my son. His granny died two years ago. This has been our home ever sence, an' not once, since little Jack has been with me, have I done a wrong deed. Often an' often we've slipt up to hear you preach — what you've said went home to me."

" Jack," said the old man suddenly aroused —" was

that you — was it you been puttin' them twenty dollar
gol' pieces in the church Bible — between the leds,
ever' month for the las' two years? By it I've kep' up
the po' of Cottontown. I've puzzled an' wonder'd —
I've thought of a dozen fo'ks — but I sed nothin' —
was it you? "

The outlaw smiled: " It come from the rich an' it
went to the po'. Come," he said —" that's somethin'
we must settle."

He took up the lantern and led the way into the
other room. Under a ledge of rocks, securely hid, sat,
in rows, half a dozen common water buckets, made of
red cedar, with tops fitting securely on them.

The outlaw spread a blanket on the sand, then knelt
and, taking up a bucket, removed the top and poured out
its contents on the blanket. They chuckled and rolled
and tumbled over each other, the yellow eagles and half
eagles, like thoroughbred colts turned out in the paddocks for a romp.

The old man's knees shook under him. He trembled
so that he had to sit down on the blanket. Then he
ran his hand through them — his fingers open, letting
the coins fall through playfully.

Never before had he seen so much gold. Poor as he
was and had ever been — much and often as he had suffered — he and his, for the necessities of life, even,
knowing its value and the use he might make of it, it
thrilled him with a strange, nervous longing — a childish curiosity to handle it and play with it.

Modest and brave men have looked on low-bosomed

women in the glitter of dissipative lights with the same feeling.

The old man gazed, silent — doubtless with the same awe which Keats gave to Cortez, when he first looked on the Pacific and stood

"Silent, upon a peak in Darien."

The outlaw lifted another bucket and took off the lid. It also was full. "There are five mo'," he said — "that last one is silver an' this one —" He lifted the lid of a small cedar box. In it was a large package, wrapped in water-proof. Unravelling it, he shoved out packages of bank bills of such number and denomination as fairly made the old preacher wonder.

"How much in all, Jack?"

"A little the rise of one hundred thousand dollars."

He pushed them back and put the buckets under their ledge of rocks. "I'd give it all just to have little Jack here agin — an'— an'— start out — a new man. This has cost me ten years of outlawry an' fo'teen bullets. Now I've got all this an'— well — a hole in the groun' an' little Jack in the hole. If you wanter preach a sermon cn the folly of pilin' up money," he went on half ironically, "here is yo' tex'. All me an' little Jack needed or cu'd use, was a few clothes, some bac'n an' coffee an' flour. Often I'd fill my pockets an' say: 'Well, I'll buy somethin' I want, an' that little Jack will want. I'd go to town an' see it all, an' think an' puzzle an' wonder — then I'd come home with a few toys, maybe, an' bac'n an' flour an' coffee."

"With all our money we can't buy higher than our

source, an' when we go we leave even that behind," he added.

"The world," said the old man quaintly, "is full of folks who have got a big pocket-book an' a bac'n pedigree."

"Do you know who this money belongs to?" he asked the outlaw.

"Every dollar of it," said Jack Bracken. "It come from railroads, banks and express companies. I didn't feel squirmish about takin' it, for all o' them are robbers. The only diff'r'nce betwix' them an' me is that they rob a little every day, till they get their pile, an' I take mine from 'em, all at onct."

He thought awhile, then he said: "But it must all go back to 'em, Jack. Let them answer for their own sins. Leave it here until next week — an' then we will come an' haul it fifty miles to the next town, where you can express it to them without bein' known, or havin' anybody kno' what's in the buckets till you're safe back here in this town. I'll fix it an' the note you are to write. They'll not pester you after they get their money. The crowd you've named never got hot under a gold collar. A clean shave will change you so nobody will suspect you, an' there's a good openin' in town for a blacksmith, an' you can live with me in my cabin."

"But there's one thing I've kept back for the las'," said Jack, after they had gone into the front part of the room and sat down on the deer skins there.

"That sword there "— and he pointed to the wall where it hung.

The Bishop glanced up, and as he did so he felt a

strange thrill of recognition run through him —" It belongs to Cap'n Tom," said Jack quietly.

The old man sprang up and took it reverently, fondly down.

" Jack —" he began.

" I was at Franklin," went on Jack proudly. " I charged with old Gen. Travis over the breastworks near the Carter House. I saw Cap'n Tom when he went under."

" Cap'n Tom," repeated the old man slowly.

" Cap'n Tom, yes — he saved my life once, you know. He cut me down when they were about to hang me for a spy — you heard about it? "

The Bishop nodded.

" It was his Company that caught me an' they was glad of any excuse to hang me. An' they mighty nigh done it, but Cap'n Tom came up in time to cut me down an' he said he'd make it hot for any man that teched me, that I was a square prisoner of war, an' he sent me to Johnson Island. Of course it didn't take me long to get out of that hole — I escaped."

The Bishop was silent, looking at the sword.

" Well, at Franklin, when I seed Cap'n Tom dyin' as I tho'rt, shunned by the Yankees as a traitor —"

" As a traitor? " asked the old man hotly —" what, after Shiloh — after he give up Miss Alice for the flag he loved an' his old grand sire an' The Gaffs an' all of us that loved him — you call that a traitor? "

" You never heard," said Jack, " how old Gen'l Travis charged the breastworks at Franklin and hit the line where Cap'n Tom's battery stood. Nine times they

had charged Cap'n Tom's battery that night — nine
times he stood his ground an' they melted away around
it.   But when he saw the line led by his own grand-sire
the blood in him was thicker than water and —"

" An' whut? " gasped the Bishop.

" Well, why they say it was a drunken soldier in his
own battery who struck him with the heavy hilt of a
sword.   Any way I found the old Gen'l cryin' over him:
' My Irish Gray — my Irish Gray,' he kept sayin'.
' I might have known it was you,' and the old Gen'l
charged on leaving him for dead.   An' so I found him
an' tuck him in my arms an' carried him to my own
cabin up yonder on the mountain — carried him an' —"

" An' whut? "— asked the old man, grasping the outlaw's shoulder —" Didn't he die?   We've never been
able to hear from him."

Jack shook his head.   " It 'ud been better for him if
he had "— and he touched his forehead significantly.

" Tell me, Jack — quick — tell it all," exclaimed the
old man, still gripping Jack's shoulder.

" There's nothin' to tell except that I kept him ever
sence — here — right here for two years, with little
Jack an' Ephrum, the young nigger that was his body
servant — he's been our cook an' servant.   He never
would leave Cap'n Tom, followed me offen the field of
Franklin.   An' mighty fond of each other was all three
of 'em."

The old man turned pale and his voice trembled so
with excitement he could hardly say:

" Where is he, Jack?   My God — Cap'n Tom —
he's been here all this time too — an' me awonderin'—"

" Right here, Bishop — kind an' quiet and teched in his head, where the sword-hilt crushed his skull. All these years I've cared for him — me an' Ephrum, my two boys as I called 'em — him an' little Jack. An' right here he staid contented like till little Jack died last night — then —"

" In God's name — quick! — tell me — Jack —"

" That's the worst of it — Bishop — when he found little Jack was dead he wandered off —"

" When? " almost shouted the old man.

" To-day — this even'. I have sent Eph after him — an' I hope he has found him by now an' tuck him somewhere. Eph'll never stop till he does."

" We must find him, Jack. Cap'n Tom alive — thank God — alive, even if he is teched in his head. Oh, God, I might a knowed it — an' only to-day I was doubtin' You."

He fell on his knees and Jack stood awed in the presence of the great emotion which shook the old man.

Finally he arose. " Come — Jack — let us go an' hunt for Cap'n Tom."

But though they hunted until the moon went down they found no trace of him. For miles they walked, or took turn about in riding the old blind roan.

" It's no use, Bishop," said Jack. " We will sleep a while and begin to-morrow. Besides, Eph is with him. I feel it — he'll take keer o' him."

That is how it came that at midnight, that Saturday night, the old Bishop brought home a strange man to live in the little cabin in his yard.

That is how, a week later, all the South was stirred

over the strange return of a fortune to the different corporations from which it had been taken, accompanied by a drawling note from Jack Bracken saying he returned ill-gotten gain to live a better life.

It ended laconically:

"*An' maybe you'd better go an' do likewise.*"

The dim starlight was shining faintly through the cracks of the outlaw's future home when the old man showed him in.

"Now, Jack," he said, "it's nearly mornin' an' the old woman may be wild an' raise sand. But learn to lay low an' shoe hosses. She was bohn disapp'inted — maybe because she wa'n't a boy," he whispered.

There was a whinny outside, in a small paddock, where a nearby stable stood: "That's Cap'n Tom's horse," said the old man —"I mus' go see if he's hungry."

"I've kept his horse these ten years, hopin' maybe he'd come back agin. It's John Paul Jones — the thoroughbred, that the old General give him."

"I remember him," said Jack.

The great bloodlike horse came up and rubbed his nose on the old man's shoulder.

"Hungry, John Paul?"

"It's been a job to get feed fur him, po' as I've been — but — but — he's Cap'n Tom's. You kno'—"

"An' Cap'n Tom will ride him yet," said Jack.

"Do you believe it, Jack?" asked the old man huskily —"God be praised!"

That Saturday night was one never to be forgotten

by others beside Jack Bracken and the old preacher of Cottontown.

When Helen Conway, after supper, sought her drunken father and learned that he really intended to have Lily and herself go into the cotton mills, she was crushed for the first time in her life.

An hour later she sent a boy with a note to The Gaffs to Harry Travis.

He brought back an answer that made her pale with wounded love and grief. Not even Mammy Maria knew why she had crept off to bed. But in the night the old woman heard sobs from the young girl's room where she and her sister slept.

"What is it, chile?" she asked as she slipped from her own cot in the adjoining little room and went in to Helen's.

The girl had been weeping all night — she had no mother — no one to whom she could unbosom her heart — no one but the old woman who had nursed her from her infancy. This kind old creature sat on the bed and held the girl's sobbing head on her lap and stroked her cheek. She knew and understood — she asked no questions:

"It isn't that I must work in the mill," she sobbed to the old woman —"I can do that — anything to help out — but — but — to think that Harry loves me so little as to give me up for — for — that."

"Don't cry, chile," said Mammy soothingly —"It ain't registered that you gwine wuck in that mill yit — I ain't made my afferdavit yit."

"But Harry doesn't love me — Oh, he doesn't love

me," she wept. " He would not give me up for anything if he did."

" I'm gwine give that Marse Harry a piece of my mind when I see him — see if I don't. Don't you cry, chile — hold up yo' haid an' be a Conway. Don't you ever let him know that yo' heart is bustin' for him an' fo' the year is out we'll have that same Marse Harry acrawlin' on his very marrow bones to aix our forgiveness. See if we won't."

It was poor consolation to the romantic spirit of Helen Conway. Daylight found her still heart-broken and sobbing in the old woman's lap.

PART THIRD — THE GIN

CHAPTER I

ALICE WESTMORE

IT is remarkable how small a part of our real life the
world knows — how little our most intimate friends
know of the secret influences which have proven to
be climaxes, at the turning points of our existence.

There was no more beautiful woman in Alabama than
Alice Westmore; and throughout that state, where the
song birds seem to develop, naturally, along with the
softness of the air, and the gleam of the sunshine, and
the lullaby of the Gulf's soft breeze among the pine
trees, there was no one, they say, who could sing as she
sang.

And she seemed to have caught it frcm her native
mocking-birds, so natural was it. Not when they sing
in the daylight, when everything is bright and joyous
and singing is so easy; but when they waken at midnight amid the *arbor vitæ* trees, and under the sweet,
sad influence of a winter moon, pour out their half
awakened notes to the star-sprays which fall in mist to
blend and sparkle around the soft neck of the night.

For like the star-sprays her notes were as clear; and
through them ran a sadness as of a mist of moonlight.
And just as moonbeams, when they mingle with the
mist, make the melancholy of night, so the memory of

a dead love ran through everything Alice Westmore sang.

And this made her singing divine.

Why should it be told? What right has a blacksmith to pry into a grand piano to find out wherein the exquisite harmony of the instrument lies? Who has the right to ask the artist how he blended the colors that crowned his picture with immortality, or the poet to explain his pain in the birth of a mood which moved the world?

Born in the mountains of North Alabama, she grew up there and developed this rare voice; and when her father sent her to Italy to complete her musical education, the depth and clearness of it captured even that song-nation of the world.

The great of all countries were her friends and princes sought her favors. She sang at courts and in great cathedrals, and her genius and beauty were toasts with society.

"Still, Mademoiselle will never be a great singer, perfect as her voice is,"— said her singing master to her one day — a famous Italian teacher, "until Mademoiselle has suffered. She is now rich and beautiful and happy. Go home and suffer if you would be a great singer," he said, "for great songs come only with great suffering."

If this were true, Alice Westmore was now, indeed, a great singer; for now had she suffered. And it was the death of a life with her when love died. For there be some with whom love is a separate life, and when love dies all that is worth living dies with it.

From childhood she and Cousin Tom — Captain Thomas Travis he lived to be — had been sweethearts. He was the grandson of Colonel Jeremiah Travis of " The Gaffs," and Tom and Alice had grown up together. Their love was one of those earthly loves which comes now and then that we may not altogether lose our faith in heaven.

Both were of a romantic temperament with high ideals, and with keen and sensitive natures.

Their love was the poem of their lives.

And though a toast in society, and courted by the nobility of the old world, Alice Westmore remembered only a moon-lighted night when she told Cousin Tom good-bye. For though they had loved each other all their lives, they had never spoken of it before that night. To them it had been a thing too sacred to profane with ordinary words.

Thomas Travis had just graduated from West Point, and he was at home on vacation before being assigned to duty. To-night he had ridden John Paul Jones — the pick of his grandfather's stable of thoroughbreds — a present from the sturdy old horse-racing, fox-hunting gentleman to his favorite grandson for graduating first in a class of fifty-six.

How handsome he looked in his dark blue uniform! And there was the music of the crepe-myrtle in the air — the music of it, wet with the night dew — for there are flowers so delicate in their sweetness that they pass out of the realm of sight and smell, into the unheard world of rhythm. Their very existence is the poetry of perfume. And this music of the crepe-myrtle, pulsing

10

through the shower-cooled leaves of that summer night, was accompanied by a mocking-bird from his nest in the tree.

Never did the memory of that night leave Alice Westmore. In after years it hurt her, as the dream of childhood's home with green fields about, and the old spring in the meadow, hurts the fever-stricken one dying far away from it all.

How long they sat on the rustic bench under the crepe-myrtle they did not know. At parting there was the light clasp of hands, and Cousin Tom drew her to him and put his lips reverently to hers. When he had ridden off there was a slender ring on her finger.

There was nothing in Italy that could make her forget that night, though often from her window she had looked out on Venice, moon-becalmed, while the nightingale sang from pomegranate trees in the hedgerows.

Where a woman's love is first given, that, thereafter, is her heart's sanctuary.

Alice Westmore landed at home again amid drum beats. War sweeps even sentiment from the world — sentiment that is stronger than common sense, and which moves the world.

On the retreat of the Southern army from Fort Donelson, Thomas Travis, now Captain of Artillery, followed, with Grant's army, to Pittsburg Landing. And finding himself within a day's journey of his old home, he lost no time in slipping through the lines to see Alice, whom he had not seen since her return.

He went first to her, and the sight of his blue uniform threw Colonel Westmore into a rage.

" To march into our land in that thing and claim my daughter —" he shouted. " To join that John Brown gang of abolitionists who are trying to overrun our country! Your father was a Southern gentleman and the bosom friend of my youth, but I'll see you damned before you shall ever again come under my roof, unless you can use your pistols quicker than I can use mine."

" Oh, Tom," said Alice when they were alone —" how — how could you do it? "

" But it is my side," he said quietly. " I was born, reared, educated in the love of the Union. My grand-father himself taught it to me. He fought with Jack-son at New Orleans. My father died for it in Mexico. I swore fidelity to it at West Point, and the Union gave me my military education on the faith of my oath. Farragut is a Tennessean — Thomas a Virgin-ian — and there are hundreds of others, men who love the Union more than they do their State. Alice — Alice — I do not love you less because I am true to my oath — my flag."

" Your flag," said Alice hotly —" your flag that would overrun our country and kill our people? It can never be my flag! "

She had never been angry before in all her life, but now the hot blood of her Southern clime and ancestry surged in her cheeks. She arose with a dignity she had never before imagined, even, with Cousin Tom. " You will choose between us now," she said.

" Alice — surely you will not put me to that test. I

will go —" he said, rising. " Some day, if I live, you can tell me to come back to you without sacrificing my conscience and my word of honor — my sacred oath — write me and — and — I will come."

And that is the way it ended — in tears for both.

Thomas Travis had always been his grandsire's favorite. His other grandson, Richard Travis, was away in Europe, where he had gone as soon as rumors of the war began to be heard.

That night the old man did not even speak to him. He could not. Alone in his room, he walked the floor all night in deep sorrow and thought.

He loved Thomas Travis as he did no other living being, and when morning came his great nature shook with contending emotions. It ended in the grandson receiving this note, a few minutes before he rode away:

" All my life I taught you to love the Union which I helped to make, with my blood in war and my brains in peace. I gave it my beloved boy — your father's life — in Mexico. We buried him in its flag. I sent you to West Point and made you swear to defend that flag with your life. How now can I ask you to repudiate your oath and turn your back on your rearing?

" Believing as I do in the right of the State first and the Union afterwards, I had hoped you might see it differently. But who, but God, controls the course of an honest mind?

" Go, my son — I shall never see you again. But I know you, my son, and I shall die knowing you did what you thought was right."

The young man wept when he read this — he was

neither too old nor too hardened for tears — and when
he rode away, from the ridge of the Mountain he
looked down again — the last time, on all that had been
his life's happiness.

It was an hour afterwards when the old General called
in his overseer.

" Watts," he said, " in the accursed war which is about
to wreck the South and which will eventually end in
our going back into the Union as a subdued province
and under the heel of our former slaves, there will be
many changes.   I, myself, will not live to see it.   I have
two grandsons, as you know, Tom and Richard.   Richard is in Europe; he went there following Alice Westmore, and is going to stay, till this fight is over.   Now,
I have added a codicil to my will and I wish you to
hear it."

He took up a lengthy document and read the last
codicil:

" *Since the above will was written and acknowledged,*
leaving The Gaffs to be equally divided between my two
grandsons, Thomas and Richard Travis, my country
has been precipitated into the horrors of Civil War.
In view of this I hereby change my will as above and
give and bequeath The Gaffs to that one of my grand-
sons who shall fight — it matters not to me on which
side — so that he fights.   For The Gaffs shall never go
to a Dominecker.   If both fight and survive the war,
it shall be divided equally between them as above ex-
pressed.   If one be killed it shall go to the survivor.   If
both be killed it shall be sold and the money appro-
priated among those of my slaves who have been faithful

to me to the end, one-fifth being set aside for my faithful overseer, Hilliard Watts."

In the panel of the wall he opened a small secret drawer, zinc-lined, and put the will in it.

"It shall remain there unchanged," he said, " and only you and I shall know where it is. If I die suddenly, let it remain until after the war, and then do as you think best."

CHAPTER II

T HE real heroes of the war have not been decorated yet. They have not even been pensioned,
for many of them lie in forgotten graves, and
those who do not are not the kind to clamor for honors
or emoluments.

On the last Great Day, what a strange awakening for
decorations there will be, if such be in store for the just
and the brave: Private soldiers, blue and gray, arising from neglected graves with tattered clothes and un-
marked brows. Scouts who rode, with stolid faces set,
into Death's grim door and died knowing they went out
unremembered. Spies, hung like common thieves at the
end of a rope — hung, though the bravest of the brave.

Privates, freezing, starving, wounded, dying,— un-
loved, unsoothed, unpitied — giving their life with a
last smile in the joy of martyrdom. Women, North,
whose silent tears for husbands who never came back
and sons who died of shell and fever, make a tiara
around the head of our reunited country. Women,
South, glorious Rachels, weeping for children who are
not and with brave hearts working amid desolate homes,
the star and inspiration of a rebuilded land. Slaves,
faithfully guarding and working while their masters
went to the front, filling the granaries that the war

might go on — faithful to their trust though its success meant their slavery — faithful and true.

O Southland of mine, be gentle, be just to these simple people, for they also were faithful.

Among the heroic things the four years of the American Civil War brought out, the story of Captain Thomas Travis deserves to rank with the greatest of them.

The love of Thomas Travis for the preacher-overseer was the result of a life of devotion on the part of the old man for the boy he had reared. Orphaned as he was early in life, Thomas Travis looked up to the overseer of his grandfather's plantation as a model of all that was great and good.

Tom and Alice,— on the neighboring plantations — ran wild over the place and rode their ponies always on the track of the overseer. He taught them to ride, to trap the rabbit, to boat on the beautiful river. He knew the birds and the trees and all the wild things of Nature, and Tom and Alice were his children.

As they grew up before him, it became the dream of the preacher-overseer to see his two pets married. Imagine his sorrow when the war fell like a thunderbolt out of a harvest sky and, among the thousand of other wrecked dreams, went the dream of the overseer.

The rest is soon told: After the battle of Shiloh, Hilliard Watts, Chief of Johnston's scouts, was captured and sent to Camp Chase. Scarcely had he arrived before orders came that twelve prisoners should be shot, by lot, in retaliation for the same number of Federal prisoners which had been executed, it was said, unjustly,

by Confederates. The overseer drew one of the black
balls. Then happened one of those acts of heroism
which now and then occur, perhaps, to redeem war of
the base and bloody.

On the morning before the execution, at daylight,
Thomas Travis arrived and made arrangements to save
his friend at the risk of his own life and reputation. It
was a desperate chance and he acted quickly. For Hilliard Watts went out a free man dressed in the blue uniform of the Captain of Artillery.

The interposition of the great-hearted Lincoln alone
saved the young officer from being shot.   ·

The yellow military order bearing the words of the
martyred President is preserved to-day in the library of
The Gaffs:

" *I present this young man as a Christmas gift to my
old friend, his grandsire, Colonel Jeremiah Travis.
The man who could fight his guns as he did at Shiloh,
and could offer to die for a friend, is good enough to
receive pardon, for anything he may have done or may
do, from*   A. LINCOLN."

Afterwards came Franklin and the news that Captain
Tom had been killed.

CHAPTER III

BUT General Jeremiah Travis could not keep out of the war; for toward the last, when Hood's army marched into Tennessee the Confederacy called for everything — even old age.

And so there rode out of the gates of The Gaffs a white-haired old man, who sat his superb horse well. He was followed by a negro on a mule.

They were General Jeremiah Travis and his body-servant, Bisco.

" I have come to fight for my state," said General Travis to the Confederate General.

" An' I am gwine to take keer of old marster suh," said Bisco as he stuck to his saddle girth.

It was the middle of the afternoon of the last day of November — and also the last day of many a gallant life — when Hood's tired army marched over the brow of the high ridge of hills that looked down on the town of Franklin, in front of which, from railroad to river, behind a long semicircular breastwork lay Schofield's determined army. It was a beautiful view, and as plain as looking down from the gallery into the pit of an amphitheatre.

Just below them lay the little town in a valley, admirably situated for defense, surrounded as it was on three sides by the bend of a small river, the further banks of which were of solid rocks rising above the town. On the highest of these bluffs — Roper's Knob — across and behind the town, directly overlooking it and grimly facing Hood's army two miles away, was a federal fort capped with mighty guns, ready to hurl their shells over the town at the gray lines beyond. From the high ridge where Hood's army stood the ground gradually rolled to the river. A railroad ran through a valley in the ridge to the right of the Confederates, spun along on the banks of the river past the town and crossed it in the heart of the bend to the left of the federal fort. From that railroad on the Confederate right, in front and clear around the town, past an old gin house which stood out clear and distinct in the November sunlight — on past the Carter House, to the extreme left bend of the river on the left — in short, from river to river again and entirely inclosing the town and facing the enemy — ran the newly made and hastily thrown-up breastworks of the federal army, the men rested and ready for battle.

There stands to-day, as it stood then, in front of the town of Franklin, on the highest point of the ridge, a large linden tree, now showing the effects of age. It was half-past three o'clock in the afternoon, when General Hood rode unattended to that tree, threw the stump of the leg that was shot off at Chickamauga over the pommel of his saddle, drew out his field glasses and sat looking for a long time across the valley at the enemy's position.

Strange to say, on the high river bluff beyond the

town, amid the guns of the fort, also with field glass in hand anxiously watching the confederates, stood the federal general. A sharp-shooter in either line could have killed the commanding general in the other. And now that prophesying silence which always seems to precede a battle was afloat in the air. In the hollow of its stillness it seemed as if one could hear the ticking of the death-watch of eternity. But presently it was broken by the soft strains of music which floated up from the town below. It was the federal band playing "Just Before The Battle, Mother."

The men in gray on the hill and the men in blue in the valley listened, and then each one mentally followed the tune with silent words, and not without a bit of moisture in their eyes.

"Just before the battle, Mother,
I am thinking most of thee."

Suddenly Hood closed his glasses with that nervous jerk which was a habit with him, straightened himself in the saddle and, riding back to General Stewart, said simply: "We will make the fight, General Stewart."

Stewart pressed his General's hand, wheeled and formed his corps on the right. Cheatham formed his on the left. A gun — and but few were used by Hood in the fight for fear of killing the women and children in the town — echoed from the ridge. It was the signal for the battle to begin. The heavy columns moved down the side of the ridge, the brigades marching in echelon.

At the sound of the gun, the federal army, some of whom were on duty, but the larger number loitering around at rest, or engaged in preparing their evening meal, sprang noiselessly to their places behind the breast-works, while hurried whispers of command ran down the line.

General Travis had been given a place of honor on General Hood's staff. He insisted on going into the ranks, but his commander had said: "Stay with me, I shall need you elsewhere." And so the old man sat his horse silently watching the army forming and marching down. But directly, as a Mississippi regiment passed by, he noticed at the head of one of the companies an old man, almost as old as himself, his clothes torn, and ragged from long marching; shoeless, his feet tied up in sack-cloth and his old slouch hat aflop over his ears. But he did not complain, he stood erect, and gamely led his men into battle. As the company halted for a moment, General Travis rode up to the old man whose thin clothes could not keep him from shivering in the now chill air of late afternoon, for it was then past four o'clock, saluted him and said:

"Captain, will you do me the favor to pull off this boot?" Withdrawing his boot from the stirrup and thrusting it towards the old man, the latter looked at him a moment in surprise but sheathed his sword and complied with the request. "And now the other one?" said Travis as he turned his horse around. This, too, was pulled off.

"Just put them on, Captain, if you please," said the rider. "I am mounted and do not need them as much as you do?" and before the gallant old Captain could refuse, he rode away for duty — in his stocking feet!

And now the battle began in earnest.

The confederates came on in splendid form. On the extreme right, Forrest's cavalry rested on the river; then Stewart's corps of Loring, Walthall, French, from right to left in the order named. On the left Cheatham's corps, of Cleburne, Brown, Bate, and Walker. Behind Cheatham marched Johnston's and Clayton's brigade for support, thirty thousand and more of men, in solid lines, bands playing and flags fluttering in the afternoon wind.

Nor had the federals been idle. Behind the breastworks lay the second and third divisions of the 23rd Corps, commanded in person by the gallant General J. D. Cox. From the railroad on the left to the Carter's Creek pike on the right, the brigades of these divisions stood as follows: Henderson's, Casement's, Reilly's, Strickland's, Moore's. And from the right of the Carter's Creek pike to the river lay Kimball's first division of the Fourth Corps. In front of the breastworks, across the Columbia pike, General Wagner, commanding the second division of the Fourth Corps, had thrown forward the two brigades of Bradley and Lane to check the first assault of the confederates, while Opdyck's brigade of the same division was held in the town as a reserve. Seven splendid batteries growled along the line of breastworks, and showed their teeth to the advancing foe, while three more were caged in the fort above and beyond the town.

Never did men march with cooler courage on more

formidable lines of defense. Never did men wait an
attack with cooler courage. Breastworks with abatis in
front through which the mouth of cannon gaped; artillery and infantry on the right to enfilade; siege guns in
the fort high above all, to sweep and annihilate.

Schofield, born general that he was, simply lay in a
rock-circled, earth-circled, water-circled, iron-and-steel-
circled cage, bayonet and flame tipped, proof against the
armies of the world!

But Hood's brave army never hesitated, never doubted.

Even in the matter of where to throw up his breastworks, Schofield never erred. On a beautiful and seemingly level plain like this, a less able general might have
thrown them up anywhere, just so that they encircled
the town and ran from river to river.

But Schofield took no chances. His quick eye de-
tected that even in apparent level plains there are slight
undulations. And so, following a gentle rise all the
way round, just on its top he threw up his breastworks.
So that, besides the ditch and the abatis, there was a
slight depression in his immediate front, open and clear,
but so situated that on the gentle slope in front, down
which the confederates must charge, the background of
the slope brought them in bold relief — gray targets for
the guns. On that background the hare would loom up
as big as the hound.

There were really two federal lines, an outer and an
inner one. The outer one consisted of Bradley's and
Lane's brigades which had retired from Spring Hill before the Confederate army, and had been ordered to halt
in front of the breastworks to check the advance of the

army. They were instructed to fire and then fall back to
the breastworks, if stubbornly charged by greatly their
superiors in numbers. They fired, but, true to American
ideas, they disliked to retreat. When forced to do so,
they were swept away with the enemy on their very heels
and as they rushed in over the last line at the breastworks on the Columbia pike the eager boys in gray
rushed over with them, swept away portions of Reilly's
and Strickland's troops, and bayoneted those that remained.

It was then that Schofield's heart sank as he looked
down from the guns of the fort. But Cox had the
forethought to place Opdyck's two thousand men in
reserve at this very point. These sprang gallantly
forward and restored the line.

They saved the Union army!

The battle was now raging all around the line.
There was a succession of yells, a rattle, a shock and
a roar, as brigade after brigade struck the breastworks,
only to be hurled back again or melt and die away in
the trenches amid the abatis. Clear around the line
of breastworks it rolled, at intervals, like a magazine
of powder flashing before it explodes, then the roar
and upheaval, followed anon and anon by another.
The ground was soon shingled with dead men in gray,
while down in the ditches or hugging the bloody sides
of the breastworks right under the guns, thousands,
more fortunate or daring than their comrades, lay,
thrusting and being thrust, shooting and being shot.
And there they staid throughout the fight — not strong
enough to climb over, and yet all the guns of the

federal army could not drive them away. Many a gray regiment planted its battle-flag on the breastworks and then hugged those sides of death in its efforts to keep it there, as bees cling around the body of their queen.

"I have the honor to forward to the War Department nine stands of colors," writes General Cox to General Geo. L. Thomas; "these flags with eleven others were captured by the Twenty-third Army Corps along the parapets."

Could Bonaparte's army have planted more on the ramparts of Mount St. Jean?

The sun had not set; yet the black smoke of battle had set it before its time. God had ordained otherwise; but man, in his fury had shut out the light of heaven against the decree of God, just as, equally against His decree, he has now busily engaged in blotting out many a brother's bright life, before the decree of its sunset. Again and again and again, from four till midnight — eight butchering hours — the heart of the South was hurled against those bastions of steel and flame, only to be pierced with ball and bayonet.

And for every heart that was pierced there broke a dozen more in the shade of the southern palmetto, or in the shadow of the northern pine. After nineteen hundred years of light and learning, what a scientific nation of heart-stabbers and brother-murderers we Christians are!

It was now that the genius of the confederate cavalry leader, Forrest, asserted itself. With nearly ten thousand of his intrepid cavalry-men, born in the saddle, who

11

carried rifles and shot as they charged, and whom with
wonderful genius their leader had trained to dismount
at a moment's notice and fight as infantry — he lay on
the extreme right between the river and the railroad.
In a moment he saw his opportunity, and rode furiously
to Hood's headquarters. He found the General sitting
on a flat rock, a smouldering fire by his side, half way
down the valley, at the Winstead House, intently
watching the progress of the battle.

"Let me go at 'em, General," shouted Forrest in his
bluff way, "and I'll flank the federal army out of its
position in fifteen minutes."

"No! Sir," shouted back Hood. "Charge them out!
charge them out!"

Forrest turned and rode back with an oath of disgust. Years afterwards, Colonel John McGavock,
whose fine plantation lay within the federal lines and
who had ample opportunity for observation, says that
when in the early evening a brigade of Forrest's cavalry
deployed across the river as if opening the way for the
confederate infantry to attack the federal army in flank
and rear, hasty preparations were made by the federal
army for retreat. And thus was Forrest's military wisdom corroborated. "Let me flank them out," was military genius. "No, charge them out," was dare-devil
blundering!

The shock, the shout and the roar continued. The
flash from the guns could now plainly be seen as night
descended. So continuous was the play of flame around
the entire breastwork that it looked to the general at
headquarters like a circle of prairie fire, leaping up at

intervals along the breastworks, higher and higher where the batteries were ablaze.

In a black-locust thicket, just to the right of the Columbia turnpike and near the Carter House, with abatis in front, the strongest of the batteries had been placed. It mowed down everything in front. Seeing it, General Hood turned to General Travis and said: "General, my compliments to General Cleburne, and say to him I desire that battery at his hands."

The old man wheeled and was gone. In a moment, it seemed, the black smoke of battle engulfed him. Cleburne's command was just in front of the old gin house, forming for another charge. The dead lay in heaps in front. They almost filled the ditch around the breastworks. But the command, terribly cut to pieces, was forming as coolly as if on dress parade. Above them floated a peculiar flag, a field of deep blue on which was a crescent moon and stars. It was Cleburne's battle flag and well the enemy knew it. They had seen and felt it at Shiloh, Murfreesboro, Ringgold Gap, Atlanta. "I tip my hat to that flag," said General Sherman years after the war. "Whenever my men saw it they knew it meant fight."

As the old man rode up, the division charged. Carried away in the excitement he charged with them, guiding his horse by the flashes of the guns. As they rushed on the breastworks a gray figure on a chestnut horse rode diagonally across the front of the moving column at the enemy's gun. The horse went down within fifty yards of the breastwork. The rider arose, waved his sword and led his men on foot to the very ramparts.

Then he staggered and fell, pierced with a dozen minie balls. It was Cleburne, the peerless field-marshal of confederate brigade commanders; the genius to infantry as Forrest was to cavalry. His corps was swept back by the terrible fire, nearly half of them dead or wounded.

Ten minutes afterwards General Travis stood before General Hood.

"General Cleburne is dead, General"— was all he said. Hood did not turn his head.

"My compliments to General Adams," he said, "and tell him I ask that battery at his hands."

Again the old man wheeled and was gone. Again he rode into the black night and the blacker smoke of battle.

General Adams's brigade was in Walthall's division. As the aged courier rode up, Adams was just charging. Again the old man was swept away with the charge. They struck the breastworks where Stile's and Casement's brigades lay on the extreme left of the federal army. "Their officers showed heroic examples and self-sacrifice," wrote General Cox in his official report, "riding up to our lines in advance of their men, cheering them on. One officer, Adams, was shot down upon the parapet itself, his horse falling across the breastworks." Casement himself, touched by the splendor of his ride, had cotton brought from the old gin house and placed under the dying soldier's head. "You are too brave a man to die," said Casement tenderly; "I wish that I could save you." " 'Tis the fate of a soldier to die for his country," smiled 'he dying soldier. Then he passed away.

It was a half hour before the old man reached Hood's headquarters again, his black horse wet with sweat.

" General Adams lies in front of the breastworks — dead! His horse half over it — dead "— was all he said.

Hood turned pale. His eyes flashed with indignant grief.

" Then tell General Gist," he exclaimed. The old man vanished again and rode once more into the smoke and the night. Gist's brigade led the front line of Brown's division, Cheatham's corps. It was on the left, fronting Strickland's and Moore's, on the breastworks. The Twenty-fourth South Carolina Infantry was in front of the charging lines. " In passing from the left to the right of the regiment," writes Colonel Ellison Capers commanding the South Carolina regiment above named, " the General (Gist) waved his hat to us, expressed his pride and confidence in the Twenty-fourth and rode away in the smoke of battle never more to be seen by the men he had commanded on so many fields. His horse was shot, and, dismounting, he was leading the right of the brigade when he fell, pierced through the heart. On pressed the charging lines of the brigade, driving the advance force of the enemy pell-mell into a locust abatis where many were captured and sent to the rear; others were wounded by the fire of their own men. This abatis was a formidable and fearful obstruction. The entire brigade was arrested by it. But Gist's and Gordon's brigade charged on and reached the ditch, mounted the works and met the enemy in close combat. The colors of the Twenty-fourth were planted and defended on the parapet, and the enemy retired in our front some distance, but soon rallied and came back in turn to charge us.   He never succeeded in retaking the line we held.   Torn and exhausted, deprived of every general officer and nearly every field officer, the division had only strength enough left to hold its position."

The charging became intermittent.   Then out of the night, as Hood sat listening, again came the old man, his face as white as his long hair, his horse once black, now white with foam.

" General Gist too, is dead," he said sadly.

" Tell Granbury, Carter, Strahl — General!   Throw them in there and capture that battery and break that line."

The old man vanished once more and rode into the shock and shout of battle.

General Strahl was leading his brigade again against the breastworks.   " Strahl's and Carter's brigade came gallantly to the assistance of Gist's and Gordon's " runs the confederate report sent to Richmond, " but the enemy's fire from the houses in the rear of the line and from guns posted on the far side of the river so as to enfilade the field, tore their line to pieces before it reached the locust abatis."

General Carter fell mortally wounded before reaching the breastworks, but General Strahl reached the ditch, filled with dead and dying men, though his entire staff had been killed.   Here he stood with only two men around him, Cunningham and Brown.   " Keep firing " said Strahl as he stood on the bodies of the dead and passed up guns to the two privates.   The next instant

Brown fell heavily; he, too, was dead. "What shall I do, General?" asked Cunningham. "Keep firing," said Strahl. Again Cunningham fired. "Pass me another gun, General," said Cunningham. There was no answer — the general was dead.

Not a hundred yards away lay General Granbury, dead. He died leading the brave Texans to the works.

To the commanding General it seemed an age before the old man returned. Then he saw him in the darkness afar off, before he reached the headquarters. The General thought of death on his pale horse and shivered.

"Granbury, Carter, Strahl — all dead, General," he said. "Colonels command divisions, Captains are commanding brigades."

"How does Cheatham estimate his loss?" asked the General.

"At half his command killed and wounded," said the old soldier sadly.

"My God! — my God! — this awful, awful day!" cried Hood.

There was a moment's silence and then: "General?" It came from General Travis.

The General looked up.

"May I lead the Tennessee troops in — I have led them often before."

Hood thought a moment, then nodded and the horse and the rider were gone. It was late — nearly midnight. The firing on both sides had nearly ceased,— only a desultory rattling — the boom of a gun now and then. But O, the agony, the death, the wild confusion!

This was something like the babel that greeted the old soldier's ears as he rode forward:

" The Fourth Mississippi — where is the Fourth Mississippi? " " Here is the Fortieth Alabama's standard — rally men to your standard! " " Where is General Cleburne, men? Who has seen General Cleburne? " " Up, boys, and let us at 'em agin! Damn 'em, they've wounded me an' I want to kill some more! "

" Water! — water — for God's sake give us water! " This came from a pile of wounded men just under the guns on the Columbia pike. It came from a sixteen year old boy in blue. Four dead comrades lay across him.

" And this is the curse of it," said General Travis, as he rode among the men.

But suddenly amid the smoke and confusion, the soldiers saw what many thought was an apparition — an old, old warrior, on a horse with black mane and tail and fiery eyes, but elsewhere covered with white sweat and pale as the horse of death. The rider's face too, was deadly white, but his keen eyes blazed with the fire of many generations of battle-loving ancestors.

The soldiers flocked round him, half doubting, half believing. The terrible ordeal of that bloody night's work; the poignant grief from beholding the death and wounds of friends and brothers; the weird, uncanny groans of the dying upon the sulphurous-smelling night air; the doubt, uncertainty, and yet, through it all, the bitter realization that all was in vain, had shocked, benumbed, unsettled the nerves of the stoutest; and many of them scarcely knew whether they were really alive, confronting in the weird hours of the night ditches of blood, and breastworks of death, or were really dead — dead from concussion, from shot or shell, and were now wandering on a spirit battle-field till some soul-leader should lead them away.

And so, half dazed and half dreaming, and yet half alive to its realization, they flocked around the old warrior, and they would not have been at all surprised had he told them he came from another world.

Some thought of Mars. Some thought of death and his white horse. Some felt of the animal's mane and touched his streaming flanks and cordy legs to see if it were really a horse and not an apparition, while " What is it?" and " Who is he?" was whispered down the lines.

Then the old rider spoke for the first time, and said simply:

" Men, I have come to lead you in."

A mighty shout came up. " It's General Lee! — he has come to lead us in," they shouted.

" No, no, men,"— said the old warrior quickly. " I am not General Lee. But I have led Southern troops before. I was at New Orleans. I was —"

" It's Ole Hick'ry — by the eternal! — Ole Hick'ry — and he's come back to life to lead us!" shouted a big fellow as he threw his hat in the air.

" Ole Hickory! Ole Hickory!" echoed and re-echoed down the lines, till it reached the ears of the dying soldiers in the ditch itself, and many a poor, brave fellow, as his heart strings snapped and the broken chord gurgled out into the dying moan, saw amid the blaze and

light of the new life, the apparition turn into a reality
and a smile of exquisite satisfaction was forever ,frozen
on his face in the mould of death, as he whispered with
his last breath:

"It's Old Hickory — my General — I have fought
a good fight — I come!"

Then the old warrior smiled — a smile of simple
beauty and grandeur, of keen satisfaction that such an
honor should have been paid him, and he tried to speak
to correct them. But they shouted the more, and
drowned out his voice and would not have it otherwise.
Despairing, he rode to the front and drew his long,
heavy, old, revolutionary sword. It flashed in the air.
It came to "attention"— and then a dead silence followed.

"Men," he said, "this is the sword of John Sevier,
the rebel that led us up the sides of King's Mountain
when every tyrant gun that belched in our face called
us — rebels!"

"Old Hick'ry! Old Hick'ry, forever!" came back
from the lines.

Again the old sword came to attention, and again a
deep hush followed.

"Men," he said, drawing a huge rifled barreled pistol
—"this is the pistol of Andrew Jackson, the rebel that
whipped the British at New Orleans when every gun that
thundered in his face, meant death to liberty!"

"Old Hickory! Old Hickory!!" came back in a
frenzy of excitement.

Again the old sword came to attention — again, the
silence. Then the old man fairly stood erect in his

stirrups — he grew six inches taller and straighter and the black horse reared and rose as if to give emphasis to his rider's assertion:

" Men," he shouted, " rebel is the name that tyranny gives to patriotism! And now, let us fight, as our forefathers fought, for our state, our homes and our firesides! And then clear and distinct there rang out on the night air, a queer old continental command:

" Fix, pieces! "

They did not know what this meant at first. But some old men in the line happened to remember and fixed their bayonets. Then there was clatter and clank down the entire line as others imitated their examples.

" Poise, fo'k! " rang out again more queerly still. The old men who remembered brought their guns to the proper position. " Right shoulder, fo'k! "— followed. Then, " Forward, March! " came back and they moved straight at the batteries — now silent — and straight at the breastworks, more silent still. Proudly, superbly, they came on, with not a shout or shot — a chained line with links of steel — a moving mass with one heart — and that heart,— victory.

On they came at the breastworks, walking over the dead who lay so thick they could step from body to body as they marched. On they came, following the old cocked hat that had once held bloodier breastworks against as stubborn foe.

On — on — they came, expecting every moment to see a flame of fire run round the breastworks, a furnace of flame leap up from the batteries, and then — victory or death — behind old Hickory! Either was honor enough!

And now they were within fifty feet of the breast-works, moving as if on dress parade. The guns must thunder now or never! One step more — then, an electrical bolt shot through every nerve as the old man wheeled his horse and again rang out that queer old continental command, right in the mouth of the enemy's ditch, right in the teeth of his guns:

" Charge, pieces! "

It was Tom Travis who commanded the guns where the Columbia Pike met the breastworks at the terrible deadly locust thicket. All night he had stood at his post and stopped nine desperate charges. All night in the flash and roar and the strange uncanny smell of blood and black powder smoke, he had stood among the dead and dying calling stubbornly, monotonously:

" Ready! "

" Aim! "

" Fire! "

And now it was nearly midnight and Schofield, finding the enemy checked, was withdrawing on Nashville.

Tom Travis thought the battle was over, but in the glare and flash he looked and saw another column, ghostly gray in the starlight, moving stubbornly at his guns.

" Ready! " he shouted as his gunners sprang again to their pieces.

On came the column — beautifully on. How it thrilled him to see them! How it hurt to think they were his people!

" *Aim!* " he thundered again, and then as he looked through the gray torch made, starlighted night, he quailed in a cold sickening fear, for the old man who led them on was his grandsire, the man whom of all on earth he loved and revered the most.

Eight guns, with grim muzzles trained on the old rider and his charging column, waited but for the captain's word to hurl their double-shotted canisters of death.

And Tom Travis, in the agony of it, stood, sword in hand, stricken in dumbness and doubt. On came the column, the old warrior leading them — on and: —

" The command — the command! Give it to us, Captain," shouted the gunners.

" *Cease firing!* "

The gunners dropped their lanyards with an oath, trained machines that they were.

It was a drunken German who brought a heavy sword-hilt down on the young officer's head with:

" You damned traitor! "

A gleam of gun and bayonet leaped in the misty light in front, from shoulder to breast — a rock wall, tipped with steel swept crushingly forward over the trenches over the breastworks.

Under the guns, senseless, his skull crushed, an upturned face stopped the old warrior. Down from his horse he came with a weak, hysterical sob.

" O Tom — Tom, I might have known it was you — my gallant, noble boy — my Irish Gray! "

He kissed, as he thought, the dead face, and went on with his men.

It was just midnight.

" At midnight, all being quiet in front, in accordance with orders from the commanding Generals," writes General J. D. Cox in his official report, " I withdrew my command to the north bank of the river."

" The battle closed about twelve o'clock at night," wrote General Hood, " when the enemy retreated rapidly on Nashville, leaving the dead and wounded in our hands. We captured about a thousand prisoners and several stands of colors."

Was this a coincidence — or as some think — did the boys in blue retreat before they would fire on an old Continental and the spirit of '76?

An hour afterwards a negro was sadly leading a tired old man on a superb horse back to headquarters, and as the rider's head sank on his breast he said:

" Lead me, Bisco, I'm too weak to guide my horse. Nothing is left now but the curse of it."

And O, the curse of it!

Fifty-seven Union dead beside the wounded, in the little front yard of the Carter House, alone.   And they lay around the breastworks from river to river, a chain of dead and dying.   In front of the breastworks was another chain — a wider and thicker one.   It also ran from river to river, but was gray instead of blue. Chains are made of links, and the full measure of " the curse of it " may have been seen if one could have looked over the land that night and have seen where the dead links lying there were joined to live under the roof trees of far away homes.

But here is the tale of a severed link: About two

o'clock lights began to flash about over the battle-field
— they were hunting for the dead and wounded.
Among these, three had come out from the Carter House.
A father, son and daughter; each carried a lantern and
as they passed they flashed their lights in the faces of
the dead.

"May we look for brother?" asked the young girl,
of an officer. "We hope he is not here but fear he is.
He has not been home for two years, being stationed in
another state. But we heard he could not resist the
temptation to come home again and joined General
Bate's brigade. And O, we fear he has been killed for
he would surely have been home before this."

They separated, each looking for "brother." Directly the father heard the daughter cry out. It was in
the old orchard near the house. On reaching the spot
she was seated on the ground, holding the head of her
dying brother in her lap and sobbing:

"Brother's come home! Brother's come home!"
Alas, she meant — gone home!

"Captain Carter, on staff duty with Tyler's brigade," writes General Wm. B. Bate in his official report, "fell mortally wounded near the works of the
enemy and almost at the door of his father's home. His
gallantry I witnessed with much pride, as I had done
on other fields, and here take pleasure in mentioning it
especially."

The next morning in the first light of the first day of
that month celebrated as the birth-month of Him who
declared long ago that war should cease, amid the dead
and dying of both armies, stood two objects which

should one day be carved in marble — One, to represent the intrepid bravery of the South, the other, the cool courage of the North, and both —" the curse of it."

The first was a splendid war-horse, dead, but lying face forward, half over the federal breastworks. It was the horse of General Adams.

The other was a Union soldier — the last silent sentinel of Schofield's army. He stood behind a small locust tree, just in front of the Carter House gate. He had drawn his iron ram-rod which rested under his right arm pit, supporting that side. His gun, with butt on the ground at his left, rested with muzzle against his left side, supporting it. A cartridge, half bitten off was in his mouth. He leaned heavily against the small tree in front. He was quite dead, a minie ball through his head; but thus propped he stood, the wonder of many eyes, the last sentinel of the terrible night battle.

*   *   *   *   *   *   *   *

But another severed link cut deepest of all. In the realization of her love for Thomas Travis, Alice Westmore's heart died within her. In the years which followed, if suffering could make her a great singer, now indeed was she great.

PART FOURTH — THE LINT

177

12

CHAPTER I

S LAVERY clings to cotton.
    When the directors of a cotton mill, in a
Massachusetts village, decided, in the middle
'70's, to move their cotton factory from New England to
Alabama, they had two objects in view — cheaper labor
and cheaper staple.

And they did no unwise thing, as the books of the
company from that time on showed.

In the suburbs of a growing North Alabama town,
lying in the Tennessee Valley and flanked on both sides
by low, regularly rolling mountains, the factory had
been built.

It was a healthful, peaceful spot, and not unpictur-
esque. North and south the mountains fell away in an
undulating rhythmical sameness, with no abrupt gorges
to break in and destroy the poetry of their scroll against
the sky. The valley supplemented the effect of the
mountains; for, from the peak of Sunset Rock, high up
on the mountain, it looked not unlike the chopped up
waves of a great river stiffened into land — especially
in winter when the furrowed rows of the vast cotton
fields lay out brown and symmetrically turned under the
hazy sky.

The factory was a low, one-story structure of half

179

burnt bricks. Like a vulgar man, cheapness was written all over its face. One of its companions was a wooden store house near by, belonging to the company. The other companion was a squatty low-browed engine room, decorated with a smoke-stack which did business every day in the week except Sunday. A black, soggy exhaust-pipe stuck out of a hole in its side, like a nicotine-soaked pipe in an Irishman's mouth, and so natural and matter-of-fact was the entire structure that at evening, in the uncertain light, when the smoke was puffing out of its stack, and the dirty water running from its pipes, and the reflected fire from the engine's furnace blazed through the sunken eyes of the windows, begrizzled and begrimed, nothing was wanted but a little imagination to hear it cough and spit and give one final puff at its pipe and say: " Lu'd but o'ive wur-rek hard an' o'im toired to-day!"

Around it in the next few years had sprung up Cottontown.

The factory had been built on the edge of an old cotton-field which ran right up to the town's limit; and the field, unplowed for several years, had become sodded with the long stolens of rank Bermuda grass, holding in its perpetual billows of green the furrows which had been thrown up for cotton rows and tilled years before.

This made a beautiful pea-green carpet in summer and a comfortable straw-colored matting in winter; and it was the only bit of sentiment that clung to Cottontown.

All the rest of it was practical enough: Rows of scurvy three-roomed cottages, all exactly alike, even to the gardens in the rear, laid off in equal breadth and running with the same unkept raggedness up the flinty side of the mountain.

There was not enough originality among the worked-to-death inhabitants of Cottontown to plant their gardens differently; for all of them had the same weedy turnip-patch on one side, straggling tomatoes on another, and half-dried mullein-stalks sentineling the corners. For years these cottages had not been painted, and now each wore the same tinge of sickly yellow paint. It was not difficult to imagine that they had had a long siege of malarial fever in which the village doctor had used abundant plasters of mustard, and the disease had finally run into " yaller ja'ndice," as they called it in Cottontown.

And thus Cottontown had stood for several years, a new problem in Southern life and industry, and a paying one for the Massachusetts directors.

In the meanwhile another building had been put up — a little cheaply built chapel, of long-leaf yellow pine. It was known as the Bishop's church, and sat on the side of the mountain, half way up among the black-jacks, exposed to the blistering suns of summer and the winds of winter.

It had never been painted: " An' it don't need it," as the Bishop had said when the question of painting it had been raised by some of the members.

" No, it don't need it, for the hot sun has drawed all the rosin out on its surface, an' pine rosin's as good a paint as any church needs. Jes' let God be, an' He'll fix His things like He wants 'em any way. He put the paint in the pine-tree when He made it. Now man is mighty smart,— he can make paint, but he can't make a pine tree."

It was Sunday morning, and as the Bishop drove along to church he was still thinking of Jack Bracken and Captain Tom, and the burial of little Jack. When he arose that morning Jack was up, clean-shaved and neatly dressed. As Mrs. Watts, the Bishop's wife, had become used, as she expressed it, to his " fetchin' any old thing, frum an old hoss to an old man home, wharever he finds 'em,"— she did not express any surprise at having a new addition to the family.

The outlaw looked nervous and sorrow-stricken. Several times, when some one came on him unexpectedly, the Bishop saw him feeling nervously for a Colt's revolver which had been put away. Now and then, too, he saw great tears trickling down the rough cheeks, when he thought no one was noticing him.

" Now, Jack," said the Bishop after breakfast, " you jes' get on John Paul Jones an' hunt for Cap'n Tom. I know you'll not leave no stone unturned to find him. Go by the cave and see if him an' Eph ain't gone back. I'm not af'eard — I know Eph will take care of him, but we want to fin' him. After meetin' if you haven't found him I'll join in the hunt myself — for we must find Cap'n Tom, Jack, befo' the sun goes down. I'd ruther see him than any livin' man. Cap'n Tom — Cap'n Tom — him that's been as dead all these years! Fetch him home when you find him — fetch him home to me. He shall never want while I live. An', Jack,

remember — don't forget yo'se'f and hold up anybody.
I'll expec' you to jine the church nex' Sunday."

" I ain't been in a church for fifteen years," said the
other.

" High time you are going, then. You've put yo'
hands to the plough—turn not back an' God'll straight-
en out everything."

Jack was silent. " I'll go by the cave fus' an' jus'
look where little Jack is sleepin'. Po' little feller, he
must ha' been mighty lonesome last night."

It was ten o'clock and the Bishop was on his way to
church. He was driving the old roan of the night before. A parody on a horse, to one who did not look
closely, but to one who knows and who looks beyond the
mere external form for that hidden something in both
man and horse which bespeaks strength and reserve
force, there was seen through the blindness and the ugliness and the sleepy, ambling, shuffling gait a clean-cut
form, with deep chest and closely ribbed; with well
drawn flanks, a fine, flat steel-turned bone, and a powerful muscle, above hock and forearms, that clung to the
leg as the Bishop said, " like bees a'swarmin'."

At his little cottage gate stood Bud Billings, the best
slubber in the cotton mill. Bud never talked to any one
except the Bishop; and his wife, who was the worst
Xantippe in Cottontown, declared she had lived with
him six months straight and never heard him come
nearer speaking than a grunt. It was also a saying
of Richard Travis, that Bud had been known to break
all records for silence by drawing a year's wages at the

mill, never missing a minute and never speaking a word.

Nor had he ever looked any one full in the eye in his life.

As the Bishop drove shamblingly along down the road, deeply preoccupied in his forthcoming sermon, there came from out of a hole, situated somewhere between the grizzled fringe of hair that marked Bud's whiskers and the grizzled fringe above that marked his eye-brows, a piping, apologetic voice that sounded like the first few rasps of an old rusty saw; but to the occupant of the buggy it meant, with a drawl:

"Howdy do, Bishop?"

A blind horse is quick to observe and take fright at anything uncanny. He is the natural ghost-finder of the highways, and that voice was too much for the old roan. To him it sounded like something that had been resurrected. It was a ghost-voice, arising after many years. He shied, sprang forward, half wheeled and nearly upset the buggy, until brought up with a jerk by the powerful arms of his driver. The shaft-band had broken and the buggy had run upon the horse's rump, and the shafts stuck up almost at right angles over his back. The roan stood trembling with the half turned, inquisitive muzzle of the sightless horse — a paralysis of fear all over his face. But when Bud came forward and touched his face and stroked it, the fear vanished, and the old roan bobbed his tail up and down and wiggled his head re-assuringly and apologetically.

"Wal, I declar, Bishop," grinned Bud, "kin yo' critter fetch a caper?"

The Bishop got leisurely out of his buggy, pulled down the shafts and tied up the girth before he spoke. Then he gave a puckering hitch to his underlip and deposited in the sand, with a puddling *plunk*, the half cup of tobacco juice that had closed up his mouth.

He stepped back and said very sternly:

" Whoa, Ben Butler! "

" Why, he'un's sleep a'ready," grinned Bud.

The Bishop glanced at the bowed head, cocked hind foot and listless tail: " Sof'nin' of the brain, Bud," smiled the Bishop; " they say when old folks begin to take it they jus' go to sleep while settin' up talkin'. Now, a horse, Bud," he said, striking an attitude for a discussion on his favorite topic, " a horse is like a man — he must have some meanness or he c'udn't live, an' some goodness or nobody else c'ud live. But git in, Bud, and let's go along to meetin'—'pears like it's gettin' late."

This was what Bud had been listening for. This was the treat of the week for him — to ride to meetin' with the Bishop. Bud, a slubber-slave — henpecked at home, browbeaten and cowed at the mill, timid, scared, " an' powerful slow-mouthed," as his spouse termed it, worshipped the old Bishop and had no greater pleasure in life, after his hard week's work, than " to ride to meetin' with the old man an' jes' hear him narrate."

The Bishop's great, sympathetic soul went out to the poor fellow, and though he had rather spend the next two miles of Ben Butler's slow journey to church in thinking over his sermon, he never failed, as he termed it, " to pick up charity even on the road-side," and it was pretty to see how the old man would turn loose his crude histrionic talent to amuse the slubber.   He knew, too, that Bud was foolish about horses, and that Ben Butler was his model!

They got into the old buggy, and Ben Butler began to draw it slowly along the sandy road to the little church, two miles away up the mountain side.

CHAPTER II

B UD was now in a seventh heaven. He was riding behind Ben Butler, the greatest horse in the world, and talking to the Bishop, the only person who ever heard the sound of his voice, save in deprecatory and scary grunts.

It was touching to see how the old man humored the simple and imposed-upon creature at his side. It was beautiful to see how, forgetting himself and his sermon, he prepared to entertain, in his quaint way, this slave to the slubbing machine.

Bud looked fondly at the Bishop — then admiringly at Ben Butler. He drew a long breath of pure air, and sitting on the edge of the seat, prepared to jump if necessary; for Bud was mortally afraid of being in a runaway, and his scared eyes seemed to be looking for the soft places in the road.

" Bishop," he drawled after a while, " huc-cum you name sech a hoss "— pointing to the old roan —" sech a grand hoss, for sech a man — sech a man as he was," he added humbly.

" Did you ever notice Ben Butler's eyes, Bud? " asked the old man, knowingly.

" Blind," said Bud sadly, shaking his head —" too bad — too bad — great — great hoss! "

187

"Yes, but the leds, Bud — that hoss, Ben Butler there, holds a world's record — he's the only cock-eyed hoss in the world."

"You don't say so — that critter! — cock-eyed?" Bud laughed and slapped his leg gleefully. "Didn't I always tell you so? World's record — great — great!"

Then it broke gradually through on Bud's dull mind.

He slapped his leg again. "An' him — his namesake — he was cock-eyed, too — I seed him onct at New 'Leens."

"Don't you never trust a cock-eyed man, Bud. He'll flicker on you in the home-stretch. I've tried it an' it never fails. Love him, but don't trust him. The world is full of folks we oughter love, but not trust."

"No — I never will," said Bud as thoughtfully as he knew how to be —"nor a cock-eyed 'oman neither. My wife's cock-eyed," he added.

He was silent a moment. Then he showed the old man a scar on his forehead: "She done that last month — busted a plate on my head."

"That's bad," said the Bishop consolingly —"but you ortenter aggravate her, Bud."

"That's so — I ortenter — least-wise, not whilst there's any crockery in the house," said Bud sadly.

"There's another thing about this hoss," went on the Bishop —"he's always spoony on mules. He ain't happy if he can't hang over the front gate spoonin' with every stray mule that comes along. There's old long-eared Lize that he's dead stuck on — if he c'u'd write he'd be composin' a sonnet to her ears, like poets do to their lady love's — callin' them Star Pointers of a Greater Hope, I reck'n, an' all that. Why, he'd ruther hold hands by moonlight with some old Maria mule than to set up by lamplight with a thoroughbred filly."

"Great — great!" said Bud slapping his leg — "didn't I tell you so?"

"So I named him Ben Butler when he was born. That was right after the war, an' I hated old Ben so an' loved hosses so, I thought ef I'd name my colt for old Ben maybe I'd learn to love him, in time."

Bud shook his head. "That's agin nature, Bishop."

"But I have, Bud — sho' as you are born I love old Ben Butler." He lowered his voice to an earnest whisper: "I ain't never told you what he done for po' Cap'n Tom."

"Never heurd o' Cap'n Tom."

The Bishop looked hurt. "Never mind, Bud, you wouldn't understand. But maybe you will ketch this, listen now."

Bud listened intently with his head on one side.

"I ain't never hated a man in my life but what God has let me live long enough to find out I was in the wrong — dead wrong. There are Jews and Yankees. I useter hate 'em worse'n sin — but now what do you reckon?"

"One on 'em busted a plate on yo' head?" asked Bud.

"Jesus Christ was a Jew, an' Cap'n Tom jined the Yankees."

"Bud," he said cheerily after a pause, "did I ever tell you the story of this here Ben Butler here?"

Bud's eyes grew bright and he slapped his leg again.

"Well," said the old man, brightening up into one of his funny moods, "you know my first wife was named Kathleen — Kathleen Galloway when she was a gal, an' she was the pretties' gal in the settlement an' could go all the gaits both saddle an' harness. She was han'som' as a three-year-old an' cu'd out-dance, out-ride, out-sing an' out-flirt any other gal that ever come down the pike. When she got her Sunday harness on an' began to move, she made all the other gals look like they were nailed to the road-side. It's true, she needed a little weight in front to balance her, an' she had a lot of ginger in her make-up, but she was straight and sound, didn't wear anything but the harness an' never teched herself anywhere nor cross-fired nor hit her knees."

"Good — great!" said Bud, slapping his leg.

"O, she was beautiful, Bud, with that silky hair that 'ud make a thoroughbred filly's look coarse as sheep's wool, an' two mischief-lovin' eyes an' a heart that was all gold. Bud — Bud "— there was a huskiness in the old man's voice —"I know I can tell you because it will never come back to me ag'in, but I love that Kathleen now as I did then. A man may marry many times, but he can never love but once. Sometimes it's his fust wife, sometimes his secon', an' often its the sweetheart he never got — but he loved only one of 'em the right way, an' up yander, in some other star, where spirits that are alike meet in one eternal wedlock, they'll be one there forever."

"Her daddy, old man Galloway, had a thoroughbred filly that he named Kathleena for his daughter, an' she c'ud do anything that the gal left out. An' one day when she took the bit in her teeth an' run a quarter in twenty-five seconds, she sot 'em all wild an' lots of fellers tried to buy the filly an' get the old man to throw in the gal for her keep an' board."

" I was one of 'em. I was clerkin' for the old man an' boardin' in the house, an' whenever a young feller begins to board in a house where there is a thoroughbred gal, the nex' thing he knows he'll be —"

" Buckled in the traces," cried Bud slapping his leg gleefully, at this, his first product of brilliancy.

The old man smiled: " 'Pon my word, Bud, you're gittin' so smart. I don't know what I'll be doin' with you — so 'riginal an' smart. Why, you'll quit keepin' an old man's company — like me. I won't be able to entertain you at all. But, as I was sayin', the next thing he knows, he'll be one of the family."

" So me an' Kathleen, we soon got spoony an' wanted to marry. Lots of 'em wanted to marry her, but I drawed the pole an' was the only one she'd take as a runnin' mate. So I went after the old man this a way: I told him I'd buy the filly if he'd give me Kathleen. I never will forget what he said: ' They ain't narry one of 'em for sale, swap or hire, an' I wish you young fellers 'ud tend to yo' own business an' let my fillies alone. I'm gwinter bus' the wurl's record wid 'em both — Kathleena the runnin' record an' Kathleen the gal record. so be damn to you an' don't pester me no mo'.' "

" Did he say *damn?* " asked Bud aghast — that such a word should ever come from the Bishop.

" He sho' did, Bud. I wouldn't lie about the old man,

now that he's dead. It ain't right to lie about dead people — even to make 'em say nice an' proper things they never thought of whilst alive. If we'd stop lyin' about the ungodly dead an' tell the truth about 'em, maybe the livin' 'ud stop tryin' to foller after 'em in that respect. As it is, every one of 'em knows that no matter how wicked he lives there'll be a lot o' nice lies told over him after he's gone, an' a monument erected, maybe, to tell how good he was. An' there's another lot of half pious folks in the wurl it 'ud help — kind o' sissy pious folks — that jus' do manage to miss all the fun in the world an' jus' are mean enough to ketch hell in the nex'. Get religion, but don't get the sissy kind. So I am for tellin' it about old man Galloway jus' as he was.

"You orter heard him swear, Bud — it was part of his religion. An' wherever he is to-day in that other world, he is at it yet, for in that other life, Bud, we're just ourselves on a bigger scale than we are in this. He used to cuss the clerks around the store jus' from habit, an' when I went to work for him he said:

" ' Young man, maybe I'll cuss you out some mornin', but don't pay no 'tention to it — it's just a habit I've got into, an' the boys all understand it.'

" ' Glad you told me,' I said, lookin' him square in the eye —' one confidence deserves another. I've got a nasty habit of my own, but I hope you won't pay no 'tention to it, for it's a habit, an' I can't help it. I don't mean nothin' by it, an' the boys all understand it, but when a man cusses me I allers knock him down — do it befo' I think '— I said —' jes' a habit I've got.'

" Well, he never cussed me all the time I was there.
My stock went up with the old man an' my chances was
good to get the gal, if I hadn't made a fool hoss-trade;
for with old man Galloway a good hoss-trade covered
all the multitude of sins in a man that charity now does
in religion. In them days a man might have all the
learnin' and virtues an' graces, but if he cudn't trade
hosses he was tinklin' brass an' soundin' cymbal in that
community.

" The man that throwed the silk into me was Jud Carpenter — the same feller that's now the Whipper-in for
these mills. Now, don't be scared," said the old man
soothingly as Bud's scary eyes looked about him and he
clutched the buggy as if he would jump out —" he'll
not pester you now — he's kept away from me ever since.
He swapped me a black hoss with a star an' snip,
that looked like the genuine thing, but was about the
neatest turned gold-brick that was ever put on an unsus-
pectin' millionaire.

" Well, in the trade he simply robbed me of a fine
mare I had, that cost me one-an'-a-quarter. Kathleen
an' me was already engaged, but when old man Galloway
heard of it, he told me the jig was up an' no such
double-barrel idiot as I was shu'd ever leave any of my
colts in the Galloway paddock — that when he looked
over his gran'-chillun's pedigree he didn't wanter see all
of 'em crossin' back to the same damned fool! Oh, he
was nasty. He said that my colts was dead sho' to be
luffers with wheels in their heads, an' when pinched
they'd quit, an' when collared they'd lay down. That
there was a yaller streak in me that was already pilin'

13

up coupons on the future for tears and heartaches an',
maybe a gallows or two, an' a lot of uncomplimentary
talk of that kind.

" Well, Kathleen cried, an' I wept, an' I'll never forgit the night she gave me a little good-bye kiss out
under the big oak tree an' told me we'd hafter part.

" The old man maybe sized me up all right as bein' a
fool, but he missed it on my bein' a quitter. I had no
notion of being fired an' blistered an' turned out to grass
that early in the game. I wrote her a poem every other
day, an' lied between heats, till the po' gal was nearly
crazy, an' when I finally got it into her head that if it
was a busted blood vessel with the old man, it was a
busted heart with me, she cried a little mo' an' consented
to run off with me an' take the chances of the village
doctor cuppin' the old man at the right time.

" The old lady was on my side and helped things
along. I had everything fixed even to the moon which
was shinin' jes' bright enough to carry us to the Justice's without a lantern, some three miles away, an' into
the nex' county.

" I'll never forgit how the night looked as I rode over
after her, how the wild-flowers smelt, an' the fresh dew
on the leaves. I remember that I even heard a mockin'-
bird wake up about midnight as I tied my hoss to a lim'
in the orchard nearby, an' slipped aroun' to meet Kathleen at the bars behin' the house. It was a half mile
to the house an' I was slippin' through the sugar-maple
trees along the path we'd both walked so often befo'
when I saw what I thought was Kathleen comin' towards
me. I ran to meet her. It wa'n't Kathleen, but her

mother — an' she told me to git in a hurry, that the old
man knew all, had locked Kathleen up in the kitchen,
turned the brindle dog loose in the yard, an' was hidin'
in the woods nigh the barn, with his gun loaded with
bird-shot, an' that if I went any further the chances were
I'd not sit down agin for a year. She had slipped
around through the woods just to warn me.

"Of course I wanted to fight an' take her anyway —
kill the dog an' the old man, storm the kitchen an' run
off with Kathleen in my arms as they do in novels. But
the old lady said she didn't want the dog hurt — it being
a valuable coon-dog,— and that I was to go away out
of the county an' wait for a better time.

"It mighty nigh broke me up, but I decided the old
lady was right an' I'd go away. But 'long towards the
shank of the night, after I had put up my hoss, the moon
was still shinin', an' I cudn't sleep for thinkin' of Kathleen. I stole afoot over to her house just to look at her
window. The house was all quiet an' even the brindle
dog was asleep. I threw kisses at her bed-room window, but even then I c'udn't go away, so I slipped around
to the barn and laid down in the hay to think over my
hard luck. My heart ached an' burned an' I was nigh
dead with love.

"I wondered if I'd ever get her, if they'd wean her
from me, an' give her to the rich little feller whose fine
farm j'ined the old man's an' who the old man was
wuckin' fur — whether the two wouldn't over-persuade
her whilst I was gone. For I'd made up my mind I'd
go befo' daylight — that there wasn't anything else for
me to do.

" I was layin' in the hay, an' boylike, the tears was rollin' down. If I c'ud only kiss her han' befo' I left — if I c'ud only see her face at the winder!

" I must have sobbed out loud, for jus' then I heard a gentle, sympathetic whinny an' a cold, inquisitive little muzzle was thrust into my face, as I lay on my back with my heart nearly busted. It was Kathleena, an' I rubbed my hot face against her cool cheek — for it seemed so human of her to come an' try to console me, an' I put my arms around her neck an' kissed her silky mane an' imagined it was Kathleen's hair.

" Oh, I was heart-broke an' silly.

" Then all at onct a thought came to me, an' I slipped the bridle an' saddle on her an' led her out at the back door, an' I scratched this on a slip of paper an' stuck it on the barn do':

" '*To old man Galloway:*
" ' *You wouldn't let me 'lope with yo' dorter, so I've 'loped with yo' filly, an' you'll never see hair nor hide of her till you send me word to come back to this house an' fetch a preacher.*'
(Signed)   *Hilliard Watts.*' "

The old man smiled, and Bud slapped his leg gleefully.

" Great — great! Oh my, but who'd a thought of it? " he grunted.

" They say it 'ud done you good to have been there the nex' mornin' an' heurd the cussin' recurd busted — but me an' the filly was forty miles away. He got out a warrant for me for hoss-stealin', but the sheriff was for me, an' though he hunted high an' low he never could find me."

" Well, it went on for a month, an' I got the old man's note, sent by the sheriff:

" ' *To Hilliard Watts, Wher-Ever Found.*

" ' *Come on home an' fetch yo' preacher. Can't afford to loose the filly, an' the gal has been off her feed ever since you left.* *Jobe Galloway.*'

" Oh, Bud, I'll never forgit that home-comin' when she met me at the gate an' kissed me an' laughed a little an' cried a heap, an' we walked in the little parlor an' the preacher made us one.

" Nor of that happy, happy year, when all life seemed a sweet dream now as I look back, an' even the memory of it keeps me happy. Memory is a land that never changes in a world of changes, an' that should show us our soul is immortal, for memory is only the reflection of our soul."

His voice grew more tender, and low: " Toward the last of the year I seed her makin' little things slyly an' hidin' 'em away in the bureau drawer, an' one night she put away a tiny half-finished little dress with the needle stickin' in the hem — just as she left it — just as her beautiful hands made the last stitch they ever made on earth. . . .

" O Bud, Bud, out of this blow come the sweetest thought I ever had, an' I know from that day that this life ain't all, that we'll live agin as sho' as God lives an'

is just — an' no man can doubt that.   No — no — Bud,
this life ain't all, because its God's unvarying law to
finish things.   That tree there is finished, an' them birds,
they are finished, an' that flower by the roadside an'
the mountain yonder an' the world an' the stars an' the
sun.   An' we're mo' than they be, Bud — even the tini-
es' soul, like Kathleen's little one that jes' opened its
eyes an' smiled an' died, when its mammy died.   It had
something that the trees an' birds an' mountains didn't
have — a soul — an' don't you kno' He'll finish all such
lives up yonder?   He'll pay it back a thousandfold for
what he cuts off here."

Bud wept because the tears were running down the
old man's cheeks.   He wanted to say something, but he
could not speak.   That queer feeling that came over
him at times and made him silent had come again.

CHAPTER III

AN ANSWER TO PRAYER

THEN the old man remembered that he was making Bud suffer with his own sorrow, and when Bud looked at him again the Bishop had wiped his eyes on the back of his hand and was smiling.

Ben Butler, unknown to either, had come to a standstill.

The Bishop broke out in a cheery tone:

" My, how far off the subject I got! I started out to tell you all about Ben Butler, and — and — how he come in answer to prayer," said the Bishop solemnly.

Bud grinned: " It muster been, ' *Now I lay me down to sleep.*' "

The Bishop laughed: " Well I'll swun if he ain't sound asleep sho' 'nuff." He laughed again: " Bud, you're gittin' too bright for anything. I jes' don't see how the old man's gwinter talk to you much longer 'thout he goes to school agin."

" No — Ben Butler is a answer to prayer," he went on.

" The trouble with the world is it don't pray enough. Prayer puts God into us, Bud — we're all a little part of God, even the worst of us, an' we can make it big or let it die out accordin' as we pray. If we stop prayin' God jes' dies out in us. Of course God don't answer any fool prayer, for while we're here we are nothin' but a bundle of laws, an' the same unknown law that moves the world around makes yo' heart beat.   But God is behind the law, an' if you get in harmony with God's laws an' pray, He'll answer them.   Christ knowed this, an' there was some things that even He wouldn't ask for.   When the Devil tempted Him to jump off the top of the mountain, He drawed the line right there, for He knowed if God saved Him by stoppin' the law of gravitation it meant the wreck of the world."

"Bud," he went on earnestly, "I've lived a long time an' seed a heap o' things, an' the plaines' thing I ever seed in my life is that two generations of scoffers will breed a coward, an' three of 'em a thief, an' that the world moves on only in proportion as it's got faith in God.

"I was ruined after the war — broken — busted — ruined!   An' I owed five hundred dollars on the little home up yander on the mountain.   When I come back home from the army I didn't have nothin' but one old mare, — a daughter of that Kathleena I told you about. I knowed I was gone if I lost that little home, an' so one night I prayed to the Lord about it an' then it come to me as clear as it come to Moses in the burnin' bush. God spoke to me as clear as he did to Moses."

"How did he say it?" asked Bud, thoroughly frightened and looking around for a soft spot to jump and run.

"Oh, never mind that," went on the Bishop —"God don't say things out loud — He jes' brings two an' two together an' expects you to add 'em an' make fo'.   He gives you the soil an' the grain an' expects you to plant, assurin' you of rain an' sunshine to make the crop, if you'll only wuck. He comes into yo' life with the laws of life an' death an' takes yo' beloved, an' it's His way of sayin' to you that this life ain't all. He shows you the thief an' the liar an' the adulterer all aroun' you, an' if you feel the shock of it an' the hate of it, it's His voice tellin' you not to steal an' not to lie an' not to be impure. You think only of money until you make a bad break an' loose it all. That's His voice tellin' you that money ain't everything in life. He puts opportunities befo' you, an' if you grasp 'em it's His voice tellin' you to prosper an' grow fat in the land. No, He don't speak out, but how clearly an' unerringly He does speak to them that has learned to listen for His voice!

"I rode her across the river a hundred miles up in Marshall County, Tennessee, and mated her to a young horse named Tom Hal. Every body knows about him now, but God told me about him fust.

"Then I knowed jes' as well as I am settin' in this buggy that that colt was gwinter give me back my little home an' a chance in life. Of course, I told everybody 'bout it an' they all laughed at me — jes' like they all laughed at Noah an' Abraham an' Lot an' Moses, an' if I do say it — Jesus Christ. But thank God it didn't pester me no more'n it did them."

"Well, the colt come ten years ago — an' I named him Ben Butler — cause I hated old Ben Butler so. He had my oldest son shot in New Orleans like he did many other rebel prisoners. But this was God's colt an' God had told me to love my enemies an' do good to them that did wrong to me, an' so I prayed over it an' named him Ben Butler, hopin' that God 'ud let me love my enemy for the love I bore the colt. An' He has."

Bud shook his head dubiously.

"He showed me I was wrong, Bud, to hate folks, an' when I tell you of po' Cap'n Tom an' how good Gen. Butler was to him, you'll say so, too.

"From the very start Ben Butler was a wonder. He came with fire in his blood an' speed in his heels.

"An' I trained him. Yes — from the time I was Gen. Travis' overseer I had always trained his hosses. I'm one of them preachers that believes God intended the world sh'ud have the best hosses, as He intended it sh'ud have the best men an' women. Take all His works, in their fitness an' goodness, an' you'll see He never 'lowed for a scrub an' a quitter anywhere. An' so when He gave me this tip on Ben Butler's speed I done the rest.

"God gives us the tips of life, but He expects us to make them into the dead cinches.

"Oh, they all laughed at us, of course, an' nicknamed the colt Mister Isaacs, because, like Sarah's son, he came in answer to prayer. An' when in his two-year-old form, I led him out of the stable one cold, icy day, an' he was full of play an' r'ared an' fell an' knocked down his hip, they said that 'ud fix Mister Isaacs.

"But it didn't pester me at all. I knowed God had done bigger things in this world than fixin' a colt's hip, an' it didn't shake my faith. I kept on prayin' an' kept on trainin'.

" Well, it soon told. His hip was down, but it didn't
stop him from flyin'. As a three-year-old he paced the
Nashville half mile track in one-one flat, an' though
they offered me then an' there a thousand dollars for
Ben Butler, I told 'em no,— he was God's colt an' I
didn't need but half of that to raise the mortgage, an'
he'd do that the first time he turned round in a race.

" I drove him that race myself, pulled down the five
hundred dollar purse, refused all their fine offers for
Ben Butler, an' me an' him's been missionaryin' round
here ever since."

" Great hoss — great! " said Bud, his eyes sparkling,
—" allers told you so! Think I'll get out and hug
him."

This he did while the Bishop sat smiling. But in the
embrace Ben Butler planted a fore foot on Bud's great
toe. Bud came back limping and whimpering with pain.

" Now there, Bud," said the Bishop, consolingly.
" God has spoken to you right there."

" What 'ud He say? " asked Bud, looking scary
again.

" Why, he said through Nature's law an' voice that
you mustn't hug a hoss if you don't want yo' toes
tramped on."

" Who must you hug then? " asked Bud.

" Yo' wife, if you can't do no better," said the Bishop
quietly.

" My wife's wussern a hoss," said Bud sadly —" she
bites. I'm sorry you didn't take that thar thousan' dollars for him," he said," looking at his bleeding toe.

" Bud," said the old man sternly, " don't say that

no mo'. It mou't make me think you are one of them
selfish dogs that thinks money'll do anything. Then
I'd hafter watch you, for I'd know you'd do anything
for money."

Bud crawled in rather crest-fallen, and they drove on.

CHAPTER IV

THE Bishop laughed outright as his mind went back again.

"Well," he went on reminiscently, " I'll have to finish my tale an' tell you how I throwed the cold steel into Jud Carpenter when I got back. I saw I had it to do, to work back into my daddy-in-law's graces an' save my reputation.

"Now, Jud had lied to me an' swindled me terribly, when he put off that old no-count hoss on me. Of course, I might have sued him, for a lie is a microbe which naturally develops into a lawyer's fee. But while it's a terrible braggart, it's really cowardly an' delicate, an' will die of lock-jaw if you only pick its thumb.

"So I breshed up that old black to split-silk fineness, an' turned him over to Dr. Sykes, a friend of mine living in the next village. An' I said to the Doctor, ' Now remember he is yo' hoss until Jud Carpenter comes an' offers you two hundred dollars for him.'

" ' Will he be fool enough to do it? ' he asked, as he looked the old counterfeit over.

" ' Wait an' see,' I said.

"I said nothin', laid low an' froze an' it wa'n't long befo' Jud come 'round as I 'lowed he'd do. He expected me to kick an' howl; but as I took it all so nice he didn't understand it. Nine times out of ten the best thing to do when the other feller has robbed you is to freeze. The hunter on the plain knows the value of that, an' that he can freeze an' make a deer walk right up to him, to find out what he is. Why, a rabbit will do it, if you jump him quick, an' he gets confused an' don't know jes' what's up; an' so Jud come as I thort he'd do. He couldn't stan' it no longer, an' he wanted to rub it in. He brought his crowd to enjoy the fun.

"'Oh, Mr. Watts,' he said grinnin', 'how do you like a coal black stump-sucker?

"'Well,' I said indifferent enough —'I've knowed good judges of hosses to make a hones' mistake now an' then, an' sell a hoss to a customer with the heaves thinkin' he's a stump-sucker. But it 'ud turn out to be only the heaves an' easily cured.

"'Is that so?' said Jud, changing his tone.

"'Yes,' I said, 'an' I've knowed better judges of hosses to sell a nervous hoss for a balker that had been balked onct by a rattle head. But in keerful hands I've seed him git over it,' I said, indifferent like.

"'Indeed?' said Jud.

"'Yes, Jud,' said I, 'I've knowed real hones' hoss traders to make bad breaks of that kind, now and then — honest intentions an' all that, but bad judgment,' — sez I —'an' I'll cut it short by sayin' that I'll just give you two an' a half if you'll match that no-count, wind broken black as you tho'rt, that you swapped me.'

"'Do you mean it?' said Jud, solemn-like.

"'I'll make a bond to that effect,' I said solemnly.

" Jud went off thoughtful.   In a week or so he come
back.   He hung aroun' a while an' said:

" ' I was up in the country the other day, an' do you
kno' I saw a dead match for yo' black?   Only a little
slicker an' better lookin'— same star an' white hind foot.
As nigh like him as one black-eyed pea looks like another.'

" ' Jud,' I said, ' I never did see two hosses look exactly
alike.   You're honestly mistaken.'

" ' They ain't a hair's difference,' he said.   ' He's
a little slicker than yours — that's all — better groomed
than the one in yo' barn.'

" ' I reckon he is,' said I, for I knew very well there
wa'n't none in my barn.   ' That's strange,' I went on,
' but you kno' what I said.'

" ' Do you still hold to that offer? ' he axed.

" ' I'll make bond with my daddy-in-law on it,' I said.

" ' Nuff said,' an' Jud was gone.   The next day he
came back leading the black, slicker an' hence no-counter
than ever, if possible.

" ' Look at him,' he said proudly —' a dead match for
yourn.   Jes' han' me that two an' a half an' take him.
You now have a team worth a thousan'.'

" I looked the hoss over plum' surprised like.

" ' Why, Jud,' I said as softly as I cu'd, for I was
nigh to bustin, an' I had a lot of friends come to see the
sho', an' they standin' 'round stickin' their old hats in
their mouths to keep from explodin'—' Why, Jud, my
dear friend,' I said, ' ain't you kind o' mistaken about
this?   I said a *match* for the black, an' it peers to me
like you've gone an' bought the black hisse'f an' is

tryin' to put him off on me. No — no — my kind
frien', you'll not fin' anything no-count enuff to be his
match on this terrestrial ball.'

" By this time you cu'd have raked Jud's eyes off his
face with a soap-gourd.

" ' What? w-h-a-t?   He — why — I bought him of
Dr. Sykes.'

" ' Why, that's funny,' I said, ' but it comes in handy
all round.   If you'd told me that the other day I might
have told you,' I said —' yes, I might have, but I doubt
it — that I'd loaned him to Dr. Sykes an' told him whenever you offered him two hundred cash for him to let him
go.   Jes' keep him,' sez I, ' till you find his mate, an'
I'll take an oath to buy 'em.' "

Bud slapped his leg an' yelled with delight.

" Whew," said the Bishop —" not so loud.   We're at
the church.

" But remember, Bud, it's good policy allers to freeze.
When you're in doubt — freeze ! "

CHAPTER V

THE FLOCK

THE Bishop's flock consisted of two distinct classes: Cottontowners and Hillites.

"There's only a fair sprinklin' of Hillites that lives nigh about here," said the Bishop, "an' they come because it suits them better than the high f'lutin' services in town. When a Christian gits into a church that's over his head, he is soon food for devil-fish."

The line of demarcation, even in the Bishop's small flock, was easily seen. The Hillites, though lean and lanky, were swarthy, healthy and full of life. "But Cottontown," said the Bishop, as he looked down on his congregation —" Cottontown jes' naturally feels tired."

It was true. Years in the factory had made them dead, listless, soulless and ambitionless creatures. To look into their faces was like looking into the cracked and muddy bottom of a stream which once ran.

Their children were there also — little tots, many of them, who worked in the factory because no man nor woman in all the State cared enough for them to make a fight for their childhood.

They were children only in age. Their little forms were not the forms of children, but of diminutive men and women, on whose backs the burden of earning their

14   209

living had been laid, ere the frames had acquired the strength to bear it.

Stunted in mind and body, they were little solemn, pygmy peoples, whom poverty and overwork had canned up and compressed into concentrated extracts of humanity. The flavor — the juices of childhood — had been pressed out.

" 'N no wonder," thought the Bishop, as he looked down upon them from his crude platform, " for them little things works six days every week in the factory from sun-up till dark, an' often into the night, with jes' forty minutes at noon to bolt their food. O God," he said softly to himself, "You who caused a stream of water to spring up in the wilderness that the life of an Ishmaelite might be saved, make a stream of sentiment to flow from the heart of the world to save these little folks."

Miss Patsy Butts, whose father, Elder Butts of the Hard-shell faith, owned a fertile little valley farm beyond the mountain, was organist. She was fat and so red-faced that at times she seemed to be oiled.

She was painfully frank and suffered from acute earnestness.

And now, being marriageable, she looked always about her with shy, quick, expectant glances.

The other object in life, to Patsy, was to watch her younger brother, Archie B., and see that he kept out of mischief. And perhaps the commonest remark of her life was:

" Maw, jus' look at Archie B.! "

This was a great cross for Archie B., who had been

known to say concerning it: " If I ever has any kids,
I'll never let the old'uns nuss the young'uns. They
gits into a bossin' kind of a habit that sticks to 'em all
they lives."

To-day Miss Patsy was radiantly shy and happy,
caused by the fact that her fat, honest feet were encased
in a pair of beautiful new shoes, the uppers of which
were clasped so tightly over her ankles as to cause the
fat members to bulge in creases over the tops, as uncomfortable as two Sancho Panzas in armor.

" Side-but'ners," said Mrs. Butts triumphantly to
Mrs. O'Hooligan of Cottontown,—" side-but'ners — I
got 'em for her yistiddy — the fust that this town's ever
seed. La, but it was a job gittin' 'em on Patsy. I
had to soak her legs in cold water nearly all night, an'
then I broke every knittin' needle in the house abut'nin'
them side but'ners.

" But fashion is fashion, an' when I send my gal out
into society, I'll send her in style. Patsy Butts," she
whispered so loud that everybody on her side of the
house heard her —" when you starts up that ole wheez-
in' one gallus organ, go slow or you'll bust them side-
but'ners wide open."

When the Bishop came forward to preach his ser-
mon, or talk to his flock, as he called it, his surplice would
have astonished anyone, except those who had seen him
thus attired so often. A stranger might have laughed,
but he would not have laughed long — the old man's
earnestness, sincerity, reverence and devotion were over-
shadowing. Its pathos was too deep for fun.

Instead of a clergyman's frock he wore a faded coat of

blue buttoned up to his neck. It had been the coat of an officer in the artillery, and had evidently passed through the Civil War. There was a bullet hole in the shoulder and a sabre cut in the sleeve.

CHAPTER VI

A BISHOP MILITANT

NO one had ever heard the Bishop explain his curious surplice but once, and that had been several years before, when the little chapel, by the aid of a concert Miss Alice gave, contributions from the Excelsior Mill headed by Mr. and Mrs. Kingsley, and other sources had been furnished, and the Bishop came forward to make his first talk:

" This is the only church of its kind in the worl', I reckin," he said. " I've figured it out an' find we're made up of Baptis', Metherdis', Presbyterian, 'Piscopalian, Cam'elites an' Hard-shells. You've 'lected me Bishop, I reckon, 'cause I've jined all of 'em, an' so far as I know I am the only man in the worl' who ever done that an' lived to tell the tale. An' I'm not ashamed to say it, for I've allers foun' somethin' in each one of 'em that's a little better than somethin' in the other. An' if there's any other church that'll teach me somethin' new about Jesus Christ, that puffect Man, I'll jine it. I've never seed a church that had Him in it that wa'n't good enough for me."

The old man smiled in humorous retrospection as he went on:

" The first company of Christians I jined was the Hard-shells. I was young an' a raw recruit an' nachully

213

fell into the awkward squad. I liked their solar plexus way of goin' at the Devil, an' I liked the way they'd allers deal out a good ration of whiskey, after the fight, to ev'ry true soldier of the Cross — especially if we got our feet too wet, which we mos' always of'ntimes gen'ally did."

This brought out visible smiles all down the line, from the others at the Hard-shells and their custom of foot-washing.

" But somehow," went on the old man, " I didn't grow in grace — spent too much time in singin' an' takin' toddies to keep off the effect of cold from wet feet. Good company, but I wanted to go higher, so I drapt into the Baptis' rigiment, brave an' hones', but they spen' too much time a-campin' in the valley of the still water, an' when on the march, instid of buildin' bridges to cross dry-shod over rivers an' cricks, they plunge in with their guns stropped to their backs, their powder tied up in their socks in their hats, their shoes tied 'round their necks an' their butcher-knife in their teeth. After they lan' they seem to think it's the greates' thing in the worl' that they've been permitted to wade through water instead of crossin' on a log, an' they spen' the balance of their time marchin' 'roun' an' singin':

" ' Billows of mercy, over me roll,
    Oceans of Faith an' Hope, come to my soul.'

" Don't want to fly to heaven — want to swim there. An' if they find too much lan' after they get there, they'll spen' the res' of eternity prayin' for a deluge.

"Bes' ole relig'un in the worl', tho,— good fighters, too, in the Lord's cause. Ole timey, an' a trifle keerless about their accoutrements, an' too much water nachully keeps their guns rusty an' their powder damp, but if it comes to a square-up fight agin the cohorts of sin, an' the powder in their pans is too damp for flashin', they'd jes' as soon wade in with the butcher-knife an' the meat axe. I nachully out-grow'd 'em, for I seed if the Great Captain 'ud command us all to jine armies an' fight the worl', the Baptis' 'ud never go in, unless it was a sea-fight.

"From them to the Cam'elites was easy, for I seed they was web-footed, too. The only diff'rence betwix' them an' the Baptis' is that they are willin' to jine in with any other rigiment, provided allers that you let them 'pint the sappers an' miners an' blaze out the way. Good fellers, tho', an' learned me lots. They beats the worl' for standin' up for each other an' votin' allers for fust place. If there's a promotion in camp they want it; 'n' when they ain't out a-drillin' their companies they're sho' to be in camp 'sputin' with other rigiments as to how to do it. Good, hones' fighters, tho', and tort me how to use my side arms in a tight place. Scatterin' in some localities, but like the Baptises, whenever you find a mill-dam there'll be their camp an' plenty o' corn.

"Lord, how I did enjoy it when I struck the Methodis' rigiment! The others had tort me faith an' zeal, but these tort me discipline. They are the best drilled lot in the army of the Lord, an' their drill masters run all the way from wet-nurses to old maids. For furagin'

an' free love for ev'rything they beats the worl', an'
they pay mo' 'tenshun to their com'sary department
than they do to their ord'nance. They'll march anywhere you want 'em, swim rivers or build bridges, fight
on ship or sho', strong in camp-meetin's or battle songs,
an' when they go, they go like clockwuck an' carry their
dead with 'em!

" The only thing they need is an incubator, to keep
up their hennery department an' supply their captains
with the yellow legs of the land. Oh, but I love them
big hearted Methodists!

" I foun' the Presbyterian phalanx a pow'ful army,
steady, true an' ole-fashioned, their powder strong of
brimstone an' sulphur an' their ordnance antique.
Why, they're usin' the same old mortars John Knox
fired at the Popes, an' the same ole blunderbusses that
scatter wide enough to cover all creation an' is as liable
to kick an' kill anything in the rear as in front. They
won't sleep in tents an' nothin' suits 'em better'n being
caught in a shower on the march. In battle they know
no fear, for they know no ball is goin' to kill you if
you're predistined to be hung. In the fight they know
no stragglers an' fallers from grace.

" Ay, but they're brave. I jined 'em Sunday night
after the battle of Shiloh, when I saw one of their captains stan' up amid the dead an' dyin' of that bloody
field, with the shells from the Yankee gun-boats fallin'
aroun' him. Standin' there tellin' of God an' His forgiveness, until many a po' dyin' soldier, both frien' an'
foe, like the thief on the cross, found peace at the last
hour.

"Befo' I jined the 'Piscopal corps I didn't think I cu'd stan' 'em — too high furlutin' for my raisin'. They seemed to pay mo' attenshun to their uniforms than their ordnance, an' their drum-majors outshine any other churches' major generals. An' drillin'? They can go through mo' monkey manoeuvers in five minutes than any other church can in a year. It's drillin'— drillin' with 'em all the time, an' red-tape an' knee breeches, an' when they ain't drillin' they're dancin'. They have signs an' countersigns, worl' without end, ah-men. An' I've knowed many of them to put all his three months' pay into a Sunday uniform for dress parade.

"Weepons? They've got the fines' in the worl' an' they don't think they can bring down the Devil les' they shoot at him with a silver bullet. Everything goes by red-tape with 'em, an' the ban'-wagon goes in front.

"But I jined 'em," went on the old man, " an' I'll tell you why."

He paused — his voice trembled, and the good natured, bubbling humor, which had floated down the smooth channel of his talk, vanished as bubbles do when they float out into the deep pool beyond.

"Here," he said, lifting his arm, and showing the coat of the Captain of Artillery —" this is what made me jine 'em. This is the coat of Cap'n Tom, that saved my life at the risk of his own an' that was struck down at Franklin; an' no common man of clay, as I be, ever befo' had so God-like a man of marble to pattern after. I saw him in the thick of the fight with his guns parked an' double-shotted, stop our victorious rush almos' up to the river bank an' saved Grant's army from defeat

an' capture.   I was on the other side, an' chief of scouts
for Albert Sidney Johnston, but I see him now in his
blue Yankee coat, fightin' his guns like the hero that
he was.   I was foolish an' rushed in.   I was captured
an' in a prison pen, I drawed the black ball with 'leven
others that was sentenced to be shot.   It was Cap'n Tom
who came to me in the early dawn of the day of the
execution an' said: 'They shall not shoot you, Bishop
— put on my blue coat an' go through the lines.   I owe
much to my country — I am giving it all.

"'I owe something to you.   They shall not shoot
you like a dog.   I will tell my colonel what I have done
to-morrow.   If they think it is treason they may shoot
me instead.   I have nothing to live for — you, all.   Go.'

" I have never seed him sence.

" We are mortals and must think as mortals.   If we
conceive of God, we can conceive of Him only as in
human form.   An' I love to think that the blessed an'
brave an' sweet Christ looked like Cap'n Tom looked
in the early dawn of that morning when he come an'
offered himself,— captain that he was — to be shot, if
need be, in my place — so gran', so gentle, so brave,
so forgivin', so like a captain — so like God."

His voice had dropped lower and lower still.   It died
away in a sobbing murmur, as a deep stream purls and
its echo dies in a deeper eddy.

" It was his church an' I jined it.   This was his coat,
an' so, let us pray."

CHAPTER VII

MARGARET ADAMS

THERE passed out of the church, after the service, a woman leading a boy of twelve.

He was a handsome lad with a proud and independent way about him. He carried his head up and there was that calmness that showed good blood. There was even a haughtiness which was pathetic, knowing as the village did the story of his life.

The woman herself was of middle age, with neat, well-fitting clothes, which, in the smallest arrangement of pattern and make-up, bespoke a natural refinement.

Her's was a sweet face, with dark eyes, and in their depths lay the shadow of resignation.

Throughout the sermon she had not taken her eyes off the old man in the pulpit, and so interested was she, and so earnestly did she drink in all he said, that any one noticing could tell that, to her, the plain old man in the pulpit was more than a pastor.

She sat off by herself. Not one of them in all Cottontown would come near her.

" Our virtue is all we po' fo'ks has got — if we lose that we ain't got nothin' lef'," Mrs. Banks of grass-widow fame had once said, and saying it had expressed Cottontown's opinion.

Mrs. Banks was very severe when the question of

woman's purity was up. She was the fastest woman at
the loom in all Cottontown. She was quick, with a
bright, deep-seeing eye. She had been pretty — but
now at forty-five she was angular and coarse-looking,
with a sharp tongue.

The Bishop had smiled when he heard her say it, and
then he looked at Margaret Adams sitting in the corner with her boy. In saying it, Mrs. Banks had elevated her nose as she looked in the direction where sat
the Magdalene.

The old man smiled, because he of all others knew
the past history of Mrs. Banks, the mistress of the
loom.

He replied quietly: " Well, I dun'no — the best
thing that can be said of any of us in general is, that
up to date, it ain't recorded that the Almighty has ap-
pinted any one of us, on account of our supreme purity,
to act as chief stoner of the Universe. Mighty few of
us, even, has any license to throw pebbles."

Of all his congregation there was no more devoted
member than Margaret Adams —" an' as far as I kno',"
the old man had often said, " if there is an angel on
earth, it is that same little woman."

When she came into church that day, the old man
noticed that even the little Hillites drew away from her.
Often they would point at the little boy by her side and
make faces at him. To-day they had carried it too
far when one of them, just. out in the church yard,
pushed him rudely as he walked proudly by the side of
his mother, looking straight before him, in his military
way, and not so much as giving them a glance.

"Wood's-colt," sneered the boy in his ear, as he pushed him.

"No — thoroughbred"— came back, and with it a blow which sent the intruder backward on the grass.

Several old men nodded at him approvingly as he walked calmly on by the side of his mother.

"Jimmie — Jimmie!" was all she said as she slipped into the church.

"I guess you must be a new-comer," remarked Archie B. indifferently to the boy who was wiping the blood from his face as he arose from the ground and looked sillily around. "That boy Jim Adams is my pardner an' I could er tole you what you'd git by meddlin' with him. He's gone in with his mother now, but him an' me — we're in alliance — we fights for each other. Feel like you got enough?"— and Archie B. got up closer and made motions as if to shed his coat.

The other boy grinned good naturedly and walked off.

To-day, just outside of the church Ben Butler had been hitched up and the Bishop sat in the old buggy.

Bud Billings stood by holding the bit, stroking the old horse's neck and every now and then striking a fierce attitude, saying "Whoa — whoa — suh!"

As usual, Ben Butler was asleep.

"Turn him loose, Bud," said the old man humoring the slubber —"I've got the reins an' he can't run away now. I can't take you home to-day — I'm gwinter take Margaret, an' you an' Jimmie can come along together."

No other man could have taken Margaret Adams home and had any standing left, in Cottontown.

And soon they were jogging along down the mountain side, toward the cabin where the woman lived and supported herself and boy by her needle.

To-day Margaret was agitated and excited — more than the Bishop had ever known her to be. He knew the reason, for clean-shaved and neatly dressed, Jack Bracken passed her on the road to church that morning, and as they rode along the Bishop told her it was indeed Jack whom she had seen, " an' he loves you yet, Margaret," he said.

She turned pink under her bonnet. How pretty and fresh she looked — thought the Bishop — and what purity in a face to have such a name.

" It *was* Jack, then," she said simply —" tell me about him, please."

" By the grace of God he has reformed," said the old man —" and — Margaret — he loves you yet, as I sed. He is going under the name of Jack Smith, the blacksmith here, an' he'll lead another life — but he loves you yet," he whispered again.

Then he told her what had happened, knowing that Jack's secret would be safe with her.

When he told her how they had buried little Jack, and of the father's admission that his determination to lead the life of an outlaw had come when he found that she had been untrue to him, she was shaken with grief. She could only sit and weep. Not even at the gate, when the old man left her, did she say anything.

Within, she stopped before a picture which hung over the mantle-piece and looked at it, through eyes that filled again and again with tears. It was the picture of a pretty mountain girl with dark eyes and sensual lip.

Margaret knelt before it and wept

The boy had come and stood moodily at the front gate. The hot and resentful blood still tinged in his cheek. He looked at his knuckles — they were cut and swollen where he had struck the boy who had jeered him. It hurt him, but he only smiled grimly.

Never before had any one called him a wood's-colt. He had never heard the word before, but he knew what it meant. For the first time in his life, he hated his mother. He heard her weeping in the little room they called home. He merely shut his lips tightly and, in spite of the stoicism that was his by nature, the tears swelled up in his eyes.

They were hot tears and he could not shake them off. For the first time the wonder and the mystery of it all came over him. For the first time he felt that he was not as other boys,— that there was a meaning in this lonely cabin and the shunned woman he called mother, and the glances, some of pity, some of contempt, which he had met all of his life.

As he stood thinking this, Richard Travis rode slowly down the main road leading from the town to The Gaffs. And this went through the boy successively — not in words, scarcely — but in feelings:

" What a beautiful horse he is riding — it thrills me to see it — I love it naturally — oh, but to own one!

" What a handsome man he is — and how like a gentleman he looks! I like the way he sits his horse. I like that way he has of not noticing people. He has got the same way about him I have got — that I've always had — that I love — a way that shows me I'm not afraid, and that I have got nerve and bravery.

"He sits that horse just as I would sit him — his head — his face — the way that foot slopes to the stirrup — why that's me —"

He stopped — he turned pale — he trembled with pride and rage. Then he turned and walked into the room where Margaret Adams sat. She held out her arms to him pleadingly.

But he did not notice her, and never before had she seen such a look on his face as he said calmly:

"Mother, if you will come to the door I will show you my father."

Margaret Adams had already seen. She turned white with a hidden shame as she said:

"Jimmie — Jimmie — who — who —?"

"No one," he shouted fiercely —"by God "— she had never before heard him swear —" I tell you no one — on my honor as a Travis — no one! It has come to me of itself — I know it — I feel it."

He was too excited to talk. He walked up and down the little room, his proud head lifted and his eyes ablaze.

"I know now why I love honesty, why I despise those common things beneath me — why I am not afraid — why I struck that boy as I did this morning — why —" he walked into the little shed room that was his own and came back with a long single barrel pistol in his hand and fondled it lovingly —"why all my life I have been able to shoot this as I have —"

He held in his hand a long, single barrel, rifle-bored duelling pistol — of the type used by gentlemen at the beginning of the century. Where he had got it she did not know, but always it had been his plaything.

"O Jimmie — you would not —" exclaimed the woman rising and reaching for it.

"Tush —" he said bitterly —" tush — that's the way Richard Travis talks, ain't it? Does not my very voice sound like his? No — but I expect you now, mother" — he said it softly —" tell me — tell me all about it."

For a moment Margaret Adams was staggered. She only shook her head.

He looked at her cynically — then bitterly. A dangerous flash leaped into his eyes.

"Then, by God," he cried fiercely, "this moment will I walk over to his house with this pistol in my hand and I will ask him. If he fails to tell me — damn him — I dare him —"

She jumped up and seized him in her arms.

"Promise me that if I tell you all — all, Jimmy, when you are fifteen — promise me — will you be patient now — with poor mother, who loves you so?" And she kissed him fondly again and again.

He looked into her eyes and saw all her suffering there.

The bitterness went out of his.

"I'll promise, mother," he said simply, and walked back into his little room.

15

CHAPTER VIII

HARD-SHELL SUNDAY

"THIS bein' Hard-shell Sunday," said the Bishop that afternoon when his congregation met, " cattle of that faith will come up to the front rack for fodder. Elder Butts will he'p me conduct these exercises."

" It's been so long sence I've been in a Hard-shell lodge, I may be a little rusty on the grip an' pass word, but I'm a member in good standin' if I am rusty."

There was some laughing at this, from the other members, and after the Hard-shells had come to the front the Bishop caught the infection and went on with a sly wink at the others.

" The fact is, I've sometimes been mighty sorry I jined any other lodge; for makin' honorable exception, the other churches don't know the diff'r'nce betwixt twenty-year-old Lincoln County an' Michigan pine-top.

" The Hard-shells was the fust church I jined, as I sed. I hadn't sampled none of the others "— he whispered aside —" an' I didn't know there was any better licker in the jug. But the Baptists is a little riper, the Presbyterians is much mellower, an' compared to all of them the 'Piscopalians rises to the excellence of syllabub an' champagne.

" A hones' dram tuck now an' then, prayerfully, is

a good thing for any religion. I've knowed many a man to take a dram jes' in time to keep him out of a divorce court. An' I've never knowed it to do anybody no harm but old elder Shotts of Clay County. An' ef he'd a stuck to it straight he'd abeen all right now. But one of these old-time Virginia gentlemen stopped with him all night onct, an' tor't the old man how to make a mint julip; an' when I went down the next year to hold services his wife told me the good old man had been gathered to his fathers. ' He was all right ' she 'lowed, ' till a little feller from Virginia came along an' tort 'im ter mix greens in his licker, an' then he jes drunk hisself to death.'

"There's another thing I like about two of the churches I'm in — the Hard-shells an' the Presbyterians — an' that is special Providence. If I didn't believe in special Providence I'd lose my faith in God.

" My father tuck care of me when I was a babe, an' we're all babes in God's sight.

" The night befo' the battle of Shiloh, I preached to some of our po' boys the last sermon that many of 'em ever heard. An' I told 'em not to dodge the nex' day, but to stan' up an' 'quit themselves like men, for ever' shell an' ball would hit where God intended it should hit.

" In the battle nex' day I was chaplain no longer, but chief of scouts, an' on the firin' line where it was hot enough. In the hottest part of it General Johnston rid up, an' when he saw our exposed position he told us to hold the line, but to lay down for shelter. A big tree

was nigh me an' I got behin' it. The Gineral seed me
an' he smiled an' sed:

" ' Oh, Bishop,' "— his voice fell to a proud and tender tone —" did you know it was Gineral Johnston that
fust named me the Bishop? "

" ' Oh, Bishop,' he said, ' I can see you puttin' a tree
betwixt yo'se'f an' special Providence.' ' Yes, Gineral,'
I sed, ' an' I looks on it as a very special Providence jus'
at this time.'

" He laughed, an' the boys hoorawed an' he rid off.

" Our lives an' the destiny of our course is fixed as
firmly as the laws that wheel the planets. Why, I have
knowed men to try to hew out their own destiny an'
they'd make it look like a gum-log hewed out with a
broad axe, until God would run the rip-saw of His
purpose into them, an' square them out an' smooth them
over an' polish them into pillars for His Temple.

" What is, was goin' to be; an' the things that's got
to come to us has already happened in God's mind.

" I've knowed poor an' unpretentious, God-fearin'
men an' women to put out their hands to build shanties
for their humble lives, an' God would turn them into
castles of character an' temples of truth for all time.

" Elder Butts will lead in prayer."

It was a long prayer and was proceeding smoothly,
until, in its midst, from the front row, Archie B.'s
head bobbed cautiously up. Keeping one eye on his
father, the praying Elder, he went through a pantomime
for the benefit of the young Hillites around him, who,
like himself, had had enough of prayer. Before coming
to the meeting he had cut from a black sheep's skin a

gorgeous set of whiskers and a huge mustache.   These
now adorned his face.

There was a convulsive snicker among the young Hillites behind him.   The Elder opened one eye to see what
it meant.   They were natural children, whose childhood
had not been dwarfed in a cotton mill, and it was ex-
ceedingly funny to them.

But the young Cottontowners laughed not.   They
looked on in stoical wonder at the presumption of the
young Hillites who dared to do such a deed.

Humor had never been known to them.   There is no
humor in the all-day buzz of the cotton factory; and
fun and the fight of life for daily bread do not sleep
in the same crib.

The Hillites tittered and giggled.

"Maw," whispered Miss Butts, " look at Archie B."

Mrs. Butts hastily reached over the bench and yanked
Archie B. down.   His whiskers were confiscated and in
a moment he was on his knees and deeply devotional,
while the young Hillites nudged each other, and giggled and the young Cottontowners stared and wondered, and looked to see when Archie B. would be hung
up by the thumbs.

The Bishop was reading the afternoon chapter when
the animal in Archie B. broke out in another spot.   The
chapter was where Zacharias climbed into a sycamore
tree to see his passing Lord.   There was a rattling of
the stove pipe in one corner.

" Maw," whispered Miss Butts, " Jes' look at Archie
B.— he's climbin' the stove pipe like Zacharias did the
sycamo'."

Horror again swept over Cottontown, while the Hill-ites cackled aloud. The Elder settled it by calmly lay-ing aside his spectacles and starting down the pulpit steps. But Archie B. guessed his purpose and before he had reached the last step he was sitting demurely by the side of his pious brother, intently engaged in reading the New Testament.

Without his glasses, the Elder never knew one twin from the other, but presuming that the studious one was Ozzie B., he seized the other by the ear, pulled him to the open window and pitched him out on the grass.

It was Ozzie B. of course, and Archie B. turned cau-tiously around to the Hillites behind, after the Elder had gone back to his chapter, and whispered:

" *Venture peewee under the bridge — bam — bam — bam.*"

Throughout the sermon Archie B. kept the young Hillites in a paroxysm of smirks.

Elder Butts' legs were brackets, or more properly parentheses, and as he preached and thundered and ges-ticulated and whined and sang his sermon, he forgot all earthly things.

Knowing this, Archie B. would crawl up behind his father and thrusting his head in between his legs, where the brackets were most pronounced, would emphasize all that was said with wry grimaces and gestures.

No language can fittingly describe the way Elder Butts delivered his discourse. The sentences were whined, howled or sung, ending always in the vocal ex-pletive —" *ah — ah.*"

When the elder had finished and sat down, Archie B. was sitting demurely on the platform steps.

Then the latest Scruggs baby was brought forward to be baptised. There were already ten in the family.

The Bishop took the infant tenderly and said: "Sister Scruggs, which church shall I put him into?"

"'Piscopal," whispered the good Mrs. Scruggs.

The Bishop looked the red-headed young candidate over solemnly. There was a howl of protest from the lusty Scruggs.

"He's a Cam'elite," said the Bishop dryly —"ready to dispute a'ready"— here the young Scruggs sent out a kick which caught the Bishop in the mouth.

"With Baptis' propensities," added the Bishop. "Fetch the baptismal fount."

"Please, pap," said little Appamattox Watts from the front bench, "but Archie B. has drunk up all the baptismal water endurin' the first prayer."

"I had to," spoke up Archie B., from the platform steps —"I et dried mackerel for breakfas'."

"We'll postpone the baptisin' till nex' Sunday," said the Bishop.

CHAPTER IX

IT was Sunday and Jack Bracken had been out all the afternoon, hunting for Cap'n Tom — as he had been in the morning, when not at church. Hitching up the old horse, the Bishop started out to hunt also.

He did not go far on the road toward Westmoreland, for as Ben Butler plodded sleepily along, he almost ran over a crowd of boys in the public road, teasing what they took to be a tramp, because of his unkempt beard, his tattered clothes, and his old army cap.

They had angered the man and with many gestures he was endeavoring to expostulate with his tormentors, at the same time attempting imprecations which could not be uttered and ended in a low pitiful sound. He shook his fist at them — he made violent gestures, but from his mouth came only a guttural sound which had no meaning.

At a word from the Bishop his tormentors vanished, and when he pulled up before the uncouth figure he found him to be a man not yet in his prime, with an open face, now blank and expressionless, overgrown with a black, tangled, and untrimmed beard.

He was evidently a demented tramp.

But at a second look the Bishop started. It was the man's eyes which startled him. There was in them

something so familiar and yet so unknown that the
Bishop had to study a while before he could remember.

Then there crept into his face a wave of pitying sorrow as he said to himself:

" Cap'n Tom — Cap'n Tom's eyes."

And from that moment the homeless and demented
tramp had a warm place in the old man's heart.

The Bishop watched him closely. His tattered cap
had fallen off, showing a shock of heavy, uncut hair,
streaked prematurely with gray.

" What yo' name? " asked the Bishop kindly.

The man, flushed and angered, still gesticulated and
muttered to himself. But at the sound of the Bishop's
voice, for a moment there flashed into his eyes almost
the saneness of returned reason. His anger vanished.
A kindly smile spread over his face. He came toward
the Bishop pleadingly — holding out both hands and
striving to speak. Climbing into the buggy, he sat down
by the old man's side, quite happy and satisfied — and
as a little child.

" Where are you from? " asked the Bishop again.

The man shook his head. He pointed to his head
and looked meaningly at the Bishop.

" Can't you tell me where you're gwine, then? "

He looked at the Bishop inquisitively, and for a moment, only, the same look — almost of intelligence —
shone in his eyes. Slowly and with much difficulty —
ay, even as if he were spelling it out, he said:

" A-l-i-c-e "—

The old man turned quickly. Then he paled tremblingly to his very forehead. The word itself — the

sound of that voice sent the blood rushing to his heart.

"Alice? — and what does he mean? An' his voice an' his eyes — Alice — my God — it's Cap'n Tom!"

Tenderly, calmly he pulled the cap from off the strange being's head and felt amid the unkempt locks. But his hands trembled so he could scarcely control them, and the sight of the poor, broken, half demented thing before him — so satisfied and happy that he had found a voice he knew — this creature, the brave, the chivalrous, the heroic Captain Tom! He could scarcely see for the tears which ran down his cheeks.

But as he felt, in the depth of his shock of hair, his finger slipped into an ugly scar, sinking into a cup-shaped hollow fracture which gleamed in his hair.

"Cap'n Tom, Cap'n Tom," he whispered —"don't you know me — the Bishop?"

The man smiled reassuringly and slipped his hand, as a child might, into that of the old man.

"A-l-i-c-e"— he slowly and stutteringly pronounced again, as he pointed down the road toward Westmoreland.

"My God," said the Bishop as he wiped away the tears on the back of his hand —"my God, but that blow has spiled God's noblest gentleman." Then there rushed over him a wave of self-reproach as he raised his head heavenward and said:

"*Almighty Father, forgive me! Only this morning I doubted You; and now, now, You have sent me po' Cap'n Tom!*"

"You'll go home with me, Cap'n Tom!" he added cheerily.

The man smiled and nodded.

" A-l-i-c-e," again he repeated.

There was the sound of some one riding, and as the Bishop turned Ben Butler around Alice Westmore rode up, sitting her saddle mare with that natural grace which comes only when the horse and rider have been friends long enough to become as one. Richard Travis rode with her.

The Bishop paled again: " My God," he muttered —" but she mustn't know this is Cap'n Tom! I'd ruther she'd think he's dead — to remember him only as she knowed him last."

The man's eyes were riveted on her — they seemed to devour her as she rode up, a picture of grace and beauty, sitting her cantering mare with the ease of long years of riding. She smiled and nodded brightly at the Bishop, as she cantered past, but scarcely glanced at the man beside him.

Travis followed at a brisk gait:

" Hello, Bishop," he said banteringly —" got a new boarder to-day? "

He glanced at the man as he spoke, and then galloped on without turning his head.

" Alice! — Alice! "— whispered the man, holding out his hands pleadingly, in the way he had held them when he first saw the Bishop. " Alice! "— but she disappeared behind a turn in the road. She had not noticed him.

The Bishop was relieved.

" We'll go home, Cap'n Tom — you'll want for nothin' whilst I live. An' who knows — ay, Cap'n Tom, who

knows but maybe God has sent you here to-day to begin
the unraveling of the only injustice I've ever knowed
Him to let go so long.   It 'ud be so easy for Him —
He's done bigger things than jes' to straighten out little tangles like that.   Cap'n Tom!   Cap'n Tom!" he
said excitedly —" God'll do it — God'll do it — for He
is just!"

As he turned to go a negro came up hurriedly: " I
was fetchin' him to you, Marse Hilliard — been lookin'
for yo' home all day.   I had gone to the spring for
water an' 'lowed I'd be back in a minute."

" Why, it's Eph," said the Bishop.   " Come on to my
home, Eph, we'll take keer of Cap'n Tom."

It was Sunday night.   They had eaten their supper,
and the old man was taking his smoke before going to
bed.   Shiloh, as usual, had climbed up into his lap and
lay looking at the distant line of trees that girdled the
mountain side.   There was a flush on her cheeks and
a brightness in her eyes which the old man had noticed
for several weeks.

Shiloh was his pet — his baby.   All the affection of
his strong nature found its outlet in this little soul —
this motherless little waif, who likewise found in the old
man that rare comradeship of extremes — the inex-
plicable law of the physical world which brings the snow-
flower in winter.   The one real serious quarrel the
old man had had with his stubborn and ignorant old wife
had been when Shiloh was sent to the factory.   But it
was always starvation times with them; and when
aroused, the temper and tongue of Mrs. Watts was more
than the peaceful old man could stand up against.   And

as there were a dozen other tots of her age in the factory, he had been forced to acquiesce.

Long after all others had retired — long after the evening star had arisen, and now, high overhead, looked down through the chinks in the roof of the cabin on the mountain side, saying it was midnight and past, the patient old man sat with Shiloh on his lap, watching her quick, restless breathing, and fearing to put her to bed, lest he might awaken her.

He put her in bed at last and then slipped into Captain Tom's cabin before he himself lay down.

To his surprise he was up and reading an old dictionary — studying and puzzling over the words. It was the only book except the Bible the Bishop had in his cabin, and this book proved to be Captain Tom's solace.

After that, day after day, he would sit out under the oak tree by his cabin intently reading the dictionary.

Eph, his body servant, slept on the floor by his side, and Jack Bracken sat near him like a sturdy mastiff guarding a child. Sympathy, pity — were written in the outlaw's face, as he looked at the once splendid manhood shorn of its strength, and from that day Jack Bracken showered on Captain Tom all the affection of his generous soul — all that would have gone to little Jack.

" For he's but a child — the same as little Jack was," he would say.

" Put up yo' novel, Cap'n Tom," said the old man cheerily, when he went in, " an' let's have prayers."

The sound of the old man's voice was soothing to

Captain Tom. Quickly the book was closed and down on their knees went the three men.

It was a queer trio — the three kneeling in prayer.

"Almighty God," prayed the old man —"me an' Cap'n Tom an' Jack Bracken here, we thank You for bein' so much kinder to us than we deserves. One of us, lost to his friends, is brought back home; one of us, lost in wickedness but yestiddy, is redeemed to-day; an' me that doubted You only yestiddy, to me You have fotcht Cap'n Tom back, a reproach for my doubts an' my disbelief, lame in his head, it is true, but You've fotcht him back where I can keer for him an' nuss him. An' I hope You'll see fit, Almighty God, You who made the worl' an' holds it in the hollow of Yo' han', You, who raised up the dead Christ, to give po' Cap'n Tom back his reason, that he may fulfill the things in life ordained by You that he should fulfill since the beginning of things.

"An' hold Jack Bracken to the mark, Almighty God, — let him toe the line an' shoot, hereafter, only for good. An' guide me, for I need it — me that in spite of all You've done for me, doubted You but yestiddy. Amen."

It was a simple, homely prayer, but it comforted even Captain Tom, and when Jack Bracken put him to bed that night, even the outlaw felt that the morning of a new era would awaken them.

CHAPTER X

IT was twilight when Mrs. Westmore heard the clatter of horses' hoofs up the gravelled road-way, and two riders cantered up.

Richard Travis sat his saddle horse in the slightly stooping way of the old fox-hunter — not the most graceful seat, but the most natural and comfortable for hard riding. Alice galloped ahead — her fine square shoulders and delicate but graceful bust silhouetted against the western sky in the fading light.

Mrs. Westmore sat on the veranda and watched them canter up. She thought how handsome they were, and how well they would look always together.

Alice sprang lightly from her mare at the front steps.

"Did you think we were never coming back? Richard's new mare rides so delightfully that we rode farther than we intended. Oh, but she canters beautifully!"

She sat on the arm of her mother's chair, and bent over and kissed her cheek. The mother looked up to see her finely turned profile outlined in a pale pink flush of western sky which glowed behind her. Her cheeks were of the same tinge as the sky. They glowed with the flush of the gallop, and her eyes were bright with the happiness of it. She sat telling of the new mare's

239

wonderfully correct saddle gaits, flipping her ungloved hand with the gauntlet she had just pulled off.

Travis turned the horses over to Jim and came up.

" Glad to see you, Cousin Alethea," he said, as she arose and advanced gracefully to meet him —" no, no — don't rise," he added in his half jolly, half commanding way. " You've met me before and I'm not such a big man as I seem." He laughed: " Do you remember Giant Jim, the big negro Grandfather used to have to oversee his hands on the lower place? Jim, you know, in consideration of his elevation, was granted several privileges not allowed the others. Among them was the privilege of getting drunk every Saturday night. Then it was he would stalk and brag among those he ruled while they looked at him in awe and reverence. But he had the touch of the philosopher in him and would finally say: ' Come, touch me, boys; come, look at me; come, feel me — I'm nothin' but a common man, although I appear so big.' "

Mrs. Westmore laughed in her mechanical way, but all the while she was looking at Alice, who was watching the mare as she was led off.

Travis caught her eye and winked mischievously as he added: " Now, Cousin Alethea, you must promise me to make Alice ride her whenever she needs a tonic — every day, if necessary. I have bought her for Alice, and she must get the benefit of her before it grows too cold."

He turned to Alice Westmore: " You have only to tell me which days — if I am too busy to go with you — Jim will bring her over."

She smiled: "You are too kind, Richard, always thinking of my pleasure. A ride like this once a week is tonic enough."

She went into the house to change her habit. Her brother Clay, who had been sitting on the far end ot the porch unobserved, arose and, without noticing Travis as he passed, walked into the house.

"I cannot imagine," said Mrs. Westmore apologetically, "what is the matter with Clay to-day."

"Why?" asked Travis indifferently enough.

"He has neglected his geological specimens all day, nor has he ever been near his laboratory — he has one room he calls his laboratory, you know. To-night he is moody and troubled."

Travis said nothing. At tea Clay was not there.

When Travis left it was still early and Alice walked with him to the big gate. The moon shone dimly and the cool, pure light lay over everything like the first mist of frost in November. Beyond, in the field, where it struck into the open cotton bolls, it turned them into December snow-banks.

Travis led his saddle horse, and as they walked to the gate, the sweet and scarcely perceptible odor of the crepe-myrtle floated out on the open air.

The crepe-myrtle has a way of surprising us now and then, and often after a wet fall, it gives us the swan-song of a bloom, ere its delicate blossoms, touched to death by frost, close forever their scalloped pink eyes, on the rare summer of a life as spiritual as the sweet soft gulf winds which brought it to life.

Was it symbolic to-night,— the swan-song of the ro-

mance of Alice Westmore's life, begun under those very
trees so many summers ago?

They stopped at the gate. Richard Travis lit a cigar
before mounting his horse. He seemed at times to-night
restless, yet always determined.

She had never seen him so nearly preoccupied as he
had been once or twice to-night.

" Do you not think? " he asked, after a while as they
stood by the gate, " that I should have a sweet answer
soon? "

Her eyes fell. The death song of the crepe-myrtle,
aroused by a south wind suddenly awakened, smote her
painfully.

" You know — you know how it is, Richard "—

" How it was — Alice. But think — life is a practical — a serious thing. We all have had our romances.
They are the heritage of dreaming youth. We outlive
them — it is best that we should. Our spiritual life follows the law of all other life, and spiritually we are not
the same this year that we were last. Nor will we be the
next. It is always change — change — even as the body
changes. Environment has more to do with what we
are, what we think and feel — than anything else. If
you will marry me you will soon love me — it is the law
of love to beget love. You will forget all the lesser
loves in the great love of your life. Do you not know it,
feel it, Sweet? "

She looked at him surprised. Never before had he
used any term of endearment to her. There was a hard,
still and subtle yet determined light in his eyes.

" Richard — Richard — you — I "—

" See," he said, taking from his vest pocket a magnificent ring set in an exquisite old setting — inherited from his grandmother, and it had been her engagement ring. " See, Alice, let me put this on to-night."

He took her hand — it thrilled him as he had never been thrilled before. This impure man, who had made the winning of women a plaything, trembled with the fear of it as he took in his own the hand so pure that not even his touch could awaken sensuality in it. The odor of her beautiful hair floated up to him as he bent over. A wave of hot passion swept over him — for with him love was passion — and his reason, for a moment, was swept from its seat. Then almost beside himself for love of this woman, so different from any he had ever known, he opened his arms to fold her in one overpowering, conquering embrace.

It was but a second and more a habit than thought — he who had never before hesitated to do it.

She stepped back and the hot blood mounted to her cheek. Her eyes shone like outraged stars, dreaming earthward on a sleeping past, unwarningly obscured by a passing cloud, and then flashing out into the night, more brightly from the contrast.

She did not speak and he crunched under his feet, purposely, the turf he was standing on, and so carrying out, naturally, the gesture of clasping the air, in establishing his balance — as if it was an accident.

She let him believe she thought it was, and secured relief from the incident.

" Alice — Alice ! " he exclaimed. " I love you — love

you — I must have you in my life! Can you not wear
this now? See!"

He tried to place it on her finger. He held the small
beautiful hand in his own. Then it suddenly withdrew
itself and left him holding his ring and looking wonderingly at her.

She had thrown back her head, and, half turned, was
looking toward the crepe-myrtle tree from which the
faint odor came.

"You had better go, Richard," was all she said.

"I'll come for my answer — soon?" he asked.

She was silent.

"Soon?" he repeated as he rose in the stirrup —
"soon — and to claim you always, Alice."

He rode off and left her standing with her head still
thrown back, her thoughtful face drinking in the odor
of the crepe-myrtle.

Travis did not understand, for no crepe-myrtle had
ever come into his life. It could not come. With him
all life had been a passion flower, with the rank, strong
odor of the sensuous, wild honeysuckle, which must climb
ever upon something else, in order to open and throw
off the rank, brazen perfume from its yellow and streaked
and variegated blossoms.

And how common and vulgar and all-surfeiting it is,
loading the air around it with its sickening imitation of
sweetness, so that even the bees stagger as they pass
through it and disdain to stop and shovel, for the mere
asking, its musky and illicit honey.

But, O mystic odor of the crepe-myrtle — O love

which never dies — how differently it grows and lives and blooms!

In color, constant — a deep pink. Not enough of red to suggest the sensual, nor yet lacking in it when the full moment of ripeness comes. How delicately pink it is, and yet how unfadingly it stands the summer's sun, the hot air, the drought! How quickly it responds to the Autumn showers, and long after the honeysuckle has died, and the bees have forgotten its rank memory, this beautiful creature of love blooms in the very lap of Winter.

O love that defies even the breath of death!

The yellow lips of the honeysuckle are thick and sensual; but the beautiful petals of this cluster of love-cells, all so daintily transparent, hanging in pink clusters of loveliness with scalloped lips of purity, that even the sunbeam sends a photograph of his heart through them and every moonbeam writes in it the romance of its life. And the skies all day long, reflecting in its heart, tells to the cool green leaves that shadow it the story of its life, and it catches and holds the sympathy of the tiniest zephyr, from the way it flutters to the patter of their little feet.

All things of Nature love it — the clouds, the winds, the very stars, and sun, because love — undying love — is the soul of God, its Maker.

The rose is red in the rich passion of love, the lily is pale in the poverty of it; but the crepe-myrtle is pink in the constancy of it.

O bloom of the crepe-myrtle! And none but a lover ever smelled it — none but a lover ever knew!

She ran up the gentle slope to the old-fashioned garden and threw herself under the tree from whence the dying odor came. She fell on her knees — the moonlight over her in fleckings of purification. She clung to the scaly weather-beaten stem of the tree as she would have pressed a sister to her breast. Her arms were around it — she knew it — it's very bark.

She seized a bloom that had fallen and crushed it to her bosom and her cheek.

"O Tom — Tom — why — why did you make me love you here and then leave me forever with only the memory of it? "

" Twice does it bloom, dear Heart,— can not my love bloom like it — twice? "

" A-l-i-c-e! "

The voice came from out the distant woods nearby.

The blood leaped and then pricked her like sharp-pointed icicles, and they all seemed to freeze around and prick around her heart. She could not breathe. . . . Her head reeled. . . . The crepe-myrtle fell on her and smothered her. . . .

When she awoke Mrs. Westmore sat by her side and was holding her head while her brother was rubbing her arms.

" You must be ill, darling," said her mother gently. " I heard you scream. What —"

They helped her to rise. Her heart still fluttered violently — her head swam.

" Did you call me before — before "— she was excited and eager.

"Why, yes"— smiled her mother. "I said, 'Alice — Alice!'"

"It was not that — no, that was not the way it sounded." she said as they led her into the house.

CHAPTER XI

RICHARD TRAVIS could not sleep that night — why, he could not tell.

After he returned from Westmoreland, Mammy Charity brought him his cocktail, and tidied up his room, and beat up the feathers in his pillows and bed — for she believed in the old-fashioned feather-bed and would have no other kind in the house.

The old clock in the hall — that had sat there since long before he, himself, could remember — struck ten, and then eleven, and then, to his disgust, even twelve.

At ten he had taken another toddy to put himself to sleep.

There is only one excuse for drunkenness, and that is sleeplessness. If there is a hell for the intellectual it is not of fire, as for commoner mortals, but of sleeplessness — the wild staring eyes of an eternity of sleeplessness following an eon of that midnight mental anguish which comes with the birth of thoughts.

But still he slept not, and so at ten he had taken another toddy — and still another, and as he felt its life and vigor to the ends of his fingers, he quaffed his fourth one; then he smiled and said: "And now I don't care if I never go to sleep!"

He arose and dressed. He tried to recite one of his

favorite poems, and it angered him that his tongue seemed thick.

His head slightly reeled, but in it there galloped a thousand beautiful dreams and there were visions of Alice, and love, and the satisfaction of conquering and the glory of winning.

He could feel his heart-throbs at the ends of his fingers. He could see thoughts — beautiful, grand thoughts — long before they reached him,— stalking like armed men, helmeted and vizored, stalking forward into his mind.

He walked out and down the long hall.

The ticking of the clock sounded to him so loud that he stopped and cursed it.

Because, somehow, it ticked every time his heart beat; and he could count his heart-beats in his fingers' ends, and he didn't want to know every time his heart beat. It made him nervous.

It might stop; but it would not stop. And then, somehow, he imagined that his heart was really out in the yard, down under the hill, and was pumping the water — as the ram had done for years — through the house. It was a queer fancy, and it made him angry because he could not throw it off.

He walked down the hall, rudely snatched the clock door open, and stopped the big pendulum. Then he laughed sillily.

The moonbeams came in at the stained glass windows, and cast red and yellow and pale green fleckings of light on the smooth polished floor.

He began to feel uncanny. He was no coward and he cursed himself for it.

Things began to come to him in a moral way and mixed in with the uncanniness of it all. He imagined he saw, off in the big square library across the way, in the very spot he had seen them lay out his grandfather — Maggie, and she arose suddenly from out of his grandfather's casket and beckoned to him with —

" I love you so — I love *you* so ! "

It was so real, he walked to the spot and put his hands on the black mohair Davenport. And the form on it, sitting bolt upright, was but the pillow he had napped on that afternoon.

He laughed and it sounded hollow to him and echoed down the hall :

" How like her it looked ! "

He walked into Harry's room and lit the lamp there. He smiled when he glanced around the walls. There were hunting scenes and actresses in scant clothing. Tobacco pipes of all kinds on the tables, and stumps of ill-smelling cigarettes, and over the mantel was a crayon picture of Death shaking the dice of life. Two old cutlasses crossed underneath it.

On his writing desk Travis picked up and read the copy of the note written to Helen the day before.

He smiled with elevated eyebrows. Then he laughed ironically :

" The little yellow cur — to lie down and quit — to throw her over like that ! Damn him — he has a yellow streak in him and I'll take pleasure in pulling down the purse for him. Why, she was born for me anyway !

That kid, and in love with Helen! Not for The Gaffs would I have him mix up with that drunken set — nor — nor, well, not for The Gaffs to have him quit like that."

And yet it was news to him. Wrapped in his own selfish plans, he had never bothered himself about Harry's affairs.

But he kept on saying, as if it hurt him: " The little yellow cur — and he a Travis!" He laughed: " He's got another one, I'll bet — got her to-night and by now is securely engaged. So much the better — for my plans."

Again he went into the hall and walked to and fro in the dim light. But the Davenport and the pillow instantly formed themselves again into Maggie and the casket, and he turned in disgust to walk into his own room.

Above his head over the doorway in the hall, on a pair of splendid antlers — his first trophy of the chase,— rested his deer gun, a clean piece of Damascus steel and old English walnut, imported years before. The barrels were forty inches and choked. The small bright hammers rested on the yellow brass caps deep sunk on steel nippers. They shone through the hammer slit fresh and ready for use.

He felt a cold draught of air blow on him and turned in surprise to find the hall window, which reached to the veranda floor, open; and he could see the stars shining above the dark green foliage of the trees on the lawn without.

At the same instant there swept over him a nervous

fear, and he reached for his deer gun instinctively. Then there arose from the Davenport coffin a slouching unkempt form, the fine bright eyes of which, as the last rays of the moonlight fell on them, were the eyes of his dead cousin, Captain Tom, and it held out its hands pleadingly to him and tenderly and with much effort said:

"*Grandfather, forgive. I've come back again.*"

Travis's heart seemed to freeze tightly. He tried to breathe — he only gasped — and the corners of his mouth tightened and refused to open. He felt the blood rush up from around his loins, and leave him paralyzed and weak. In sheer desperation he threw the gun to his shoulder, and the next instant he would have fired the load into the face of the thing with its voice of the dead, had not something burst on his head with a staggering, overpowering blow, and despite his efforts to stand, his knees gave way beneath him and it seemed pleasant for him to lie prone upon the floor. . . .

When he awakened an hour afterwards, he sat up, bewildered. His gun lay beside him, but the window was closed securely and bolted. No night air came in. The Davenport and pillow were there as before. His head ached and there was a bruised place over his ear. He walked into his own room and lit the lamp.

"I may have fallen and struck my head," he said, bewildered with the strangeness of it all. "I may have," he repeated —"but if I didn't see Tom Travis's ghost to-night there is no need to believe one's senses."

He opened the door and let in two setters which

fawned upon him and licked his hand.   All his nervousness vanished.

" No one knows the comfort of a dog's company," he said, " who does not love a dog? "

Then he bathed his face and head and went to sleep.

It was after midnight when Jack Bracken led Captain Tom in and put him to bed.

" A close shave for you, Cap'n Tom," he said —" I struck just in time. I'll not leave you another night with the door unlocked."   Then: " But poor fellow — how can we blame him for wandering off, after all those years, and trying to get back again to his boyhood home."

CHAPTER XII

JACK BRACKEN rolled himself in his blanket on
the cot, placed in the room next to Captain Tom,
and prepared to sleep again.

But the excitement of the night had been great; his
sudden awakening from sleep, his missing Captain Tom,
and finding him in time to prevent a tragedy, had
aroused him thoroughly, and now sleep was far from his
eyes.

And so he lay and thought of his past life, and as it
passed before him it shook him with nervous sleeplessness.

It hurt him. He lay and panted with the strong sorrow of it.

Perhaps it was that, but with it were thoughts also of
little Jack, and the tears came into the eyes of the big-
hearted outlaw.

He had his plans all arranged — he and the Bishop —
and now as the village blacksmith he would begin the life
of an honest man.

Respected — his heart beat proudly to think of it.

Respected — how little it means to the man who is,
how much to the man who is not.

" Why," he said to himself —" perhaps after a while
people will stop and talk to me an' say as they pass my

shop: 'Good mornin', neighbor. how are you to-day?'
Little children — sweet an' innocent little children —
comin' from school may stop an' watch the sparks fly
from my anvil, like they did in the poem I onct read,
an' linger aroun' an' talk to me, shy like; maybe, after
awhile I'll get their confidence, so they will learn to love
me, an' call me Uncle Jack — Uncle Jack," he repeated
softly.

" An' I won't be suspectin' people any mo' an' none of
'em will be my enemy. I'll not be carryin' pistols an'
havin' buckets of gold an' not a friend in the worl'."

His heart beat fast — he could scarcely wait for the
morning to come, so anxious was he to begin the life of
an honest man again. He who had been an outlaw se
long, who had not known what it was to know human
sympathy and human friendship — it thrilled him with
a rich, sweet flood of joy.

Then suddenly a great wave swept over him — a wave
of such exquisite joy that he fell on his knees and cried
out: " O God, I am a changed man — how happy I
am! jus' to be human agin an' not hounded! How can
I thank You — You who have given me this blessed
Man the Bishop tells us about — this Christ who reaches
out an' takes us by the han' an' lifts us up. O God,
if there is divinity given to man, it is given to that man
who can lift up another, as the po' outlaw knows."

He lay silent and thoughtful. All day and night —
since he had first seen Margaret, her eyes had haunted
him. He had not seen her before for many years; but
in all that time there had not been a day when he had
not thought of — loved — her.

Margaret — her loneliness — the sadness of her life, all haunted him. She lived, he knew, alone, in her cottage — an outcast from society. He had looked but once in her eyes and caught the lingering look of appeal which unconsciously lay there. He knew she loved him yet — it was there as plain as in his own face was written the fact that he loved her. He thought of himself — of her. Then he said:

"For fifteen years I have robbed — killed — oh, God — killed — how it hurts me now! All the category of crime in bitter wickedness I have run. And she — once — and now an angel — Bishop himself says so."

"I am a new man — I am a respectable and honest man,"— here he arose on his cot and drew himself up — "I am Jack Smith — Mr. Jack Smith, the blacksmith, and my word is my bond."

He slipped out quietly. Once again in the cool night, under the stars which he had learned to love as brothers and whose silent paths across the heavens were to him old familiar footpaths, he felt at ease, and his nervousness left him.

He had not intended to speak to Margaret then — for he thought she was asleep. He wished only to guard her cabin, up among the stunted old field pines — while she slept — to see the room he knew she slept in — the little window she looked out of every day.

The little cabin was a hallowed spot to him. Somehow he knew — he felt that whatever might be said — in it he knew an angel dwelt. He could not understand — he only knew.

There is a moral sense within us that is a greater teacher than either knowledge or wisdom.

For an hour he stood with his head uncovered watching the little cabin where she lived. Everything about it was sacred, because Margaret lived there. It was pretty, too, in its neatness and cleanliness, and there were old-fashioned flowers in the yard and old-fashioned roses clambered on the rock wall.

He sat down in the path — the little white sanded path down which he knew she went every day, and so made sacred by her footsteps.

" Perhaps, I am near one of them now," he said — and he kissed the spot.

And that night and many others did the outlaw watch over the lonely cabin on the mountain side. And she, the outcast woman, slept within, unconscious that she was being protected by the man who had loved her all his life.

CHAPTER XIII

THE THEFT OF A CHILDHOOD

THE Watts children were up the next morning by
four o'clock.

Mrs. Watts ate, always, by candle-light.
The sun, she thought, would be dishonored, were he to
find her home in disorder, her breakfast uncooked, her
day's work not ready for her, with his first beams.

For Mrs. Watts did not consider that arising at four,
and cooking and sweeping and tidying up the cabin, and
quarreling with the Bishop as " a petty old bundle of
botheration "— and storming around at the children —
all by sun-up — this was not work at all.

It was merely an appetizer.

The children were aroused by her this morning with
more severity than usual. Half frightened they rolled
stupidly out of their beds — Appomattox, Atlanta, and
Shiloh from one, and the boys from another. Then
they began to put on their clothes in the same listless,
dogged, mechanical way they had learned to do everything — learned it while working all day between the
whirl of the spindle and the buzz of the bobbin.

The sun had not yet risen, and a cold gray mist crept
up from the valley, closing high up and around the
wood-girdled brow of the mountain as billows around
a rock in the sea. The faint, far-off crowing of cocks

added to the weirdness; for their shrill voices alone broke through the silence which came down with the mist. Around the brow of Sand Mountain the vapor made a faint halo — touched as it was by the splendid flush of the East.

It was all grand and beautiful enough without, but within was the poverty of work, and the two — poverty and work — had already had their effect on the children, except, perhaps, Shiloh. She had not yet been in the mill long enough to be automatonized.

Looking out of the window she saw the star setting behind the mountain, and she thought it slept, by day, in a cavern she knew of there.

"Wouldn't it be fine, Mattox," she cried, "if we didn't have to work at the mill to-day an' cu'd run up on the mountain an' pick up that star? I seed one fall onct an' I picked it up."

For a moment the little face was thoughtful — wistful — then she added:

"I wonder how it would feel to spen' the day in the woods onct. Archie B. says it's just fine and flowers grow everywhere. Oh, jes' to be 'quainted with one Jeree — like Archie B. is — an' have him come to yo' winder every mornin' an' say, ' *Wake up, Pet! Wake up, Pet! Wake up, Pet!* ' An' then hear a little 'un over in another tree say, ' *So-s-l-ee-py — So-s-l-ee-py!* ' .

Her chatter ceased again. Then: "Mattox, did you ever see a rabbit? I seen one onct, a settin' up in a fence corner an' a spittin' on his han's to wash his face."

She laughed at the thought of it. But the other children, who had dressed, sat listlessly in their seats, looking at her with irresponsive eyes, set deep back into tired, lifeless, weazened faces.

"I'd ruther a rabbit 'ud wash his face than mine," drawled Bull Run.

Mrs. Watts came in and jerked the chair from under him and he sat down sprawling. Then he lazily arose and deliberately spat, between his teeth, into the fire-place.

There was not enough of him alive to feel that he had been imposed upon.

For breakfast they had big soda biscuits and fried bacon floating in its own grease. There was enough of it left for the midday lunch. This was put into a tin pail with a tight fitting top. The pail, when opened, smelt of the death and remains of every other soda biscuit that had ever been laid away within this tightly closed mausoleum of tin.

They had scarcely eaten before the shrill scream of the mill-whistle called them to their work.

Shiloh, at the sound, stuck her small fingers into her ears and shuddered.

Then the others struck out across the yard, and Shiloh followed.

To this child of seven, who had already worked six months in the factory, the scream of the whistle was the call of a frightful monster, whose black smoke-stack of a snout, with its blacker breath coming out, and the flaming eyes of the engine glaring through the smoke, completed the picture of a wild beast watching her. Within, the whirr and tremble of shuttle and machinery were the purr and pulsation of its heart.

She was a nervous, sensitive child, who imagined far more than she saw; and the very uncanniness of the dark misty morning, the silence, broken only by the tremble and roar of the mill, the gaunt shadows of the overtopping mountain, filled her with childish fears.

Nature can do no more than she is permitted; and the terrible strain of twelve hours' work, every day except Sunday, for the past six months, where every faculty, from hand and foot to body, eye and brain, must be alert and alive to watch and piece the never-ceasing breaking of the threads, had already begun to undermine the half-formed frame-work of that little life.

As she approached the mill she clung to the hand of Appomattox, and shrinking, kept her sister between herself and the Big Thing which put the sweet morning air a-flutter around its lair. As she drew near the door she almost cried out in affright — her little heart grew tight, her lips were drawn.

" Oh, it can't hurt you, Shiloh," said her sister pulling her along. " You'll be all right when you get inside."

There was a snarling clatter and crescendo tremble, ending in an all-drowning roar, as the big door was pushed open for a moment, and Shiloh, quaking, but brave, was pulled in, giving the tiny spark of her little life to add to the Big Thing's fire.

Within, she was reassured; for there was her familiar spinning frame, with its bobbins ready to be set to spinning and whirling; and the room was full of people, many as small as she.

The companionship, even of fear, is helpful.

Besides, the roar and clatter drowned everything else.

Shiloh was too small to see, to know; but had she
looked to the right as she entered, she had seen a sight
which would have caused a stone man to flush with pity.
It was Byrd Boyle, one of the mill hands who ran a
slubbing machine, and he held in his arms (because
they were too young to walk so far) twins, a boy and
a girl. And they looked like half made up dolls left
out on the grass, weather-beaten by summer rains.
They were too small to know where their places were
in the room, and as their father sat them down, in their
proper places, it took the two together to run one side
of a spinner, and the tiny little workers could scarcely
reach to their whirling bobbins.

To the credit of Richard Travis, this working of children under twelve years of age in the mills was done
over his protest. Not so with Kingsley and his wife,
who were experienced mill people from New England
and knew the harm of it — morally, physically. Travis
had even made strict regulations on the subject, only to
be overruled by the combined disapproval of Kingsley
and the directors and, strange to say, of the parents of
the children themselves. His determination that only
children of twelve years and over should work in the
mill came to naught, more from the opposition of the
parents themselves than that of Kingsley. These, to
earn a little more for the family, did not hesitate to bring
a child of eight to the mill and swear it was twelve.
This and the ruling of the directors,— and worse than
all, the lack of any state law on the subject,— had
brought about the pitiful condition which prevailed
then as now in Southern cotton mills.

There was no talking inside the mill. Only the Big Thing was permitted to talk. No singing — for songs come from the happy heart of labor, unshackled. No noise of childhood, though the children were there. They were flung into an arena for a long day's fight against a thing of steel and steam, and there was no ime for anything save work, work, work — walk, walk, walk — watch, forever watch,— the interminable flying whirl of spindle and spool.

Early as it was, the children were late, and were soundly rebuffed by the foreman.

The scolding hurt only Shiloh — it made her tremble and cry. The others were hardened — insensible — and took it with about the same degree of indifference with which caged and starved mice look at the man who pours over their wire traps the hot water which scalds them to death.

The fight between steel, steam and child-flesh was on.

Shiloh, Appomattox and Atlanta were spinners.

Spinners are small girls who walk up and down an aisle before a spinning-frame and piece up the threads which are forever breaking. There were over a hundred spindles on each side of the frame, each revolving with the rapidity of an incipient cyclone and snapping every now and then the delicate white thread that was spun out like spiders' web from the rollers and the cylinders, making a balloon-like gown of cotton thread, which settled continuously around the bobbin.

All day long and into the night, they must walk up and down, between these two rows of spinning-frames, amid the whirling spindles, piecing the broken threads which were forever breaking.

It did not require strength, but a certain skill, which, unfortunately, childhood possessed more than the adult. Not power, but dexterity, watchfulness, quickness and the ability to walk — as children walk — and watch — as age should watch.

No wonder that in a few months the child becomes, not the flesh and blood of its heredity, but the steel and wood of its environment.

Bull Run and Seven Days were doffers, and confined to the same set of frames. They followed their sisters, taking off the full bobbins and throwing them into a cart and thrusting an empty bobbin into its place. This requires an eye of lightning and a hand with the quickness of its stroke.

For it must be done between the pulsings of the Big Thing's heart — a flash, a snap, a snarl of broken thread — up in the left hand flies the bobbin from its disentanglement of thread and skein, and down over the buzzing point of steel spindles settles the empty bobbin, thrust over the spindle by the right.

It is all done with two quick movements — a flash and a jerk of one hand up, and the other down, the eye riveted to the nicety of a hair's breadth, the stroke downward gauged to the cup of a thimble, to settle over the point of the spindle's end; for the missing of a thread's breadth would send a spindle blade through the hand, or tangle and snap a thread which was turning with a thousand revolutions in a minute.

Snap — bang! Snap — bang! One hundred and

twenty times — *Snap* — *bang!* and back again, went the deft little workers pushing their cart before them.

Full at last, their cart is whirled away with flying heels to another machine.

It was a steady, lightning, endless track. Their little trained fingers betook of their surroundings and worked like fingers of steel. Their legs seemed made of India rubber. Their eyes shot out right and left, left and right, looking for the broken threads on the whirling bobbins as hawks sweep over the marsh grass looking for mice, and the steel claws, which swooped down on the bobbins when they found it, made the simile not unsuitable.

Young as she was, Shiloh managed one of these harnessed, fiery lines of dancing witches, pirouetting on boards of hardened oak or hickory. Up and down she walked — up and down, watching these endless whirling figures, her bare fingers pitted against theirs of brass, her bare feet against theirs shod with iron, her little head against theirs insensate and unpitying, her little heart against theirs of flame which throbbed in the boiler's bosom and drove its thousand steeds with a whip of fire.

In the bloodiest and cruelest days of the Roman Empire, man was matched against wild beasts. But in the man's hand was the blade of his ancestors and over his breast the steel ribs which had helped his people to conquer the world.

And in the Beast's body was a heart!

Ay, and the man was a man — a trained gladiator — and he was nerved by the cheers of thousands of sympathizing spectators.

And now, centuries after, and in the age of so-called kindness, comes this battle to be fought over. And the fight, now as then, is for bread and life.

But how cruelly unfair is the fight of to-day, when the weak and helpless child is made the gladiator, and the fight is for bread, and the Beast is of steel and steam, and is soulless and heartless. Steel — that by which the old gladiator conquered — that is the heart of the Thing the little one must fight. And the cheers — the glamour of it is lacking, for the little one cannot hear even the sound of its own voice — in the roar of the thousand-throated Thing which drives the Steel Beast on.

Seven o'clock — eight o'clock — Shiloh's head swam — her shoulders ached, her ears quivered with sensitiveness, and seemed not to catch sounds any more, but sharp and shooting pains. She was dazed already and weak; but still the Steam Thing cheered its steel legions on.

Up and down, up and down she walked, her baby thoughts coming to her as through the roar of a Niagara, through pain and sensitiveness, through aches and a dull, never-ending sameness.

Nine o'clock! Oh, she was so tired of it all!

Hark, she thought she heard a bird sing in a far off, dreamy way, and for a moment she made mud pies in the back yard of the hut on the mountain, under the black-oak in the yard, with the glint of soft sunshine over everything and the murmur of green leaves in the trees above, as the wind from off the mountain went through them, and the anemone, and bellworts, and daisies grew beneath and around. Was it a bluebird?

She had never seen but one and it had built its nest in a hole in a hollow tree, the summer before she went into the mill to work.

She listened again — yes, it did sound something like a bluebird, peeping in a distant far off way, such as she had heard in the cabin on the mountain before she had ever heard the voice of the Big Thing at the mill. She listened, and a wave of disappointment swept over her baby face; for, listening closely, she found it was an un-oiled separator, that peeped in a bluebird way now and then, above the staccato of some rusty spindle.

But in the song of that bluebird and the glory of an imaginary mud pie, all the disappointment of what she had missed swept over her.

Ten o'clock — the little fingers throbbed and burned, the tiny legs were stiff and tired, the little head seemed as a block of wood, but still the Steam Thing took no thought of rest.

Eleven o'clock — oh, but to rest awhile! To rest under the trees in the yard, for the sunshine looked so warm and bright out under the mill-windows, and the memory of that bluebird's song, though but an imitation, still echoed in her ear. And those mud pies! — she saw them all around her and in such lovely bits of old broken crockery and —   .   .   .

She felt a rude punch in the side. It was Jud Carpenter standing over her and pointing to where a frowzled broken thread was tangling itself around a separator. She had dreamed but a minute — half a dozen threads had broken.

It was a rude punch and it hurt her side and fright-

ened her.   With a snarl and a glare he passed on while
Shiloh flew to her bobbin.

This fright made her work the next hour with less
fatigue.   But she could not forget the song of the bluebird, and once, when Appomattox looked at her, she was
working her mouth in a song,— a Sunday School song
she had picked up at the Bishop's church.   Appomattox
could not hear it — no one had a license to hear a song
in the Beast Thing's Den — nothing was ever privileged
to sing but it,— but she knew from the way her mouth
was working that Shiloh was singing.

Oh, the instinct of happiness in the human heart!   To
sing through noises and aches and tired feet and stunned,
blocky heads.   To sing with no hope before her and the
theft of her very childhood — ay, her life — going on
by the Beast Thing and his men.

God intended us to be happy, else He had never put
so strong an instinct there.

Twelve o'clock.   The Steam Beast gave a triumphant
scream heard above the roar of shuttle and steel.   It
was a loud, defiant, victorious roar which drowned all
others.

Then it purred and paused for breath — purred softer
and softer and — slept at last.

It was noon.

The silence now was almost as painful to Shiloh as
the noise had been.   The sudden stopping of shuttle and
wheel and belt and beam did not stop the noise in her
head.   It throbbed and buzzed there in an echoing ache,
as if all the previous sounds had been fire-waves and
these the scorched furrows of its touch.   Wherever she

turned, the echo of the morning's misery sounded in her ears.

And now they had forty minutes for noon recess.

They sat in a circle, these five children — and ate their lunch of cold soda biscuits and fat bacon.

Not a word did they say — not a laugh nor a sound to show they were children,— not even a sigh to show they were human.

Silently, like wooden things they choked it down and then — O men and women who love your own little ones — look!

Huddled together on the great, greasy, dirty floor of this mill, in all the attitudes of tired-out, exhausted childhood, they slept. Shiloh slept bolt upright, her little head against the spinning-frame, where all the morning she had chased the bobbins up and down the long aisle. Appomattox and Atlanta were grouped against her. Bull Run slept at her feet and Seven Days lay, half way over on his bobbin cart, so tired that he went to sleep as he tried to climb into it.

In other parts of the mill, other little ones slept and even large girls and boys, after eating, dozed or chatted. Spoolers, weavers, slubbers, warpers, nearly grown but all hard-faced, listless — and many of them slept on shawls and battings of cotton.

They were awakened by the big whistle at twenty minutes to one o'clock. At the same time, Jud Carpenter, the foreman, passed down the aisles and dashed cold water in the sleeping faces. Half laughingly he did it, but the little ones arose instantly, and with stooped forms, and tired, cowed eyes, in which the Anglo-Saxon

spirit of resentment had been killed by the Yankee spirit
of greed, they looked at the foreman, and then began
their long six hours' battle with the bobbins.

Three o'clock! The warm afternoon's sun poured on
the low flat tin roof of the mill and warmed the interior
to a temperature which was uncomfortable.

Shiloh grew sleepy — she dragged her stumbling little feet along, and had she stopped but a moment, she
had paid the debt that childhood owes to fairy-land.
The air was close — stifling. Her shoulders ached —
her head seemed a stuffy thing of wood and wooly lint.

As it was she nodded as she walked, and again the
song of the bluebird peeped dreamily from out the un-
oiled spindle. She tried to sing to keep awake, and
then there came a strange phantasy to mix with it all,
and out of the half-awake world in which she now staggered along she caught sight of something which made
her open her eyes and laugh outright.

*Was it — could it be?   In very truth it was —
Dolls!*

*And oh, so many!   And all in a row dressed in match-
less gowns of snowy white.   She would count them up to
ten — as far as she had learned to count.   .   .   .   But
there were ten,— yes, and many more than ten —
.   .   .   and just to think of whole rows of them —
.   .   .   all there —   .   .   .   and waiting for her to
reach out and fondle and caress.*

*And she — never in her life before had she been so for-
tunate as to own one.   .   .   .*

A smile lit up her dreaming eyes. *Rows upon rows
of dolls.   .   .   .   And not even Appomattox and At-*

*lanta had ever seen so many before; and now how funny
they acted, dancing around and around and bobbing their
quaint bodies and winking and nodding at her. . . .
It was Mayday with them and down the long line of spindles these cotton dolls were dancing around their May
Queen, and beckoning Shiloh to join them. . . .*

*It was too cute — too cunning — ! they were dancing
and drawing her in — they were actually singing —
. . . humming and chanting a May song. . . .*

O lovely — lovely dolls! . . . . . .

Jud Carpenter found her asleep in the greasy aisle,
her head resting on her arm, a smile on her little face —
a hand clasping a rounded well-threaded doll-like bobbin
to her breast.

It is useless to try to speak in a room in which the
Steam Beast's voice drowns all other voices. It is useless to try to awaken one by calling. One might as
well stand under Niagara Falls and whistle to the little
fishes. No other voice can be heard while the Steam
Beast speaks.

Shiloh was awakened by a dash of cold water and a
rough kick from the big boot of that other beast who
called himself the overseer. He did not intend to jostle
her hard, but Shiloh was such a little thing that the
kick she got in the side accompanied by the dash of
water shocked and frightened her instantly to her feet,
and with scared eyes and blanched face she darted down
to the long line of bobbins, mending the threads.

If, in the great Mystic Unknown,— the Eden of Balance,— there lies no retributive Cause to right the injustice of that cruel Effect, let us hope there is no Here-

after; that we all die and rot like dogs, who know no justice; that what little kindness and sweetness and right, man, through his happier dreams, his hopeful, cheerful idealism, has tried to establish in the world, may no longer stand as mockery to the Sweet Philosopher who long ago said: " *Suffer the little children to come unto me.*" .   .   .   .   .

They were more dead than alive when, at seven o'clock, the Steam Beast uttered the last volcanic howl which said they might go home.

Outside the stars were shining and the cool night air struck into them with a suddenness which made them shiver. They were children, and so they were thoughtless and did not know the risk they ran by coming out of a warm mill, hot and exhausted, into the cool air of an Autumn night. Shiloh was so tired and sleepy that Bull Run and Seven Days had to carry her between them.

Everybody passed out of the mill — a speechless, haggard, over-worked procession. Byrd Boyle, with a face and form which seemed to belong to a slave age, carried his twins in his arms.

Their heads lay on his shoulders. They were asleep.

Scarcely had the children eaten their supper of bissuit and bacon, augmented with dandelion salad, ere they, too, were asleep — all but Shiloh.

She could not sleep — now that she wanted to — and she lay in her grandfather's lap with flushed face and hot, overworked heart. The strain was beginning to tell, and the old man grew uneasy, as he watched the flush on her cheeks and the unusual brightness in her eyes.

"Better give her five draps of tub'bentine an' put her to bed," said Mrs. Watts as she came by. "She'll be fittin' an' good by mornin'."

The old man did not reply — he only sang a low melody and smoothed her forehead.

It was ten o'clock, and now she lay on the old man's lap asleep from exhaustion. A cricket began chirping in the fire-place, under a hearth-brick.

"What's that, Pap?" asked Shiloh half asleep.

"That's a cricket, Pet," smiled the old man.

She listened a while with a half-amused smile on her lips:

"Well, don't you think his spindles need oilin', Pap?"

There was little but machinery in her life.

Another hour found the old man tired, but still holding the sleeping child in his arms:

"If I move her she'll wake," he said to himself. "Po' little Shiloh."

He was silent a while and thoughtful. Then he looked up at the shadow of Sand Mountain, falling half way down the valley in the moonlight.

"The shadow of that mountain across that valley," he said, "is like the shadow of the greed of gain across the world. An' why should it be? What is it worth? Who is happier for any money more than he needs in life?"

He bowed his head over the sleeping Shiloh.

"Oh, God," he prayed —"You, who made the world

18

an' said it might have a childhood — remember what it means to have it filched away. It's like stealin' the bud from the rose-bush, the dew from the grass, hope from the heart of man. Take our manhood — O God — it is strong enough to stand it — an' it has been took from many a strong man who has died with a smile on his lips. Take our old age — O God — for it's jus' a memory of Has Beens. But let them not steal that from any life that makes all the res' of it beautiful with dreams of it. If, by some inscrutable law which we po' things can't see through, stealin' in traffic an' trade must go on in the world, O God, let them steal our purses, but not our childhood. Amen."

CHAPTER XIV

THE whistle of the mill had scarcely awakened Cottontown the next morning before Archie B., hatless and full of excitement, came over to the Bishop with a message from his mother. No one was astir but Mrs. Watts, and she was sweeping vigorously.

"What's the matter. Archie B.?" asked the old man when he came out.

"Uncle Dave Dickey is dyin' an' maw told me to run over an' tell you to hurry quick if you wanted to see the old man die."

"Oh, Uncle Dave is dyin', is he? Well, we'll go, Archie B., just as soon as Ben Butler can be hooked up. I've got some more calls to make anyway."

Ben Butler was ready by the time the children started for the mill. Little Shiloh brought up the rear, her tiny legs bravely following the others. Archie B. looked at them curiously as the small wage-earners filed past him for work.

"Say, you little mill-birds," he said, "why don't you chaps come over to see me sometimes an' lem'me show you things outdoors that's made for boys an' girls?"

"Is they very pretty?" asked Shiloh, stopping and all ears at once. "Oh, tell me 'bout 'em! I am jus' hungry to see 'em. I've learned the names of three birds myself an' I saw a gray squirrel onct."

"Three birds — shucks!" said Archie B., "I could sho' you forty, but I'll tell you what's crackin' good fun an' it'll test you mor'n knowin' the birds — that's easy. But the hard thing is to find their nests an' then to tell by the eggs what bird it is. That's the cracker-jack trick."

Shiloh's eyes opened wide: "Why, do they lay eggs, Archie B.? Real eggs like a hen or a duck?"

Archie B. laughed: "Well, I should say so — an' away up in a tree, an' in the funniest little baskets you ever saw. An' some of the eggs is white, an' some blue, and some green, an, some speckled an' oh, so many kind. But I'll tell you a thing right now that'll help you to remember — mighty nigh every bird lays a egg that's mighty nigh like the bird herself. The cat bird's eggs is sorter blue — an' the woodpecker's is white, like his wing, an' the thrasher's is mottled like his breast."

Ben Butler was hitched to the old buggy and the Bishop drove up. He had a bunch of wild flowers for Shiloh and he gave it with a kiss. "Run along now, Baby, an' I'll fetch you another when I come back."

They saw her run to catch up with the others and breathlessly tell them of the wonderful things Archie B. had related. And all through the day, in the dust and the lint, the thunder and rumble of the Steam Thing's war, Shiloh saw white and blue and mottled eggs, in tiny baskets, with homes up in the trees where the winds rocked the cradles when the little birds came; and young as she was, into her head there crept a thought that something was wrong in man's management of things when little birds were free and little children must work.

As she ran off she waved her hand to her grandfather.

" I'll fetch you another bunch when I come back, Pet," he called.

" You'd better fetch her somethin' to eat, instead of prayin' aroun' with old fools that's always dyin'," called Mrs. Watts to him from the kitchen door where she was scrubbing the cans.

" The Lord will always provide, Tabitha — he has never failed me yet."

She watched him drive slowly over the hill: " That means I had better get a move on me an' go to furagin'," she said to herself.

" Hillard Watts has mistuck me for the Almighty mighty nigh all his life. It's about time the blackberries was a gittin' ripe anyway."

The Bishop found the greatest distress at Uncle Dave Dickey's. Aunt Sally Dickey, his wife, was weeping on the front porch, while Tilly, Uncle Dave's pretty grown daughter, her calico dress tucked up for the morning's work, showing feet and ankles that would grace a duchess, was lamenting loudly on the back porch. A coon dog of uncertain lineage and intellectual development, tuned to the howling pitch, doubtless, by the music of Tilly's sobs, joined in the chorus.

" Po' Davy is gwine — he's most gone — boo — boo — oo!" sobbed Aunt Sally.

" Pap — Pap — don't leave us," echoed Tilly from the back porch.

" Ow — wow — oo — oo," howled the dog.

The Bishop went in sad and subdued, expecting to find Uncle Davy breathing his last. Instead, he found him sitting bolt upright in bed, and sobbing even more lustily than his wife and daughter. He stretched out his hands pitiably as his old friend went in.

" Most gone "— he sobbed —" Hillard — the old man is most gone. You've come jus' in time to see your old friend breathe his las' an' to witness his will," and he broke out sobbing afresh, in which Aunt Sally and Tilly and the dog, all of whom had followed the Bishop in, joined.

The Bishop took in the situation at a glance. Then he broke into a smile that gradually settled all over his kindly face.

" Look aheah, Davy, you ain't no mo' dyin' than I am."

" What — what? " said Uncle Davy between his sobs —" I ain't a dyin', Hillard? Oh, yes, I be. Sally and Tilly both say so."

" Now, look aheah, Davy, it ain't so. I've seed hundreds die — yes, hundreds — strong men, babes — women and little tots, strong ones, and weak and frail ones, given to tears, but I've never seed one die yet sheddin' a single tear, let alone blubberin' like a calf. It's agin nature. Davy, dyin' men don't weep. It's always all right with 'em. It's the one moment of all their lives, often, that everything is all right, seein' as they do, that all life has been a dream — all back of death jes' a beginnin' to live, an' so they die contented. No — no, Davy, if they've lived right they want to smile, not weep."

There was an immediate snuffing and drying of tears all around. Uncle Davy looked sheepishly at Aunt Sally, she passed the same look on to Tilly, and Tilly passed it to the coon dog. Here it rested in its birth-place.

" Come to think of it, Hillard," said Uncle Dave after a while, " but I believe you are right."

Tilly came back, and she and Aunt Sally nodded their heads: " Yes, Hillard, you're right," went on Uncle Davy, " Tilly and Sally both say so."

" How come you to think you was dyin' anyway? " asked the Bishop.

" Hillard,— you kno', Hillard — the old man's been thinkin' he'd go sudden-like a long time." He raised his eyes to heaven: " Yes, Lord, thy servant is even ready."

" Last night I felt a kind o' flutterin' of my heart an' I cudn't breathe good. I thought it was death — death, — Hillard, on the back of his pale horse. Tilly and Sally both thought so."

The Bishop laughed. " That warn't death on the back of a horse, Davy — that was jus' wind on the stomach of an ass."

This was too much for Uncle Davy — especially when Tilly and Sally made it unanimous by giggling out-right.

" You et cabbages for supper," said the Bishop.

Uncle Davy nodded, sheepishly.

" Then I sed my will an' Tilly writ it down an', oh, Hillard, I am so anxious to hear you read it. I wanter see how it'ull feel fer a man to have his will read after he is dead — an'— an' how his widder takes it," he

added, glancing at Aunt Sally —" an' his friends. I
wanter heah you read it, Hillard, in that deep organ
way of yours,— like you read the Old Testament. In
that *In-the-Beginning-God-Created-the-Heaven-an'-the-
Earth-Kinder* voice! Drap your voice low like a organ,
an' let the old man hear it befo' he goes. I fixed it when
I thought I was a-dyin'."

"Makin' yo' will ain't no sign you're dyin'," said the
Bishop.

"But Tilly an' Aunt Sally both said so," said Uncle
Davy, earnestly.

"All yo' needs," said the Bishop going to his saddle
bags, " is a good straight whiskey. I keep a little — a
very, very little bit in my saddle bags, for jes' sech occa-
sions as these. It's twenty years old," he said, " an'
genuwine old Lincoln County. I keep it only for folks
that's dyin'," he winked, " an' sometimes, Davy, I feel
mighty like I'm about to pass away myself."

He poured out a very small medicine glass of it, shining and shimmering in the morning light like a big
ruby,— and handed it to Uncle Davy.

"You say that's twenty years old, Hillard?" asked
Uncle Davy as he wiped his mouth on the back of his
hand and again held the little glass out entreatingly:

"Hillard, ain't it mighty small for its age —'pears
to me it orter be twins to make it the regulation size.
Don't you think so?"

The Bishop gave him another and took one himself,
remarking as he did so, " I was pow'ful flustrated when I
heard you was dyin' again, Davy, an' I need it to stiddy
my nerves. Now, fetch out yo' will, Davy," he added.

As he took it the Bishop adjusted his big spectacles, buttoned up his coat, and drew himself up as he did in the pulpit. He blew his nose to get a clear sonorous note:

"I've got a verse of poetry that I allers tunes my voice up to the occasion with," he said. "I do it sorter like a fiddle; tunes up his fiddle. Its a great poem an' I'll put it agin anything in the Queen's English for real thunder music an' a sentiment that Shakespeare an' Milton nor none of 'em cud a writ. It stirs me like our park of artillery at Shiloh, an' it puts me in tune with the great dead of all eternity. It makes me think of Cap'n Tom an' Albert Sidney Johnston."

Then in a deep voice he repeated:

> " 'The muffled drum's sad roll has beat
>   The soldier's last tattoo —
> No more on earth's parade shall meet
>   That brave and fallen few.
> On Fame's eternal camping ground
>   Their silent tents are spread
> And glory guards with solemn sound
>   The Bivouac of the Dead.' "

"Now give me yo' will."

Uncle Davy sat up solemnly, keenly, expectantly. Tilly and Aunt Sally sat subdued and sad, with that air of solemn importance and respect which might be expected of a dutiful daughter and bereaved widow on such an occasion. It was too solemn for Uncle Davy. He began to whimper again: "I didn't think I would

ever live to see the day when I'd hear my own will read
after I was dead, an' Hillard a-readin' it around my
own corpse. Its Tilly's handwrite," he explained, as
he saw the Bishop scrutinizing the testament closely.
" I can't write, as you kno', but I've made my mark at
the end, an' I want you to witness it."

Pitching his voice to organ depths, the Bishop read:

" ' *In the name of God, amen: I, Davy Dickey, of
the County of* ———, *and State of Alabama, being
of sound mind and retentive memory, but knowing the
uncertainty of life and the certainty of death, do hereby
make and ordain this — my last will and testamen —*' "

Uncle Davy had lain back, his eyes closed, his hands
clasped, drinking it all in.

" O, Hillard — Hillard, read it agin — it makes me
so happy! It does me so much good. It sounds like
the first chapter of Genesis, an' Daniel Webster's reply
to Hayne an' the 19th Psalm all put together."

The Bishop read it again.

" So happy — so happy —" sobbed Uncle Davy, in
which Aunt Sally and Tilly and the coon dog joined.

" ' *First,*' " read on the Bishop, following closely
Tilly's pretty penmanship; " ' *Concerning that part of
me called the soul or spirit which is immortal, I will it
back again to its Maker, leaving it to Him to do as He
pleases with, without asking any impertinent questions
or making any fool requests.*' "

The Bishop paused. " That's a good idea, Davy —
Givin' it back to its Maker without asking any im-
pert'n'ent questions."

" ' *Second,*' " read the Bishop, " ' *I wills to be buried*

*alongside of Dan'l Tubbs, on the Chestnut Knob, the
same enclosed with a rock wall, forever set aside for me
an' Dan'l and running west twenty yards to a black
jack, then east to a cedar stump three rods, then south
to a stake twenty yards and thence west back to me an'
Dan'l. I wills the fence to be built horse high, bull
strong and pig tight, so as to keep out the Widow Sim-
mon's old brindle cow; the said cow having pestered us
nigh to death in life, I don't want her to worry us back
to life after death.*

" *'Third. All the rest of the place except that occu-
pied as aforesaid by me an' Dan'l, and consisting of
twenty acres, more or less, I will to go to my dutiful
wife, Sally Ann Dickey, providing, of course, that she
do not marry again.' "*

" David? " put in Aunt Sallie, promptly, wiping her
eyes, " I think that last thing mout be left out."

" Well, I don't kno'," said Uncle Davy —" you sho'ly
ain't got no notion of marryin' agin, have you, Sally? "

" No — no —" said Aunt Sallie, thoughtfully, " but
there aint no tellin' what a po' widder mout have to do if
pushed to the wall."

" Well," sagely remarked Uncle Davy, " we'll jes' let
it stan' as it is. It's like a dose of calomel for disorder
of the stomach — if you need it it'll cure you, an' if you
don't it won't hurt you. This thing of old folks fallin'
in love ain't nothin' but a disorder of the stomach any-
how."

Aunt Sally again protested a poor widow was often
pushed to the wall and had to take advantage of cir-
cumstances, but Uncle Davy told the Bishop to read on.

At this point Tilly got up and left the room.

" '*Fourth. I give and bequeath to my devoted daughter, Tilly, and her husband, Charles C. Biggers, all my personal property, including the crib up in the loft, the razor my grandfather left me, the old mare and her colt, the best bed in the parlor, and —*' "

The Bishop stopped and looked serious.

" Davy, ain't you a trifle previous in this? " he asked.

" Not for a will," he said. " You see this is supposed to happen and be read after you're dead. You see Charles has been to see her twice and writ a poem on her eyes."

The Bishop frowned: " You'll have to watch that Biggers boy — he is a wild reckless rake an' not in Tilly's class in anything."

" He's pow'ful sweet on Tilly," said Aunt Sallie.

" Has he asked her to marry him? " asked the Bishop astonished.

" S-S-h — not yet," said Uncle Davy, " but he's comin' to it as fast as a lean hound to a meat block. He's got the firs' tech now — silly an' poetic. After a while he'll get silly an' desperate, an' jes' 'fo' he kills hisse'l Tilly'll fix him all right an' tie him up for life. The good Lord makes every man crazy when he is ripe for matrimony, so he can mate him off befo' he comes to."

The Bishop shook his head: " I am glad I came out here to-day — if for nothin' else to warn you to let that Biggers boy alone. He don't study nothin' but fast horses an' devilment."

" I never seed a man have a wuss'r case," said Aunt

Sally. "Won't Tilly be proud of herse'f as the daughter of Old Judge Biggers? An' me — jes' think of me as the grandmother of Biggerses — the riches' an' fines' family in the land."

"An' me? — I'll be the gran'pap of 'em — won't I, Sally?"

"You forgit, Davy," said Aunt Sally — "this is yo' will — you'll be dead."

"I did forgit," said Uncle Davy sadly — "but I'd sho' love to live an' take one of them little Biggerses on my knees an' think his gran'pap had bred up to this. Me an' old Judge Biggers — gran'paws of the same kids! Now, you see, Hillard, he met Tilly at a party an' he tuck her in to supper. The next day he writ her a poem, an' I think its a pretty good start on the gran'pap business."

The Bishop smiled: "It does look like he loves her," he added, dryly. "If I was the devil an' wanted to ketch a woman I'd write a poem to her every day an' lie between heats. Love lives on lies."

"Now, I've ca'culated them things out," said Uncle Davy, "an' it'll be this away: Tilly is as pretty as a peach an' Charlie is gittin' stuck wus'n wus'n every day. By the time I am dead they will be married good an' hard. I am almost gone as it is, the ole man he's liable to drap off any time — yea, Lord, thy servant is ready to go — but I do hope that the good master will let me live long enough to hold one of my Biggers grandboys on my knees."

"All I've got to say," said the Bishop, "is jus' to watch yo' son-in-law. Every son-in-law will stan' watchin' after the ceremony, but yours will stan' it all the time."

" ' *Lastly,*' " read the Bishop, " ' *I wills it that things be left just as they be on the place — no moving around of nothing, especially the well, it being eighty foot deep, and with good cool water; and finally I leave anything else I've got, mostly my good will, to the tender mercies of the lawyers and courts.*' "

The Bishop witnessed it, gave Uncle Davy another toddy, and, after again cautioning him to watch young Biggers closely, rode away.

CHAPTER XV

A CROSS the hill the old man rode to Millwood, and as he rode his head was bent forward in troubled thought.

He had heard that Edward Conway had come to the sorest need — even to where he would place his daughters in the mill. None knew better than Hilliard Watts what this would mean socially for the granddaughters of Governor Conway.

Besides, the old preacher had begun to hate the mill and its infamous system of child labor with a hatred born of righteousness. Every month he saw its degradation, its slavery, its death.

He preached, he talked against it. He began to be pointed out as the man who was against the mill. Ominous rumors had come to his ears, and threats. It was whispered to him that he had better be silent, and some of the people he preached to — some of those who had children in the mill and were supported in their laziness by the life blood of their little ones — these were his bitterest enemies.

To-day, the drunken proprietor of Millwood sat in his accustomed place on the front balcony, his cob-pipe in his mouth and ruin all around him.

Like others, he had a great respect for the Bishop — a

man who had been both his own and his father's friend. Often as a lad he had hunted, fished, and trapped with the preacher-overseer, who lived near his father's plantation. He had broken all of the stubborn colts in the overseer's care; he had ridden them even in some of their fiercest, hardest races, and he had felt the thrill of victory at the wire and known the great pride which comes to one who knows he has the confidence of a brave and honest man.

The old trainer's influence over Edward Conway had always been great.

To-day, as he saw the Bishop ride up, he thought of his boyhood days, and of Tom Travis. How often had they gone with the old man hunting and fishing! How he reverenced the memory of his gentleness and kindness!

The greatest desire of Hilliard Watts had been to reform Edward Conway. He had prayed for him, worked for him. In spite of his drunkenness the old man believed in him.

"God'll save him yet," he would say. "I've prayed for it an' I kno' it — tho' it may be by the crushing of him. Some men repent to God's smile, some to His frown, and some to His fist. I'm afraid it will take a blow to save Ned, po' boy."

For Ned was always a boy to him.

Conway was drunker than usual to-day. Things grew worse daily, and he drank deeper.

It is one of the strangest curses of whiskey that as it daily drags a man down, deeper and deeper, it makes him believe he must cling to his Red God the closer.

He met the old overseer cordially, in a half drunken endeavor to be natural. The old man glanced sadly up at the bloated, boastful face, and thought of the beautiful one it once had been. He thought of the fine, brilliant mind and marveled that with ten years of drunkenness it still retained its strength. And the Bishop remembered that in spite of his drinking no one had ever accused Edward Conway of doing a dishonorable thing. "How strong is that man's character rooted for good," he thought, "when even whiskey cannot undermine it."

"Where are the babies, Ned?" he asked, after he was seated.

The father called and the two girls came running out.

The old man was struck with the developing beauty of Helen — he had not seen her for a year. Lily hunted in his pockets for candy, as she had always done — and found it — and Helen — though eighteen and grown, sat thoughtful and sad, on a stool by his side.

The old man did not wonder at her sadness.

"Ned," he said, as he stroked Helen's hand, "this girl looks mo' like her mother every day, an' you know she was the handsomest woman that ever was raised in the Valley."

Conway took his pipe out of his mouth. He dropped his head and looked toward the distant blue hills. What Memory and Remorse were whispering to him the old man could only guess. Silently — nodding — he sat and looked and spoke not.

"She ain't gwineter be a bit prettier than my little Lil, when she gits grown," said a voice behind them.

It was Mammy Maria who, as usual, having dressed

19

the little girl as daintily as she could, stood nearby to
see that no harm befell her.

"Wal, Aunt Maria," drawled the Bishop. "Whar
did you come from? I declar' it looks like ole times to
see you agin'."

There is something peculiar in this, that those un-
lettered, having once associated closely with negroes,
drop into their dialect when speaking to them. Perhaps
it may be explained by some law of language — some
rule of euphony, now unknown. The Bishop unconsciously did this; and, from dialect alone, one could not
tell which was white and which was black.

Aunt Maria had always been very religious, and the
Bishop arose and shook her hand gravely.

"Pow'ful glad to see you," said the old woman.

"How's religion — Aunt Maria," he asked.

"Mighty po'ly — mighty po'ly" — she sighed. "It
looks lak the Cedars of Lebanon is dwarfed to the scrub
pine. The old time religin' is passin' away, an' I'm
all that's lef' of Zion."

The Bishop smiled.

"Yes, you see befo' you all that's lef' of Zion. I'se
been longin' to see you an' have a talk with you —
thinkin' maybe you cud he'p me out. You kno' me and
you is Hard-shells."

The Bishop nodded.

"We 'blieves in repentince an' fallin' from grace, an'
backslidin' an' all that," she went on. "Well, they've
lopped them good ole things off one by one an' they
don't 'bleeve in nothin' now but jes' jin'in'. They think
jes' jin'in' fixes 'em — that it gives 'em a free pass into

the pearly gates. So of all ole Zion Church up at the hill, sah, they've jes' jined an' jined around, fust one church an' then another, till of all the ole Zion Church that me an' you loved so much, they ain't none lef' but Parson Shadrack, the preacher, sister Tilly, an' me — We wus Zion."

" Pow'ful bad, pow'ful bad," said the Bishop —" and you three made Zion."

" We *wus*," said Aunt Maria, sadly —" but now there ain't but one lef'. *I'm Zion.* It's t'arrable, but it's true. As it wus in the days of Lot, so it is to-day in Sodom."

" Why, how did that happen? " asked the Bishop.

Aunt Maria's eyes kindled: " It's t'arrable, but it's true — last week Parson Shadrack deserts his own wife an' runs off with Sis Tilly. It looked lak he mouter tuck me, too, an' kept the fold together as Abraham did when he went into the Land of the Philistines. But thank God, if I am all that's lef', one thing is mighty consolin'— I can have a meetin' of Zion wherever I is. If I sets down in a cheer to meditate I sez to myself — ' Be keerful, Maria, for the church is in session.' When I drink, it is communion — when I bathes, it is baptism, when I walks, I sez to myself: ' Keep a straight gait, Maria, you are carryin' the tabbernackle of al' goodness.' Aunt Tilly got the preacher, but thank God, I got Zion."

" But I mus' go. Come on, Lily," she said to the little girl,— " let ole Zion fix up yo' curls."

She took her charge and curtsied out, and the Bishop knew she would die either for Zion or the little girl.

The old man sat thinking — Helen had gone in and was practising a love song.

"Ned," said the Bishop, "I tell you a man ain't altogether friendless when he's got in his home a creature as faithful as she is. She'd die for that child. That one ole faithful 'oman makes me feel like liftin' my hat to the whole nigger race. I tell you when I get to heaven an' fail to see ole Mammy settin' around the River of Life, I'll think somethin' is wrong."

The Bishop was silent a while, and then he asked: "Ned, it can't be true that you are goin' to put them girls in the factory?"

"It's all I can do," said Conway, surlily — "I'll be turned out of home soon — out in the public road. Everything I've got has been sold. I've no'where to go, an' but for Carpenter's offer from the Company of the cottage, I'd not have even a home for them. The only condition I could go on was that —"

"That you sell your daughters into slavery," said the Bishop quietly.

"You don't seem to think it hurts your's," said Conway bluntly.

"If I had my way they'd not work there a day," — the old man replied hastily. "But its different with me, an' you know it. My people take to it naturally. I am a po' white, an underling by breedin' an' birth, an' if my people build, they must build up. But you — you are tearing down when you do that. Po' as I am, I'd rather starve than to see little children worked to death in that trap, but Tabitha sees it different, and she is the one bein' in the world I don't cross — the

General "— he smiled —" she don't understand, she's built different."

He was silent a while. Then he said: "I am old an' have nothin'."

He stopped again. He did not say that what little he did have went to the poor and the sorrow-stricken of the neighborhood. He did not add that in his home, besides its poverty and hardness, he faced daily the problem of far greater things.

"If I only had my health," said Conway, "but this cursed rheumatism!"

"Some of us has been so used to benefits," said the old man, "that it's only when they've withdrawn that we miss 'em. We're always ready to blame God for what we lose, but fail to remember what He gives us. We kno' what diseases an' misfortunes we have had, we never know, by God's mercy, what we have escaped. Death is around us daily — in the very air we breathe — and yet we live.

"I'll talk square with you, Ned — though you may hate me for it. Every misfortune you have, from rheumatism to loss of property, is due to whiskey. Let it alone. Be a man. There's greatness in you yet. You'd have no chance if you was a scrub. But no man can estimate the value of good blood in man or hoss — its the unknown quantity that makes him ready to come again. For do the best we can, at last we're in the hands of God an' our pedigree."

"Do you think I've got a show yet?" asked Conway, looking up.

"Do I? Every man has a chance who trusts God an'

prays. You can't down that man. Your people were
men — brave an' honest men. They conquered themselves first, an' all this fair valley afterwards. They
overcame greater obstacles than you ever had, an' in
bringin' you into the world they gave you, by the very
laws of heredity, the power to overcome, too. Why do
you grasp at the shadow an' shy at the form? You
keep these hound dogs here, because your father rode
to hounds. But he rode for pleasure, in the lap of
plenty, that he had made by hard licks. You ride,
from habit, in poverty. He rode his hobbies — it was
all right. Your hobbies ride you. He fought chickens
for an hour's pastime, in the fullness of the red blood
of life. You fight them for the blood of the thing —
as the bred-out Spaniards fight bulls. He took his
cocktails as a gentleman — you as a drunkard."

The old man was excited, indignant, fearless.

Conway looked at him in wonder akin to fear. Even
as the idolators of old looked at Jeremiah and Isaiah.

" Why — why is it "— went on the old man earnestly,
rising and shaking his finger ominously —" that two
generations of cocktails will breed cock-fighters, and two
generations of whiskey will breed a scrub? Do you
know where you'll end? In bein' a scrub? No, no —
you will be dead an' the worms will have et you — but "
— he pointed to the house —" you are fixin' to make
scrubs of them — they will breed back.

" Go back to the plough — quit this whiskey and be
the man your people was. If you do not," he said rising to go —" God will crush you — not kill you, but
mangle you in the killin'."

" He has done that already," said Conway bitterly.
" He has turned the back of His hand on me."

" Not yet "— said the Bishop —" but it will fall and
fall there." He pointed to Helen, whose queenly head
could be seen in the old parlor as she trummed out a
sad love song.

Conway blanched and his hand shook. He felt a
nameless fear — never felt before. He looked around,
but the old man was gone. Afterwards, as he remembered that afternoon, he wondered if, grown as the old
man had in faith, God had not also endowed him with
the gift of prophecy.

CHAPTER XVI

A N HOUR afterward, the old nurse found Helen at the piano, her head bowed low over the old yellow keys. " It's gittin' t'wards dinner time, chile," she said tenderly, " an' time I was dressin' my queen gal for dinner an sendin' her out to get roses in her cheeks."

" Oh, Mammy, don't — don't dress me that way any more. I am — I am to be — after this — just a mill girl, you know? "

There was a sob and her head sank lower over the piano.

" You may be for a while, but you'll always be a Conway "— and the old woman struck an attitude with her arms akimbo and stood looking at the portraits which hung on the parlor wall.

" That — that — makes it worse, Mammy." She wiped away her tears and stood up, and her eyes took on a look Aunt Maria had not seen since the old Governor had died. She thought of ghosts and grew nervous before it.

" If my father sends me to work in that place — if he does —" she cried with flaming eyes —" I shall feel that I am disgraced. I cannot hold my head up again. Then you need not be surprised at anything I do."

296

"It ain't registered that you're gwine there yet," and Mammy Maria stroked her head. "But if you does — it won't make no difference whar you are nor what you have to do, you'll always be a Conway an' a lady."

An hour afterwards, dressed as only Mammy Maria could dress her, Helen had walked out again to the rock under the wild grape vine.

How sweet and peaceful it was, and yet how changed since but a short time ago she had sat there watching for Harry!

"Harry"— she pulled out the crumpled, tear-stained note from her bosom and read it again. And the reading surprised her. She expected to weep, but instead when she had finished she sat straight up on the mossy rock and from her eyes gleamed again the light before which the political enemies of the old dead Governor had so often quailed.

Nor did it change in intensity, when, at the sound of wheels and the clatter of hoofs, she instinctively dropped down on the moss behind the rock and saw through the grape leaves one of Richard Travis's horses, steaming hot, and stepping,— right up to its limit — a clipping gait down the road.

She had dropped instinctively because she guessed it was Harry. And instinctively, too, she knew the girl with the loud boisterous laugh beside him was Nellie.

The buggy was wheeled so rapidly past that she heard only broken notes of laughter and talk. Then she sat again upon her rock, with the deep flush in her eyes, and said:

" I hate — him — I hate him — and oh — to think
—"

She tore his note into fragments, twisted and rolled
them into a ball and shot it, as a marble, into the gulch
below.

Then, suddenly she remembered, and reaching over
she looked into a scarred crevice in the rock. Twice
that summer had Clay Westmore left her a quaint love
note in this little rock-lined post-office. Quaint indeed,
and they made her smile, for they had been queer mix-
tures of geology and love. But they were honest —
and they had made her flush despite the fact that she did
not love him.

Still she would read them two or three times and sigh
and say: " Poor Clay —" after every reading.

" Surely there will be one this afternoon," she thought
as she peeped over.

But there was not, and it surprised her to know how
much she was disappointed.

" Even Clay has forgotten me," she said as she arose
hastily to go.

A big sob sprang up into her throat and the Conway
light of defiance, that had blazed but a few moments
before in her eyes, died in the depths of the cloud of
tears which poured between it and the open.

A cruel, dangerous mood came over her. It enveloped
her soul in its sombre hues and the steel of it struck
deep.

She scarcely remembered her dead mother — only
her eyes. But when these moods came upon Helen
Conway — and her life had been one wherein they had

fallen often — the memory of her mother's eyes came to her and stood out in the air before her, and they were sombre and sad, and full, too, of the bitterness of hopes unfulfilled.

All her life she had fought these moods when they came. But now — now she yielded to the subtle charm of them — the wild pleasure of their very sinfulness.

" And why not," she cried to herself when the consciousness of it came over her, and like a morphine fiend carrying the drug to his lips, she knew that she also was pressing there the solace of her misery.

" Why should I not dissipate in the misery of it, since so much of it has fallen upon me at once?

" Mother? — I never knew one — only the eyes of one, and they were the eyes of Sorrow. Father? "— she waved her hand toward the old home —" drunk-wrecked — he would sell me for a quart of whiskey.

" Then I loved — loved an image which is — mud — mud "— she fairly spat it out. " One poor friend I had — I scorned him, and he has forgotten me, too. But I did know that I had social standing — that my name was an honored one until — now."

" Now! "— she gulped it down. " Now I am a common mill girl."

She had been walking rapidly down the road toward the house. So rapidly that she did not know how flushed and beautiful she had become. She was swinging her hat impatiently in her hand, her fine hair half falling and loose behind, shadowing her face as rosy sunset clouds the temple on Mt. Ida. A face of more classic beauty, a skin of more exquisite fairness, flushed

with the bloom of youth, Richard Travis had never before seen.

And so, long before she reached him, he reined in his
trotters and sat silently watching her come. What a
graceful step she had — what a neck and head and hair
— half bent over with eyes on the ground, unconscious
of the beauty and grace of their own loveliness.

She almost ran into his buggy — she stopped with a
little start of surprise, only to look into his clean-cut
face, smiling half patronizingly, half humorously, and
with a look of command too, and of patronage withal,
of half-gallant heart-undoing.

It was the look of the sharp-shinned hawk hovering
for an instant, in sheer intellectual abandon and physical
exuberance, above the unconscious oriole bent upon its
morning bath.

He was smiling down into her eyes and repeating half
humorously, half gallantly, and altogether beautifully,
she thought, Keats' lines:

> " A thing of beauty is a joy forever;
>   Its loveliness increases; it will never
>   Pass into nothingness; but will keep
>   A bower quiet for us, and a sleep
>   Full of sweet dreams and health and
>   Quiet breathing." .   .   .

Even Helen could not tell how it was done nor why
she had consented. . . .

" No — no — you are hot and tired and you shall
not walk. . . . I will give you just a little spin

before Mammy Maria calls you to dinner. . . .
Yes, Lizzette and Sadie B. always do their best when a
pretty girl is behind them."

How refreshing the air — hot and tired as she was.
And such horses — she had never before ridden behind
anything so fine. How quickly he put her at her ease
— how intellectual he was — how much of a gentleman.
And was it not a triumph — a social triumph for her?
A mill girl, in name, to have him notice her? It made
her heart beat quickly to think that Richard Travis
should care enough for her to give her this pleasure and
at a time when — when she always saw her mother's
eyes.

Timidly she sat by him scarce lifting her eyes to
speak, but conscious all the time that his eyes were
devouring her, from her neck and hair to her slippered
foot, sticking half way out from skirts of old lace-
trimmed linen.

She reminded him at last that they should go back
home.

No — he would have her at home directly. Yes, he'd
have her there before the old nurse missed her.

She knew the trotters were going fast, but she did
not know just how fast, until presently, in a cloud of
whirling dust they flew around a buggy whose horse,
trot as fast as it could, seemed stationary to the speed
the pair showed as they passed.

It was Harry and Nellie. She glanced coldly at him,
and when he raised his hat she cut him with a smile of
scorn. She saw his jaw drop dejectedly as Richard
Travis sang out banteringly:

"Sweets to the sweet, and good-bye to the three-minute class."

It was a good half hour, but it seemed but a few minutes before he had her back at the home gate, her cheeks burning with the glory of that burst of speed, and rush of air.

He had helped her out and stood holding her hand as one old enough to be her father. He smiled and, looking down at her glowing face, and hair, and neck, repeated:

"What thou art we know not.
    What is most like thee?
  From rainbow clouds there flow not
    Drops so bright to see
  As from thy presence showers a rain of melody."

Then he changed as she thanked him, and said: "When you go into the mill I shall have many pleasant surprises for you like this."

He bent over her and whispered: "I have arranged for your pay to be double — we are neighbors, you know — your father and I,— and a pretty girl, like you, need not work always."

She started and looked at him quickly.

The color went from her cheeks. Then it came again in a crimson tide, so full and rich, that Richard Travis, like Titian with his brush, stood spellbound before the work he had done.

Fearing he had said too much, he dropped his voice and with a twinkle in his eye said:

"For there is Harry — you know."

All her timidity vanished — her hanging of the head, her silence, her blushes. Instead, there leaped into her eyes that light which Richard Travis had never seen before — the light of a Conway on mettle.

"I hate him."

"I do not blame you," he said. "I shall be a — father to you if you will let me."

He pressed her hand, and raising his hat, was gone.

As he drove away he turned and looked at her slipping across the lawn in the twilight. In his eyes was a look of triumphant excitement.

"To own her — such a creature — God — it were worth risking my neck."

The mention of Harry brought back all her bitter recklessness to Helen. She was but a child and her road, indeed, was hard. And as she turned at the old gate and looked back at the vanishing buggy she said:

"Had he asked me this evening I'd — yes — I'd go to the end of the world with him. I'd go — go — go — and I care not how."

Richard Travis was in a jolly mood at the supper table that night, and Harry became jolly also, impertinently so. He had not said a word about his cousin being with Helen, but it burned in his breast, and he awaited his chance to mention it.

"I have thought up a fable since I have been at supper, Cousin Richard. Shall I tell you?"

"Oh" — with a cynical smile — "do!"

"Well," began Harry unabashed, and with many

sly winks and much histrionic effort, " it is called the
' Fox and the Lion.'   Now a fox in the pursuit ran
down a beautiful young doe and was about to devour her
when the lion came up and with a roar and a sweep of
his paw, took her saying . . ."

" ' Get out of the way, you whelp,' " said his cousin,
carrying the fable on, " for I perceive you are not even
a fox, but a coyote, since no fox was ever known to run
down a doe."

The smile was gradually changed on his face to a
cruel sneer, and Harry ceased talking with a suddenness
that was marked.

CHAPTER XVII

WHEN the mill opened the next day, there was work for Jud Carpenter. He came in and approached the superintendent's desk briskly.

"Well, suh, hu' many to-day?" he asked.

Kingsley looked over his list of absentees.

"Four, and two of them spinners. Carpenter, you must go at once and see about it. They are playing off, I am sure."

"Lem'me see the list, suh,"—and he ran his eye over the names.

"Bud Billings — plague his old crotchetty head —. He kno's that machine's got to run, whether no. Narthin's the matter with him — bet a dollar his wife licked him last night an' he's mad about it."

"That will do us no good," said Kingsley —" what he is mad about. That machine must be started at once. The others you can see afterwards."

Carpenter jerked his slouch hat down over his eyes and went quickly out.

In half an hour he was back again. His hat was off, his face was red, his shaggy eyebrows quivered with angry determination, as, with one hand in the collar of the frightened Bud, he pulled the slubber into the superintendent's presence.

Following her husband came Mrs. Billings — a small, bony, wiry, black-eyed woman, with a firmly set mouth and a perpetual thunder-cloud on her brow — perhaps the shadow of her coarse, crow-black hair.

While Jud dragged him, she carried a stick and prodded Bud in the rear.   Nor was she chary in abuse.

Jerked into the superintendent's presence, Bud's scared eyes darted here and there as if looking for a door to break through, and all the time they were silently protesting.   His hands, too, joined in the protest; one of them wagged beseechingly behind appealing to his spouse to desist — the other went through the same motion in front begging Jud Carpenter for mercy.

But not a word did he utter — not even a grunt did he make.

They halted as quickly as they entered.   Bud's eyes sought the ceiling, the window, the floor,— anywhere but straight ahead of him.

His wife walked up to the superintendent's desk — she was hot and flushed.   Her small black eyes, one of which was cocked cynically, flashed fire, her coarse hair fell across her forehead, or was plastered to her head with perspiration.

It was pathetic to look at Bud, with his deep-set, scared eyes.   Kingsley had never heard him speak a word, nor had he even been able to catch his eye.   But he was the best slubber in the mill — tireless, painstaking.   His place could not be filled.

Bud was really a good-natured favorite of Kingsley and when the superintendent saw him, scared and panting, his tongue half out, with Jud Carpenter's hand still in his collar, he motioned to Jud to turn him loose.

" Uh — uh — grunted Jud "— he will bolt sho ! "

Kingsley noticed that Bud's head was bound with a cloth.

" What's the matter, Bud? " he asked kindly.

The slubber never spoke, but glanced at his wife, who stood glaring at him. Then she broke out in a thin, drawling, daring, poor-white voice — a ring of impertinence and even a challenge in it:

" I'll tell you'uns what's the matter with Bud. Bud Billings is got what most men needs when they begin to raise sand about their vittels for nothin'. I've busted a plate over his head."

She struck an attitude before Kingsley which plainly indicated that she might break another one. It was also an attitude which asked: " What are you going to do about it? "

Bud nodded emphatically — a nod that spoke more than words. It was a positive, unanimous assertion on his part that the plate had been broken there.

" Ne'ow, Mister Kingsley, you know yo'se'f that Bud is mighty slow mouthed — he don't talk much an' I have to do his talkin' fur him. Ne'ow Bud don't intend for to be so mean "— she added a little softer —" but every month about the full of the moon, Bud seems to think somehow that it is about time fur him to make a fool of hisse'f again. He wouldn't say nothin' fur a month — he is quiet as a lam' an' works steady as a clock — then all to once the fool spell 'ud hit him an' then some crockery 'ud have to be wasted.

" They ain't no reason for it, Mister Kingsley —
Bud cyant sho' the rappin' of yo' finger fur havin'
sech spells along towards the full of the moon. Bud
cyant tell you why, Mister Kingsley, to save his soul —
'cept that he jes' thinks he's got to do it an' put me to
the expense of bustin' crockery.

" I stood it mighty nigh two years arter Bud and me
was spliced, thinkin' maybe it war ther bed-bugs a-bitin'
Bud, long towards the full of the moon. So I watched
that pint an' killed 'em all long towards the first quarter
with quicksilver an' the white of an egg. Wal, Bud
never sed a word all that month. He never opened his
mouth an' he acted jes' lak a puf'fec' gentleman an'
a dutiful dotin' husband —(Bud wiped away a tear)
— until the time come for the fool spell to hit 'im,
an 'all to once you never seed sech a fool spell hit a
man befo'.

" What you reckin' Bud done, Mister Kingsley? Bud
Billins thar, what did he do? Got mad about his biscuits — it's the funny way the fool spell allers hits him,
he never gits mad about anything but his biscuits.
Why I cud feed Bud on dynamite an' he'd take it all
right if he cu'd eat it along with his biscuits. Onct I
put concentrated lye in his coffee by mistake. I'd never
knowed it if the pup hadn't got some of it by mistake
an' rolled over an' died in agony. I rushed to the mill
thinkin' Bud ud' be dead, sho'— but he wa'nt. He
never noticed it. I noticed his whiskers an' eyebrows
was singed off an' questioned 'im 'bout it and he 'lowed
he felt sorter quare arter he drunk his coffee, an' full
like, an' he belched an' it sot his whiskers an' eyebrows

a-fiah, which ther same kinder puzzled him fur a while; but it must be biscuits to make him raise cain. It happened at the breakfas' table. Mind you, Mister Kingsly, Bud didn't say it to my face — no, he never says anything to my face — but he gits up an' picks up the cat an' tells ther cat what he thinks of me — his own spliced an' wedded wife — sland'in' me to the cat."

She shook her finger in his face —" You know you did, Bud Billins — an' what you reckin he told ther cat, Mister Kingsley — told her I was a — a —"

She gasped — she clinched her fist. Bud dodged an' tried to break away.

" Told him I was a — a — heifer! "

Bud looked sheepishly around — he tried even to run, but Jud Carpenter held him fast. She shook her finger in his face. " I heard you say it, Bud Billins, you know I did an' I busted a plate over yo' head."

" But, my dear Madam," said Kingsley, " that was no reason to treat him so badly."

" Oh, it wa'nt? " she shrieked —" to tattle-tale to the house-cat about yo' own spliced an' wedded wife? In her own home an' yard — her that you've sworn to love an' cherish agin bed an' board — ter call her a heifer? "

She slipped her hand under her apron and produced a deadly looking blue plate of thick cheap ware. Her eyes blazed, her voice became husky with anger.

" An' you don't think that was nothin'? " she shrieked.

" You don't understand me, my dear Madam," said Kingsley quickly. " I meant that it was no reason why

you should continue to treat him so after he has suffered
and is sorry. Of course you have got to control Bud."

She softened and went on.

"Wal, it was mighty nigh a year befo' Bud paid any
mo' 'tention to the cat. The full moon quit 'fectin'
him — he even quit eatin' biscuits. Then the spell
commenced to come onct a year an' he cu'dn't pass over
blackberry winter to save his life. Mind you he never
sed anything to me about it, but one day he ups an'
gits choked on a chicken gizzerd an' coughs an' wheezes
an' goes on so like a fool that I ups with the cheer an'
comes down on his head a-thinkin' I'd make him cough
it up. I mout a bin a little riled an' hit harder'n I
orter, but I didn't mean anything by it, an' he did
cough it up on my clean floor, an' I'm willin' to say
agin' I was a little hasty, that's true, in callin' him a
lop-sided son of a pigeon-toed monkey, for Bud riled
me mighty. But what you reckin he done?"

She shook her finger in his face again. Bud tried to
run again.

"You kno' you done it, Bud Billins — I followed you
an' listened when you tuck up the cat an' you whispered
in the cat's year that your spliced an' wedded wife was
a — a — *she devil!* "

"It tuck two plates that time, Mister Kingsley —
that's the time Bud didn't draw no pay fur two weeks.

"Wal, that was over a year ago, an' Bud he's been
a behavin' mighty well, untwell this mornin'. It's true
he didn't say much, but he sed 'nuff fur me to see ther
spell was acomin' on an' I'd better bust it up befo' it
got into his blood an' sot 'im to cultivate the company

of the cat. I seed I had to check the disease afore it
got too strong, fur I seed Bud was tryin' honestly to
taper off with them spells an' shake with the cat if he
cu'd, so when he kinder snorted a little this mornin' because he didn't have but one aig an' then kinder began to
look aroun' as if he was thinkin' of mice, I busted a saucer
over his head an' fotched 'im too, grateful la'k an'
happy, to be hisse'f agin. I think he's nearly c'wored
an' I'm mighty glad you is, Bud Billins, fur its costin'
a lot of mighty good crockery to c'wore you.

"Now you all jes' lem'me 'lone, Mister Kingsley —
lem'me manage Bud. He's slo' mouthed as I'm tellin'
you, but he's gittin' over them spells an' I'm gwinter
c'wore him if I hafter go into the queensware bus'ness
on my own hook. Now, Bud Billins, you jes' go in
there now an' go to tendin' to that slubbin' machine, an'
don't you so much as look at a cat twixt now an' next
Christmas."

Bud needed no further admonition. He bolted for
the door and was soon silently at work.

CHAPTER XVIII

SAMANTHA CAREWE

BUT Jud Carpenter did not finish his work by starting the slubbing machine. Samantha Carewe, one of the main loom women, was absent. Going over to her cottage, he was told by her mother, a glinty-eyed, shrewd looking, hard featured woman — that Samantha was " mighty nigh dead."

" Oh, she's mighty nigh dead, is she," said Jud with a tinge of sarcasm —" I've heurn of her bein' mighty nigh dead befo'. Well, I wanter see her."

The mother looked at him sourly, but barred the doorway with her form. Jud fixed his hard cunning eyes on her.

" Cyant see her, I tell you — she's mighty po'ly."

" Well, cyant you go an' tell her that Mister Jud Cyarpenter is here an' 'ud like to kno' if he can be of any sarvice to her in orderin' her burial robe an' coffin, or takin' her last will an' testerment."

With that he pushed himself in the doorway, rudely brushing the woman aside. " Now lem'me see that gyrl —" he added sternly —" that loom is got to run or you will starve, an' if she's sick I want to kno' it. I've seed her have the toe-ache befo'."

The door of the room in which Samantha lay was open, and in plain view of the hall she lay with a look

312

of pain, feigned or real, on her face. She was a woman past forty — a spinster truly — who had been in the mill since it was first started, and, as she came from a South Carolina mill to the Acme, had, in fact, been in a cotton mill, as she said —" all her life." For she could not remember when, as a child even, she had not worked in one.

Her chest was sunken, her shoulders stooped, her whole form corded and knotted with the fight against machinery. Her skin, bronzed and sallow, looked not unlike the hard, fine wood-work of the loom, oiled with constant use.

Jud walked in unceremoniously.

" What ails you, Samanthy? " he asked, with feigned kindness.

" Oh, I dunno, Jud, but I've got a powerful hurtin' in my innards."

" The hurtin' was so bad," said her mother, " that I had to put a hot rock on her stomach, last night."

She motioned to a stone lying on the hearth. Jud glanced at it — its size staggered him.

" Good Lord! an' you say you had that thing on her stomach? Why didn't you send her up to the mill an' let us lay a hot steam engine on her? "

" What you been eatin', Samanthy? " he asked suddenly.

" Nuthin', Jud — I aint got no appetite at all! "

" No, she aint eat a blessed thing, hardly, to-day," said her mother —" jes' seemed to have lost her appetite from a to izzard."

" I wish the store'd keep wild cherry bark and whiskey

— somethin' to make us eat. We cyant work unless we can eat," said Samantha, woefully.

" Great Scott," said Jud, " what we want to do is to keep you folks from eatin' so much. Lem'me see," he added after a pause, as if still thinking he'd get to the source of her trouble —" Yistidday was Sunday — you didn't have to work — now what did you eat for breakfast? "

" Nothin'— oh, I aint got no appetite at all "— whined Miss Samantha.

" Well, what did you eat — I wanter find out what ails you? "

" Well, lem'me see," said Miss Samantha, counting on her fingers —" a biled mackrel, some fried bacon, two pones of corn bread — kinder forced it down."

" Ur-huh —" said Jud, thoughtfully —" of course you had to drink, too."

" Yes "— whined Miss Samantha woefully —" two glasses of buttermilk."

Jud elevated his eye-brows " An' for dinner? "

" O, Lor'. Jes' cu'dn't eat nothin' fur dinner," she wailed. " If the Company'd only get some cherry bark an' whiskey "—

" At dinner," said Mrs Carewe, stroking her chin — " we had some sour-kraut — she eat right pe'rtly of that — kinder seemed lak a appetizer to her. She mixed it with biled cabbage an' et right pe'rtly of it."

" An' some mo' buttermilk — it kinder cools my stomach," whined Miss Samantha. " An' hog-jowl, an' corn-bread — anything else Maw? "

" A raw onion in vinegar," said her mother —" It's

the only thing that seems to make you want to eat a little. An' reddishes — we had some new reddishes fur dinner — didn't we, Samanthy? "

" Good Lord," snapped Jud —" reddishes an' buttermilk — no wonder you needed that weight on your stomach — it's all that kept you from floatin' in the air. Cyant eat — O good Lord! "

They were silent — Miss Samantha making wry faces with her pain.

" Of course you didn't eat no supper? " he asked.

" No — we don' eat no supper Sunday night," said Mrs. Carewe.

" Didn't eat none at all," asked Jud —" not even a little? "

" Well, 'bout nine o'clock I thought I'd eat a little, to keep me from gittin' hungry befo' day, so I et a raw onion, an' some black walnuts, and dried prunes, an'— an'—"

" A few apples we had in the cellar," added her mother, " an' a huckleberry pie, an' buttermilk —"

Jud jumped up —" Good Lord, I thought you was a fool when you said you put that stone on her stomach, but now I know you done the right thing — you might have anchored her by a chain to the bed post, too, in case the rock didn't hold her down. Now look here," he went on to Mrs. Carewe, " I'll go to the sto' an' send you a half pound of salts, a bottle of oil an' turbb'ntine. Give her plenty of it an' have her at the mill by tomorrow, or I'll cut off all your rations. As it is I don't see that you need them, anyway, to eat "— he sneered —" for you ' aint got no appetite at all.' "

From the Carewe cottage Jud went to a small yellow cottage on the farthest side of the valley. It was the home of John Corbin, and Willis, his ten-year-old son, was one of the main doffers. The father was lounging lazily on the little front verandah, smoking his pipe.

" What's the matter with Willis? " asked Jud after he had come up.

" Why, nothin'—" drawled the father. " Aint he at the mill? "

" No — the other four children of your'n is there, but Willis aint."

The man arose with more than usual alacrity. " I'll see that he is there —" he declared —" it's as much as we can do to live on what they makes, an' I don't want no dockin' for any sickness if I can he'p it."

Willis, a pale over-worked lad, was down with tonsilitis. Jud heard the father and mother in an angry dispute. She was trying to persuade him to let the boy stay at home. In the end hot words were used, and finally the father came out followed by the pale and hungry-eyed boy.

" He'd better die at the mill at work than here at home," the father added brutally, as Jud led him off, " fur then the rest of us will have that much ahead to live on."

He settled lazily back in his chair, and resumed his smoking.

CHAPTER XIX

A QUICK CONVERSION

IT happened that morning that the old Bishop was on his daily round, visiting the sick of Cottontown. He went every day, from house to house, helping the sick, cheering the well, and better than all things else, putting into the hearts of the disheartened that priceless gift of coming again.

For of all the gifts the gods do give to men, that is the greatest — the ability to induce their fallen fellow man to look up and hope again. The gift to spur others onward — the gift to make men reach up. His flock were all mill people, their devotion to him wonderful. In the rush and struggle of the strenuous world around them, this humble old man was the only being to whom they could go for spiritual help.

To-day in his rounds, one thing impressed him more sadly than anything else — for he saw it so plainly when he visited their homes — and that was that with all their hard work, from the oldest to the youngest, with all their traffic in human life, stealing the bud along with the broken and severed stem — as a matter of fact, the Acme mills paid out to the people but very little money. Work as they might, they seldom saw anything but an order on a store, for clothes and provisions sold to them at prices that would make a Jew peddler blush for shame.

The Bishop found entire families who never saw a piece of money the year round.

There are families and families, and some are more shiftless than others.

In one of the cottages the old man found a broken down little thing of seven, sick. For just such trips he kept his pockets full of things, and such wonderful pockets they would have been to a healthful natural child! Ginger cakes — a regular Noah's Ark, and apples, red and yellow. Sweet gum, too, which he had himself gathered from the trees in the woods. And there were even candy dolls and peppermints.

"Oh, well, maybe I can help her, po' little thing," the Bishop said when the mother conducted him in. But one look at her was enough — that dead, unmeaning look, not unconscious, but unmeaning — deadened — a disease which to a robust child would mean fever and a few days' sickness — to this one the Bishop knew it meant atrophy and death. And as the old man looked at her, he thought it were better that she should go. For to her life had long since lost its individuality, and dwarfed her into a nerveless machine — the little frame was nothing more than one of a thousand monuments to the cotton mill — a mechanical thing, which might cease to run at any time.

"How old is she?" asked the Bishop, sitting down by the child on the side of the bed.

"We put her in the mill two years ago when she was seven," said the mother. "We was starvin' an' had to do somethin'." She added this with as much of an apologetic tone as her nature would permit. "We told the mill men she was ten," she added. "We had to do it. The fust week she got two fingers mashed off."

The Bishop was silent, then he said: "It's bes' always to tell the truth. Liar is a fast horse, but he never runs but one race."

Although there were no laws in Alabama against child labor, the mill drew the lines then as now, if possible, on very young children. Not that it cared for the child — but because it could be brought to the mill too young for any practical use, unless it was wise beyond its age.

He handed the little thing a ginger man. She looked at it — the first she had ever seen,— and then at the giver in the way a wild thing would, as if expecting some trick in the proffered kindness; but when he tried to caress her and spoke kindly, she shrank under the cover and hid her head with fear.

It was not a child, but a little animal — a wild being of an unknown species in a child's skin — the missing link, perhaps; the link missing between the natural, kindly instinct of the wild thing, the brute, the monkey, the anthropoid ape, which protects its young even at the expense of its life, and civilized man of to-day, the speaking creature, the so-called Christian creature, who sells his young to the director-Devils of mills and machinery and prolongs his own life by the death of his offspring.

Biology teaches that many of the very lowest forms

of life eat their young. Is civilized man merely a case,
at last, of reversion to a primitive type?

She hid her head and then peeped timidly from under
the cover at the kindly old man. He had seen a fox
driven into its hole by dogs do the same thing.

She did not know what a smile meant, nor a caress,
nor a proffered gift. Tremblingly she lay, under the
dirty quilt, expecting a kick, a cuff.

The Bishop sat down by the bedside and took out a
paper. "It'll be an hour or so I can spend," he said
to the mother —" maybe you'd like to be doin' about
a little."

"Come to think of it, I'm pow'ful obleeged to you,"
she said. "I've all my mornin' washin' to do yit, only
I was afraid to leave her alone."

"You do yo' washin'— I'll watch her. I'm a pretty
good sort of a hoss doctor myse'f."

The child had nodded off to sleep, the Bishop was
reading his paper, when a loud voice was heard in the
hallway and some rough steps that shook the little
flimsily made floor of the cottage, and made it rock with
the tramp of them. The door opened suddenly and Jud
Carpenter, angry, boisterous, and presumptuous, entered. The child had awakened at the sound of Carpenter's foot fall, and now, frightened beyond control,
she trembled and wept under the cover.

There are natural antipathies and they are God-given.
They are the rough cogs in the wheel of things. But
uneven as they are, rough and grating, strike them off
and the wheel would be there still, but it would not

turn. It is the friction of life that moves it. And movement is the law of life.

Antipathies — thank God who gave them to us! But for them the shepherd dog would lie down with the wolf.

The only man in Cottontown who did not like the Bishop was Jud Carpenter, and the only man in the world whom the Bishop did not love was Jud Carpenter. And many a time in his life the old man had prayed: " O God, teach me to love Jud Carpenter and despise his ways."

Carpenter glared insolently at the old man quietly reading his paper, and asked satirically. " Wal, what ails her, doctor? "

" Mill-icious fever," remarked the Bishop promptly with becoming accent on the first syllable, and scarcely raising his eyes from the paper.

Carpenter flushed. He had met the Bishop too often in contests which required courage and brains not to have discovered by now that he was no match for the man who could both pray and fight.

" They aint half as sick as they make out an' I've come to see about it," he added. He felt the child's pulse. " She ain't sick to hurt. That spinner is idle over yonder an' I guess I'll jes' be carryin' her back. Wuck — it's the greatest tonic in the worl'—it's the Hostetter's Bitters of life," he added, trying to be funny.

The Bishop looked up. " Yes, but I've knowed men to get so drunk on bitters they didn't kno' a mill-dam from a dam'-mill! "

Carpenter smiled: " Wal, she ain't hurt — guess

21

I'll jes' git her cloze on an' take her over "— still feeling the child's wrist while she shuddered and hid under
the cover. Nothing but her arm was out, and from the
nervous grip of her little claw-like fingers the old man
could only guess her terrible fear.

" You sho'ly don't mean that, Jud Carpenter? " said
the Bishop, with surprise in his heretofore calm tone.

" Wal, that's jus' what I do mean, Doctor," remarked
Carpenter dryly, and in an irritated voice.

" Jud Carpenter," said the old man rising —" I am
a man of God — it is my faith an' hope. I'm gettin'
old, but I have been a man in my day, an' I've still got
strength enough left with God's he'p to stop you. You
shan't tech that child."

In an instant Carpenter was ablaze — profane, abu-
sive, insolent — and as the old man stepped between
him and the bed, the Whipper-in's anger overcame all
else.

The child under the cover heard a resounding whack
and stuck her head out in time to see the hot blood leap
to the old man's cheeks where Carpenter's blow had
fallen. For a moment he paused, and then the child
saw the old overseer's huge fist gripping spasmodically,
and the big muscles of his arms and shoulders rolling
beneath the folds of his coat, as a crouching lion's skin
rolls around beneath his mane before he springs.

Again and again it gripped, and relaxed — gripped
and relaxed again. Mastering himself with a great
effort, the old man turned to the man who had slapped
him.

" Strike the other cheek, you coward, as my Master sed you would."

Even the child was surprised when Carpenter, half wickedly, in rage, half tauntingly slapped the other cheek with a blow that almost sent the preacher reeling against the bed. Again the great fist gripped convulsively, and the big muscles that had once pitched the Mountain Giant over a rail fence worked — rolled beneath their covering.

" What else kin I do for you at the request of yo' Master? " sneered Carpenter.

" As He never said anything further on the subject," said the old man, in a dry pitched voice that told how hard he was trying to control himself, " I take it He intended me to use the same means that He employed when He run the thieves an' bullies of His day out of the temple of God."

The child thought they were embracing. It was the old hold and the double hip-thrust, by which the overseer had conquered so often before in his manhood's prime. Nor was his old-time strength gone. It came in a wave of righteous indignation, and like the gust of a whirlwind striking the spars of a rotting ship. Never in his life had Carpenter been snapped so nearly in two. It seemed to him that every bone in his body broke when he hit the floor. . . . It was ten minutes before his head began to know things again. Dazed, he opened his eyes to see the Bishop sitting calmly by his side bathing his face with cold water. The blood had been running from his nose, for the rag and water were colored. His head ached.

Jud Carpenter had one redeeming trait — it was an appreciation of the humorous. No man has ever been entirely lost or entirely miserable, who has had a touch of humor in him. As the Bishop put a pillow under his head and then locked the door to keep any one else out, the ridiculousness of it all came over him, and he said sillily:

" Wal, I reckin you've 'bout converted me this time."

" Jud Carpenter," said the Bishop, his face white with shame, " for God's sake don't tell anybody I done that —"

Jud smiled as he arose and put on his hat. " I can stan' bein' licked," he added good naturedly —" because I remember now that I've run up agin the old champion of the Tennessee Valley — ain't that what they useter call you? — but it does hurt me sorter, to think you'd suppose I'd be such a damned fool as to tell it."

He felt the child's wrist again. " 'Pears lak she's got a little fever since all this excitement — guess I'll jes' let her be to-day."

" I do think it 'ud be better, Jud," said the Bishop gently.

And Jud pulled down his hat and slipped quietly out.

The mother never did understand from the child just what happened. When she came in the Bishop had her so much better that the little thing actually was playing with his ginger cake dolls, and had eaten one of them.

It was bed time that night before the child finally

whispered it out: "Maw, did you ever see two men hug each other?"

"No — why?"

"Why, the Bishop he hugged Jud Carpenter so hard he fetched the bleed out of his nose!"

It was her first and last sight of a ginger-man. Two days later she was buried, and few save the old Bishop knew she had died; for Cottontown did not care.

CHAPTER XX

THE next Sunday was an interesting occasion — voted so by all Cottontown when it was over. There was a large congregation out, caused by the announcement of the Bishop the week before.

" Nex' Sunday I intend to preach Uncle Dave Dickey's funeral sermon. I've talked to Dave about it an' he tells me he has got all kinds of heart disease with a fair sprinklin' of liver an' kidney trouble an' that he is liable to drap off any day.

" I am one of them that believes that whatever bouquets we have for the dead will do 'em mo' good if given while they can smell; an' whatever pretty things we've got to say over a coffin had better be said whilst the deceased is up an' kickin' around an' can hear — an' so Dave is pow'ful sot to it that I preach his fun'ral whilst he's alive. An' I do hope that next Sunday you'll all come an' hear it. An' all the bouquets you expect to give him when he passes away, please fetch with you."

To-day Uncle Dave was out, dressed in his long-tail jeans frock suit with high standing collar and big black stock. His face had been cleanly shaved, and his hair, coming down to his shoulders, was cut square away around his neck in the good old-fashioned way. He sat

326

on the front bench and looked very solemn and deeply impressed. On one side of him sat Aunt Sally, and on the other, Tilly; and the coon dog, which followed them everywhere, sat on its tail, well to the front, looking the very essence of concentrated solemnity.

But the coon dog had several peculiar idiosyncrasies; one of them was that he was always very deeply affected by music — especially any music which sounded anything like a dinner horn. As this was exactly the way Miss Patsy Butts' organ music sounded, no sooner did she strike up the first notes than the coon dog joined in, with his long dismal howl — much to the disgust of Uncle Dave and his family.

This brought things to a standstill, and all the Hillites to giggling, while Archie B. moved up and took his seat with the mourners immediately behind the dog.

Tilly looked reproachfully at Aunt Sally; Aunt Sally looked reproachfully at Uncle Dave, who passed the reproach on to the dog.

. " There now," said Uncle Dave — "Sally an' Tilly both said so! They both said I mustn't let him come."

He gave the dog a punch in the ribs with his huge foot. This hushed him at once.

" Be quiet Dave," said the Bishop, sitting near — " it strikes me you're pow'ful lively for a corpse. It's natural for a dog to howl at his master's fun'ral."

The coon dog had come out intending to enter fully into the solemnity of the occasion, and when the organ started again he promptly joined in.

" I'm sorry," said the Bishop, " but I'll have to rise an' put the chief mourner out."

It was unnecessary, for the chief mourner himself arose just then, and began running frantically around the pulpit with snaps, howls and sundry most painful barks.

Those who noticed closely observed that a clothes-pin had been snapped bitingly on the very tip end of his tail, and as he finally caught his bearing, and went down the aisle and out of the door with a farewell howl, they could hear him tearing toward home, quite satisfied that live funerals weren't the place for him.

What he wanted was a dead one.

"Maw!" said Miss Patsy Butts —"I wish you'd look after Archie B."

Everybody looked at Archie B., who looked up from a New Testament in which he was deeply interested, surprised and grieved.

The organ started up again.

But it grew irksome to Miss Samantha Carewe seated on the third bench.

"Ma," she whispered, "I've heard o' fun'rals in Ire-lan' where they passed around refreshments —d'ye reckin this is goin' to be that kind? I'm gittin' pow'ful hungry."

"Let us trust that the Lord will have it so," said her mother devoutly.

Amid great solemnity the Bishop had gone into the pulpit and was preaching:

"It may be a little onusual," he said, "to preach a man's fun'ral whilst he's alive, but it will certn'ly do him mo' good than to preach it after he's dead. If we're goin' to do any good to our feller man, let's do it while he's alive.

" Kind words to the livin' are more than monuments to the dead.

" Come to think about it, but ain't we foolish an' hypocritical the way we go on over the dead that we have forgot an' neglected whilst they lived?

" If we'd reverse the thing how many a po' creature that had given up the fight, an' shuffled off this mortal coil fur lack of a helpin' han' would be alive to-day!

" How many another that had laid down an' quit in the back stretch of life would be up an' fightin'! Why, the money spent for flowers an' fun'rals an' monuments for the pulseless dead of the world would mighty nigh feed the living dead that are always with us.

" What fools we mortals be! Why, we're not a bit better than the heathen Chinee that we love to send missionaries to and call all kinds of hard names. The Chinee put sweet cakes an' wine an' sech on the graves of their departed, an' once one of our missionaries asked his servant, Ching Lu, who had just lost his brother an' had put all them things on his grave, when he thought the corpse 'ud rise up an' eat them; an' Ching Lu told him he thought the Chinee corpse 'ud rise up an' eat his sweetmeats about the same time that the Melican man's corpse 'ud rise up an' smell all the bouquets of sweet flowers spread over him.

" An' there we are, right on the same footin' as the heathen an' don't know it.

" David Dickey, the subject of this here fun'ral discourse, was born on the fourth day of July, 1810, of

pious, godly parrents. Dave as a child was always a
good boy, who loved his parrents, worked diligently
and never needed a lickin' in his life "—

" Hold on, Bishop," said Uncle Davy, rising and
protesting earnestly —" this is my fun'ral an' I ain't
agoin' to have nothin' told but the exact facts: Jes'
alter that by sayin' I was a *tollerbul* good boy, *tollerbul*
diligent, with a big sprinklin' o' meanness an' laziness
in me, an' that my old daddy,— God bless his memory
for it — in them days cleared up mighty nigh a ten
acre lot of guv'ment land cuttin' off the underbrush for
my triflin' hide."

Uncle Dave sat down. The Bishop was confused a
moment, but quickly said: " Now bretherin, there's another good p'int about preachin' a man's fun'ral whilst
he's alive. It gives the corpse a chance to correct any
errors. Why, who'd ever have thought that good old
Uncle Dave Dickey was that triflin' when he was young?
Much obliged, Dave, much obliged, I'll try to tell the
exact facts hereafter."

Then he began again:

" In manner Uncle Dave was approachable an' with
a kind heart for all mankind, an' a kind word an' a
helpin' han' for the needy. He was *tollerbul* truthful "
— went on the Bishop — with a look at Uncle Davy as
if he had profited by previous interruptions.

" Tell it as it was, Hillard,"— nodded Uncle Dave,
from the front bench —" jes' as it was — no lies at
my fun'ral."

" *Tollerbul* truthful," went on the Bishop, " on all
subjects he wanted to tell the truth about. An' I'm

proud to say, bretherin, that after fifty odd years of intermate acquantance with our soon-to-be-deceased brother, you cu'd rely on him tellin' the truth in all things except "—

" Tell it as it was, Hillard — no — filigree work at my fun'ral —" said Uncle Dave.

—" Except," went on the Bishop, " returnin' any little change he happen'd to borry from you, or swoppin' horses, or tellin' the size of the fish he happened to ketch. On them p'ints, my bretherin, the lamented corpse was pow'ful weak; an' I'm sorry to have to tell it, but I've been warned, as you all kno', to speak the exact facts."

" Hillard Watts," said Uncle Dave rising hotly — " that's a lie an' you know it! "

" Sit down, Dave," said the Bishop calmly, " I've been preachin' fun'rals fur fifty years an' that is the fus' time I ever was sassed by a corpse. You know it's so an' besides I left out one thing. You're always tellin' what kinder weather it's gwinter be to-morrow an' missin' it. You burnt my socks off forty years ago on the only hoss-trade I ever had with you. You owe me five dollars you borrowed ten years ago, an' you never caught a half pound perch in yo' life that you didn't tell us the nex' day it was a fo' pound trout. So set down. Oh, I'm tellin' the truth without any filigree, Dave."

Aunt Sally and Tilly pulled Uncle Dave down while they conversed with him earnestly. Then he arose and said:

" Hillard, I beg yo' pardon. You've spoken the truth

— Sally and Tilly both say so. I tell yo', bretherin,"
he said turning to the congregation —" it'd be a good
thing if we c'ud all have our fun'ral sermon now and
then correctly told. There would be so many points
brought out as seen by our neighbors that we never
saw ourselves."

" The subject of this sermon "— went on the Bishop
—" the lamented corpse-to-be, was never married but
once — to his present loving widow-to-be, and he never
had any love affair with any other woman — she bein'
his fust an' only love —"

" Hillard," said Uncle Dave rising, " I hate to —"

" Set down, David Dickey," whispered Aunt Sally,
hotly, as she hastily jerked him back in his seat with a
snap that rattled the teeth in his head:

" If you get up at this time of life to make any post-
mortem an' dyin' declaration on that subject in my
presence, ye'll be takin' out a corpse sho' 'nuff! "

Uncle Dave very promptly subsided.

" An' the only child he's had is the present beautiful
daughter that sits beside him."

Tilly blushed.

" David, I am very sorry to say, had some very
serious personal faults. He always slept with his mouth
open. I've knowed him to snore so loud after dinner
that the folks on the adjoining farm thought it was the
dinner horn."

" Now Hillard," said Uncle Dave, rising —" do you
think it necessary to bring in all that? "

" A man's fun'ral," said the Bishop, " ain't intended
to do him any good — it's fur the coming generation.

Boys and girls, beware of sleepin' with yo' mouth open an' eatin' with yo' fingers an' drinkin' yo' coffee out of the saucer, an' sayin' *them molasses* an' *I wouldn't choose any* when you're axed to have somethin' at the table.

" Dave Dickey done all that.

" Brother Dave Dickey had his faults as we all have. He was a sprinklin' of good an' evil, a mixture of diligence an' laziness, a brave man mostly with a few yaller crosses in him, truthful nearly always, an' lyin' mostly fur fun an' from habit; good at times an' bad at others, spiritual at times when it looked like he cu'd see right into heaven's gate, an' then again racked with great passions of the flesh that swept over him in waves of hot desires, until it seemed that God had forgotten to make him anything but an animal.

" Come to think of it, an' that's about the way with the rest of us?

" But he aimed to do right, an' he strove constantly to do right, an' he prayed constantly fur help to do right, an' that's the main thing. If he fell he riz agin, fur he had a Hand outstretched in his faith that cu'd lift him up, an' knew that he could go to a Father that always forgave — an' that's the main thing. Let us remember, when we see the faults and vices of others — that we see only what they've done — as Bobby Burns says, we don't kno' what they have resisted. Give 'em credit for that — maybe it over-balances. Balancin' — ah, my bretherin, that's a gran' thing. It's the thing on which the whole Universe hangs — the law of balance. The pendulum every whar swings as fur back as it did furra'd, an' the very earth hangs in space by this same law.   An' it holds in the moral worl' as well as the t'other one — only man is sech a liar an' so bigoted he can't see it.   But here comes into the worl' a man or woman filled so full of passion of every sort,— passions they didn't make themselves either — regular thunder clouds in the sky of life.   Big with the rain, the snow, the hail — the lightning of passion.   A spark, a touch, a strong wind an' they explode, they fall from grace, so to speak.   But what have they done that we ain't never heard of?   All we've noticed is the explosion, the fall, the blight.   They have stirred the sky, whilst the little white pale-livered untempted clouds floated on the zephyrs — they've brought rain that made the earth glad, they've cleared the air in the very fall of their lightnin'.   The lightnin' came — the fall — but give 'em credit fur the other.   The little namby-pamby, white livered, zephyr clouds that is so divine an' useless, might float forever an' not even make a shadow to hide men from the sun.

" So credit the fallen man or woman, big with life an' passion, with the good they've done when you debit 'em with the evil.   Many a 'oman so ugly that she wasn't any temptation even for Sin to mate with her, has done more harm with her slanderin' tongue an' hypocrisy than a fallen 'oman has with her whole body.

" We're mortals an' we can't he'p it — animals, an' God made us so.   But we'll never fall to rise no mo' 'less we fail to reach up fur he'p.

" What then is our little sins of the flesh to the big goodness of the faith that is in us?

" For forty years Uncle Dave has been a consistent

member of the church — some church — it don't matter which. For forty years he has trod the narrer path,
stumpin' his toe now an' then, but allers gettin' up agin,
for forty years he has he'ped others all he cu'd, been
charitable an' forgivin', as hones' as the temptation
would permit, an' only a natural lie now an' then as to
the weather or the size of a fish, trustin' in God to make
it all right.

"An' now, in the twilight of life, when his sun is
'most set an' the dews of kindness come with old age,
right gladly will he wake up some mornin' in a better
lan', the scrub in him all bred out, the yaller streak
gone, the sins of the flesh left behind. An' that's
about the way with the most of us,— no better an' maybe wuss — Amen ! "

Uncle Dave was weeping :

" Oh, Hillard — Hillard," he said, " say all that
over agin about the clouds an' the thunder of passion —
say all the last part over agin — it sounds so good ! "

The congregation thronged around him and shook his
hand. They gave him the flowers they had brought ;
they told him how much they thought of him, how
sorry they would be to see him dead, how they had always intended to come to see him, but had been so busy,
and to cheer up that he wasn't dead yet.

" No "— said Uncle Dave, weeping —" no, an' now
since I see how much you all keer fur me I don't b'lieve
— I — I wanter die at all."

CHAPTER XXI

JACK AND THE LITTLE ONES

NO one would ever have supposed that the big blacksmith at the village was Jack Bracken. All the week he worked at his trade — so full of his new life that it shone continually in his face — his face strong and stern, but kindly. With his leathern apron on, his sleeves rolled up, his hairy breast bare and shining in the open collar, physically he looked more like an ancient Roman than a man of to-day.

His greatest pleasure was to entice little children to his shop, talking to them as he worked. To get them to come, he began by keeping a sack of ginger snaps in his pockets. And the villagers used to smile at the sight of the little ones around him, especially after sunset when his work was finished. Often a half dozen children would be in his lap or on his knees at once, and the picture was so beautiful that people would stop and look, and wonder what the big strong man saw in all those noisy children to love.

They did not know that this man had spent his life a hunted thing; that the strong instinct of home and children had been smothered in him, that his own little boy had been taken, and that to him every child was a saint.

But they soon learned that the great kind-hearted, simple man was a tiger when aroused. A small child from the mill, sickly and timid, was among those who stopped one morning to get one of his cakes.

Not knowing it was a mill child on its way to work, Jack detained it in all the kindness of his heart, and the little thing was not in a hurry to go. Indeed, it forgot all about the mill until its father happened along an hour after it should have been at work. His name was Joe Hopper, a ne'er-do-well whose children, by working at the mill, supported him in idleness.

Catching the child, he berated it and boxed its ears soundly. Jack was at work, but turning, and seeing the child chastised, he came at the man with quiet fury. With one huge hand in Joe Hopper's collar, he boxed his ears until he begged for mercy. " Now go," said Jack, as he released him, " an' know hereafter how it feels for the strong to beat the weak."

Of all things, Jack wanted to talk with Margaret Adams; but he could never make up his mind to seek her out, though his love for this woman was the love of his life. Often at night he would slip away from the old preacher's cabin and his cot by Captain Tom's bed, to go out and walk around her little cottage and see that all was safe.

James, her boy, peculiarly interested Jack, but it was some time before he came to know him. He knew the boy was Richard Travis's son, and that he alone had stood between him and his happiness. That but for him — the son of his mother — he would never have been the outlaw that he was, and even now but for this

22

son he would marry her. But outlaw that he was,
Jack Bracken had no free-booting ideas of love. Never
did man revere purity in woman more than he — that
one thing barred Margaret Adams forever from his life,
though not from his heart.

He felt that he would hate James Adams; but instead
he took to the lad at once — his fine strange ways, his
dignity, courage, his very aloofness and the sorrow he
saw there, drew him to the strange, silent lad.

One day while at work in his shop he looked up and
saw the boy standing in the door watching him closely
and with evident admiration.

" Come in, my lad," said Jack, laying down his big
hammer.   " What is yo' name? "

" Well, I don't know that that makes any difference,"
he replied smiling, " I might ask you what is yours."

Jack flushed, but he pitied the lad.

He smiled: " I guess you an' I could easily understan' each other, lad — what can I do for you? "

" I wanted you to fix my pistol for me, sir — and —
and I haven't anything to pay you."

Jack looked it over — the old duelling pistol. He
knew at once it was Colonel Jeremiah Travis's. The
boy had gotten it somehow. The hair-spring trigger
was out of fix. Jack soon repaired it and said:

" Now, son, she's all right, and not a cent do I charge
you."

" I didn't mean that," said the boy, flushing.   " I
have no money, but I want to pay you, for I need this
pistol — need it very badly."

" To shoot rabbits? " smiled Jack.

The boy did not smile. He ran his hand in his pocket and handed Jack a thin gold ring, worn almost to a wire; but Jack paled, and his hand shook when he took it, for he recognized the little ring he himself had given Margaret Adams years ago.

"It's my mother's," said the boy, "and some man gave it to her once — long ago — for she is foolish about it. Now, of late, I think I have found out who that man was, and I hate him as I do hell itself. I am determined she shall never see it again. So take it, or I'll give it to somebody else."

"If you feel that way about it, little 'un," said Jack kindly, "I'll keep it for you," and he put the precious relic in his pocket.

"Now, look here, lad," he said, changing the subject, "but do you know you've got an' oncommon ac'rate gun in this old weepon?"

The boy smiled — interested.

"It's the salt of the earth," said Jack, "an' I'll bet its stood 'twixt many a gentleman and death. Can you shoot true, little 'un?"

"Only fairly — can you?"

"Some has been kind enough to give me that character"— he said promptly. "Want me to give you a few lessons?"

The boy warmed to him at once. Jack took him behind the shop, tied a twine string between two trees and having loaded the old pistol with cap and powder and ball, he stepped off thirty paces and shot the string in twain.

"Good," said the boy smiling, and Jack handed him

the pistol with a boyish flush of pride in his own face.

"Now, little 'un, it's this away in shootin' a weepon like this -- it's the aim that counts most. But with my Colts now — the self-actin' ones — you've got to cal'c'late chiefly on another thing — a kinder thing that ain't in the books — the instinct that makes the han' an' the eye act together an' 'lowin', at the same time, for the leverage on the trigger." The lad's face glowed with excitement. Jack saw it and said: "Now I'll give you a lesson to-day. Would you like to shoot at that tree?" he asked kindly.

"Do you suppose I could hit the string?" asked the boy innocently.

Jack had to smile. "In time — little 'un — in time you might. You're a queer lad," he said again laughing. "You aim pretty high."

"Oh, then I'll never hit below my mark. Let me try the string, please."

To humor him, Jack tied the string again, and the boy stepped up to the mark and without taking aim, but with that instinct which Jack had just mentioned, that bringing of the hand and eye together unconsciously, he fired and the string flew apart.

"You damned little cuss," shouted Jack enthusiastically, as he grabbed the boy and hugged him —" to make a sucker of me that way! To take me in like that!"

"Oh," said the boy, "I do nothing but shoot this thing from morning till night. It was my great grandfather's."

And from that time the two were one.

But another thing happened which cemented the tie more strongly. One Saturday afternoon Jack took a crowd of his boy friends down to the river for a plunge. The afternoon was bright and warm; the frost of the morning making the water delightful for a short plunge. It was great sport. They all obeyed him and swam in certain places he marked off — all except James Adams. He boldly swam out into the deep current of the river and came near losing his life. Jack plunged in in time to reach him, but had to dive to get him, he having sunk the third time. It required hard work to revive him on the bank, but the man was strong and swung the lad about by the heels till he got the water out of his lungs, and his circulation started again. James opened his eyes at last, and Jack said, smiling: " That's all right, little 'un, but I feared onct, you was gone."

He took the boy home, and then it was that for the first time for fifteen years he saw and talked to the woman he loved.

" Mother," said the boy, " this is the new blacksmith that I've been telling you about, and he is great guns — just pulled me out of the bottom of the Tennessee river."

Jack laughed and said: " The little 'un ca'n't swim as well as he can shoot, ma'am."

There was no sign of recognition between them, nothing to show they had ever seen each other before, but Jack saw her eyes grow tender at the first word he uttered, and he knew that Margaret Adams loved him then, even as she had loved him years ago.

He stayed but a short while, and James Adams never saw the silent battle that was waged in the eyes of each. How Jack Bracken devoured her with his eyes,— the comely figure, the cleanliness and sweetness of the little cottage — his painful hungry look for this kind of peace and contentment — the contentment of love.

And James noticed that his mother was greatly embarrassed, even to agitation, but he supposed it was because of his narrow escape from drowning, and it touched him even to caressing her, a thing he had never done before.

It hurt Jack — that caress. Richard Travis's boy — she would have been his but for him. He felt a terrible bitterness arising. He turned abruptly to go.

Margaret had not spoken. Then she thanked him and bade James change his clothes. As the boy went in the next room to do this, she followed Jack to the little gate and stood pale and suffering, but not able to speak.

"Good-bye," he said, giving her his hand —" you know, Margaret, my life — why I am here, to be near you,— how I love you, have loved you."

"And how I love you, Jack," she said simply.

The words went through him with a fierce sweetness that shook him.

"My God — don't say that — it hurts me so, after — what you've done."

"Jack," she whispered sadly —" some day you'll know — some day you'll understand that there are things in life greater even than the selfishness of your own heart's happiness."

"They can't be," said Jack bitterly —"that's what all life's for — heart happiness — love. Why, hunger and love, them's the fust things; them's the man an' the woman; them's the law unto theyselves, the animal, the instinct, the beast that's in us; the things that makes God excuse all else we do to get them — we have to have 'em. He made us so; we have to have 'em — it's His own doin'."

"But," she said sweetly —"suppose it meant another to be despised, reviled, made infamous."

"They'd have to be," he said sternly, for he was thinking of Richard Travis —"they'd have to be, for he made his own life."

"Oh, you do not understand," she cried. "And you cannot now — but wait — wait, and it will be plain. Then you'll know all and — that I love you, Jack."

He turned bitterly and walked away.

CHAPTER XXII

THE BROKEN THREAD

FOR the first time in years, the next Sunday the little church on the mountain side was closed, and all Cottontown wondered. Never before had the old man missed a Sabbath afternoon since the church had been built. This was to have been Baptist day, and that part of his congregation was sorely disappointed.

For an hour Bud Billings had stood by the little gate looking down the big stretch of sandy road, expecting to see the familiar shuffling, blind old roan coming:

" Sum'pins happened to Ben Butler," said Bud at last — and at thought of such a calamity, he sat down and shed tears.

His simple heart yearned for pity, and feeling something purring against him he picked up the cat and coddled it.

" You seem to be cultivatin' that cat again, Bud Billings," came a sharp voice from the cabin window.

Bud dropped the animal quickly and struck out across the mountain for the Bishop's cabin.

But he was not prepared for the shock that came to his simple heart: Shiloh was dying — the Bishop himself told him so — the Bishop with a strange, set, hard look in his eyes — a look which Bud had never seen

there before, for it was sorrow mingled with defiance —
in that a great wrong had been done and done over his
protest. It was culpable sorrow too, somewhat, in that
he had not prevented it, and a heart-hardening sorrow
in that it took the best that he loved.

"She jes' collapsed, Bud — sudden't like — wilted
like a vi'let that's stepped on, an' the Doctor says she's
got no sho' at all, ther' bein' nothin' to build on. She
don't kno' nothin'— ain't knowed nothin' since last
night, an' she thinks she's in the mill — my God, it's
awful! The little thing keeps reaching out in her delirium an' tryin' to piece the broken threads, an' then
she falls back pantin' on her pillow an' says, pitful like
—' *the thread — the thread is broken!* ' an' that's jes'
it, Bud — the thread *is* broken!"

Tears were running down the old man's cheeks, and
that strange thing which now and then came up in Bud's
throat and stopped him from talking came again. He
walked out and sat under a tree in the yard. He looked
at the other children sitting around stupid — numbed
— with the vague look in their faces which told that a
sorrow had fallen, but without the sensitiveness to know
or care where. He saw a big man, bronzed and hard-
featured, but silent and sorrowful, walking to and fro.
Now and then he would stop and look earnestly through
the window at the little still figure on the bed, and then
Bud would hear him say —" *like little Jack — like little
Jack.*"

The sun went down — the stars came up — but Bud
sat there. He could do nothing, but he wanted to be
there.

When the lamp was lighted in the cabin he could see all within the home and that an old man held on a large pillow in his lap a little child, and that he carried her around from window to window for air, and that the child's eyes were fixed, and she was whiter than the pillow. He also saw an old woman, lantern-jawed and ghostly, tidying around and she mumbling and grumbling because no one would give the child any turpentine.

And still Bud sat outside, with that lump in his throat, that thing that would not let him speak.

Late at night another man came up with saddle bags, and hitching his horse within a few feet of Bud, walked into the cabin.

He was a kindly man, and he stopped in the doorway and looked at the old man, sitting with the sick child in his lap. Then he pulled a chair up beside the old man and took the child's thin wrist in his hand. He shook his head and said:

" No use, Bishop — better lay her on the bed — she can't live two hours."

Then he busied himself giving her some drops from a vial.

" When you get through with your remedy and give her up," said the old man slowly —" I'm gwinter try mine."

The Doctor looked at the old man sorrowfully, and after a while he went out and rode home.

Then the old man sent them all to bed. He alone would watch the little spark go out.

And Bud alone in the yard saw it all. He knew he

should go home — that it was now past midnight, but somehow he felt that the Bishop might need him.

He saw the moon go down, and the big constellations shine out clearer. Now and then he could see the old nurse reach over and put his ear to the child's mouth to see if it yet breathed. But Bud thought maybe he was listening for it to speak, for he could see the old man's lips moving as he did when he prayed at church. And Bud could not understand it, but never before in his life did he feel so uplifted, as he sat and watched the old man holding the little child and praying. And all the hours that he sat there, Bud saw that the old man was praying as he had never prayed before. The intensity of it increased and began to be heard, and then Bud crept up to the window and listened, for he dearly loved to hear the Bishop, and amid the tears that ran down his own cheek, and the quick breathing which came quicker and quicker from the little child in the lap, Bud heard:

"*Save her, oh, God, an' if I've done any little thing in all my po' an' blunderin' life that's entitled to credit at Yo' han's, give it now to little Shiloh, for You can if You will. If there's any credit to my account in the Book of Heaven, hand it out now to the little one robbed of her all right up to the door of death. She that is named Shiloh, which means rest. Do it, oh, God,— take it from my account if she ain't got none yet her-se'f, an' I swear to You with the faith of Abraham that henceforth I will live to light a fire-brand in this valley that will burn out this child slavery, upheld now by ig-*

*norance and the greed of the gold lovers. Save little
Shiloh, for You can."*

Bud watched through the crisis, the shorter and
shorter breaths, the struggle — the silence when, only by
holding the lighted candle to her mouth, could the old
man tell whether she lived or not. And Bud stood outside and watched his face, lit up like a saint in the light
of the candle falling on his silvery hair, whiter than
the white sand of Sand Mountain, a stern, strong face
with lips which never ceased moving in prayer, the eyes
riveted on the little fluttering lips. And watching the
stern, solemn lips set, as Bud had often seen the white
stern face of Sunset Rock, when the clouds lowered
around it, suddenly he saw them relax and break silently,
gently, almost imperceptibly into a smile which made
the slubber think the parting sunset had fallen there;
and Bud gripped the window-sill outside, and swallowed
and swallowed at the thing in his throat, and stood terse-
ly wiggling on his strained tendons, and then almost
shouted when he saw the smile break all over the old
man's face and light up his eyes till the candle's flicker-
ing light looked pale, and saw him bow his head and
heard him say:

*"Lord God Almighty . . . My God . . .
My own God . . . an' You ain't never gone back
on me yet. . . . 'Bless the Lord all my soul, an'
all that is within me; bless His Holy Name!'"*

Bud could not help it. He laughed out hysterically.
And then the old face, still smiling, looked surprised
at the window and said: "Go home, Bud. God is the
Great Doctor, an' He has told me she shall live."

Then, as he turned to go, his heart stood still, for he heard Shiloh say in her little piping child voice, but, oh, so distinctly, and so sweetly, like a bird in the forest:

" Pap, sech a sweet dream — an' I went right up to the gate of heaven an' the angel smiled an' kissed me an' sed:

" ' Go back, little Shiloh — not yet — not yet! ' "

Then Bud slipped off in the dawn of the coming light.

CHAPTER XXIII

GOD WILL PROVIDE

IN a few days Shiloh was up, but the mere shadow of a little waif, following the old man around the place. She needed rest and good food and clothes; and Bull Run and Seven Days and Appomattox and Atlanta needed them, and where to get them was the problem which confronted the grandfather.

Shiloh's narrow escape from death had forever settled the child-labor question with him — he would starve, " by the Grace of God," as he expressed it, before one of them should ever go into the mill again.

He had a bitter quarrel about it with Mrs. Watts; but the good old man's fighting blood was up at last — that hatred of child-slavery, which had been so long choked by the smoke of want, now burst into a blaze when the shock of it came in Shiloh's collapse — a blaze which was indeed destined " to light the valley with a torch of fire."

On the third day Jud Carpenter came out to see about it; but at sight of him the old man took down from the rack over the hall door the rifle he had carried through the war, and with a determined gesture he stopped the employment agent at the gate: " I am a man of God, Jud Carpenter," he said in a strange voice, rounded with a deadly determination, " but in the name of God an' humanity, if you come into that gate after my little 'uns, I'll kill you in yo' tracks, jes' as a bis'n bull 'ud stamp the life out of a prowlin' coyote."

And Jud Carpenter went back to town and spread the report that the old man was a maniac, that he had lost his mind since Shiloh came so near dying.

The problem which confronted the old man was serious.

" O Jack, Jack," he said one night, " if I jes' had some of that gold you had!"

Jack replied by laying ten silver dollars in the old man's hand.

" I earned it,"— he said simply —" this week — shoeing horses — it's the sweetest money I ever got."

" Why, Jack," said the Bishop —" this will feed us for a week. Come here, Tabitha," he called cheerily — " come an' see what happens to them that cast their bread upon the waters. We tuck in this outcast an' now behold our bread come back ag'in."

The old woman came up and took it gingerly. She bit each dollar to test it, remarking finally: " Why, hit's genuwine!"—

Jack laughed.

" Why, hit's mo' money'n I've seed fur years," she said —" I won't hafter hunt fur 'sang roots to-morrow."

" Jack," said the Bishop, after the others had retired, and the two men sat in Captain Tom's cabin —" Jack, I've been thinkin' an' thinkin'— I must make some money."

" How much?" asked Jack.

" A thousand or two."

" That's a lot of money," said the outlaw quickly.
" A heap fur you to need."

" It's not fur me," he said —" I don't need it — I
wouldn't have it for myself. It's for him — see ! " he
pointed to the sleeping man on the low cot. " Jack,
I've been talkin' to the Doctor — he examined Cap'n
Tom's head, and he says it'd be an easy job — that it's
a shame it ain't been done befo'— that in a city to the
North,— he gave me the name of a surgeon there who
could take that pressure from his head and make him
the man he was befo'— the *man*, mind you, the *man* he
was befo'."

Jack sat up excited. His eyes glittered.

" Then there's Shiloh," went on the old man —" it'll
mean life to her too — life to git away from the mill.

" Cap'n Tom and Shiloh — I must have it, Jack —
I must have it. God will provide a way. I'd give my
home — I'd give everything — just to save them two —
Cap'n Tom and little Shiloh."

He felt a touch on his shoulder and looked up.

Jack Bracken stood before him, clutching the handle
of his big Colt's revolver, and his hat was pulled low
over his eyes. He was flushed and panting. A glitter
was in his eyes, the glitter of the old desperado spirit
returned.

" Bishop," he said, " ever' now and then it comes
over me ag'in, comes over me — the old dare-devil feelin'." He held up his pistol: " All week I've missed
somethin'. Last night I fingered it in my sleep."

He pressed it tenderly. " Jes' you say the word,"
he whispered, " an' in a few hours I'll be back here with

the coin. Shipton's bank is dead easy an' he is a money devil with a cold heart." The old man laughed and took the revolver from him.

" It's hard, I know, Jack, to give up old ways. I must have made po' Cap'n Tom's and Shiloh's case out terrible to tempt you like that. But not even for them — no — no — not even for them. Set down."

Jack sat down, subdued. Then the Bishop pulled out a paper from his pocket and chuckled.

" Now, Jack, you're gwinter have the laugh on me, for the old mood is on me an' I'm yearnin' to do this jes' like you yearn to hold up the bank ag'in. It's the old instinct gettin' to wurk. But, Jack, you see — this — mine — ain't so bad. God sometimes provides in an on-expected way."

" What is it? " asked Jack.

The old man chuckled again. Then Jack saw his face turn red — as if half ashamed: " Why should I blame you, Jack, fur I'm doin' the same thing mighty nigh — I'm longin' for the flesh pots of Egypt. As I rode along to-day thinkin'— thinkin'— thinkin'— how can I save the children an' Cap'n Tom, *how can I get a little money to send Cap'n Tom off to the Doctor* — an' also repeatin' to myself —' *The Lord will provide* — *He will provide* —' I ran up to this, posted on a tree, an' kinder starin' me an' darin' me in the face."

He laughed again: " Jes' scolded you, Jack, but see here. See how the old feelin' has come over me at sight of this bragging, blow-hard challenge. It makes my blood bile.

" Race horse? — Why, Richard Travis wouldn't
23

know a real race horse if he had one by the tail. It's disgustin'— these silk-hat fellers gettin' up a three-cornered race, an' then openin' it up to the valley — knowin' they've put the entrance fee of fifty dollars so high that no po' devil in the County can get in, even if he had a horse equal to theirs.

"Three thousan' dollars! — think of it! An' then Richard Travis rubs it in. He's havin' fun over it — he always would do that. Read the last line ag'in — in them big letters:

" ' *Open to anything raised in the Tennessee Valley.*"

"Fine fun an' kinder sarcastic, but, Jack, Ben Butler cu'd make them blooded trotters look like steers led to slaughter."

Jack sat looking silently in the fire.

"If I had the entrance fee I'd do it once — jes' once mo' befo' I die? Once mo' to feel the old thrill of victory! An' for Cap'n Tom an' Shiloh. God'll provide, Jack — God'll provide!"

CHAPTER XXIV

BONAPARTE'S WATERLOO

BONAPARTE lay on the little front porch — the loafing place which opened into Billy Buch's bar-room. Apparently, he was asleep and basking in the warm Autumn sunshine. In reality he was doing his star trick and one which could have originated only in the brains of a born genius. Feigning sleep, he thus enticed within striking distance all the timid country dogs visiting Cottontown for the first time, and viewing its wonders with a palpitating heart. Then, like a bolt from the sky, he would fall on them, appalled and paralyzed — a demon with flashing teeth and abbreviated tail.

When finally released, with lacerated hides and wounded feelings, they went rapidly homeward, and they told it in dog language, from Dan to Beersheba, that Cottontown was full of the terrible and the unexpected.

And a great morning he had had of it — for already three humble and unsuspecti g curs, following three humble and unsuspecting countrymen who had walked in to get their morning's dram, had fallen victims to his guile.

Each successful raid of Bonaparte brought forth shouts of laughter from within, in which Billy Buch, the Dutch proprietor, joined. It always ended in Bona-

parte being invited in and treated to a cuspidor of beer
— the drinking, with the cuspidor as his drinking horn,
being part of his repertoire. After each one Billy
Buch would proudly exclaim:

"Mine Gott, but dat Ponyparte ees one greet dog!"

Then Bonaparte would reel around in a half drunken
swagger and go back to watch for other dogs.

"I tell you, Billy," said Jud Carpenter —"Jes'
watch that dog. They ain't no dog on earth his e'kal
when it comes to brains. Them country dogs aflyin' up
the road reminds me of old Uncle Billy Alexander who
paid for his shoes in bacon, and paid every spring in
advance for the shoes he was to get in the fall. But
one fall when he rid over after his shoes, the neighbors said the shoemaker had gone — gone for good —
to Texas to live — gone an' left his creditors behin'.
Uncle Billy looked long an' earnestly t'wards the settin' sun, raised his han's to heaven an' said: "Good-
bye, my bacon!'"

Billy Buch laughed loudly.

"Dat ees goot — goot — goot-bye, mine bac'n! I
dus remember dat."

Bonaparte had partaken of his fourth cuspidor of
beer and was in a delightful state of swagger and fight
when he saw an unusual commotion up the street. What
was it, thought Bonaparte — a crowd of boys and men
surrounding another man with an organ and leading a
little devil of a hairy thing, dressed up like a man.

His hair bristled with indignation. That little thing
dividing honors with him in Cottontown? It was not
to be endured for a moment!

Bonaparte stood gazing in indignant wonder. He slowly arose and shambled along half drunkenly to see what it all meant. A crowd had gathered around the thing — the insignificant thing which was attracting more attention in Cottontown than himself, the champion dog. Among them were some school boys, and one of them, a red-headed lad, was telling his brother all about it.

"Now, Ozzie B., this is a monkey — the furst you've ever seed. He looks jes' like I told you — sorter like a man an' sorter like a nigger an' sorter like a groun' hog."

"The pretties' thing I ever seed," said Ozzie B., walking around and staring delightedly.

The crowd grew larger. It was a show Cottontown had never seen before.

Then two men came out of the bar-room — one, the bar-keeper, fat and jolly, and the other lank and with malicious eyes.

This gave Bonaparte his cue and he bristled and growled.

"Look out, mister," said the tender-hearted Ozzie B. to the Italian, "watch this here dog, Bonaparte; he's terrible 'bout fightin'. He'll eat yo' monkey if he gets a chance."

"Monk he noo 'fear'd ze dog," grinned the Italian. "Monk he whup ze dog."

"Vot's dat?" exclaimed Billy Buch —"Vot's dat, man, you say? Mine Gott, I bet ten to one dat Ponyparte eats him oop!"

To prove it Bonaparte ran at the monkey savagely.

But the monkey ran up on the Italian's shoulder, where he grinned at the dog.

The Italian smiled. Then he ran his hand into a dirty leathern belt which he carried around his waist — and slowly counted out some gold coins. With a smile fresh as the skies of Italy, full of all sweetness, gentleness and suavity:

" Cover zees, den, py Gar! "

Billy gasped and grasped Jud around the neck where he clung, with his Dutch smile frozen on his lips. Jud, with collapsed under jaw, looked sheepishly around. Bonaparte tried to stand, but he, too, sat down in a heap.

The crowd cheered the Italian.

" We will do it, suh," said Jud, who was the first to recover, and who knew he would get his part of it from Billy.

" Ve vill cover eet," said Billy, with ashen face.

" We will! " barked Bonaparte, recovering his equilibrium and snarling at the monkey.

There was a sob and a wail on the outskirts of the crowd.

" Oh, don't let him kill the monkey — oh, don't! "

It was Ozzie B.

Archie B. ran hastily around to him, made a cross mark in the road with his toe and spat in it.

" You're a fool as usual, Ozzie B.," he said, shaking his brother. " Can't you see that Italian knows what he's about? If he'd risk that twenty, much as he loves money, he'd risk his soul. *Venture pee-wee under the bridge — bam — bam — bam!* "

Ozzie B. grew quieter. Somehow, what Archie B. said always made things look differently. Then Archie B. came up and whispered in his ear: " I'm fur the monkey — the Lord is on his side."

Ozzie B. thought this was grand.

Then Archie B. hunted for his Barlow pocket knife. Around his neck, tied with a string, was a small greasy, dirty bag, containing a piece of gum asafœtida and a ten-dollar gold piece. The asafœtida was worn to keep off contagious diseases, and the gold piece, which represented all his earthly possessions, had been given him by his grandmother the year she died.

Archie B. was always ready to " swap sight under seen." He played marbles for keeps, checkers for apples, ran foot-races for stakes, and even learned his Sunday School lessons for prizes.

The Italian still stood, smiling, when a small redheaded boy came up and touched him on the arm. He put a ten-dollar gold piece into the Italian's hand.

" Put this in for me, mister — an' make 'em put up a hundred mo'. I want some of that lucre."

The Italian was touched. He patted Archie B.'s head:

" Breens," he said, " breens uppa da."

Again he shook the gold in the face of Jud and Bill.

" Now bring on ze ten to one, py Gar! "

The cheers of the crowd nettled Billy and Jud.

" Jes' wait till we come back," said Jud. " ' He laughs bes' who laughs las'. ' "

They retired for consultation.

Bonaparte followed.

Within the bar-room they wiped the cold perspiration from their faces and looked speechlessly into each other's eyes. Billy spoke first.

" Mine Gott, but we peek it oop in de road, Jud? "

" It seems that way to me — a dead cinch."

Bonaparte was positive — only let him get to the monkey, he said with his wicked eyes.

Billy looked at Bonaparte, big, swarthy, sinewy and savage. He thought of the little monkey.

" Dees is greet! — dees is too goot! — Jud, we peek it oop in de road, heh? "

" I'm kinder afraid we'll wake an' find it a dream, Billy — hurry up. Get the cash."

Billy was thoughtful: " Tree hun'd'd dollars — Jud — eef — eef —" he shook his head.

" Now, Billy," said Jud patronizingly —" that's nonsense. Bonaparte will eat him alive in two minutes. Now, he bein' my dorg, jes' you put up the coin an' let me in on the ground floor. I'll pay it back — if we lose —" he laughed. " *If* we lose — it's sorter like sayin' if the sun don't rise."

" Dat ees so, Jud, we peek eet oop in de road. But eef we don't peek eet oop, Billy ees pusted! "

" Oh," said Jud, " it's all like takin' candy from your own child."

The news had spread and a crowd had gathered to see the champion dog of the Tennessee Valley eat up a monkey. All the loafers and ne'er-do-wells of Cottontown were there. The village had known no such excitement since the big mill had been built.

They came up and looked sorrowfully at the monkey,

as they would look in the face of the dead. But, considering that he had so short a time to live, he returned the grin with a reverence which was sacreligious.

"So han'sum — so han'sum," said Uncle Billy Caldwell, the squire. "So bright an' han'sum an' to die so young!"

"It's nothin' but murder," said another.

This proved too much for Ozzie B.—

"Don't — d-o-n-'t — let him kill the monkey," he cried.

There was an electric flash of red as Archie B. ran around the tree and kicked the sobs back into his brother.

"Just wait, Ozzie B., you fool."

"For — what?" sobbed Ozzie.

"For what the monkey does to Bonaparte," he shouted triumphantly.

The crowd yelled derisively: "*What the monkey does to Bonaparte — that's too good?*"

"Boy," said Uncle Billy kindly —"don't you know it's ag'in nachur — why, the dorg'll eat him up!"

"That's rot," said Archie B. disdainfully. Then hotly: "Yes, it wus ag'in nachur when David killed Goliath — when Sampson slew the lion, and when we licked the British. Oh, it wus ag'in nachur then, but it looks mighty nach'ul now, don't it? Jes' you wait an' see what the monkey does to Bonaparte. I tell you, Uncle Billy, the Lord's on the monkey's side — can't you see it?"

Uncle Billy smiled and shook his head. He was interrupted by low laughter and cheers. A villager had drawn a crude picture on a white paste-board and was

showing it around.   A huge dog was shaking a lifeless
monkey and under it was written:

"What Bonaparte Done To The Monkey!"

Archie B. seized it and spat on it derisively: "Oh,
well, that's the way of the worl'," he said.   "God makes
one wise man to see befo', an' a million fools to see afterwards."

The depths of life's mysteries have never yet been
sounded, and one of the wonders of it all is that one
small voice praying for flowers in a wilderness of thorns
may live to see them blossom at his feet.

"I've seed stranger things than that," remarked Uncle Billy thoughtfully.   "The boy mout be right."

And now Jud and Billy were seen coming out of the
store, with their hands full of gold.

"Eet's robbery — eet's stealin' "— winked Billy at
the crowd —" eet's like takin' it from a babe —"

With one accord the crowd surged toward the back
lot, where Bonaparte, disgusted with the long delay,
had lain down on a pile of newly-blown leaves and slept.
Around the lot was a solid plank fence, with one gate
open, and here in the lot, sound asleep in the sunshine,
lay the champion.

The Italian brought along the monkey in his arms.
Archie B. calmly and confidently acting as his bodyguard.   Jud walked behind to see that the monkey did
not get away, and behind him came Ozzie B. sobbing in
his hiccoughy way:

"Don't let him kill the po' little thing!"

He could go no farther than the gate.   There he
stood weeping and looking at the merciless crowd.

Bonaparte was still asleep on his pile of leaves. Jud would have called and wakened him, but Archie B. said: " Oh, the monkey will waken him quick enough — let him alone."

In the laugh which followed, Jud yielded and Archie B. won the first blood in the battle of brains.

The crowd now stood silent and breathless in one corner of the lot. Only Ozzie B.'s sobs were heard. In the far corner lay Bonaparte.

The Italian stooped, and unlinking the chain of the monkey's collar, sat him on the ground and, pointing to the sleeping dog, whispered something in Italian into his pet's ear.

The crowd scarcely drew its breath as it saw the little animal slipping across the yard to its death.

Within three feet of the dog he stopped, then springing quickly on Bonaparte, with a screeching, blood-curdling yell, grabbed his stump of a tail in both hands, and as the crowd rushed up, they heard its sharp teeth close on Bonaparte's most sensitive member with the deadly click of a steel trap.

The effect was instantaneous. A battery could not have brought the champion to his feet quicker. With him came the monkey — glued there — a continuation of the dog's tail.

Around and around went Bonaparte, snarling and howling and making maddening efforts to reach the monkey. But owing to the shortness of Bonaparte's tail, the monkey kept just out of reach, its hind legs braced against the dog, its teeth and nails glued to the two inches of tail.

Around and around whirled Bonaparte, trying to throw off the things which had dropped on him, seemingly, from the skies. His growls of defiance turned to barks, then to howls of pain and finally, as he ran near to Archie B., he was heard to break into yelps of fright as he broke away dashing around the lot in a whirlwind of leaves and dust.

The champion dog was running!

" Sick him, Bonaparte, grab him — turn round an' grab him! " shouted Jud pale to his eyes, and shaking with shame.

" Seek heem, Ponyparte — O mine Gott, seek him," shouted Billy.

Jud rushed and tried to head the dog, but the champion seemed to have only one idea in his head — to get away from the misery which brought up his rear.

Around he went once more, then seeing the gate open, he rushed out, knocking Ozzie B. over into the dust, and when the crowd rushed out, nothing could be seen except a cloud of dust going down the village street, in the hind most cloud of it a pair of little red coat tails flapping in the breeze.

Then the little red coat tails suddenly dropped out of the cloud of dust and came running back up the road to meet its master.

Jud watched the vanishing cloud of dust going toward the distant mountains.

" My God — not Bonaparte — not the champion," he said.

Billy stood also looking with big Dutch tears in his

eyes. He watched the cloud of dust go over the distant hills. Then he waved his hand sadly —

"Goot-pye, mine bac'n!"

The monkey came up grinning triumphantly.

Thinking he had done something worthy of a penny, he added to Billy Buch's woe by taking off his comical cap and passing it around for a collection.

He was honest in it, but the crowd took it as irony, and amid their laughter Jud and Billy slipped away.

Uncle Billy, the stake-holder, in handing the money over to the Italian, remarked:

"Wal, it don't look so much ag'in nachur now, after all."

"Breens uppa dar"—smiled the Italian as he put ten eagles into Archie B.'s hand. All of which made Archie B. vain, for the crowd now cheered him as they had jeered before.

"Come, let's go, Ozzie B.," he said. "They ain't no man livin' can stand too much heroism."

CHAPTER XXV

A RCHIE B. trotted off, striking a path leading
through the wood. It was a near cut to the
log school house which stood in an old field,
partly grown up in scrub-oaks and bushes.

Down in the wood, on a clean bar where a mountain
stream had made a bed of white sand, he stopped, pulled
off his coat, counted his gold again with eyes which
scarcely believed it yet, and then turned handsprings
over and over in the white sand.

This relieved him of much of the suppressed steam
which had been under pressure for two hours. Then
he sat down on a log and counted once more his gold.

Ozzie B., pious, and now doubly so at sight of his
brother's wealth, stood looking over his shoulder:

" It was the good Lord done it," he whispered reverently, as he stood and looked longingly at the gold.

" Of course, but I helped at the right time, that's the
way the Lord does everything here."

Then Archie B. went down into his coat pocket and
brought out a hollow rubber ball, with a small hole in
one end. Ozzie B. recognized his brother's battery of
Gypsy Juice.

" How — when, oh, Archie B.! "

" -S-h-h — Ozzie B. It don't pay to show yo' hand

even after you've won — the other feller might remember it nex' time. 'Taint good business sense. But I pumped it into Bonaparte at the right time when he was goin' round an' round an' undecided whether he'd take holt or git. This settled him — he got. The Lord was on the monkey's side, of course, but He needed Gypsy Juice at the right time."

Then he showed Ozzie B. how it was done. " So, with yo' hand in yo' pocket — so! Then here comes Bonaparte round an' round an' skeered mighty nigh to the runnin' point. So — then sczit! It wus enough."

Ozzie B. shuddered: " You run a terrible risk doin' that. They'd have killed you if they'd seen it, Jud an' Billy. An' all yo' money up too."

" Of course," said his brother, " but Ozzie B., when you bluff, bluff bold; when you bet, bet big; when you steal, steal straight."

Ozzie B. shook his head. Then he looked up at the sun high above the trees.

He sprang up from the log, pale and scared.

" Archie B.— Archie B., jes' look at the sun! It must be 'leven o'clock an — an think what we'll ketch for bein' late at school. Oh, but I clean forgot — oh — "

He started off trembling.

" Hold on, hold on!" said his brother running and catching Ozzie B. in the coat collar. " Now you sho'ly ain't goin' to be sech a fool as that? It's too late to go now; we'll only ketch a whuppin'. We are goin' to play hookey to-day."

But Ozzie B. only shook his head. " That's wrong

— so wrong. The Lord — He will not bless us — maw says so. Oh, I can't, Archie B."

"Now look here, Ozzie B. The Lord don't expec' nobody but a fool to walk into a tan-hidin'. If you go to school now, old Triggers will tan yo' hide, see? Then he'll send word to paw an' when you get home to-night you'll git another one."

"Maw said I was to allers do my duty. Oh, I can't tell him a lie!"

"You've got to lie, Ozzie B. They's times when everybody has got to lie. Afterwards when it's all over an' understood they can square it up in other ways. When a man or 'oman is caught and downed it's all over — they can't tell the truth then an' get straight — an' there's no come ag'in! But if they lie an' brazen it out they'll have another chance yet. Then's the time to stop lyin'— after yo' ain't caught."

"Oh, I can't," said Ozzie B., trying to pull away. "I must — must go to school."

"Rats "— shouted Archie B., seizing him with both hands and shaking him savagely —" here I am argu'in' with you about a thing that any fool orter see when I cu'd a bin yonder a huntin' for that squirrel nest I wus tellin' you about. Now what'll happen if you go to school? Ole Triggers 'll find out where you've been an' what adoin'— he'll lick you. Paw 'll know all about it when you git home — he'll lick you."

Ozzie B. only shook his head: "It's my duty — hate to do it, Archie B.— but it's my duty. If the Lord wills me a lickin' for tellin' the truth, I'll, I'll hafter take it —" and he looked very resigned.

" Oh, you're playin' for martyrdom again! "

" There was Casabianca, Archie B.— him that stood on the burnin' deck "— he ventured timidly.

" Tarnashun! " shouted his brother —" an' I hope he is still standin' on a burnin' deck in the other worl'— don't mention that fool to me! — to stay there an' git blowed up after the ship was afire an' his dad didn't sho' up." He spat on a mark: " *Venture pee-wee under the bridge — bam — bam — bam.*"

" There was William Tell's son," ventured his brother again.

" Another gol-darn id'jut, Ozzie B., like his dad that put him up to it. Why, if the ole man had missed, the two would'er gone down in history as the champion ass an' his colt. The risk was too big for the odds. Why, he didn't have one chance in a hundred. Besides, them fellers actin' the fool don't hurt nobody but theyselves. Now you —"

" How's that, Archie B.? "

Archie B. lowered his voice to a gentle persuasive whisper: " Don't do it, ole man — come now — be reasonable. If we stay here in the woods, Triggers 'll think we're at home. Dad will think we're in school. They'll never know no better. It's wrong, but we'll have plenty o' time to make it right — we've got six months mo' of school this year. Now, if you do go — you'll be licked twice an' — an', Ozzie B., I'll git licked when paw hears of it to-night."

" Oh," said Ozzie B., " that's it, is it? "

" Yes, of course; if a man don't look out for his own

24

hide, whose goin' to do it for him? Come now, ole man."

Ozzie B. was silent. His brother saw the narrow forehead wrinkling in indecision. He knew the different habits — not principles — of his nature were at work for mastery. Finally the hypocrite habit prevailed, when he said piously: "We have sowed the wind, Archie B.— we'll hafter reap the whirlwind, like paw says."

"Go!" shouted his brother. "Go!" and he helped him along with a kick —"Go, since I can't save you. You'll reap the whirlwind, but I won't if my brains can save me."

He sat down on a log and watched his brother go down the path, sobbing as usual, when he felt that he was a martyr. He sat long and thought.

"It's bad," he sighed —"a man cu'd do so much mo' in life if he didn't hafter waste so much time arguin' with fools. Well, I'm here fur the day an' I'll learn somethin'. Now, I wanter know if one squirrel er two squirrels stays in the same hole in winter. Then there's the wild-duck. I wanter kno' when the mallards go south."

In a few minutes he had hid himself behind a tree in a clump of brush. He was silent for ten minutes, so silent that only the falling leaves could be heard. Then very cautiously he imitated the call of the gray squirrel — once, twice, and still again. He had not long to wait. In a hole high up in a hickory a little gray head popped out — then a squirrel came out cautiously — first its head, then half of its body, and each time it moved looking and listening, with its cunning, bright eyes, taking in everything. Then it frisked out with a flirt of its tail, and sat on a limb nearby. It was followed by another and another. Archie B. watched them for a half hour, a satisfied smile playing around his lips. He was studying squirrel. He saw them run into the hole again and bring out each a nut and sit on a nearby limb and eat it.

"That settles that," he said to himself. "I thought they kept their nuts in the same hole."

There was the sound of voices behind him and the squirrels vanished. Archie B. stood up and saw an old man and some children gathering nuts.

"It's the Bishop an' the little mill-mites. I'll bet they've brought their dinner."

This was the one thing Archie B. needed to make his day in the woods complete.

"Hello," he shouted, coming up to them.

"Why, it's Archie B.," said Shiloh, delighted.

"Why, it is," said her grandfather. "What you doin', Archie B.?"

"Studyin' squirrels right now. What you all doin'?"

"I've tuck the kids out of the mill an' I'm givin' 'em their fus' day in the woods. Shiloh, there, has been mighty sick and is weak yet, so we're goin' slow. Mighty glad to run upon you, Archie B. Can't you sho' Shiloh the squirrels? She's never seed one yet, have you, pet?"

"No," said Shiloh thoughtfully. "Is they like them little jorees that say *Wake-up, pet! Wake-up, pet?*

Oh, do sho' me the squirrel! 'Mattox, ain't this jes' fine, bein' out of the mill?'"

Archie B.'s keen glance took in the well-filled lunch basket. At once he became brilliantly entertaining. In a few minutes he had Shiloh enraptured at the wood-lore he told her,— even Bull Run and Seven Days, Atlanta and Appomattox were listening in amazement, so interesting becomes nature's story when it finds a reader.

And so all the morning Archie B. went with them, and never had they seen so much and enjoyed a day as they had this one.

And the lunch — how good it tasted! It was a new life to them. Shiloh's color came in the healthful exercise, and even Bull Run began to look out keenly from his dull eyes.

After lunch Shiloh went to sleep on a soft carpet of Bermuda grass with the old man's coat for a blanket, while the other children waded in the branch, and gathered nuts till time to go back home.

It was nearly sun-down when they reached the gate of the little hut on the mountain.

"We must do this often, Archie B," said the Bishop, as the children went in, tired and hungry, leaving him and Archie B. at the gate. "I've never seed the little 'uns have sech a time, an' it mighty nigh made me young ag'in."

All afternoon Archie B. had been thinking. All day he had felt the lumpy, solid thing in the innermost depths of his jeans pocket, which told him one hundred dollars in gold lay there, and that it would need an explanation when he reached home or he was in for the

worst whipping he ever had.   Knowing this, he had not
been thinking all the afternoon for nothing.   The old
man bade him good-night, but still Archie B. lingered,
hesitated, hung around the gate.

"Won't you come in, Archie B.?"

"No-o — thank you, Bishop, but I'd — I'd like to,
really tho', jes' to git a little spirt'ul g'idance"— a
phrase he had heard his father use so often.

"Why, what's the matter, Archie B.?"

Archie B. rubbed his chin thoughtfully.   "I'm — I'm
— thinkin' of j'inin' the church, Bishop."

"Bless yo' h'art — that's right.   I know'd you'd
quit yo' mischeev'us ways an' come in — an' I honor you
fur it, Archie B.— praise the Lord!"

Archie B. still stood pensive and sobered:

"But a thing happened to-day, Bishop, an' it's wor-
ryin' me very much.   It makes me think, perhaps —
I — ain't — ain't worthy of — the bestowal of — the
grace — you know, the kind I heard you speak of?"

"Tell me, Archie B., lad — an' I'll try to enlighten
you in my po' way."

"Well, now; it's this — jes' suppose you wus goin'
along now — say to school, an' seed a dorg, say his
name was Bonaparte, wantin' to eat up a little monkey; an' a lot of fellers, say like Jud Carpenter an'
Billy Buch, a-bettin' he cu'd do it in ten minutes an'
a-sickin' him on the po' little monkey — this big savage
dorg.   An' suppose now you feel sorry for the monkey
an' somethin'— you can't tell what — but somethin'
mighty plain tells you the Lord wus on the monkey's
side — so plain you cu'd read it — like it told David —

an' the dorg wus as mean an' bostful as Goliah wus —"

" Archie B., my son, I'd a been fur the monkey, I sho'
would," said the Bishop impressively.

Archie B. smiled: "Bishop, you've called my hand
— I *wus* for that monkey."

The old man smiled approvingly: "Good — good
— Archie B."

"Now, what happened? I'm mighty inter'sted —
oh, that is good. I'm bettin' the monkey downed him,
the Lord bein' on his side."

"But, s'pose furst," went on Archie B. argumenta-
tively, "that you wanted to give some money fur a
little church that you wanted to j'ine — up on the mountain side, a little po'-fo'k church, that depended on
charity —"

"I understan's, I understan's, Archie B., that wus
the Lord's doin's,— ten to one on the monkey, Archie —
ten to one!"

"An' that you had ten dollars in gold around yo'
neck in a little bag, given you by your ole Granny when
she died — an' knowin' how the Lord wus for the monkey, an' it bein' a dead cinch, an' all that — an' these
fellers blowin' an' offerin' to bet ten to one — an' seein'
you c'ud pick it up in the road — all for the little
church, mind you, Bishop —"

"Archie B.," exclaimed the old man excitedly,
"them bein' the facts an' the thing at stake, with that
ole dorg an' Jud Carpenter at the bottom of it, I'd a
put it up on the monkey, son — fur charity, you know,
an' fur the principle of it,— I'd a put it up, Archie B.,
if I'd lost ever' cent!"

"Exactly, Bishop, an' I did — at ten to one — think of the odds! Ten to one, mighty nigh as great as wus ag'in David."

"An' you won, of course, Archie B., you won in a walk?" said the old man breathlessly. "God was fur you an' the monkey."

Archie B. smiled triumphantly and pulled out his handful of gold. The old man sat down on a log, dazed.

"Archie B., sho'ly, sho'ly, not all that? An' licked the dorg, an' that gang, an' cleaned 'em up?"

Archie B. told him the story with all the quaint histrionic talent of his exuberant nature.

The Bishop sat and laughed till the tears came.

"An' Bonaparte went down the road with the monkey holt his tail — the champion dorg — an' you won all that?"

"All fur charity, Bishop, except, you know, part fur keeps as a kinder nes' egg."

"Of co-u-r-se — Archie B., of — course, no harm in the worl' — if — if — my son — *if you carry out your original ideas*, or promise, ruther; it won't work if you go back on yo' promise to God. 'God moves in a mysterious way his wonders to perform,'" added the Bishop solemnly.

Archie B. slipped fifty of his dollars into the old man's hands.

"Do you know, Archie B., I prayed for this las' night? Now you tell me God don't answer prayers?"

He was silent, touched. Seldom before had a prayer of his been answered so directly.

"Fur charity, Archie B., fur charity. I'll take it, an' little you know what this may mean."

Archie B. was silent. So far so good, but it was plain from his still thoughtful looks that he had only half won out yet. He had heard the old man speak, and there had been a huskiness about his voice.

"Now there is paw, Bishop — you know he ain't jes like you — he don't see so far. He might not under' stan' it. Would you mind jes' droppin' him a line, you know? I'll take it to him — in case he looks at the thing differently, you know, fur whut you write will go a long way with him."

The old man smiled: "Of course, Archie B.— he must understan' it. Of course, it 'ud never do to have him spile as good a thing as that — an' fur charity, all fur the Lord —"

"An' why I didn't go to school, helpin' you all in the woods," put in Archie B.

"Of course, Archie B., why of course, my son; I'll fix it right."

And he scribbled a few lines on the fly leaf of his note book for Archie B. to take home:

"God bless you, my son, good-night."

Archie B. struck out across the fields jingling his remaining gold and whistling. At home it was as he expected. Patsy met him at the gate. One look into her expectant face showed him that she was delighted at the prospect of his punishment. It was her hope deferred, now long unfulfilled. He had always gotten out before, but now —

"Walk in, Mister Gambler, Mr. Hookey — walk in — paw is waitin' fur you," she said, smirking.

The Deacon stood in the door, silent, grim, determined. In his hand were well-seasoned hickories. By him stood his wife more silent, more grim, more determined.

" Pull off yo' coat, Archie B.," said the Deacon, " I'm gwinter lick you fur gamblin'."

" Pull off yo' coat, Archie B.," said his mother, " I'm goin' to lick you fur playin' hookey."

" Pull it off, Archie B.," said his sister bossily, " I'm goin' to stan' by an' see."

Archie B. pulled off his coat deliberately.

" That's all right," he said, " Many a man has been licked befo' fur bein' on the Lord's side."

" You mean to tell me, Archie B. Butts, you bet on a dorg fight sho' nuff," said his father, nervously handling his hickories.

" An' played hookey? " chimed in his mother.

" Tell it, Archie B., tell the truth an' shame the devil," mocked Patsy.

" Yes, I done all that — fur charity," he said boldly, and with a victorious ring in his voice.

" Did you put up that ten dollars yo' Granny lef' you? " screamed his mother.

" Did you dare, Archie B.," said Patsy.

His father paled at the thought of it: " An' lost it, Archie B., lost it, my son. Oh, I mus' teach you how sinful it is to gamble."

Archie B. replied by running his hand deep down

into his pocket and bringing up a handful of gold —
five eagles!

His father dropped the switches and stared. His
mother sat down suddenly in a chair and Patsy reached
out, took it and counted it deliberately:—

"One — two — three — fo'— five — an' all gold —
my gracious, Maw!"

"That's jes' ha'f of it," said Archie B. indifferently.
"I gave the old Bishop five of 'em — fur — charity.
Here's his note."

The Deacon read it and rubbed his chin thoughtfully: "That's a different thing," he said after a
while. "Entirely different proposition, my son."

"Yes, it 'pears to be," said his mother counting the
gold again. "We'll jes' keep three of 'em, Archie B.
They'll come in handy this winter."

"Put on yo' coat, my son," said the Deacon gently.

"Patsy, fetch him in the hot waffles an' syrup — the
lad 'pears to be a leetle tired," said his mother.

"How many whippings did you git, Archie B.?"
whispered his brother as Archie B., after entertaining
the family for an hour, all about the great fight, crawled
into bed: "I got three," went on Ozzie B. "Triggers
fust, then paw, then maw."

"None," said Archie B., as he put his two pieces of
gold under his pillow.

"I can't see why that was," wailed Ozzie B. "I
done nothin' an'— an'— got all — all — the — lickin'!"

"You jes' reaped my whirlwind," sneered his brother
—"All fools do!"

But later he felt so sorry for poor Ozzie B. because he could not lie on his back at all, that he gave him one of his beautiful coins to go to sleep.

CHAPTER XXVI

BEN BUTLER'S LAST RACE

IT was the last afternoon of the fair, and the great race was to come off at three o'clock.

There is nothing so typical as a fair in the Tennessee Valley. It is the one time in the year when everybody meets everybody else. Besides being the harvest time of crops, of friendships, of happy interchange of thought and feeling, it is also the harvest time of perfected horseflesh.

The forenoon had been given to social intercourse, the display of livestock, the exhibits of deft women fingers, of housewife skill, of the tradesman, of the merchant, of cotton — cotton, in every form and shape.

At noon, under the trees, lunch had been spread — a bountiful lunch, spreading as it did from the soft grass of one tree to that of another — as family after family spread their linen — an almost unbroken line of fried chicken, flanked with pickles and salad, and all the rich profusion of the country wife's pantry.

And now, after lunch, the grand stand had been quickly filled, for the fame of the great race had spread up and down the valley, and the valley dearly loved a horse-race.

Five hundred dollars was considered a large purse, but this race was three thousand!

Three thousand! It would buy a farm. It would buy thirty mules, and twice that many steers. It would make a family independent for life.

And to-day it was given to see which one, of three rich men, owned the best horse.

No wonder that everybody for miles around was there.

Sturdy farmers with fat daughters, jaded wives, and lusty sons who stepped awkwardly on everything on the promenade, and in trying to get off stepped on themselves. They went about, with broad, strong, stooping shoulders, and short coats that sagged in the middle, dropping under-jaws, and eyes that were kindly and shrewd.

The town people were better dressed and fed than the country people, and but only half way in fashion between the city and country, yet knowing it not.

The infield around the judges' stand, and in front of the grand-stand, was thronged with surreys and buggies, and filled with ladies and their beaux. A ripple of excitement had gone up when Richard Travis drove up in a tally-ho. It was filled with gay gowns and alive with merriment and laughter, and though Alice Westmore was supposed to be on the driver's box with the owner, she was not there.

Tennesseans were there in force to back Flecker's gelding — Trumps, and they played freely and made much noise. Col. Troup's mare — Trombine — had her partisans who were also vociferous. But Travis's entry, Lizzette, was a favorite, and, when he appeared on the track to warm up, the valley shouted itself hoarse.

Then Flecker shot out of the draw-gate and spun merrily around the track, and Col. Troup joined him with Trombine, and the audience watched the three trotters warm up and shouted or applauded each as it spun past the grand-stand.

Then the starting-judge held up a silk bag in the center of the wire. It held three thousand dollars in gold, and it swung around and then settled, to a shining, shimmering silken sack, swaying the wire as it flashed in the sun.

The starting-judge clanged his bell, but the drivers, being gentlemen, were heedless of rules and drove on around still warming up.

The starting-judge was about to clang again — this time more positively — when there appeared at the draw-gate a new comer, the sight of whose horse and appointments set the grand-stand into a wild roar of mingled laughter and applause.

As he drove demurely on the track, he lifted quaintly and stiffly his old hat and smiled.

He was followed by the village blacksmith, whose very looks told that they meant business and were out for blood. The audience did not like the looks of this blacksmith — he was too stern for the fun they were having. But they recognized the shambling creature who followed him as Bud Billings, and they shouted with laughter when they saw he had a sponge and bucket!

" Bud Billings a swipe! "

Cottontown wanted to laugh, but it was too tired. It merely grinned and nudged one another. For Trav's had given a half holiday and all Cottontown was there.

The old man's outfit brought out the greatest laughter. The cart was a big cheap thing, new and brightly repainted, and it rattled frightfully. The harness was a combination — the saddle was made of soft sheep skin, the wool next to the horse, as were also the head-stall of the bridle, the breast-strap and the breeching. The rest of it was undressed leather, and the old man had evidently made it himself.

But Ben Butler — never had he looked so fine. Blind, cat-hammed and pacing along,— but his sides were slick and hard, his quarters rubber.

The old man had not been training him on the sandy stretches of Sand Mountain for nothing.

A man with half an eye could have seen it, but the funny people in the grand-stand saw only the harness, and the blind sunken eyes of the old horse. So they shouted and cat-called and jeered. The outfit ambled up to the starting judge, and the old driver handed him fifty dollars.

The starter laughed as he recovered himself, and winking at the others, asked:

" What's this for, old man? "

" Oh, jes' thought I'd j'ine in —" smiling.

" Why, you can't do it. What's your authority? "

The Bishop ran his hand in his pocket, while Bud held Ben Butler's head and kept saying with comical seriousness: " Whoa — whoa, sah! "

Pending it all, and seeing that more talk was coming, Ben Butler promptly went to sleep. Finally the old man brought out a faded poster. It was Travis's challenge and conditions.

" Jes' read it," said the old driver, " an' see if I ain't
under the conditions."

The starting judge read: " *Open to the Tennessee
Valley — trot or pace. Parties entering, other than the
match makers, to pay fifty dollars at the wire.*"

" Phew! " said the starting judge, as he scratched
his head. Then he stroked his chin and re-read the
conditions, looking humorously down over his glasses
at the queer combination before him.

The audience took it in and began to shout: " Let
him in! Let him in! It's fair! "

But others felt outraged and shouted back: " No —
put him out! Put him out! "

The starting judge clanged his bell again, and the
other three starters came up.

Flecker, good-natured and fat, his horse in a warm-
ing-up foam, laughed till he swayed in the sulky. Col.
Troup, dignified and reserved, said nothing. But Travis
swore.

" It's preposterous! — it will make the race a farce.
We're out for blood and that purse. This is no com-
edy," he said.

The old man only smiled and said: " I'm sorry to
spile the sport of gentlemen, but bein' gentlemen, I
know they will stan' by their own rules."

" It's here in black and white, Travis," said the starter,
" You made it yourself."

" Oh, hell," said Travis hotly, " that was mere form
and to satisfy the Valley. I thought the entrance fee
would bar any outsider."

"But it didn't," said the Judge, "and you know the rules."

"Let him start, let the Hill-Billy start!" shouted the crowd, and then there was a tumult of hisses, groans and cat-calls.

Then it was passed from mouth to mouth that it was the old Cottontown preacher, and the excitement grew intense.

It was the most comical, most splendid joke ever played in the Valley. Travis was not popular, neither was the dignified Col. Troup. Up to this time the crowd had not cared who won the purse; nor had they cared which of the pretty trotters received the crown. It meant only a little more swagger and show and money to throw away.

But here was something human, pathetic. Here was a touch of the stuff that made the grand-stand kin to the old man. The disreputable cart, the lifeless, blind old pacer, the home-made harness, the seediness of it all — the pathos.

Here was the quaint old man, who, all his life, had given for others, here was the ex-overseer and the ex-trainer of the Travis stables, trying to win the purse from gentlemen.

"Ten to one," said a prosperous looking man, as he looked quietly on — "the Bishop wants it for charity or another church. Like as not he knows of some poverty-stricken family he's going to feed."

"If that's so," shouted two young fellows who were listening, and who were partisans of Flecker of Ten-

nessee, " if that's the way of it, we'll go over and take
a hand in seeing that he has fair play."

They arose hastily, each shifting a pistol in his pocket, and butted through the crowd which was thronged
around the Judge's stand, where the old man sat quietly
smiling from his cart, and Travis and Troup were talking earnestly.

" Damned if I let Trombine start against such a
combination as that, sah. I'll drive off the track now,
sah — damned if I don't, sah! "

But the two young men had spoken to big fat Flecker
of Tennessee, and he arose in his sulky-seat and said:
" Now, gentlemen, clear the track and let us race. We
will let the old man start. Say, old man," he laughed,
" you won't feel bad if we shut you out the fust heat,
eh? "

" No," smiled the Bishop — " an, I 'spec you will.
Why, the old hoss ain't raced in ten years."

" Oh, say, I thought you were going to say twenty,"
laughed Flecker.

Some rowdy had crowded around the old cart and
attempted to unscrew the axle tap. But some one
reached over the head of the crowd and gripped him
where his shoulder and arm met, and pulled him forward
and twirled him around like a top.

It was enough. It was ten minutes before he could
lift up his arm at all; it felt dead.

" Don't hurt nobody, Jack," whispered the old man,
" be keerful."

The crowd were for the old man. They still shouted

—" Fair play, fair play — let him start," and they came thronging and crowding on the track.

" Clear the track," cried the starting-judge to a deputy sheriff in charge —" I'll let him start."

This set the crowd in a roar.

" Square man," they yelled — " Square man! "

Travis bit his lips and swore.

" Why, damn him," he said, " we'll lose him the first heat. I'll shut him out myself."

" We will, sah, we will! " said Col. Troup.   " But if that rattling contraption skeers my mare, I'll appeal to the National Association, sah.   I'll appeal — sah," and he drove off up the stretch, hotter than his mare.

And now the track was cleared — the grand stand hummed and buzzed with excitement.

It was indeed the greatest joke ever played in the Tennessee Valley. Not that there was going to be any change in the race, not that the old preacher had any chance, driving as he did this bundle of ribs and ugliness, and hitched to such a cart — but that he dared try it at all, and against the swells of horsedom.   There would be one heat of desperate fun and then —

A good-natured, spasmodic gulp of laughter ran clear through the grand-stand, and along with it, from excited groups, from the promenade, from the track and infield and stables, even, came such expressions as these:

" Worth ten dollars to see it! "

" Wouldn't take a hoss for the sight! "

" If he *did* happen to beat that trio of sports! "

" Boss, it's gwinter to be a hoss race from wire to wire! "

"Oh, pshaw! one heat of fun — they'll shut him out!"

In heart, the sympathy of the crowd was all with the old preacher.

The old man had a habit when keyed to high pitch, emotionally, of talking to himself. He seemed to regard himself as a third person, and this is the way he told it, heat by heat:

"Fus' heat, Ben Butler — Now if we can manage to save our distance an' leave the flag a few yards, we'll be doin' mighty well. Long time since you stretched them ole muscles of yo's in a race — long time —an' they're tied up and sore. Ever' heat'll be a wuck out to you till you git hot. If I kin only stay in till you git hot — (*Clang — clang — clang*). That's the starter's bell. Yes — we'll score now — the fus' heat'll be our wuss. They've got it in fur us — they'll set the pace an' try to shet us out an', likely es not, do it. God he'p us — Shiloh — Cap'n Tom — it's only for them, Ben Butler — fur them. (*Clang! — Clang!*) Slow there — heh — heh — Steady — ah-h!"

Clang — clang-clang! vigorously. The starter was calling them back.

They had scored down for the first time, but the hotheads had been too fast for the old ambler. In their desire to shut him out, they rushed away like a whirlwind. The old pacer followed, rocking and rolling in his lazy way. He wiggled, shuffled, skipped, and when the strain told on the sore old muscles, he winced, and was left at the wire!

The crowd jeered and roared with laughter.

" He'll never get off! "

" He's screwed there — fetch a screw driver! "

" Pad his head, he'll fall on it nex'! "

" Go back, gentlemen, go back," shouted the starter, " and try again. The old pacer was on a break "— *Clang — clang — clang!* and he jerked his bell vigorously.   •

Travis was furious as he drove slowly back. " I had to pull my mare double to stop her," he called to the starter. " We were all aligned but the old pacer — why didn't you let us go? "

" Because I am starting these horses by the rules, Mr. Travis. I know my business," said the starter hotly.

Col. Troup was blue in the face with rage.

Flecker laughed.

They all turned again and came down, the numbers on the drivers' arms showing 1, 2, 3, 4 — Travis, Troup, Flecker, and the old Bishop, respectively.

" Ben Butler, ole hoss, this ain't no joke — you mus' go this time. We ain't goin' to meetin' — Stretch them ole legs as you did! — oh, that's better — ef we could only score a few more times — look! — ah! "

Clang — clang — clang!

This time it was Col. Troup's mare. She broke just at the wire.

" She saved us that time, Ben Butler. We wus two rods behind — "

They came down the third time. " Now, thank God, he's jes' beginnin' to unlimber," chuckled the old man as the old pacer, catching on to the game and warming to his work, was only a length behind at the wire, as they scored the fourth time, when Flecker's mare flew up in the air and again the bell clanged.

The crowd grew impatient. The starter warned them that time was up and that he'd start them the next time they came down if he had the ghost of a chance.

Again they aligned and came thundering down. The old man was pale and silent, and Ben Butler felt the lines telegraphing nervous messages to his bitted mouth; but all he heard was: "*Shiloh — Cap'n Tom — Steady, old hoss!*"

"Go!"

It sounded like a gun-shot in the old man's ears. There was a whirr of wheels, a patter of feet grappling with dirt and throwing it all over him — another whirr and flutter and buzz as of a covey flushed, and the field was off, leaving him trailing.

"Whew, Ben Butler, we're in fur it now — the Lord 'a-mussy on our souls! Take the pole — s'artenly,— it's all yowin, since you're behin'! Steady ole hoss, there's one consolation,— they're breakin' the wind for you, an' thank God! — yes Ben Butler, look! they're after one other,— they're racin' like Tam O'Shanter an' cookin' each other to a gnat's heel — Oh, Lord what fools! It'll tell on 'em — if we can only save our distance — this heat — jes' save our distance — Wh-o-p, sah! Oh, my Lord, told you so — Troup's mare's up an' dancin' like a swamp rabbit by moonlight. Who-op, sah, steady ole hoss — there now we've passed him — Trombine and Lizette ahead — steady — let 'em go, big devil, little devil, an' pumpin' each other — Go now, go old hoss, now's the time to save our distance — go old hoss, step lively now — 'tain't no meetin', no Sunday School — it's life, bread and a chance for Cap'n Tom! Oh, but you ain't forgot entirely, no-no,— ain't forgot that you come in answer to prayer, ain't forgot that half in one-one, ain't forgot yo' pious raisin', yo' pedigree. Ain't forgot you're racin' for humanity an' a chance, ain't forgot — there! the flag — my God and safe!"

He had passed the flag. Lizzette and Trombine were already at the wire, but poor Troup — his mare had never been able to settle after her wild break, and she caught the flag square in the face.

The crowd met the old pacer with a yell of delight. He had not been shut out — marvel of marvels!

It was getting interesting indeed.

Bud and Jack met him with water and a blanket. How proud they were! But the heavy old cart had told on Ben Butler. He panted like a hound, he staggered and was distressed.

" He'll get over that," said the old driver cheerily to Bud's tearful gaze—" he ain't used to it yet—ten years, think of it," and Jack led Ben Butler blanketed away.

The old man looked at the summary the judges had hung up. It was:

1st Heat: Trumps, 1st; Lizzette, 2nd; Ben Butler, 3rd; Trombine distanced. Time, 2 :17½.

Then he heard a man swearing elegantly. It was Col. Troup. He was sitting in his sulky in front of the grand stand and talking to Travis and the genial Flecker:

" A most unprofessional thing, gentlemen,— damned

unprofessional, sah, to shut me out. Yes, sah, to shut out a gentleman, sah, an' the first heat, sah, with his horse on a break."

"What!" said Flecker excitedly — "you, Col'nel? Shut out — why, I thought it was the old pacer."

"I swear I did, too, Colonel," said Travis apologetically. "I heard something rattling and galloping along — I thought it was the old pacer and I drove like the devil to shut him out!"

"It was me, sah, me! damned unprofessional, sah; my mare throwed a boot!"

He walked around and swore for ten minutes. Then he quieted down and began to think. He was shut out — his money was gone. But — "By gad, sah," he said cracking his whip — "By gad I'll do it!"

Ten minutes later as Ben Butler, cooled and calm, was being led out for the second heat, Col. Troup puffed boisterously up to the Bishop: "Old man, by gad, sah, I want you to use my sulky and harness. It's a hundred pounds lighter than that old ox-cart you've got. I'm goin' to he'p you, sah, beat that pair of short dogs that shets out a gentleman with his horse on a break, sah!"

And that was how the old man drew first blood and came out in a new sulky and harness.

How proud Ben Butler seemed to feel! How much lighter and how smoothly it ran!

They got the word at the first score, Trumps and Lizzette going at it hammer and tongs — Ben Butler, as usual, trailing.

The old man sat pale and ashy, but driving like the born reinsman that he was.

"Steady, old hoss, steady agin '— jes' save our distance, that's all — they've done forgot us — done forgot us — don't know we're here. They'll burn up each other an' then, oh, Ben Butler, God he'p us! Cap'n Tom, Cap'n Tom an' Shiloh! Steady, whoa there! — Lord, how you're lar'nin' ! How the old clip is comin' agin! Ho — hi — there ole hoss — here we are — what a bresh of speed he's got — hi — ho!"

And the grand-stand was cheering again, and as the old man rode up the judges hung out:

2nd Heat: Trumps, 1st; Lizzette, 2nd; Ben Butler, 3rd. Time, 2:15½.

The old man looked at it in wonder: "Two fifteen an' not shet out, Ben Butler? Only five lengths behind? My God, can we make it — can we make it?"

His heart beat wildly. For the first time he began to hope.

Trumps now had two heats. As the race was best three out of five, one more heat meant that Flecker of Tennessee would win the race and the purse. But when the old man glanced at Trumps, his experienced eye told him the gallant gelding was all out — he was distressed greatly — in a paroxyism of thumps. He glanced at Lizzette. She was breathing freely and was fresh. His heart fell.

"Trumps is done fur, Ben Butler, but Lizzette — what will Travis do? — Ah, ole hoss, we're up ag'in it!"

It was too true, as the next heat proved. Away Trumps and Lizzette went, forgetful of all else, while the old man trailed behind, talking to, soothing, coaxing the old horse and driving him as only a master could.

"They're at it ag'in — ole hoss, what fools! Whoa — steady there! Trumps is done fur, an' you'll see — No sand left in his crops, cooked — watch an' see, oh, my, Ben Butler — there — he's up now — up an' done fur — Go now — move some — hi —"

Trumps and Lizzette had raced it out to the head of the stretch. But Trumps was not equal to the clip which Travis had made cyclonic, knowing the horse was sadly distressed. Trumps stood it as long as flesh and blood could, and then jumped into the air, in a heartbroken, tired break. It was then that the old man began to drive, and moving like well-balanced machinery, the old pacer caught again the spirit of his youth, as the old time speed came back, and leaving Trumps behind he even butted his bull-dog nose into the seat of Lizzette's sulky, and clung determinedly there, right up to the wire, beaten only by a length.

Lizzette had won the heat. The judge hung out:

3rd Heat: Lizzette, 1st; Ben Butler, 2nd; Trumps distanced. Time, 2:20.

Lizzette had won, but the crowd had begun to see.

"The old pacer — the old pacer!" — they yelled.

Travis bit his lip —"what did it all mean? He had won the heat. Trumps was shut out, and there they were yelling for the old pacer!"

The Bishop was pale to the roots of his hair when he got out of the sulky.

"Great hoss! great! great!" yelled Bud as he trotted along bringing the blanket.

The old man bowed his head in the sulky-seat, a moment, amid the crash of the band and the noise of the crowd:

" Dear God — my Father — I thank Thee. Not for me — not for Ben Butler — but for life — life — for Shiloh — and Cap'n Tom. Help us — old and blind — help us ! O God —"

Col. Troup grasped his hand. The Tennesseans, followers of Flecker, flocked around him. Flecker, too, was there — chagrined, maddened — he too had joined his forces with the old Bishop.

" Great Scott, old man, how you do drive ! We've hedged on you — me and the Colonel — we've put up a thousand each that you'll win. We've cooked ourselves good and hard. Now drive from hell to breakfast next heat, and Travis is yo' meat ! Fools that we were ! We've cut each other to pieces like a pair of cats tied by the tails. Travis is at your mercy."

" Yes, sah, Flecker is right. Travis is yo' meat, sah," said the Colonel, solemnly.

The old man walked around with his lips moving silently, and a great pulsing, bursting, gripping pain in his heart — a pain which was half a hope and half despair.

The crowd was on tip-toe. Never before had such a race been paced in the Tennessee Valley. Could he take the next heat from Lizzette? If he could, he had her at his mercy.

Grimly they scored down. Travis sullen that he had to fight the old pacer, but confident of shutting him out this time. Confident and maddened. The old man,

as was his wont in great emergencies, had put a bullet
in his mouth to clinch his teeth on. He had learned it
from Col. Jeremiah Travis, who said Jackson did it
when he killed Dickinson, and at Tallapoosa, and at
New Orleans.

"GO!"

And he heard Travis whirl away with a bitter curse
that floated back. Then the old man shot out in the
long, stealing, time-eating stride the old pacer had, and
coming up just behind Lizzette's sulky he hung there in
a death struggle.

One quarter, half, three-quarters, and still they swung
around — locked — Travis bitter with hot oaths and the
old man pale with prayer. He could see Travis's eyes
flashing lightning hatred across the narrow space between them — hatred, curses, but the old man prayed on.

"The flag — now — ole hoss — for Jesus' sake! —"

He reached out in the old way, lifted his horse by
sheer great force and fairly flung him ahead! —

"Flu-r-r-r!" it was Lizzette's breath as he went
by her. He shot his eyes quickly sideways as she
flailed the air with her forefeet within a foot of his
head. Her eyes glowed, sunken,— beat — in their
sockets; with mouth wide open, collapsed, frantic, in
heart-broken dismay, she wabbled, staggered and quit!

"Oh, God bless you, Ben Butler! —"

But that instant in the air with her mouth wide open
within a foot of the old man's head her lower teeth
exposed, the old driver saw she was only four years old.
Why had he noticed it? What mental telepathy in

great crises cause us to see the trifles on which often the destiny of our life hangs?

Ben Butler, stubborn, flying, was shaking his game old head in a bull-dog way as he went under the wire. It maddened him to be pulled up.

" So, softly, softly old fellow! We've got 'em licked, you've got religin' in yo' heels, too. Ain't been goin' to church for ten years for nothin'! "

The old man wanted to shout, and yet he was actually shedding tears, talking hysterically and trembling all over. He heard in a dazed way the yells and thunder from the grand-stand. But he was faint and dizzy, and worst of all, as he laughed to himself and said: " Kinder sissy an' soft in spots."

Jack and Bud had Ben Butler and were gone. No wonder the grand-stand pulsed with human emotion. Never before had anything been done like this. The old, blind pacer,— the quaint old preacher — the thing they were going to shut out,— the pathos, the splendor of it all,— shook them as humanity will ever be shaken when the rejected stone comes up in the beauty of purest marble. Here it was:

4th Heat: Ben Butler, 1st; Lizzette, 2nd. Time, 2:19½.

What a record it was for the old pacer! Starting barely able to save his distance, he had grown in speed and strength and now had the mare at his mercy — the two more heats he had yet to win would be a walk around for him.

Oh, it was glorious — glorious!

" Oh, by gad, sah," shouted Col. Troup, pompously.

"I guess I've hedged all right. Travis will pay my thousand. He'll know how to shet out gentlemen the nex' time. Oh, by gad, sah!"

Flecker and the Tennesseans took drinks and shouted themselves hoarse.

Then the old preacher did something, but why he never could explain. It seemed intuition when he thought of it afterwards. Calling Col. Troup to him he said: "I'm kinder silly an' groggy, Col'nel, but I wish you'd go an' look in her mouth an' see how old Lizzette is."

The Colonel looked at him, puzzled.

"Why?"

"Oh, I dunno, Col'nel — but when a thing comes on me that away, maybe it's because I'm so nervous an' upsot, but somehow I seem to have a second sight when I git in this fix. I wanted you to tell me."

"What's it got to do with the race, sah! There is no bar to age. Have you any susp —"

"Oh, no — no — Col'nel, it's jes' a warnin', an intuition. I've had 'em often, it's always from God. I b'leeve it's Him tellin' me to watch, watch an' pray. I had it when Ben Butler come, thar, come in answer to prayer —"

Colonel Troup smiled and walked off. In a short while he sauntered carelessly back:

"Fo' sah, she was fo' years old this last spring."

"Thank ye, Col'nel!"

The Colonel smiled and whispered: "Oh, how cooked she is! Dead on her feet, dead. Don't drive yo' ole pacer hard — jes' walk around him, sah. Do as you please, you've earned the privilege. It's yo' walk over an' yo' money."

The fifth heat was almost a repetition of the fourth, the old pacer beating the tired mare cruelly, pacing her to a standstill.   It was all over with Lizzette, anyone could see that.   The judges hung out:

5th Heat: Ben Butler, 1st; Lizzette, 2nd.   Time, 2:24.

Travis's face was set, set in pain and disappointment when he went to the stable. He looked away off, he saw no one. He smoked. He walked over to the stall where they were cooling Lizzette out.

" Take the full twenty minutes to cool her, Jim."

In the next stall stood Sadie B.   She had been driven around by Jud Carpenter, between heats, to exercise her, he had said.   She was warmed up, and ready for speed.

Travis stood watching Lizzette cool out. Jud came up and stood looking searchingly at him.   There was but a glance and a nod, and Travis walked over to the grand-stand, light-hearted and even jolly, where he stood in a group of society folks.

He was met by a protest of feminine raillery: " Oh, our gloves, our candy!   Oh, Mr. Travis, to get beat that way!"

He laughed: " I'll pay all you ladies lose. I was just playing with the old pacer. Bet more gloves and candy on the next heat!"

" Oh — oh," they laughed. " No — no-o! We've seen enough!"

Travis smiled and walked off. He turned at the gate and threw them back a bantering kiss.

" You'll see —" was all he said.

The old man spent the twenty minutes helping to rub off Ben Butler.

" It does me good — kinder unkeys me," he said to Bud and Jack. He put his ear to the old horses' flank — it pulsed strong and true.

Then he laughed to himself. It vexed him, for it was half hysterical and he kept saying over to himself:

" Holy, holy, holy, Lord God Almighty —
All Thy works shall praise Thy name, in earth and
    sky and sea;
Holy, holy, holy, merciful and mighty —"

Some one touched his arm. It was Jack: " Bishop, Bishop, time's up! We're ready. Do you hear the bell clanging? "

The Bishop nodded, dazed:

" Here, you're kinder feeble, weak an', an' sorter silly. Why, Bishop, you're recitin' poetry —" said Jack apologetically. " A man's gone when he does that — here! "

He had gone to the old man's saddle bags, and brought out his ancient flask.

" Jes' a swaller or two, Bishop," he said coaxingly, as one talking to a child — " Quick, now, you're not yo'self exactly — you've dropped into poetry."

" I guess I am a little teched, Jack, but I don't need that when I can get poetry, sech poetry as is now in me. Jack, do you want to hear the gran'est verse ever writ in poetry? "

"No — no, Bishop, don't! Jack Bracken's yo'
friend, he'll freeze to you. You'll be all right soon.
It's jes' a little spell. Brace up an' drop that stuff."

The old man smiled sadly as if he pitied Jack. Then
he repeated slowly:

"Holy, holy, holy, all the saints adore Thee
  Castin' down their golden crowns around the glassy
    sea;
Cherubim an' Seraphim, fallin' down before Thee
Which wert an' art, an' ever more shall be."

Feebly he leaned on Jack, the tears ran down his
cheek: "'Tain't weakness, Jack, 'tain't that — it's joy,
it's love of God, Whose done so much for me. It's the
glory, glory of them lines — Oh, God — what a line
of poetry!

"Castin' down their golden crowns around the glassy
  sea!"

Ben Butler stood ready, the bell clanged again. Jack
helped him into the sulky; never had he seen the old
man so feeble. Travis was already at the post.

They got the word immediately, but to the old man's
dismay, Travis's mare shot away like a scared doe,
trotting as frictionless as a glazed emery wheel.

The old man shook up Ben Butler and wondered why
he seemed to stand so still. The old horse did his best,
he paced as he never had before, but the flying thing

like a red demon flitted always just before him, a thing with tendons of steel and feet of fire.

"Oh, God, Ben Butler, what is it — what? Have you quit on me, ole hoss? — you, Ben Butler, you that come in answer to prayer? My God, Cap'n Tom, Shiloh!"

And still before him flew the red thing with wings.

At the half, at the three-quarters: "Now ole hoss!" And the old horse responded gamely, grandly. He thundered like a cyclone bursting through a river-bed. Foot by foot, inch by inch, he came up to Travis's mare. Nose to nose they flew along. There was a savage yell — a loud cracking of Travis' whip in the blind horse's ears. Never had the sightless old horse had such a fright! He could not see — he could only hear the terrible, savage yell. Frightened, he forgot, he dodged, he wavered —

"Steady, Ben Butler, don't — oh — "

It was a small trick of Travis', for though the old pacer came with a rush that swept everything before it, the drive had been made too late. Travis had the heat won already.

Still there was no rule against it. He could yell and crack his whip and make all the noise he wished, and if the other horse was frightened, it was the fault of his nerves. Everybody who knew anything of racing knew that.

A perfect tornado of hisses met Travis at the grand-stand.

But he had won the heat! What did he care? He could scarcely stop his mare. She seemed like a bird and as fresh. He pulled her double to make her turn and come back after winning, and as she came she still fought the bit.

As he turned, he almost ran into the old pacer jogging, broken-hearted behind. The mare's mouth was wide open, and the Bishop's trained eye fell on the long tusk-like lower teeth, flashing in the sun.

Startled, he quivered from head to foot. He would not believe his own eyes. He looked closely again. There was no doubt of it — she was eight years old!

In an instant he knew — his heart sank, "We're robbed, Cap'n Tom — Shiloh — my God!"

Travis drove smilingly back, amid hisses and cheers and the fluttering of ladies' handkerchiefs in the boxes.

"How about the gloves and candy now?" he called to them with his cap in his hand.

Above the judges had hung out:

6th Heat: Lizzette, 1st; Ben Butler, 2nd.   Time, 2:14.

When Flecker of Tennessee saw the time hung out, he jumped from his seat exclaiming: "Six heats and the last heat the fastest? Who ever heard of a tired mare cutting ten seconds off that way? By the eternal, but something's wrong there."

"Six heats an' the last one the fastest — By gad, sah," said Col. Troup, "It is strange. That mare Lizzette is a wonder, an' by gad, sah, didn't the old pacer come? By gad, but if he'd begun that drive jus' fifty yards sooner — our money "—

Flecker groaned: "We're gone, Colonel — one thousand we put up and the one we hedged with."

"By gad, sah, but, Flecker, don't you think Lizzette went smoother that last heat? She had a different stride, a different gait."

Flecker had not noticed it. "But it was a small thing," he said —" to frighten the old horse. No rule against it, but a gentleman —"

The Colonel smiled: "Damn such gentlemen, sah. They're a new breed to me."

The old man went slowly back to the stable. He said nothing. He walked dazed, pale, trembling, heart-broken. But never before had he thought so keenly.

Should he expose Travis? —Ruin him, ruin him — here? Then there passed quickly thoughts of Cap'n Tom — of Miss Alice. What a chance to straighten every thing out, right every wrong — to act for Justice, Justice long betrayed — for God. For God? And had not, perhaps, God given him this opportunity for this very purpose? Was not God,— God, the ever merciful but ever just, behind it all? Was it not He who caused him to look at the open mouth of the first mare? Was it not He giving him a chance to right a wrong so long, so long delayed? If he failed to speak out would he not be doing every man in the race a wrong, and Cap'n Tom and Shiloh, and even Miss Alice, so soon to marry this man — how it went through him! —'even God — even God a wrong!

He trembled; he could not walk. He sat down; Jack and Bud had the horse, the outlaw's eyes flashing fire as he led him away. But Bud, poor Bud, he was follow-ing, broken-hearted, blubbering and still saying between his sobs: "Great — hoss — he skeered him!"

The grand-stand sat stupefied, charged to the explosive point with suppressed excitement. Six terrible heats and no horse had won three. But now Lizzette and Ben Butler had two each — who would win the next, the decisive heat. God help the old preacher, for he had no chance. Not after the speed that mare showed.

Colonel Troup came up: "By gad, sah, Bishop — don't give up — you've got one mo' chance. Be as game as the ole hoss."

"We are game, sir — but — but, will you do as I tell you an' swear to me on yo' honor as a gentleman never to speak till I say the word? Will you swear to keep sacred what I show you, until I let you tell?"

The Colonel turned red: "What do you mean, sah?"

"Swear it, swear it, on yo' honor as a gentleman —"

"On my honor as a gentleman, sah? I swear it."

"Go," said the old man quickly, "an' look in the mouth of the mare they are jes' bringin' in — the mare that won that heat. Go, an' remember yo' honor pledged. Go an' don't excite suspicion."

The old man sat down and, as he waited, he thought. Never before had he thought so hard. Never had such a burden been put upon him. When he looked up Colonel Troup stood pale and silent before him — pale with close-drawn lips and a hot, fierce, fighting gleam in his eyes.

"You've explained it, sah —" he said. Then he fumbled his pistol in his pocket. "Now — now, give me back my promise, my word. I have two thousand dollars at stake, and — and clean sport, sah,— clean sport.   Give me back my word."

" Sit down," said the old man quietly.

The Colonel sat down so still that it was painful. He was calm but the Bishop saw how hard the fight was.

Then the old man broke out: " I can't — O God, I can't!   I can't *make* a character, why should I *take* one?   It's so easy to take a word — a nod — it is gone! And if left maybe it 'ud come agin.   Richard Travis — it looks bad — he may be bad — but think what he may do yet — if God but touch him?   No man's so bad but that God can't touch him — change him.   We may live to see him do grand and noble things — an' God will touch him," said the old man hotly, " He will yet."

" If you are through with me," said Colonel Troup, coolly, " and will give me back my promise, I'll go and touch him — yes, damn him, I'll shoot him as he should be."

" But I ain't gwine to give it back," smiled the old man.

Colonel Troup flushed: " What'll you do, then? Let him rob you an' me, sah?   Steal my two thousand, and Flecker's?   Your purse that you've already won — yours — yours, right this minute?   Rob the public in a fake race, sah?   You've won the purse, it is yours, sah.   He forfeited it when he brought out that other mare.   Think what you are doing, sah!"

" Cap'n Tom an' Shiloh, too "— winced the old man. " But I forgot — you don't kno' — yes "— and he smiled triumphantly. " Yes, Col'nel, I'll let him do all that if — if God'll let it be. But God won't let it be ! "

Colonel Troup arose disgusted — hot. " What do you mean, old man. Are you crazy, sah? Give me back my word —"

" Wait — no — no," said the Bishop. " Col'nel, you're a man of yo' word — wait ! "

And he arose and was gone.

The Colonel swore soundly. He walked around and damned everything in sight. He fumbled his pistol in his pocket, and wondered how he could break his word and yet keep it.

There was no way, and he went off to take a drink.

Bud, the tears running down his cheeks — was rubbing Ben Butler down, and saying : " Great hoss — great hoss ! "

Of all, he and the Bishop had not given up.

" I'm afeard we'll have to give it up, Bishop," said Jack.

" Me, me give it up, Jack? Me an' Ben Butler quit like yeller dogs? Why, we're jes' beginnin' to fight — with God's help."

Then he thought a moment : " Fetch me some cotton."

He took it and carefully packed it in the old horse's ears.

" It was a small trick, that yellin' and frightening the ole hoss," said Jack.

" Ben Butler," said the old man, as he stepped back and looked at the horse, " Ben Butler, I've got you now where God's got me — you can't see an' you can't hear. You've got to go by faith, by the lines of faith. But I'll be guidin' 'em, ole hoss, as God guides me — by faith."

The audience sat numbed and nerveless when they scored for the last heat. The old pacer's gallant fight had won them all — and now — now after winning two heats, with only one more to win — now to lose at last. For he could not win — not over a mare as fresh and full of speed as that mare now seemed to be. And she, too, had but one heat to win.

But Col. Troup had been thinking and he stopped the old man as he drove out on the track.

" Been thinkin', parson, 'bout that promise, an' I'll strike a bargain with you, sah. You say God ain't goin' to let him win this heat an' race an' so forth, sah."

The Bishop smiled: " I ain't give up, Col'nel — not yet."

" Well, sah, if God does let Travis win, I take it from yo' reasoning, sah, that he's a sorry sort of a God to stand in with a fraud an' I'll have nothin' to do with Him. I'll tell all about it."

" If that's the way you think — yes," said the old man, solemnly —" yes — tell it — but God will never stan' in with fraud."

" We'll see," said the Colonel. " I'll keep my word if — if — you win! "

Off they went as before, the old pacer hugging the mare's sulky wheels like a demon. Even Travis had time to notice that the old man had done something to

steady the pacer, for how like a steadied ship did he
fly along!

Driving, driving, driving — they flew — they fought
it out. Not a muscle moved in the old man's body.
Like a marble statue he sat and drove. Only his lips
kept moving as if talking to his horse, so close that
Travis heard him: " It's God's way, Ben Butler, God's
way — faith,— the lines of faith —' He leadeth me —
He leadeth me ' ! "

Up — up — came the pacer fearless with frictionless
gait, pacing like a wild mustang-king of the desert,
gleaming in sweat, white covered with dust, rolling like
a cloud of fire. The old man sang soft and low:

" He leadeth me, O blessed thought,
    O word with heavenly comfort fraught,
    Whate'er I do, whate'er I be,
    Still 'tis God's hand that leadeth me."

Inch by inch he came up. And now the home stretch,
and the old pacer well up, collaring the flying mare and
pacing her neck to neck.

Travis smiled hard and cruel as he drew out his whip
and circling it around his head, uttered again, amid
fierce crackling, his Indian yell: " Hi — hi — there —
ho — ha — ho — hi — hi — e — e ! "

But the old pacer swerved not a line, and Travis,
white and frightened now with a terrible, bitter fear
that tightened around his heart and flashed in his eyes
like the first swift crackle of lightning before the blow
of thunder, brought his whip down on his own mare,

welting her from withers to rump in a last desperate
chance.

Gamely she responded and forged ahead — the old
pacer was beaten!

They thundered along, Travis whipping his mare at
every stride. She stood it like the standard-bred she
was, and never winced, then she forged ahead farther,
and farther, and held the old pacer anchored at her
wheels, and the wire not fifty feet away!

There was nothing left for the old man to do — with
tears streaming down his cheeks he shouted —" Ben
Butler, Ben Butler — it's God's way — the chastening
rod— " and his whip fell like a blade of fire on the old
horse's flank.

It stung him to madness. The Bishop striking him,
the old man he loved, and who never struck! He shook
his great ugly head like a maddened bull and sprang savagely at the wire, where the silken thing flaunted in his
face in a burst of speed that left all behind. Nor could
the old man stop him after he shot past it, for his flank
fluttered like a cyclone of fire and presently he went down
on his knees — gently, gently, then — he rolled over!

His driver jumped to the ground. It was all he knew
except he heard Bud weeping as he knelt on the ground
where the old horse lay, and saying: " *Great hoss —
great hoss!* "

Then he remembered saying: " Now, Bud, don't cry
— if he does die, won't it be glorious, to die in harness,
giving his life for others — Cap'n Tom — Shiloh?
Think of it, Bud, to die at the wire, his race won, his

work finished, the crown his! O Bud, who would not love to go like Ben Butler?"

But he could not talk any more, for he saw Jack Bracken spring forward, and then the gleam of a whiskey flask gleamed above Ben Butler's fluttering nostrils and Jack's terrible gruff voice said: "Wait till he's dead fust. Stand back, give him air," and his great hat fluttered like a windmill as he fanned the gasping nostrils of the struggling horse.

The old man turned with an hysterical sob in his throat that was half a shout of joy.

Travis stood by him watching the struggles of the old horse for breath.

"Well, I've killed him," he said, laconically.

There was a grip like a vise on his shoulders. He turned and looked into the eyes of the old man and saw a tragic light there he had never seen before.

"Don't — for God's sake don't, Richard Travis, don't tempt me here, wait till I pray, till this devil goes out of my heart."

And then in his terrible, steel-gripping way, he pulled Richard Travis, with a sudden jerk up against his own pulsing heart, as if the owner of The Gaffs had been a child, burying his great hardened fingers in the man's arm and fairly hissing in a whisper these words: "If he dies — Richard Travis — remember he died for you . . . it tuck both yo' mares to kill him — no — no — don't start — don't turn pale . . . you are safe . . . I made Col'nel Troup give me his word . . . he'd not expose you . . . if Ben Butler won an' he saved his money. I knew what it 'ud mean

. . . that last heat . . . that it 'ud kill him
. . . but I drove it to save you . . . to keep
Troup from exposin' yo' . . . I've got his word.
An' then I was sure . . . as I live, I knew that God
will touch you yet . . . an' his touch will be as
quickening fire to the dead honor that is in you . . .
Go! Richard Travis . . . Go . . . don't
tempt me agin. . . . "

He remembered later feeling very queer because he
held so much gold in a bag, and it was his. Then he
became painfully acute to the funny thing that happened, so funny that he had to sit down and laugh. It
was on seeing Ben Butler rising slowly to his feet and
shaking himself with that long powerful shake he had
seen so often after wallowing. And the funniest thing!
— two balls of cotton flew out of his ears, one hitting
Flecker of Tennessee on the nose, the other Colonel
Troup in the eye.

"By Gad, sah," drawled Colonel Troup, "but now,
I see. I thought he cudn't ah been made of flesh an'
blood, sah, why damme he's made of cotton! An' you
saved my money, old man, an' that damned rascal's name
by that trick? Well, you kno' what I said, sah, a gentleman an' his word — but — but —" he turned quickly
on the old man — excitedly, "ah, here — I'll give you
the thousand dollars I hedged now . . . if you'll
give me back my promise — damned if I don't! Won't
do it? No? Well, it's yo' privilege. I admire yo'
charity, it's not of this world."

And then he remembered seeing Bud sitting in the
old cart driving Ben Butler home and telling every-

body what they now knew: "*Great hoss — G-r-e-a-t hoss!*"

And the old horse shuffled and crow-hopped along, and Jack followed the Bishop carrying the gold.

And then such a funny thing: Ben Butler, frightened at a mule braying in his ear, ran away and threw Bud out!

When the old man heard it he sat down and laughed and cried — to his own disgust —"like a fool, sissy man," he said, "a sissy man that ain't got no nerve. But, Lord, who'd done that but Ben Butler?"

CHAPTER XXVII

YOU'LL COME BACK A MAN

IT was after dark when the old man, pale, and his knees still shaking with the terrible strain and excitement of it all, reached his cabin on the mountain. The cheers of the grand-stand still echoed in his ears, and, shut his eyes as he would, he still saw Ben Butler, stretched out on the track struggling for the little breath that was in him.

Jack Bracken walked in behind the old man carrying a silken sack which sagged and looked heavy.

The grand-father caught up Shiloh first and kissed her. Then he sat down with the frail form in his arms and looked earnestly at her with his deep piercing eyes.

" Where's the ole hoss," began his wife, her eyes beginning to snap. " You've traded him off an' I'll bet you got soaked, Hilliard Watts — I can tell it by that pesky, sheepish look in yo' eyes. You never cu'd trade horses an' I've allers warned you not to trade the ole roan."

" Wal, yes," said the Bishop. " I've traded him for this —" and his voice grew husky with emotion —" for this, Tabitha, an', Jack, jes' pour it out on the table there."

It came out, yellow waves of gold. The light shone on them, and as the tired eyes of little Shiloh peeped

414

curiously at them, each one seemed to throw to her a kiss of hope, golden tipped and resplendent.

The old woman stood dazed, and gazing sillily. Then she took up one of the coins and bit it gingerly.

" In God's name, Hilliard Watts, what does all this mean? ˙ Why, it's genuwine gold."

" It means," said the old man cheerily, " that Shiloh an' the chillun will never go into that mill ag'in — that old Ben Butler has give 'em back their childhood an' a chance to live. It means," he said triumphantly, " that Cap'n Tom's gwinter have the chance he's been entitled to all these years — an' that means that God'll begin to unravel the tangle that man in his meanness has wound up. It means, Tabitha, that you'll not have to wuck anymo' yo'self — no mo', as long as you live —"

The old woman clutched at the bed-post: " Me? — not wuck anymo'? Not hunt 'sang an' spatterdock an' clean up an' wash an' scour an' cook an'—"

" No, why not, Tabitha? We've got a plenty to —"

He saw her clutch again at the bed-post and go down in a heap, saying:—

" Lemme die — now, if I can't wuck no mo'."

They lifted her on the bed and bathed her face. It was ten minutes before she came around and said feebly :

" I'm dyin', Hilliard, it's kilt me to think I'll not have to wuck any mo'."

" Oh, no, Tabitha, I wouldn't die fur that," he said soothingly. " It's terrible suddent like, I kno', an' hard fur you to stan', but try to bear it, honey, fur our sakes. It's hard to be stricken suddent like with riches, an' I've never seed a patient get over it, it is true.

You'll be wantin' to change our cabin into an ole Col-
onial home, honey, an' have a carriage an' a pair of
roached mules, an' a wantin' me to start a cotton factory
an' jine a whis'-club, whilst you entertain the Cottontown Pettico't Club with high-noon teas, an' cut up a
lot o' didoes that'll make the res' of the town laugh.
But you mus' fight ag'in it, Tabitha, honey. We'll
jes' try to live as we've allers lived an' not spend our
money so as to have people talk about how we're throwin'
it at the ducks. You can get up befo' day as usual an'
hunt 'sang on the mountain side, and do all the other
things you've l'arnt to do befo' breakfast."

This was most reassuring, and the old woman felt
much better. But the next morning she complained
bitterly:

" I tested ever' one o' them yaller coins las' night,
they mout a put a counterfeit in the lot, an' see heah,
Hilliard —" she grinned showing her teeth —" I wore
my teeth to the quick a testin' 'em! "

The next week, as the train took the Bishop away, he
stood on the rear platform to cry good-bye to Shiloh
and Jack Bracken who were down to see him off. By
his side was a stooped figure and as the old man jingled
some gold in his pocket he said, patting the figure on the
back:

" You'll come back a man, Cap'n Tom — thank God!
a man ag'in! "

PART FIFTH.—THE LOOM

CHAPTER I

THE autumn had deepened — the cotton had been picked. The dry stalks, sentinelling the seared ground, waved their tattered remnants of un-picked bolls to and fro — summer's battle flags which had not yet fallen.

Millwood was astir early that morning — what there was of it. One by one the lean hounds had arisen from their beds of dry leaves under the beeches, and, shaking themselves with that hound-shake which began at their noses and ended in a circular twist of their skeleton tails, had begun to hunt for stray eggs and garbage. Yet their master was already up and astir.

He came out and took a long drink from the jug behind the door. He drank from the jug's mouth, and the gurgling echo sounded down the empty hall: *Guggle — guggle — gone! Guggle — guggle — gone!* It said to Edward Conway as plainly as if it had a voice.

"Yes, you've gone — that's the last of you. Everything is gone," he said.

He sat down on his favorite chair, propped his feet upon the rotten balcony's rim and began to smoke.

Within, he heard Lily sobbing. Helen was trying to comfort her.

Conway glanced into the room. The oldest sister was

419

dressed in a plain blue cotton gown — for to-day she would begin work at the mill. Conway remembered it. He winced, but smoked on and said nothing.

" 'Tain't no use — 'tain't no use," sobbed the little one —" My mammy's gone — gone! "

Such indeed was the fact. Mammy Maria had gone. All that any of them knew was that only an hour before another black mammy had come to serve them, and all she would say was that she had come to take Mammy Maria's place — gone, and she knew not where.

Conway winced again and then swore under his breath. At first he had not believed it, none of them had. But as the morning went on and Mammy Maria failed to appear, he accepted it, saying: " Jus' like a niggah — who ever heard of any of them havin' any gratitude! "

Helen was too deeply numbed by the thought of the mill to appreciate fully her new sorrow. All she knew — all she seemed to feel — was, that go to the mill she must — go — go — and Lily might cry and the world might go utterly to ruin — as her own life was going:

" I want my mammy — I want my mammy," sobbed the little one.

Then the mother instinct of Helen — that latent motherhood which is in every one of her sex, however young — however old — asserted itself for the first time.

She soothed the younger child: " Never mind, Lily, I am going to the mill only to learn my lesson this week — next week you shall go with me. We will not be separated after that."

" I want my mammy — oh, I want my mammy," was all Lily could say.

Breakfast was soon over and then the hour came —
the hour when Helen Conway would begin her new life.
This thought — and this only — burned into her soul:
To-day her disgrace began. She was no longer a Conway. The very barriers of her birth, that which had
been thrown around her to distinguish her from the
common people, had been broken down. The foundation of her faith was shattered with it.

For the last time, as a Conway, she looked at the fields
of Millwood — at the grim peak of Sunset Rock above —
the shadowed wood below. Until then she did not know
it made such a difference in the way she looked at things.
But now she saw it and with it the ruin, the abandon-
ment of every hope, every ambition of her life. As she
stood upon the old porch before starting for the mill,
she felt that she was without a creed and without a principle.

"I would do anything," she cried bitterly —"I care
for nothing. If I am tempted I shall steal, I know I
shall — I know I shall "— she repeated.

It is a dangerous thing to change environments for
the worse. It is more dangerous still to break down
the moral barrier, however frail it may be, which our
conscience has built between the good and the evil in us.
Some, reared under laws that are loose, may withstand
this barrier breaking and be no worse for the change;
but in the case of those with whom this barrier of their
moral belief stands securely between conscience and for-
bidden paths, let it fall, and all the best of them will
fall with it.

For with them there are no degrees in degradation —

no caste in the world of sin. Headlong they rush to
moral ruin. And there are those like Helen Conway,
too blinded by the environment of birth to know that
work is not degradation. To them it is the lowering
of every standard of their lives, standards which idleness has erected. And idleness builds strange standards.

If it had occurred to Helen Conway — if she had been
reared to know that to work honestly for an honest living was the noblest thing in life, how different would
it all have been!

And so at last what is right and what is wrong de-
pend more upon what has gone before than what follows after. It is more a question of pedigree and environment than of trials and temptations.

"I shall steal," she repeated — " oh, I know I shall."

And yet, as her father drove her in the old shambling
buggy across the hill road to the town, there stood out in
her mind one other picture which lingered there all day
and for many days. She could not forget it nor cast it
from her, and in spite of all her sorrow it uplifted her
as she had been uplifted at times before when, reading
the country newspaper, there had blossomed among its
dry pages the perfume of a stray poem, whose incense
entered into her soul of souls.

It was a young man in his shirt sleeves, his face
flushed with work, his throat bare, plowing on the slope
of the hillside for the fall sowing of wheat.

What a splendid picture he was, silhouetted in the rising sun against the pink and purple background of
sunbeams!

It was Clay Westmore, and he waved his hand in his slow, calm forceful way as he saw her go by.

It was a little thing, but it comforted her. She remembered it long.

The mill had been running several hours when Kingsley looked up, and saw standing before him at his office window a girl of such stately beauty that he stood looking sillily at her, and wondering.

He did not remember very clearly afterwards anything except this first impression; that her hair was plaited in two rich coils upon her head, and that never before had he seen so much beauty in a gingham dress.

He remembered, too, that her eyes, which held him spellbound, wore more an expression of despair and even desperation than of youthful hope. He could not understand why they looked that way, forerunners as they were of such a face and hair.

And so he stood, sillily smiling, until Richard Travis arose from his desk and came forward to meet her.

She nodded at him and tried to smile, but Kingsley noticed that it died away into drawn, hard lines around her pretty mouth.

" It is Miss Conway," he said to Kingsley, taking her hand familiarly and holding it until she withdrew it with a conscious touch of embarrassment.

" She is one of my neighbors, and, by the way, Kingsley, she must have the best place in the mill."

Kingsley continued to look sillily at her. He had not heard of Helen — he did not understand.

" A place in the mill — ah, let me see," he said thoughtfully.

" I've been thinking it out," went on Travis, " and there is a drawing-in machine ready for her. I understand Maggie is going to quit on account of her health."

"I, ah — " began Kingsley — " Er — well, I never heard of a beginner starting on a drawing-in machine."

" I have instructed Maggie to teach her," said Travis shortly. Then he beckoned to Helen: " Come."

She followed Richard Travis through the mill. He watched her as she stepped in among the common herd of people — the way at first in which she threw up her head in splendid scorn. Never had he seen her so beautiful. Never had he desired to own her so much as then.

" The exquisite, grand thing," he muttered. " And I shall — she shall be mine."

Then her head sank again with a little crushed smile of helpless pity and resignation. It touched even Travis, and he said, consolingly, to her:

" You are too beautiful to have to do this and you shall not — for long. You were born to be queen of — well, The Gaffs, eh? "

He laughed and then he touched boldly her hair which lay splendidly around her temples.

She looked at him resignedly, then she flushed to her eyes and followed him.

The drawer-in is to the loom what the architect is to the building. And more — it is both architect and foundation, for as the threads are drawn in so must the cloth be.

The work is tedious and requires skill, patience, quickness, and that nicety of judgment which comes with intellect of a higher order than is commonly found in the mill. For that reason the drawer-in is removed from the noise of the main room — she sits with another drawer-in in a quiet little room nearby, and, with her trained fingers, she draws in through the eyelets the threads, which set the warp.

Maggie was busy, but she greeted him with a quaint, friendly little smile. Helen noticed two things about her at once: that there was a queer bright light in her eyes, and that beneath them glowed two bright red spots, which, when Travis approached, deepened quickly.

"Yes, I am going to leave the mill," she said, after Travis had left them together. " I jus' can't stan' it any longer. Mother is dead, you know, an' father is an invalid. I've five little brothers and sisters at home. I couldn't bear to see them die in here. It's awful on children, you know. So I've managed to keep 'em a-goin' until — well — I've saved enough an' with the help of — a — a — friend — you see — a very near friend — I've managed to get us a little farm. We're all goin' to it next week. Oh, yes, of course, I'll be glad to teach you."

She glanced at Helen's hands and smiled: " Yo' hands don't look like they're used to work. They're so white and beautiful."

Helen was pleased. Her fingers were tapering and beautiful, and she knew her hands were the hands of many generations of ladies.

" I have to make a living for myself now," she said with a dash of bitterness.

" If I looked like you," said Maggie, slyly and yet

frankly, " I'd do something in keeping with my place.
I can't bear to think of anybody like you bein' here."

Helen was silent and Maggie saw that the tears were
ready to start. She saw her half sob and she patted
her cheek in a motherly way as she said:

" Oh, but I didn't mean to hurt you so. Only I do
hate so to see — oh, I am silly, I suppose, because I am
going to get out of this terrible, terrible grind."

Her pale face flushed and she coughed, as she bent
over her work to show Helen how to draw in the threads.

" Now, I'm a good drawer-in, an' he said onct "—
she nodded at the door from which Travis had gone out
—" that I was the best in the worl'; the whole worl'."
She blushed slightly. " But, well — I've made no fortune yet — an' somehow, in yo' case now — you see —
somehow I feel sorter 'fraid — about you — like somethin' awful was goin' to happen to you."

" Why — what —" began Helen, surprised.

" Oh, it ain't nothin'," she said trying to be cheerful
—" I'll soon get over this . . . out in the air. I'm
weak now and I think it makes me nervous an' skeery.
. . . I'll throw it off that quick," she snapped her
fingers —" out in the open air again — out on the little
farm." She was silent, as if trying to turn the subject,
but she went back to it again. " You don't know how
I've longed for this — to get away from the mill. It's
day in an' day out here an' shut up like a convict. It
ain't natural — it can't be — it ain't nature. If anybody thinks it is, let 'em look at them little things over
on the other side," and she nodded toward the main room.
" Why, them little tots work twelve hours a day an'

sometimes mo'. Who ever heard of children workin' at all befo' these things come into the country? Now, I've no objection to 'em, only that they ought to work grown folks an' not children. They may kill me if they can," she laughed,—"I am grown, an' can stan' it, but I can't bear to think of 'em killin' my little brothers an' sisters — they're entitled to live until they get grown anyway."

She stopped to cough and to show Helen how to untangle some threads.

"Oh, but they can't hurt me," she laughed, as if ashamed of her cough; "this is bothersome, but it won't last long after I get out on the little farm."

She stopped talking and fell to her work, and for two hours she showed Helen just how to draw the threads through, to shift the machine, to untangle the tangled threads.

It was nearly time to go home when Travis came to see how Helen was progressing. He came up behind the two girls and stood looking at them work. When they looked up Maggie started and reddened and Helen saw her tighten her thin lips in a peculiar way while the blood flew from them, leaving a thin white oval ring in the red that flushed her face.

"You are doing finely," he said to Helen —"you will make a swift drawer-in." He stooped over and whispered: "Such fingers and hands would draw in anything — even hearts."

Helen blushed and looked quickly at Maggie, over whose face the pinched look had come again, but Maggie was busy at her machine.

"I remember when I came here five years ago," went on Maggie after Travis had left, "I was so proud an' happy. I was healthy an' well an' so happy to think I cu'd make a livin' for the home-folks — for daddy an' the little ones. Oh, they would put them in the mill, but I said no, I'll work my fingers off first. Let 'em play an' grow. Yes, they've lived on what I have made for five years — daddy down on his back, too, an' the children jus' growin', an' now they are big enough and strong enough to he'p me run the little farm — instead "— she said after a pause —"instead of bein' dead an' buried, killed in the mill. That was five years ago — five years "— she coughed and looked out of the window reflectively.

"Daddy — poor daddy — he couldn't help the tree fallin' on his back an' cripplin' him; an' little Buddy, well, he was born weakly, so I done it all. Oh, I am not braggin' an' I ain't complainin', I'm so proud to do it."

Helen was silent, her own bitterness softened by the story Maggie was telling, and for a while she forgot herself and her sorrow.

It is so always. When we would weep we have only to look around and see others who would wail.

"When I come I was as rosy as you," Maggie went on; "not so pretty now, mind you — nobody could be as pretty as you."

She said it simply, but it touched Helen.

"But I'll get my color back on the little farm — I'll be well again." She was silent a while. "I kno' you are wonderin' how I saved and got it." Helen saw her face sparkle and the spots deepen. "Mr. Travis has

been so kind to me in — in other ways — but that's a
big secret," she laughed, " I'm to tell you some day, or
rather you'll see yo'self, an' then, oh — every thing will
be all right an' I'll be ever so much happier than I am
now."

She jumped up impulsively and stood before Helen.

" Mightn't I kiss you once,— you're so pretty an'
fresh?" And she kissed the pretty girl half timidly on
the cheek.

" It makes me so happy to think of it," she went on
excitedly, " to think of owning a little farm all by ourselves, to go out into the air every day whenever you
feel like it and not have to work in the mill, nor ask
anybody if you may, but jus' go out an' see things
grow — an' hear the birds sing and set under the pretty
green trees an' gather wild flowers if you want to.   To
keep house an' to clean up an' cook instead of forever
drawin'-in, an' to have a real flower garden of yo' own
— yo' very own."

They worked for hours, Maggie talking as a child
who had found at last a sympathetic listener. Twilight came and then a clang of bells and the shaft above
them began to turn slower and slower. Helen looked
up wondering why it had all stopped so suddenly. She
met the eyes of Travis looking at her.

" I am to take you home," he said to her, " the
trotters are at the door. Oh," as he looked at her work
—" why, you have done first rate for the day."

" It's Maggie's," she whispered.

He had not seen Maggie and he stood looking at Helen

with such passionate, patronizing, commanding, masterful eyes, that she shrank for a moment, sideways.

Then he laughed: " How beautiful you are! There
are queens born and queens made — I shall call you the
queen of the mill, eh? "

He reached out and tried to take her hand, but she
shrank behind the machine and then —

" Oh, Maggie! " she exclaimed — for the girl's face
was now white and she stood with a strained mouth as if
ready to sob.

" Oh, Maggie's a good little girl," said Travis, catching her hand.

" Oh, please don't — please "— said Maggie.

Then she walked out, drawing her thin shawl around
her.

CHAPTER II

ALL the week the two girls worked together at the mill; a week which was to Helen one long nightmare, filled, as it was, with the hum and roar of machinery, the hot breath of the mill, and worst of all, the seared and deadening thought that she was disgraced.

In the morning she entered the mill hoping it might fall on and destroy her. At night she went home to a drunken father and a little sister who needed, in her childish sorrow, all the pity and care of the elder one.

And one night her father, being more brutal than ever, had called out as Helen came in: " Come in, my mill-girl! "

Richard Travis always drove her home, and each night he became more familiar and more masterful. She felt, — she knew — that she was falling under his fascinating influence.

And worse than all, she knew she did not care.

There is a depth deeper even than the sin — the depth where the doer ceases to care.

Indeed, she was beginning to make herself believe that she loved him — as he said he wished her to do — and as he loved her, he said; and with what he said and what

431

he hinted she dreamed beautiful, desperate dreams of the future.

She did not wonder, then, that on one drive she had permitted him to hold her hand in his. What a strong hand it was, and how could so weak a hand as her's resist it? And all the time he had talked so beautifully and had quoted Browning and Keats. And finally he had told her that she had only to say the word, and leave the mill with him forever.

But where, she did not even care — only to get away from the mill, from her disgrace, from her drunken father, from her wretched life.

And another night, when he had helped her out of the buggy, and while she was close to him and looking downward, he had bent over her and kissed her on the neck, where her hair had been gathered up and had left it white and fair and unprotected. And it sent a hot flame of shame to the depths of her brain, but she could only look up and say —" Oh, please don't — please don't, Mr. Travis," and then dart quickly into the old gate and run to her home.

But within it was only to meet the taunts and sneers of her father that brought again the hot Conway blood in defying anger to her face, and then she had turned and rushed back to the gate which Travis had just left, crying:

" Take me now — anywhere — anywhere. Carry me away from here."

But she heard only the sound of his trotters' feet up the road, and overcome with the reflective anguish of it

all, she had tottered and dropped beneath the tree upon
the grass — dropped to weep.

After a while she sat up, and going down the long
path to the old spring, she bathed her face and hands
in its cool depths. Then she sat upon a rock which
jutted out into the water. It calmed her to sit there and
feel the rush of the air from below, upon her hot cheeks
and her swollen eyes.

The moon shone brightly, lighting up the water, the
rocks which held the spring pool within their fortress of
gray, and the long green path of water-cresses, stretch-
ing away and showing where the spring branch ran to
the pasture.

Glancing down, she saw her own image in the water,
and she smiled to see how beautiful it was. There was
her hair hanging splendidly down her back, and in the
mirror of water beneath she saw it was tinged with that
divine color which had set the Roman world afire in Cleo-
patra's days. But then, there was her dress — her mill
dress.

She sighed — she looked up at the stars. They always filled her with great waves of wonder and reverence.

"Is mother in one of you?" she asked. "Oh,
mother, why were you taken from your two little girls?
and if the dead are immortal, can they forget us of
earth? Can they be indifferent to our fate? How
could they be happy if they knew —" She stopped and
looking up, picked out a single star that shone brighter
than the others, clinging so close to the top of Sunset
Rock as to appear a setting to his crown.

28

" I will imagine she is there "— she whispered —" in
that world — O mother — mother — will you — cannot
you help me? "

She was weeping and had to bathe her face again.
Then another impulse seized her — an impulse of childhood. Pulling off her stockings, she dipped her feet in
the cool water and splashed them around in sheer delight.

The moonbeams falling on them under the water
turned the pink into white, and she smiled to see how like
the pictures of Diana her ankles looked.

She had forgotten that the old spring was near the
public road and that the rail fence was old and fallen.
Her revery was interrupted by a bantering, half drunk-
en, jolly laugh:

" Well, I must say I never saw anything quite so
pretty! "

She sprang up in shame. Leaning on the old fence,
she saw Harry Travis, a roguish smile on his face. She
thought she would run, then she remembered her bare
feet and she sat down on the grass, covering her ankles
with her skirt. At first she wanted to cry, then she
grew indignant as he came tipsily toward her and sat
down by her side.

She was used to the smell of whiskey on the breath.
It's slightest odor she knew instantly. To her it was the
smell of death.

" Got to the Gov'ner's private bottle to-night," he
said familiarly, " and took a couple of cocktails. Going
over to see Nellie, but couldn't resist such beauties as "—
he pointed to her feet.

"It was mean of you to slip upon me as you did," she said. Then she turned the scorn of her eyes on him and coolly looked him over, the weak face, the boyish, half funny smile, the cynical eyes,— trying to be a man of the world and too weak to know what it all meant.

The Conway spirit had come to her — it always did in a critical moment. She no longer blushed or even feared him.

"How, how," she said slowly and looking him steadily over, "did I ever love such a thing as you?"

He moved up closer. "You will have to kiss me for that," he said angrily. "I've kissed you so often I know just how to do it," and he made an attempt to throw his arms around her.

She sprang away from him into the spring branch, standing knee deep in the water and among the water-cresses.

He arose hot with insolence: "Oh, you think you are too good for me now — now that the Gov'ner has set his heart on you. Damn him — you were mine before you were his. He may have you, but he will take you with Cassius' kisses on your lips."

He sprang forward, reached over the rock and seized her by the arm. But she jerked away from him and sprang back into the deeper water of the spring. She did not scream, but it seemed that her heart would burst with shame and anger. She thought of Ophelia, and as she looked down into the water she wiped away indifferently and silently the cool drops which had splashed up into her face, and she wondered if she might not be able to drop down flat and drown herself there, and thus end it all.

He had come to the edge of the rock and stood leering drunkenly down on her.

" I love you," he laughed ironically.

" I hate you," she said, looking up steadily into his eyes and moving back out of his reach.

The water had wet her dress, and she stooped and dipped some of it up and bathed her hot cheeks.

" I'll kiss you if I have to wade into that spring."

" If I had a brother,— oh, if I even had a father," she said, looking at him with a flash of Conway fire in her eyes —" and you did — you would not live till morning — you know you wouldn't."

She stood now knee-deep in water. Above her the half-drunken boy, standing on the rock which projected into the spring, emboldened with drink and maddened by the thought that she had so easily given him up, had reached out and seized her around the neck. He was rough, and it choked her as he drew her to him.

She screamed for the first time — for she thought she heard hoof beats coming down the road; then she heard a horseman clear the low fence and spur into the spring branch. The water from the horse's feet splashed over her. She remembered it only faintly — the big glasses — the old straw hat,— the leathern bag of samples around his shoulders.

" Most unusual," she heard him say, with more calmness it seemed to Helen than ever: " Quite unusual — insultingly so!"

Instinctively she held up her arms and he stooped in

the saddle and lifted her up and set her on the stone
curbing on the side farthest from Harry Travis.

Then he turned and very deliberately reached over
and seized Harry Travis, who stood on the rock, nearly
on a line with the pommel of the saddle. But the hand
that gripped the back of Harry's neck was anything
but gentle. It closed around the neck at the base of
the brain, burying its fingers in the back muscles with
paralyzing pain and jerked him face downward across
the saddle with a motion so swift that he was there before he knew it. Then another hand seized him and
rammed his mouth, as he lay across the pommel of the
saddle, into the sweaty shoulders below the horse's
withers, and he felt the horse move out and into the
road and up to the crossing of the ways just as a buggy
and two fast bay mares came around the corner.

The driver of the bays stopped as he saw his cousin
thrown like a pig over the pommel and held there kicking and cursing.

"I was looking for him," said Richard Travis quietly, "but I would like to know what it all means."

The big glasses shone in kindly humor. They did not
reflect any excitement in the eyes behind them.

"I am afraid it means that he is drunk. Perhaps he
will tell you about it. Quite unusual, I must say — he
seemed to be trying to drown a young lady in a spring."

He eased his burden over the saddle and dropped him
into the road.

Richard Travis took it in instantly, and as Clay rode
away he heard the cousin say: "You damned yellow
cur — to bear the name of Travis."

CHAPTER III

WORK IN A NEW LIGHT

IT was an hour before Clay Westmore rode back to Millwood. He had been too busy plowing that day to get, sooner, a specimen of the rock he had seen out-cropping on Sand Mountain. At night, after supper, he had ridden over for it.

And now by moonlight he had found it!

He flushed with the strength of it all as he put it in his satchel — the strength of knowing that not even poverty, nor work, nor night could keep him from accomplishing his purpose.

Then he rode back, stopping at Millwood. For he thought, too, that he might see Helen, and while he had resolved not to force himself on her after what she had said when he last saw her, still he wished very much to see her now and then.

For somehow, it never got out of his deductive head that some day she would learn to love him. Had he known the temptation, the despair that was hers, he would not have been so quietly deliberate. But she had never told him. In fact, he had loved her from a distance all his life in his quiet way, though now, by her decree, they were scarcely more than the best of friends. Some day, after he had earned enough, he would tell her just how much he loved her. At present he could not, for was he not too poor, and were not his mother and sister dependent upon him?

He knew that Harry Travis loved her in a way — a love he was certain would not last, and in the fullness and depths of his sincere nature, he felt as sure of ultimately winning her, by sheer force of strength, of consistency and devotion, as he was that every great thing in life had been done by the same force and would be to the end of time.

As sure as that, by this same force, he, himself, would one day discover the vein of coal which lay somewhere in the beautiful valley of the Tennessee.

And so he waited his time with the easy assurance of the philosopher which he was, and with that firm faith which minds of his strength always have in themselves and their ultimate success.

It surprised him, it is true — hurt him — when he found to what extent Harry Travis had succeeded in winning the love of Helen. He was hurt because he expected — hoped — she would see further into things than she had. And counting all the poverty and hardships of his life, the Sunday afternoon when he had left her in the arbor, after she had told him she was engaged to Harry Travis, he could not remember when anything had been so hard for him to bear. Later he had heard how she had gone to work in the mill, and he knew that it meant an end of her love affair with Harry.

To-night something told him it was time to see her again, not to tell her of his own love, and how it would never change, whether she was mill girl or the mistress of Millwood, but to encourage her in the misery of it all.

Work — and did not he himself love to work? Was it not the noblest thing of life?

He would tell her it was.

He was surprised when he saw what had just happened; but all his life he had controlled himself to such a degree that in critical moments he was coolest; and so what with another might have been a serious affair, he had turned into half retributive fun, but the deadliest punishment, as it afterwards turned out, that he could have inflicted on a temperament and nature such as Harry Travis'. For that young man, unable to stand the gibes of the neighborhood and the sarcasm of his uncle when it all became known, accepted a position in another town and never came back again.

To have been shot or floored in true melodramatic style by his rival, as he stood on a rock with a helpless girl in his clutch, would have been more to his liking than to be picked up bodily, by the nape of his neck, and taken from the scene of his exploits like a pig across a saddle.

That kind of a combat did not meet his ideas of chivalry.

Helen was dressed in her prettiest gown when Clay rode back to Millwood, after securing the samples he had started for. She knew he was coming and so she tied a white scarf over her head and went again to her favorite seat beneath the trees.

"I don't know how to thank you, Clay," she said, as he swung down from his saddle and threw his leathern bag on the grass.

"Now, you look more like yourself," he smiled admiringly, as he looked down on her white dress and auburn hair, drooping low over her neck and shoulders.

" Tell me about yourself and how you like it at the mill," he went on as he sat down.

" Oh, you will not be willing to speak to me now — now that I am a mill-girl," she added. " Do you know? Clay —"

" I know that, aside from being beautiful, you have just begun to be truly womanly in my sight."

" Oh, Clay, do you really think that? It is the first good word that has been spoken to me since — since my — disgrace."

He turned quickly: " Your disgrace! Do you call it disgrace to work — to make an honest living — to be independent and self-reliant? "

He picked up his bag of samples and she saw that his hands had become hard and sunburnt from the plow handles.

" Helen," he went on earnestly, " that is one of the hide-bound tyrannies that must be banished from our Southland — banished as that other tyranny, slavery, has been banished — a sin, which, with no fault of our own, we inherited from the centuries. We shall never be truly great — as God intended we should be great — until we learn to work. We have the noblest and sunniest of lands, with more resources than man now dreams of, a greater future than we know of if we will only work — work and develop them. You have set an example for every girl in the South who has been thrown upon her own resources. Never before in my life have I cared — so — much — for you."

And he blushed as he said it, and fumbled his samples.

"Then you do care some for me?" she asked pleadingly. She was heart-sick for sympathy and did not know just what she said.

He flushed and started to speak. He looked at her, and his big glasses quivered with the suppressed emotions which lay behind them in his eyes.

But he saw that she did not love him, that she was begging for sympathy and not for love. Besides, what right had he to plan to bring another to share his poverty?

He mounted his horse as one afraid to trust himself to stay longer. But he touched her hair in his awkward, funny way, before he swung himself into the saddle, and Helen, as she went into the desolate home, felt uplifted as never before.

Never before had she seen work in that light — nor love.

CHAPTER IV

MAGGIE

IT was Maggie's last day at the mill, and she had been unusually thoughtful. Her face was more pinched, Helen thought, and the sadness in her eyes had increased.

Helen had proved to be an apt pupil, and Maggie declared that thereafter she would be able to run her machine without assistance.

It was Saturday noon and Maggie was ready to go, though the mill did not shut down until six that day. And so she found herself standing and looking with tearful eyes at the machine she had learned to love, at the little room in which she had worked so long, supporting her invalid father and her little ones —as she motherly called the children. It had been hard — so hard, and the years had been long and she was so weak now, compared to what she had been. How happy she had thought the moment of her leaving would be; and yet now that it had come — now — she was weeping.

" I didn't think," she said to Helen —" I didn't think I'd — I'd care so to leave it — when — when — the time — came."

She turned and brushed away her tears in time to see Travis come smiling up.

"Why, Maggie," he said playfully flipping the tip of her ear as he passed her. "I thought you left us yesterday afternoon. You'll not be forgetting us now that you will not see us again, will you?"

She flushed and Helen heard her say: "Forget you — ever? Oh, please, Mr. Travis —" and her voice trembled.

"Oh, tut," he said, frowning quickly —"nothing like that here. Of course, you will hate to leave the old mill and the old machine. Come, Maggie, you needn't wait — you're a good girl — we all know that."

He turned to Helen and watched her as she drew in the threads. Her head was bent over, and her great coil of hair sat upon it like a queen on a throne.

What a neck and throat she had — what a beautiful queenly manner!

Travis smiled an amused smile when he thought of it — an ironical sneering smile; but he felt, as he stood there, that the girl had fascinated him in a strange way, and now that she was in his power, "now that Fate, or God has combined to throw her into my arms — almost unasked for — is it possible that I am beginning to fall in love with her?"

He had forgotten Maggie and stood looking at Helen. And in that look Maggie saw it all. He heard her sit down suddenly.

"I would go if I were you, Maggie — you are a good girl and we shall not forget you."

"May I stay a little while longer?" she asked. "I won't ever come back any more, you know."

Travis turned quickly and walked off. He came back and spoke to Helen.

"Remember, I am to take you home to-night. But it will be later than usual, on account of the pay-roll."

As he shut the door Maggie turned, and her heart being too full to speak, she came forward and dropped on her knees, burying her face in Helen's lap. "You must not notice me," she said —" don't — don't — oh, don't look at me."

Helen stroked her cheek and finally she was quiet.

Then she looked into Helen's face. "Do you know — oh, will you mind if I speak to you — or perhaps I shouldn't — but — but — don't you see that he loves you?"

Helen reddened to her ears.

"I am foolish — sick — nervous — I know I am silly an' yet I don't see how he could help it — you are so queenly — beautiful — so different from any that are here. He — he — has forgotten me —"

Helen looked at her quickly.

"Why, I don't understand," she said.

"I mean," she stammered, "he used to notice us common girls — me and the others —"

"I don't understand you," said Helen, half indignantly.

"Oh, don't pay no 'tention to me," she said. "I, I fear I am sick, you know — sicker than I thought," and she coughed violently.

She lay with her head in Helen's lap. "Please," she said timidly, looking up into Helen's face at last — " please let me stay this way a while. I never knew a

mother — nobody has ever let me do this befo', an' I am
so happy for it."

Helen stroked her face and hair anew, and Maggie
kneeled looking up at her eagerly, earnestly, hungrily,
scanning every feature of the prettier girl with wor-
shipping eyes.

"How could he he'p it — how could he he'p it," she
said softly —" yes — yes— you are his equal and so
beautiful."

"I don't understand you, Maggie — indeed I do
not."

Maggie arose quickly: " Good-bye — let me kiss you
once mo'— I feel like I'll never see you again — an'—
an'— I've learned to love you so!"

Helen raised her head and kissed her.

Then Maggie passed quickly out, and with her eyes
only did she look back and utter a farewell which carried
with it both a kiss and a tear. And something else
which was a warning.

And Helen never forgot.

CHAPTER V

IT was Saturday afternoon and pay-day, and the mill
shut down at six o'clock

When Helen went in Kingsley sat at the Superintendent's desk, issuing orders on the Secretary and
Treasurer, Richard Travis, who sat at his desk near by
and paid the wages in silver.

Connected with the mill was a large commissary or
store — a cheap modern structure which stood in another part of the town, filled with the necessaries of life
as well as the flimsy gewgaws which delight the heart
of the average mill hand. In establishing this store,
the directors followed the usual custom of cotton-mills
in smaller towns of the South; paying their employees
part in money and part in warrants on the store. It is
needless to add that the prices paid for the goods were,
in most cases, high enough to cut the wages to the
proper margin. If there was any balance at the end
of the month, it was paid in money.

Kingsley personally supervised this store, and his
annual report to the directors was one of the strong
financial things of his administration.

A crowd of factory hands stood around his desk, and
the Superintendent was busy issuing orders on the store,

or striking a balance for the Secretary and Treasurer to pay in silver.

They stood around tired, wretched, lint- and dust-covered, but expectant. Few were there compared with the number employed; for the wages of the minors went to their parents, and as minors included girls under eighteen and boys under twenty-one, their parents were there to receive their wages for them.

These children belonged to them as mercilessly as if they had been slaves, and despite the ties of blood, no master ever more relentlessly collected and appropriated the wages of his slaves than did the parents the pitiful wages of their children.

There are two great whippers-in in the child slavery of the South — the mills which employ the children and the parents who permit it — encourage it. Of these two the parents are often the worse, for, since the late enactment of child labor laws, they do not hesitate to stultify themselves by false affidavits as to the child's real age.

Kingsley had often noticed how promptly and even proudly the girls, after reaching eighteen, and the boys twenty-one, had told him hereafter to place their wages to their own credit, and not to the parent's. They seemed to take a new lease on life. Decrepit, drawn-faced, hump-shouldered and dried up before their time, the few who reached the age when the law made them their own masters, looked not like men and women who stand on the threshold of life, but rather like overworked middle-aged beings of another period.

Yet that day their faces put on a brighter look.

They stood around the office desk, awaiting their

turn. The big engine had ceased to throb and the shuttles to clatter and whirl. The mill was so quiet that those who had, year in and year out, listened to its clatter and hum, seemed to think some overhanging calamity was about to drop out of the sky of terrible calm.

"Janette Smith," called out Kingsley.

She came forward, a bony, stoop-shouldered woman of thirty-five years who had been a spooler since she was fifteen.

"Seventy-seven hours for the week"— he went on mechanically, studying the time book, "making six dollars and sixteen cents. Rent deducted two dollars. Wood thirty-five cents. Due commissary for goods furnished — here, Mr. Kidd," he said to the book-keeper, "let me see Miss Smith's account." It was shoved to him across the desk. Kingsley elevated his glasses. Then he adjusted them with a peculiar lilt — it was his way of being ironical:

"Oh, you don't owe the store anything, Miss Smith — just eleven dollars and eighty cents."

The woman stood stoically — not a muscle moved in her face, and not even by the change of an eye did she indicate that such a thing as the ordinary human emotions of disappointment and fear had a home in the heart.

"Mother was sick all last month," she said at last in a voice that came out in the same indifferent, unvarying tone. "I had to overdraw."

Kingsley gave his eye-glasses another lilt. They said as plainly as eye-glasses could: "Well, of course, I made her sick." Then he added abruptly: "We will

29

advance you two dollars this week—an' that will be all."

"I hoped to get some little thing that she could eat—some relish," she began.

"Not our business, Miss Smith—sorry—very sorry—but try to be more economical. Economy is the great objective haven of life. Emerson says so. And Browning in a most beautiful line of poetry says the same thing," he added.

"The way to begin economy is to begin it — Emerson is so helpful to me — he always comes in at the right time."

"And it's only to be two dollars," she added.

"That's all," and he pushed her the order. She took it, cashed it and went hurriedly out, her poke bonnet pulled over her face. But there were hot tears and a sob under her bonnet.

And so it went on for two hours — some drawing nothing, but remaining to beg for an order on the store to keep them running until next week.

One man with six children in the mill next came forward and drew eighteen dollars. He smiled complacently as he drew it and chucked the silver into his pocket. This gave Jud Carpenter, standing near, a chance to get in his mill talk.

"I tell you, Joe Hopper," he said, slapping the man on the back, "that mill is a great thing for the mothers an' fathers of this little settlement. What 'ud we do if it warn't for our chillun?"

"You're talkin now —" said Joe hopefully.

"It useter be," said Jud, looking around at his crowd,

"that the parents spoiled the kids, but now it is the kids spoilin' the parents."

His audience met this with smiles and laughter.

"I never did know before," went on Jud, "what that old sayin' really meant: 'A fool for luck an' a po' man for chillun.'"

Another crackling laugh.

"How much did Joe Hopper's chillun fetch 'im in this week?"

Joe jingled his silver in his pocket and spat importantly on the floor.

"I tell you, when I married," said Jud, "I seed nothin' but poverty an' the multiplication of my part of the earth ahead of me — poverty, I tell you, starvation an' every new chile addin' to it. But since you started this mill, Mister Kingsley (Kingsley smiled and bowed across the desk at him), I've turned what everybody said 'ud starve us into ready cash. And now I say to the young folks: 'Marry an' multiply an' the cash will be forthcomin'.'"

This was followed by loud laughs, especially from those who were blessed with children, and they filed up to get their wages.

Jim Stallings, who had four in the mill, was counted out eleven dollars. As he pocketed it he looked at Jud and said:

"Oh, no, Jud; it don't pay to raise chillun. I wish I had the chance old Sollerman had. I'd soon make old Vanderbilt look like shin plaster."

He joined in the laughter which followed.

In the doorway he cut a pigeon-wing in which his thin, bowed legs looked comically humorous.

Jud Carpenter was a power in the mill, standing as he did so near to the management. To the poor, ignorant ones around him he was the mouth-piece of the mill, and they feared him even more than they did Kingsley himself, Kingsley with his ironical ways and lilting eye-glasses. With them Jud's nod alone was sufficient.

They were still grouped around the office awaiting their turn. In the faces of some were shrewdness, cunning, hypocrisy. Some looked out through dull eyes, humbled and brow-beaten and unfeeling. But all of them when they spoke to Jud Carpenter — Jud Carpenter who stood in with the managers of the mill — became at once the grinning, fawning framework of a human being.

" Yes, boys," said Jud patronizingly as Stallings went out, " this here mill is a god-send to us po' folks who've got chillun to burn. They ain't a day we ortenter git down on our knees an' thank Mr. Kingsley an' Mister Travis there. You know I done took down that sign I useter have hangin' up in my house in the hall — that sign which said, *God bless our home?* I've put up another one now."

" What you done put up now, Jud? " grinned a tall weaver with that blank look of expectancy which settles over the face of the middle man in a negro minstrel troupe when he passes the stale question to the end man, knowing the joke which was coming.

" Why, I've put up," said Jud brutally, " ' *Suffer*

Little Children to Come Unto Me.' That's scriptural
authority for cotton mills, ain't it?"

The paying went on, after the uproarious laughter
had subsided, and down the long row only the clinking
of silver was heard, intermingled now and then with the
shrill voice of some creature disputing with Kingsley
about her account. Generally it ran thus: " *It cyant be
thet a-way. Sixty hours at five cents an hour — wal,
but didn't the chillun wuck no longer than that? I
cyant — I cyant — I jes' cyant live on that little bit.*"

Such it was, and it floated down the line to Helen like
the wail of a lost soul. When her time came Kingsley
met her with a smile. Then he gave her an order and
Travis handed her a bright crisp ten-dollar bill.

She looked at him in astonishment. " But — but,"
she said. " Surely, I didn't earn all this, did I? Maggie — you had to pay Maggie for teaching me this
week. It was she who earned it. I cannot take it."

Kingsley smiled: " If you must know — though we
promised her we would not tell you," he said —" no,
Miss Conway, you did not earn but five dollars this week.
The other five is Maggie's gift to you — she left it
here for you."

She looked at him stupidly — in dazed gratitude.
Travis came forward:

" I've ordered Jim to take you home to-night. I cannot leave now."

And he led her out to where the trotters stood. He
lifted her in, pressing her hand as he did so — but she
did not know it — she burned with a strange fullness
in her throat as she clutched her money, the first she

had ever earned, and thought of Maggie — Maggie, dying and unselfish.

Work — it had opened a new life to her. Work — and never before had she known the sweetness of it.

" Oh, father," she said when she reached home, " I have made some money — I can support you and Lily now."

When Travis returned Jud Carpenter met him at the door.

" I had a mess o' trouble gittin' that gal into the mill. Huh! but ain't she a beaut! I guess you 'orter tip me for throwin' sech a peach as that into yo' arms. Oh, you're a sly one —" he went on whisperingly — " the smoothest one with women I ever seed. But you'll have to thank me for that queen. Guess I'll go down an' take a dram. I want to git the lint out of my throat."

" I'll be down later," said Travis as he looked at his watch. " Charley Biggers and I. It's our night to have a little fun with the boys."

" I'll see you there," said Jud.

The clinking of silver, questions, answers, and expostulations went on. In the midst of it there was the sudden shrill wail of an angry child.

" I wants some of my money, Paw — I wants to buy a ginger man."

Then came a cruel slap which was heard all over the room, and the boy of ten, a wild-eyed and unkempt thing, staggered and grasped his face where the blow fell.

" Take that, you sassy meddling up-start — you belong to me till you are twenty-one years old. What 'ud you do with a ginger man 'cept to eat it?" He cuffed the boy through the door and sent him flying home.

It was Joe Sykes, the wages of whose children kept him in active drunkenness and chronic inertia. He was the champion loafer of the town.

In a short time he had drawn a pocketful of silver, and going out soon overtook Jud Carpenter.

"I tell you, Jud, we mus' hold these kids down — we heads of the family. I've mighty nigh broke myself down this week a controllin' mine. Goin' down to take a drink or two? Same to you."

CHAPTER VI

THE PLOT

A VILLAGE bar-room is a village hell.

Jud Carpenter and Joe Hopper were soon there, and the silver their children had earned at the mill began to go for drinks.

The drinks made them feel good. They resolved to feel better, so they drank again. As they drank the talk grew louder. They were joined by others from the town — ne'er-do-wells, who hung around the bar — and others from the mill.

And so they drank and sang and danced and played cards and drank again, and threw dice for more drinks.

It was nearly nine o'clock before the Bacchanal laugh began to ring out at intervals — so easily distinguished from the sober laugh, in that it carries in its closing tones the queer ring of the maniac's.

Only the mill men had any cash. The village loafers drank at their expense, and on credit.

" And why should we not drink if we wish," said one of them. " Our children earned the money and do we not own the children? "

Twice only were they interrupted. Once by the wife of a weaver who came in and pleaded with her husband for part of their children's money. Her tears touched the big-hearted Billy Buch, and as her husband was too drunk to know what he was doing, Billy took what money he had left and gave it to the wife. She had a sick child, she told Billy Buch, and what money she had would not even buy the medicine.

Billy squinted the corner of one eye and looked solemnly at the husband: "He ha'f ten drinks in him ag'in, already. I vil gif you pay for eet all for the child. An' here ees one dollar mo' from Billy Buch. Now go, goot voman."

The other interruption was the redoubtable Mrs. Billings; her brother, also a slubber, had arrived early, but had scarcely taken two delightful, exquisite drinks before she came on the scene, her eyes flashing, her hair disheveled, and her hand playing familiarly with something under her apron.

Her presence threw them into a panic.

"Mine Gott!" said Billy, turning pale. "Eet es Meeses Billings an' her crockery."

Half a dozen jubilants pointed out a long-haired man at a center table talking proudly of his physical strength and bravery.

"Cris Ham?" beckoned Mrs. Billings, feeling nervously under her apron. "Come with me!"

"I'll be along t'orectly, sis."

"You will come now," she said, and her hands began to move ominously beneath her apron.

"To be sho'," he said as he walked out with her. "I didn't know you felt that away about it, sis."

It was after ten o'clock when the quick roll of a

buggy came up to the door, and Richard Travis and
Charley Biggers alighted.

They had both been drinking. Slowly, surely, Travis was going down in the scale of degeneracy. Slowly
the loose life he was leading was lowering him to the
level of the common herd. A few years ago he would
not have thought of drinking with his own mill hands.
To-night he was there, the most reckless of them all.
Analyzed, it was for the most part conceit with him;
the low conceit of the superior intellect which would
mingle in infamy with the lowest to gain its ignorant
homage. For Intellect must have homage if it has to
drag it from the slums.

Charley Biggers was short and boyish, with a fat,
round face. When he laughed he showed a fine set of
big, sensual teeth. His eyes were jolly, flighty, insincere. Weakness was written all over him, from a derby
hat sitting back rakishly on his forehead to the small,
effeminate boot that fitted so neatly his small effeminate
foot. He had a small hand and his little sensual face
had not a rough feature on it. It was set off by a
pudgy, half-formed dab of a nose that let his breath
in and out when his mouth happened to be shut. His
eyes were the eyes of one who sees no wrong in anything.

They came in and pulled off their gloves, daintily.
They threw their overcoats on a chair. Travis glanced
around the circle of the four or five who were left and
said pompously:

" Come up, gentlemen, and have something at my expense." Then he walked up to the bar.

They came. They considered it both a pleasure and an honor, as Jud Carpenter expressed it, to drink with him.

" It is a good idea to mingle with them now and then," whispered Travis to Charley. " It keeps me solid with them — health, gentlemen ! "

Charley Biggers showed his good-natured teeth:

" Health, gentlemen," he grinned.

Then he hiccoughed through his weak little nose.

" Joe Hopper can't rise, gentlemen, Joe is drunk, an' — an' a widderer, besides," hiccoughed Joe from below.

Joe had been a widower for a year. His wife, after being the mother of eleven children, who now supported Joe in his drunkenness, had passed away.

Then Joe burst into tears.

" What's up, Joe? " asked Jud kindly.

" Liza's dead," he wailed.

" Why, she's been dead a year," said Jud.

" Don't keer, Jud — I'm jes'— jes' beginnin' to feel it now "— and he wept afresh.

It was too much for Charley Biggers, and he also wept. Travis looked fixedly at the ceiling and recited portions of the Episcopal burial service. Then Jud wept. They all wept.

" Gentlemen," said Travis solemnly, " let us drink to the health of the departed Mrs. Hopper. Here's to her ! "

This cheered all except Joe Hopper — he refused to be comforted. They tried to console him, but he only wept the more. They went on drinking and left him out, but this did not tend to diminish his tears.

"Oh, Mister Hopper, shet up," said Jud peremptorily —"close up — I've arranged for you to marry a grass-widder."

This cheered him greatly.

"O Jud — Jud — if I marry a grass-widder whut — whut'll I be then?"

"Why, a grasshopper, sure," said Travis.

They all roared. Then Jud winked at Travis and Travis winked at the others. Then they sat around a table, all winking except poor Joe, who continued to weep at the thought of being a grasshopper. He did not quite understand how it was, but he knew that in some way he was to be changed into a grasshopper, with long green wings and legs to match.

"Gentlemen," said Jud seriously —"it is our duty to help out po' Joe. Now, Joe, we've arranged it for you to marry Miss Kate Galloway — the grass-widder."

"Not Miss Kate," said Travis with becoming serious-ness.

"Why not her, Mr. Travis?" asked Jud, winking.

"Because his children will be Katydids," said Travis.

This brought on thundering roars of laughter and drinks all around. Only Joe wept — wept to think his children would be katydids.

"Now, Joe, it's this way. I've talked it all over and arranged it. That's what we've met for to-night — ain't it, gents?" said Jud.

"Sure — sure," they all exclaimed.

"Now, Joe, you mus' dry yo' tears an' become reconciled — we've got a nice scheme fixed for you."

"I'll never be reconciled — never," wailed Joe. "Liza's dead an'— I'm a grasshopper."

"Now, wait till I explain to you — but, dear, devoted friend, everything is ready. The widder's been seen an' all you've got to do is to come with us and get her."

"She's a mighty handsome 'oman," said Jud, winking his eye. "Dear — dear frien's — all — I'm feelin' reconciled already "— said Joe.

They all joined in the roar. Jud winked. They all winked. Jud went on:

"Joe, dear, dear Joe — we have had thy welfare at heart, as the books say. We wanted thee to become a millionaire. Thou hast eleven children to begin with. They pay you —"

"Eighteen dollars a week, clear,"— said Joe proudly.

"Well, now, Joe — it's all arranged — you marry the widder an' in the course of time you'll have eleven mo'. That's another eighteen dollars — or thirty-six dollars a week clear in the mills."

"Now, but I hadn't thought of that," said Joe enthusiastically —" that's a fact. When — when did you say the ceremony'd be performed? "

"Hold on," said Jud, " now, we've studied this thing all out for you. You're a Mormon — the only one of us that is a Mormon — openly."

They all laughed.

"Openly —" he went on —" you've j'ined the Mormon church here up in the mountains."

"But we don't practise polygamy — now "— said Joe.

" That's only on account of the Grand Jury and the
law — not yo' religion.   You see — you'll marry an' go
to Utah — but — es the kids come you'll sen' 'em all
down here to the mills — every one a kinder livin'
coupon.   All any man's got to do in this country to git
rich is to marry enough wives."

" Can I do that — do the marryin' in Utah an' keep
sendin' the — the chilluns down to the mill? "   His eyes
glittered.

" Sart'inly "— said Jud —" sure! "

" Then there's Miss Carewe "— he went on —" you
haf'ter cal'clate on feedin' several wives in one, with
her.   But say eleven mo' by her.   That's thirty-seven
mo'."

Joe jumped up.

" Is she willin'? "

" Done seen her," said Jud; " she say come on."

" Hold on," said Travis with feigned anger.   " Hold
on.   Joe is fixin' to start a cotton-mill of his own.
That'll interfere with the Acme.   No — no — we must
vote it down.   We mustn't let Joe do it."

Joe had already attempted to rise and start after his
wives.   But in the roar of laughter that followed he sat
down and began to weep again for 'Liza.

It was nearly midnight.   Only Travis, Charley Biggers and Jud remained sober enough to talk.   Charley
was telling of Tilly and her wondrous beauty.

" Now — it's this way," he hiccoughed —" I've got
to go off to school — but — but — I've thought of a
plan to marry her first, with a. bogus license and
preacher."

There was a whispered conversation among them, ending in a shout of applause.

"What's the matter with you takin' yo' queen at the same time?" asked Jud of Travis.

Travis, drunk as he was, winced to think that he would ever permit Jud Carpenter to suggest what he had intended should only be known to himself. His tongue was thick, his brain whirled, and there were gaps in his thoughts; but through the thickness and heaviness he thought how low he had fallen. Lower yet when, despite all his vanishing reserve, all his dignity and exclusiveness, he laughed sillily and said:

"Just what I had decided to do — two queens and an ace."

They all cheered drunkenly.

CHAPTER VII

MRS. WESTMORE TAKES A HAND

"WHAT are you playing, Alice?"

The daughter arose from the piano and kissed her mother, holding for a moment the pretty face, crowned with white hair, between her two palms.

"It — it is an old song which Tom and I used to love to sing."

The last of the sentence came so slowly that it sank almost into silence, as of one beginning a sentence and becoming so absorbed in the subject as to forget the speech. Then she turned again to the piano, as if to hide from her mother the sorrow which had crept into her face.

"You should cease to think of that. Such things are dreams — at present we are confronted by very disagreeable realities."

"Dreams — ah, mother mine" — she answered with forced cheeriness —"but what would life be without them?"

"For one thing, Alice" — and she took the daughter's place at the piano and began to play snatches of an old waltz tune —" it would be free from all the morbid unnaturalness, the silliness, the froth of things. There is too much hardness in every life — in the world

464

— in the very laws of life, for such things ever to have been part of the original plan. For my part, I think they are the product of man and wine or women or morphine or some other narcotic."

" We make the dreams of life, but the realities of it make us," she added.

" Oh, no, mother. 'Tis the dreams that make the realities. Not a great established fact exists but it was once the vision of a dreamer. Our dreams to-day become the realities of to-morrow."

" Do you believe Tom is not dead — that he will one day come back? " asked her mother abruptly.

It was twilight and the fire flickered, lighting up the library. But in the flash of it Mrs. Westmore saw Alice's cheek whiten in a hopeless, helpless, stricken way.

Then she walked to the window and looked out on the darkness fast closing in on the lawn, clustering denser around the evergreens and creeping ghostlike toward the dim sky line which shone clear in the open.

The very helplessness of her step, her silence, her numbed, yearning look across the lawn told Mrs. Westmore of the death of all hope there.

She followed her daughter and put her arms impulsively around her.

" I should not have hurt you so, Alice.   I only wanted to show you how worse than useless it is . . . but to change the subject, I do wish to speak to you of — our condition."

Alice was used to her mother's ways — her brilliancy — her pointed manner of going at things — her quick change of thought — of mood, and even of tempera-

30

ment. An outsider would have judged Mrs. Westmore
to be fickle with a strong vein of selfishness and even of
egotism. Alice only knew that she was her mother; who
had suffered much; who had been reduced by poverty to
a condition straitened even to hardships. To help her
the daughter knew that she was willing to make any
sacrifice. Unselfish, devoted, clear as noonday in her
own ideas of right and wrong, Alice's one weakness was
her blind devotion to those she loved. A weakness beautiful and even magnificent, since it might mean a sacrifice of her heart for another. The woman who gives
her time, her money, her life, even, to another gives
but a small part of her real self. But there is something truly heroic when she throws in her heart also.
For when a woman has given that she has given all; and
because she has thrown it in cold and dead — a lifeless
thing — matters not; in the poignancy of the giving
it is gone from her forever and she may not recall it
even with the opportunity of bringing it back to life.

She who gives her all, but keeps her heart, is as a
priest reading mechanically the Sermon on the Mount
from the Bible. But she who gives her heart never to
take it back again gives as the Christ dying on the Cross.

" Now, here is the legal paper about "—

Her voice failed and she did not finish the sentence.

Alice took the paper and glanced at it. She flushed
and thrust it into her pocket. They were silent a while
and Mrs. Westmore sat thinking of the past. Alice
knew it by the great reminiscent light which gleamed in
her eyes. She thought of the time when she had servants, money, friends unlimited — of the wealth and in-

fluence of her husband — of the glory of Westmoreland.

Every one has some secret ambition kept from the eyes of every living soul — often even to die in its keeper's breast. It is oftenest a mean ambition of which one is ashamed and so hides it from the world. It is often the one weakness. Alice never knew what was her mother's. She did not indeed know that she had one, for this one thing Mrs. Westmore had kept inviolately secret. But in her heart there had always rankled a secret jealousy when she thought of The Gaffs. It had been there since she could remember — a feeling cherished secretly, too, by her husband: for in everything their one idea had been that Westmoreland should surpass The Gaffs,— that it should be handsomer, better kept, more prosperous, more famous.

Now, Westmoreland was gone — this meant the last of it. It would be sold, even the last hundred acres of it, with the old home on it. Gone — gone —all her former glory — all her family tradition, her memories, her very name.

Gone, and The Gaffs remained!

Remained in all its intactness — its beauty — its well equipped barns with all the splendor of its former days. For so great was the respect of Schofield's army for the character of Colonel Jeremiah Travis that his home escaped the torch when it was applied to many others in the Tennessee Valley. And Richard Travis had been shrewd enough after the war to hold his own. Joining the party of the negro after the war, he had been its political ruler in the county. And the Honorable Rich-

ard Travis had been offered anything he wanted. At
present he was State Senator.   He with others called
himself a Republican — one of the great party of Lincoln to which the negroes after their enfranchisement
united themselves.   It was a fearful misnomer.   The
Republican party in the South, composed of ninety-nine
ignorant negroes to one renegade white, about as truly
represented the progressive party of Lincoln as a black
vampire the ornithology of all lands.   Indeed, since the
war, there has never been in the South either a Republican or a Democratic party.   The party line is not
drawn on belief but on race and color.   The white men,
believing everything they please from free trade to protection, vote a ticket which they call Democratic.   The
negroes, and a few whites who allied themselves with
them for the spoils of office, vote the other ticket.   Neither of them represent anything but a race issue.

To this negro party belonged Richard Travis — and
the price of his infamy had been *Honorable* before his
name.

But Mrs. Westmore cared nothing for this.   She
only knew that he was a leader of men, was handsome,
well reared and educated, and that he owned The Gaffs,
her old rival.   And that there it stood, a fortune — a
refuge — a rock — offered to her and her daughter,
offered by a man who, whatever his other faults, was
brave and dashing, sincere in his idolatrous love for her
daughter.   That he would make Alice happy she did
not doubt; for Mrs. Westmore's idea of happiness was
in having wealth and position and a splendid name.

Having no real heart, how was it possible for her to know, as Alice could know, the happiness of love?

An eyeless fish in the river of Mammoth Cave might as well try to understand what light meant.

He would make Alice happy, of course he would; he would make her happy by devotion, which he was eager to give her with an unstinted hand. Alice needed it, she herself needed it. It was common sense to accept it,— business sense. It was opportunity — fate. It was the reward of a life — the triumph of it — to have her old rival — enemy — bound and presented to her.

And nothing stood between her and the accomplishment of it all but the foolish romance of her daughter's youth.

And so she sat building her castles and thinking:

" With The Gaffs, with Richard Travis and his money would come all I wish, both for her and for me. Once more I would hold the social position I once held: once more I would be something in the world. And Alice, of course, she would be happy; for her's is one of those trusting natures which finds first where her duty points and then makes her heart follow."

But Mrs. Westmore wisely kept silent. She did not think aloud. She knew too well that Alice's sympathetic, unselfish, obedient spirit was thinking it over.

She sat down by her mother and took up a pet kitten which had come purring in, begging for sympathy. She stroked it thoughtfully.

Mrs. Westmore read her daughter's thoughts:

" So many people," the mother said after a while, " have false ideas of love and marriage. Like ignorant people when they get religion, they think a great and sudden change must come over them — changing their very lives."

She laughed her ringing little laugh: "I told you of your father's and my love affair. Why, I was engaged to three other men at the same time — positively I was. And I would have been just as happy with any of them."

"Why did you marry father, then?"

Her mother laughed and tapped the toe of her shoe playfully against the fender: "It was a silly reason; he swam the Tennessee River on his horse to see me one day, when the ferry-boat was a wreck. I married him."

"Would not the others have done as well?"

"Yes, but I knew your father was brave. You cannot love a coward — no woman can. But let a man be brave — no matter what his faults are — the rest is all a question of time. You would soon learn to love him as I did your father."

Mrs. Westmore was wise. She changed the subject.

"Have you noticed Uncle Bisco lately, mother?" asked Alice after a while.

"Why, yes; I intended to ask you about him."

"He says there are threats against his life — his and Aunt Charity's. He had a terrible dream last night, and he would have me to interpret it."

"Quite Biblical," laughed her mother. "What was it?"

"They have been very unhappy all day — you know the negroes have been surly and revengeful since the election of Governor Houston — they believe they will be put back into slavery and they know that Uncle Bisco voted with his white friends. It is folly, of course — but they beat Captain Roland's old body servant nearly to death because he voted with his old master. And Uncle Bisco has heard threats that he and Aunt Charity will be visited in a like manner. I think it will soon blow over, though at times I confess I am often worried about them, living alone so far off from us, in the cabin in the wood."

" What was Uncle Bisco's dream? " asked Mrs. Westmore.

" Why, he said an angel had brought him water to drink from a Castellonian Spring. Now, I don't know what a Castellonian Spring is, but that was the word he used, and that he was turned into a live-oak tree, old and moss-grown. Then he stood in the forest surrounded by scrub-oaks and towering over them and other mean trees when suddenly they all fell upon him and cut him down. Now, he says, these scrub-oaks are the radical negroes who wish to kill him for voting with the whites. You will laugh at my interpretation," she went on. " I told him that the small black oaks were years that still stood around him, but that finally they would overpower him and he would sink to sleep beneath them, as we must all eventually do. I think it reassured him — but, mamma, I am uneasy about the two old people."

" If the Bishop were here —"

" He would sleep in the house with a shotgun, I fear," laughed Alice.

They were silent at last: " When did you say Richard was coming again, Alice? "

"To-morrow night — and — and — I hear Clay in his laboratory. I will go and talk to him before bed time."

She stooped and kissed her mother. To her surprise, she found her mother's arms around her neck and heard her whisper brokenly:

"Alice — Alice — you could solve it all if you would. Think — think — what it would mean to me — to all of us — oh, I can stand this poverty no longer — this fight against that which we cannot overcome."

She burst into a flood of tears. Never before had Alice seen her show her emotions over their condition, and it hurt her, stabbed her to the vital spot of all obedience and love.

With moistened eyes she went into her brother's room.

And Mrs. Westmore wrote a note to Richard Travis. It did not say so in words but it meant: *"Come and be bold — you have won."*

CHAPTER VIII

"I SHALL go to Boston next week to meet the directors of the mill and give in my annual report."

The three had been sitting in Westmoreland library this Sunday night — for Richard Travis came regularly every Sunday night, and he had been talking about the progress of the mill and the great work it was doing for the poor whites of the valley. " I imagine," he added, " that they will be pleased with the report this year."

" But are you altogether pleased with it in all its features? " asked Alice thoughtfully.

" Why, what do you mean, Alice? " asked her mother, surprised.

" Just this, mother, and I have been thinking of talking to Richard about it for some time."

Travis took his cigar out of his mouth and looked at her quizzically.

She flushed under his gaze and added: " If I wasn't saying what I am for humanity's sake I would be willing to admit that it was impertinent on my part. But are you satisfied with the way you work little children in that mill, Richard, and are you willing to let it go on without a protest before your directors? You have

473

such a fine opportunity for good there," she added in all her old beautiful earnestness.

"Oh, Alice, my dear, that is none of our affair. Now I should not answer her, Richard," and Mrs. Westmore tapped him playfully on the arm.

"Frankly, I am not," he said to Alice. "I think it is a horrible thing. But how are we to remedy it? There is no law on the subject at all in Alabama —"

"Except the broader, unwritten law," she added.

Travis laughed: "You will find that it cuts a small figure with directors when it comes in conflict with the dividends of a corporation."

"But how is it there?" she asked,—"in New England?"

"They have seen the evils of it and they have a law against child labor. The age is restricted to twelve years, and every other year they must go to a public school before they may be taken back into the mill. But even with all that, the law is openly violated, as it is in England, where they have been making efforts to throttle the child-labor problem for nearly a century, and after whose law the New England law was patterned."

"Why, by the parents of the children falsely swearing to their age."

Alice looked at him in astonishment.

"Do you really mean it?" she asked.

"Why, certainly — and it would be the same here. If we had a law the lazy parents of many of them would swear falsely to their children's ages."

" There could be some way found to stop that," she said."

" It has not been found yet," he added. " What is to prevent two designing parents swearing that an eight year old child is twelve — and these little poor whites," he added with a laugh, "all look alike from eight to sixteen — scrawny — hard and half-starved. In many cases no living man could swear whether they are six or twelve."

" If you really should make it a rule to refuse all children under twelve," she added, " tell me how many would go out of your mill."

" In other words, how many under twelve do we work there? " he asked.

She nodded.

He thought a while and then said: " About one hundred and twenty-five."

She started: " That is terrible — terrible! Couldn't you — couldn't you bring the subject up before the directors for — for —"

" Your sake — yes "— he said, admiringly.

" Humanity's — God's — Right's — helpless, ignorant, dying children! "

" Do you know," he added quickly, " how many idle parents these hundred and twenty-five children support — actually support? Why, about fifty. Now do you see? The whole influence of these fifty people will be to violate the law — to swear the children are twelve or over. Yes, I am opposed to it — so is Kingsley — but we are powerless."

" My enthusiasm has been aroused, of late, on the

subject," Alice went on, " by the talks and preaching of my old friend, Mr. Watts."

Travis frowned : " The old Bishop of Cottontown," he added ironically —" and he had better stop it — he will get into trouble yet."

" Why ? "

" Because he is doing the mill harm."

" And I don't suppose one should do a corporation harm," she said quickly,—" even to do humanity good ? "

" Oh, Alice, let us drop so disagreeable a subject," said her mother. " Come, Richard and I want some music."

" Any way," said Alice, rising, " I do very much hope you will bring the subject up in your visit to the directors. It has grown on me under the talks of the old Bishop and what I have seen myself — it has become a nightmare to me."

" I don't think it is any of our business at all," spoke up Mrs. Westmore quickly.

Alice turned her big, earnest eyes and beautiful face on her mother.

" Do you remember when I was six years old ? " she asked.

" Of course I do."

" Suppose — suppose — that our poverty had come to us then, and you and papa had died and left brother and me alone and friendless. Then suppose we had been put into that mill to work fourteen hours a day — we — your own little ones — brother and I "—

Mrs. Westmore sprang up with a little shriek and put her hands over her daughter's mouth.

Richard Travis shrugged his shoulders: "I had not thought of it that way myself," he said. "That goes home to one."

Richard Travis was always uplifted in the presence of Alice. It was wonderful to him what a difference in his feelings, his behavior, his ideas, her simple presence exerted. As he looked at her he thought of last night's debauch — the bar-room — the baseness and vileness of it all. He thought of his many amours. He saw the purity and grandeur of her in this contrast — all her queenliness and beauty and simplicity. He even thought of Maggie and said to himself: "Suppose Alice should know all this. . . . My God! I would have no more chance of winning her than of plucking a star from the sky!"

He thought of Helen and it made him serious. Helen's was a different problem from Maggie's. Maggie was a mill girl — poor, with a bed-ridden father. She was nameless. But Helen — she was of the same blood and caste of this beautiful woman before him, whom he fully expected to make his wife. There was danger in Helen — he must act boldly, but decisively — he must take her away with him — out of the State, the South even. Distance would be his protection, and her pride and shame would prevent her ever letting her whereabouts or her fate be known.

Cold-bloodedly, boldly, and with clear-cut reasoning, all this ran through his mind as he stood looking at Alice Westmore.

We are strangely made—the best of us. Men have looked on the Madonna and wondered why the artist had not put more humanity there—had not given her a sensual lip, perhaps. And on the Cross, the Christ was thinking of a thief.

Two hours later he was bidding her good-bye.

" Next Sunday, do you remember — Alice — next Sunday night you are to tell me — to fix the day, Sweet? "

" Did mother tell you that? " she asked. " She should let me speak for myself."

But somehow he felt that she would. Indeed he knew it as he kissed her hand and bade her good-night.

Richard Travis had ridden over to Westmoreland that Sunday night, and as he rode back, some two miles away, and within the shadows of a dense clump of oaks which bordered the road, he was stopped by two dusky figures. They stood just on the edge of the forest and came out so suddenly that the spirited saddle mare stopped and attempted to wheel and bolt. But Travis, controlling her with one hand and, suspecting robbers, had drawn his revolver with the other, when one of them said :

" Friends, don't shoot."

" Give the countersign," said Travis with ill-concealed irritation.

" Union League, sir.   I am Silos, sir."

Travis put his revolver back into his overcoat pocket and quieted his mare.

The two men, one a negro and the other a mulatto,

came up to his saddle-skirt and stood waiting respect-fully.

"You should have awaited me at The Gaffs, Silos."

"We did, sir," said the mulatto, "but the boys are all out here in the woods, and we wanted to hold them to-gether. We didn't know when you would come home."

"Oh, it's all right," said Travis pettishly —"only you came near catching one of my bullets by mistake. I thought you were Jack Bracken and his gang."

The mulatto smiled and apologized. He was a bright fellow and the barber of the town.

"We wanted to know, sir, if you were willing for us to do the work to-night, sir?"

"Why bother me about it — no need for me to know, Silos, but one thing I must insist upon. You may whip them — frighten them, but nothing else, mind you, nothing else."

"But you are the commander of the League — we wanted your consent."

Travis bent low over the saddle and talked earnestly to the man a while. It was evidently satisfactory to the other, for he soon beckoned his companion and started off into the woods.

"Have you representatives from each camp present, Silos?"

The mulatto turned and came back.

"Yes — but the toughest we could get. I'll not stay myself to see it. I don't like such work, sir — only some one has to do it for the cause — the cause of free-dom, sir."

"Of course — why of course," said Travis. "Old

Bisco and his kind are liable to get all you negroes put back into slavery — if the Democrats succeed again as they have just done. Give them a good scare."

" We'll fix him to-night, boss," said the black one, grinning good naturedly. Then he added to himself : " Yes, I'll whip 'em — to death."

" I heard a good deal of talk among the boys, to-night, sir," said the mulatto. " They all want you for Congress next time."

" Well, we'll talk about that, Silos, later. I must hurry on."

He started, then wheeled suddenly :

" Oh, say, Silos —"

The latter came back.

" Do your work quietly to-night — Just a good scare — If you disturb "— he pointed to the roof of Westmoreland in the distance showing above the beech tops. " You know how foolish they are about old Bisco and his wife —"

" They'll never hear anything." He walked off, saying to himself : " A nigger who is a traitor to his race ought to be shot, but for fear of a noise and disturbin' the ladies — I'll hang 'em both,— never fear."

Travis touched his mare with the spur and galloped off.

Uncle Bisco and his wife were rudely awakened. It was nearly midnight when the door of their old cabin was broken open by a dozen black, ignorant negroes, who seized and bound the old couple before they could cry out. Bisco was taken out into the yard under a tree, while his wife, pleading and begging for her husband's life, was tied to another tree.

"Bisco," said the leader, "we cum heah to pay you back fur de blood you drawed frum our backs whilst you hilt de whip ob slabery an' oberseed fur white fo'ks. An' fur ebry lick you giv' us, we gwi' giv' you er dozen on your naked back, an' es fur dis ole witch," said the brute, pointing to old Aunt Charity, "we got de plain docyments on her fur witchin' Br'er Moses' little gal — de same dat she mek hab fits, an' we gwi' hang her to a lim'."

The old man drew himself up. In every respect — intelligence, physical and moral bravery — he was superior to the crowd around him. Raised with the best class of whites, he had absorbed many of their virtues, while in those around him were many who were but a few generations removed from the cowardice of darkest Africa.

"I nurver hit you a lick you didr.'t deserve, suh, I nurver had you whipped but once an' dat wus for stealin' a horg which you sed yo'se'f you stole. You ken do wid me es you please," he went on, "you am menny an' kin do it, an' I am ole an' weak. But ef you hes got enny soul, spare de po' ole 'oman who ain't nurver dun nothin' but kindness all her life. De berry chile you say she witched hes hed 'leptis fits all its life an' Cheerity ain't dun nuffin' but take it medicine to kwore it. Don't hurt de po' ole 'oman," he exclaimed.

"Let 'em do whut dey please wid me, Bisco," she said: "Dey can't do nuffin' to dis po' ole body but sen' de tired soul on dat journey wher de buterful room is

31

already fix fur it, es you read dis berry night. But spare de ole man, spare 'im fur de secun' blessin' which Gord dun promised us, an' which boun' ter cum bekase Gord can't lie. O Lord," she said suddenly, " remember thy po' ole servants dis night."

But her appeals were fruitless. Already the " witch council " of the blacks was being formed to decide their fate. And it was an uncanny scene that the moon looked down on that night, under the big trees on the banks of the Tennessee. They formed in a circle around the " Witch Finder," an old negro whose head was as white as snow, and who was so ignorant he could scarcely speak even negro dialect.

Both his father and mother were imported from Africa, and the former was " Witch Finder " for his tribe there. The negroes said the African Witch Finder had imparted his secret only to his son, and that it had thus been handed down in one family for many generations.

The old negro now sat upon the ground in the center of the circle. He was a small, bent up, wiry-looking black, with a physiognomy closely resembling a dog's, which he took pains to cultivate by drawing the plaits of his hair down like the ears of a hound, while he shaped his few straggling strands of beard into the under jaw of the same animal. Three big negroes had led him, blindfolded, into the circle, chanting a peculiar song, the music of which was weird and uncanny. And now as he sat on the ground the others regarded him with the greatest reverence and awe. It was in one of the most dismal portions of the swamp, a hundred yards or two from the road that led to the ferry at the river. Here the old people had been brought from their homes and tied to this spot where the witch council was to be held. Before seating himself the Witch Finder had drawn three rings within a circle on the ground with the thigh bone of a dog. Then, unbuttoning his red flannel shirt, he took from his bosom, suspended around his neck, a kind of purse, made from the raw-hide of a calf, with white hair on one side and red on the other, and from this bag he proceeded to take out things which would have given Shakespeare ideas for his witch scene in Macbeth. A little black ring, made of the legs of the black spider and bound together with black horse hair; a black thimble-like cup, not much longer than the cup of an acorn, made of the black switch of a mule containing the liver of a scorpion. The horny head and neck of the huge black beetle, commonly known to negroes as the black Betsy Bug; the rattle and button of a rattlesnake; the fang-tooth of a cotton-mouth moccasin, the left hind foot of a frog, seeds of the stinging nettle, and pods of peculiar plants, all incased in a little sack made of a mole's hide. These were all given sufficient charm by a small round cotton yarn, in the center of which was a drop of human blood. They were placed on the ground around him, but he held the ball of cotton yarn in his hand, and ordered that the child be brought into the ring. The poor thing was frightened nearly to death at sight of the Witch Finder, and when he began slowly to unwind his ball of cotton thread and chant his monotonous funeral song, she screamed in terror. At a signal from the " Witch Finder," Aunt Charity was dragged into the ring, her hands tied be-

hind her. The sight of such brutality was too much
for the child, and she promptly had another fit. No
other evidence was needed, and the Witch Finder declared that Aunt Charity was Queen of Witches. The
council retired, and in a few minutes their decision was
made: Uncle Bisco was to be beaten to death with hickory flails and his old wife hung to the nearest tree.
Their verdict being made, two stout negroes came forward to bind the old man to a tree with his arms around
it. At sight of these ruffians the old woman broke out
into triumphant song:

" O we mos' to de home whar we all gwi' res',
　　Cum, dear Lord, cum soon!
An' take de ole weary ones unto yo' bres',
　　Cum, dear Lord, cum soon!
Fur we ole an' we tired an' we hungry fur yo' sight,
An' our lim's dey am weary, fur we fou't er good fight,
An' we longin' fur de lan' ob lub an' light —
　　Cum, dear Lord, cum soon."

And it was well that she sang that song, for it stopped
three horsemen just as they forded the creek and turned
their horses' heads into the lane that led to the cabin.
One who was tall and with square shoulders sat his horse
as if born in the saddle. Above, his dark hair was
streaked with white, but the face was calm and sad,
though lit up now with two keen and kindly eyes which
glowed with suppressed excitement. It was the face of
splendid resolve and noble purpose, and the horse he
rode was John Paul Jones. The other was the village

blacksmith.   A negro followed them, mounted on a raw-
bone pony, and carrying his master's Enfield rifle.

The first horseman was just saying: " Things look
mighty natural at the old place, Eph; I wonder if the
old folks will know us?   It seems to me —"

He pulled up his horse with a jerk.   He heard singing just over to his left in the wood.   Both horsemen
sat listening:

O we mos' to de do' ob our Father's home —
  Lead, dear Lord, lead on!
An' we'll nurver mo' sorrer an' nurver mo' roam —
  Lead, dear Lord, lead on!
An' we'll meet wid de lam's dat's gohn on befo'
An' we lie in de shade ob de good shepherd's do',
An' he'll wipe away all ob our tears as dey flow —
  Lead, dear Lord, lead on!

" Do you know that voice, Eph?" cried the man in
front to his body servant.   " We must hurry "; and he
touched the splendid horse with the heel of his riding
boot.

But the young negro had already plunged two spurs
into his pony's flanks and was galloping toward the
cabin.

It was all over when the white rider came up.   Two
brutes had been knocked over with the short heavy barrel of an Enfield rifle.   There was wild scattering
of others through the wood.   An old man was clinging
in silent prayer to his son's knees and an old woman was
clinging around his neck, and saying:

" Praise God — who nurver lies — it's little Ephrum — come home ag'in."

Then they looked up and the old man raised his hands in a pitiful tumult of joy and fear and reverence as he said:

" An' Marse Tom, so help me God — a-ridin' John Paul Jones ! "

CHAPTER IX

M AN may breed up all animals but himself. Strive as he may, the laws of heredity are hidden. " Like produces like or the likeness of an ancestor " is the unalterable law of the lower animal. Not so with man — he is a strange anomaly. Breed him up — up — and then from his high breeding will come reversion. From pedigrees and plumed hats and ruffled shirts come not men, but pygmies — things which in the real fight of life are but mice to the eagles which have come up from the soil with the grit of it in their craws and the strength of it in their talons.

We stop in wonder — balked. Then we see that we cannot breed men — they are born; not in castles, but in cabins.

And why in cabins? For therein must be the solution. And the solution is plain: It is work — work that does it.

We cannot breed men unless work — achievement — goes with it.

From the loins of great horses come greater horses; for the pedigree of work — achievement — is there. Unlike man, the race-horse is kept from degeneracy by work. Each colt that comes must add achievement to pedigree when he faces the starter, or he goes to the shambles or the surgeon.

Why may not man learn this simple lesson — the lesson of work — of pedigree, but the pedigree of achievement?

The son who would surpass his father must do more than his father did. Two generations of idleness will beget nonentities, and three, degenerates.

The preacher, the philosopher, the poet, the ruler — it matters not what his name — he who first solves the problem of how to keep mankind achieving will solve the problem of humanity.

And now to Helen Conway for the first time in her life this simple thing was happening — she was working — she was earning — she was supporting herself and Lily and her father. Not only that, but gradually she was learning to know what the love of one like Clay meant — unselfish, devoted, true.

If to every tempted woman in the world could be given work, and to work achievement, and to achievement independence, there would be few fallen ones.

All the next week Helen went to the mill early — she wanted to go. She wanted to earn more money and keep Lily out of the mill. And she went with a light heart, because for the first time in her life since she could remember, her father was sober. Helen's earnings changed even him. There was something so noble in her efforts that it uplifted even the drunkard. In mingled shame and pride he thought it out: **Sup-ported by his daughter — in a mill and such a daugh-ter!** He arose from it all white-lipped with resolve:

"*I will be a Conway again!*"   He said it over and over.
He swore it.

It is true he was not entirely free from that sickening, sour, accursed smell with which she had associated him all her life. But that he was himself, that
he was making an earnest effort, she knew by his neatly
brushed clothes, his clean linen, his freshly shaved face,
his whole attire which betokened the former gentleman.

"How handsome he must have been when he was once
a Conway!" thought Helen.

He kissed his daughters at the breakfast table. He
chatted with them, and though he said nothing about
it, even Lily knew that he had resolved to reform.

After breakfast Helen left him, with Lily sitting on
her father's lap, her face bright with the sunshine
of it:

"If papa would always be like this"— and she patted his cheek.

Conway started. The very intonation of her voice,
her gesture, was of the long dead mother.

Tears came to his eyes. He kissed her: "Never
again, little daughter, will I take another drop."

She looked at him seriously: "Say with God's
help —" she said simply. "Mammy Maria said it
won't count unless you say that."

Conway smiled. "I will do it my own self."

But Lily only shook her head in a motherly, scolding
way.

"With God's help, then," he said.

Never was an Autumn morning more beautiful to
Helen as she walked across the fields to the mill. She

had learned a nearer way, one which lay across hill and field. The path ran through farms, chiefly The Gaffs, and cut across the hills and meadow land. Through little dells, amid fragrant groves of sweet gum and maples, their beautiful many-colored leaves now scattered in rich profusion around. Then down little hollows where the brooks sputtered and frothed and foamed along, the sun all the time darting in and out, as the waters ran first in sunshine and then in shadow. And above, the winds were so still, that the jumping of the squirrel in the hickories made the only noise among the leaves which still clung to the boughs.

All so beautiful, and never had Helen been so happy.

She was earning a living — she was saving Lily from the mill and her father from temptation.

Her path wound along an old field and plunged into scrub cedar and glady rocks. A covey of quail sprang up before her and she screamed, frightened at the sudden thunder of their wings.

Then the path ran through a sedge field, white with the tall silvered panicled-leaves of the life-everlasting.

Beyond her she saw the smoke-stack of the mill, and a short cut through a meadow of The Gaffs would soon take her there.

She failed to see a warning on the fence which said: *Keep out — Danger.*

Through the bars she went, intent only on soon reaching the mill beyond and glorying in the strong rich smell of autumn in leaf and grass and air.

" What a beautiful horse that is in the pasture," she thought, and then her attention went to a meadow lark

flushed and exultant. She heard shouts, and now —
why was Jim, the stable boy, running toward her so fast,
carrying a pitchfork in his hands and shouting: " Whoa
— there, Antar — Antar,— you, sir ! "

And the horse! One look was enough. With ears
laid back, and mouth wide open, with eyes blazing with
the fire of fury he was plunging straight at her.

Helpless, she turned in sickening doubt, to feel that
her limbs were limp in the agony of fear. She heard
the thunder of the man-eating stallion's hoofs just behind her and she butted blindly, as she sank down, into
some one who held bravely her hand as she fell, and the
next instant she heard a thundering report and smelt
a foul blast of gunpowder. She looked up in time to
see the great horse pitch back on his haunches, rear,
quiver a moment and strike desperately at the air with
his front feet and fall almost upon her.

When she revived, the stable boy stood near by the
dead stallion, pale with fright and wonder. A half-
grown boy stood by her, holding her hand.

" You are all right now," he said quietly as he helped
her to arise. In his right hand he held a pistol and
the foul smoke still oozed up from the nipple where the
exploded cap lay shattered, under the hammer.

He was perfectly cool — even haughtily so. He
scarcely looked at Helen nor at Jim, who kept saying
nervously:

" You've killed him — you've killed him — what will
Mr. Travis say? "

The boy laughed an ironical laugh. Then he walked
up and examined the shot he had made. Squarely be-

tween the great eyes the ball had gone, and scarcely had the glaring, frenzied eye-balls of the man-eater been fixed in the rigid stare of death.   He put his fingers on it, and turning, said:

" A good shot, running — and at twenty paces! "

Then he stood up proudly, and his blue eyes flashed defiance as he said:

" And what will Mr. Travis say?   Well, tell him first of all that this man-eating stallion of his caught the bullet I had intended for his woman-eating master — this being my birth-day.   And tell him, if he asks you who I am, that last week I was James Adams, but now I am James Travis.   He will understand."

He came over to Helen gallantly — his blue eyes shining through a smile which now lurked in them:

" This is Miss Conway, isn't it?   I will see you out of this."

Then, taking her hand as if she had been his big sister, he led her along the path to the road and to safety.

CHAPTER X

MARRIED IN GOD'S SIGHT

NIGHT — for night and death, are they not one? A farm cabin in a little valley beyond the mountain. An Indian Summer night in November, but a little fire is pleasant, throwing its cheerful light on a room rough from puncheon floor to axe-hewn rafters, but cleanly-tidy in its very roughness. It looked sinewy, strong, honest, good-natured. There was roughness, but it was the roughness of strength. Knots of character told of the suffering, struggles and privations of the sturdy trees in the forest, of seams twisted by the tempests; rifts from the mountain rocks; fibre, steel-chilled by the terrible, silent cold of winter stars.

And now plank and beam and rafter and roof made into a home, humble and honest, and giving it all back again under the warm light of the hearth-stone.

On a bed, white and beautifully clean, lay a fragile creature, terribly white herself, save where red live coals gleamed in her cheeks beneath the bright, blazing, fever-fire burning in her eyes above.

She coughed and smiled and lay still, smiling.

She smiled because a little one — a tiny, sickly little girl — had come up to the bed and patted her cheek and said: "Little mother — little mother!"

There were four other children in the room, and they sat around in all the solemn, awe-stricken sorrow of death, seen for the first time.

Then a man in an invalid chair, helpless and with a broken spine, spoke, as if thinking aloud:

" She's all the mother the little 'uns ever had, Bishop —'pears like it's cruel for God to take her from them."

" God's cruelty is our crown," said the old man — " we'll understand it by and by."

Then the beautiful woman who had come over the mountain arose from the seat by the fireside, and came to the bed. She took the little one in her arms and petted and soothed her.

The child looked at her timidly in childish astonishment. She was not used to such a beautiful woman holding her — so proud and fine — from a world that she knew was not her world.

" May I give you some nourishment now, Maggie? "

The girl shook her head.

" No — no — Miss Alice," and then she smiled so brightly and cheerfully that the little one in Alice Westmore's arms clapped her hands and laughed: " Little mother — be up, well, to-morrow."

Little Mother turned her eyes on the child quickly, smiled and nodded approval. But there were tears — tears which the little one did not understand.

An hour went by — the wind had ceased, and with it the rain. The children were asleep in bed; the father in his chair.

A cold sweat had broken out on the dying girl's forehead and she breathed with a terrible effort. And in it

all the two watchers beside the bed saw that there was
an agony there but not the fear of death. She kept
trying to bite her nails nervously and saying:

"There is only — ι. . . one thing — . . .
one . . . thing. . . ."

"Tell me, Maggie," said the old man, bending low
and soothing her forehead with his hands, "tell us
what's pesterin' you — maybe it hadn't oughter be.
You mustn't worry now — God'll make everything right
— to them that loves him even to the happy death.
You'll die happy an' be happy with him forever. The
little 'uns an' the father, you know they're fixed here —
in this nice home an' the farm — so don't worry."

"That's it! . . . Oh, that's it! . . . I got
it that way — . . . all for them . . . but it's
that that hurts now. . . ."

He bent down over her: "Tell us, child — me an'
Miss Alice — tell us what's pesterin' you. You mustn't
die this way — you who've got such a right to be
happy."

The hectic spark burned to white heat in her cheek.
She bit her nails, she picked at the cover, she looked
toward the bed and asked feebly: "Are they asleep?
Can I talk to you two?"

The old man nodded. Alice soothed her brow.

Then she beckoned to the old preacher, who knelt
by her side, and he put his arms around her neck and
raised her on the pillow. And his ear was close to her
lips, for she could scarcely talk, and Alice Westmore
knelt and listened, too. She listened, but with a grip-
ing, strained heartache,— listened to a dying confession

from the pale lips, and the truth for the first time came to Alice Westmore, and kneeling, she could not rise, but bent again her head and heard the pitiful, dying confession.   As she listened to the broken, gasping words, heard the heart-breaking secret come out of the ruins of its wrecked home, her love, her temptation, her ignorance in wondering if she were really married· by the laws of love, and then the great martyrdom of it all — giving her life, her all, that the others might live — a terrible tightening gathered around Alice Westmore's heart, her head fell with the flooding tears and she knelt sobbing, her bloodless fingers clutching the bed of the dying girl.

" Don't cry," said Maggie.   " I should be the one to weep, . . .   only I am so happy . . .   to think . . .   I am loved by the noblest, best, of men, . . .   an' I love him so, . . .   only he ain't here; . . .   but I wouldn't have him see me die.   Now — now . . .   what I want to know, Bishop, . . ." she tried to rise.   She seemed to be passing away.   The old man caught her and held her in his arms.

Her eyes opened: " I — is —" she went on, in the agony of it all with the same breath, " am . . . am I married . . . in God's sight . . . as well as his —"

The old man held her tenderly as if she were a child. He smiled calmly, sweetly, into her eyes as he said:

" You believed it an' you loved only him, Maggie — poor chile! "

" Oh, yes — yes —" she smiled, " an' now — even now I love him up — right up — as you see . . .

to the door, . . . to the shadow, . . . to the valley of the shadow. . . ."

" And it went for these, for these "— he said looking around at the room.

" For them — my little ones — they had no mother, you kno'— an' Daddy's back. Oh, I didn't mind the work, . . . the mill that has killed . . . killed me, . . . but, . . . but was I "— her voice rose to a shrill cry of agony —" am I married in God's sight? "

Alice quivered in the beauty of the answer which came back from the old man's lips:

" As sure as God lives, you were — there now — sleep and rest; it is all right, child."

Then a sweet calmness settled over her face, and with it a smile of exquisite happiness.

She fell back on her pillow: " In God's sight . . . married . . . married . . . my — Oh, I have never said it before . . . but now, . . . can't I? "

The Bishop nodded, smiling.

" My husband, . . . my husband, . . . dear heart, . . . Good-bye. . . ."

She tried to reach under her pillow to draw out something, and then she smiled and died.

When Alice Westmore dressed her for burial an hour afterwards, her heart was shaken with a bitterness it had never known before — a bitterness which in a man would have been a vengeance. For there was the smile still on the dead face, carried into the presence of God.

32

Under the dead girl's pillow lay the picture of Richard Travis.

The next day Alice sent the picture to Richard Travis, and with it a note.

"*It is your's,*" she wrote calmly, terribly calm — "*from the girl who died believing she was your wife. I am helping bury her to-day. And you need not come to Westmoreland to-morrow night, nor next week, nor ever again.*"

And Richard Travis, when he read it, turned white to his hard, bitter, cruel lips, the first time in all his life.

For he knew that now he had no more chance to recall the living than he had to recall the dead.

CHAPTER XI

ALL that week at the mill, Richard Travis had been making preparations for his trip to Boston. Regularly twice, and often three times a year, he had made the same journey, where his report to the directors was received and discussed. After that, there were always two weeks of theatres, operas, wine-suppers and dissipations of other kinds — though never of the grossest sort — for even in sin there is refinement, and Richard Travis was by instinct and inheritance refined.

He was not conscious — and who of his class ever are? — of the effects of the life he was leading — the tightening of this chain of immoral habits, the searing of what conscience he had, the freezing of all that was generous and good within him.

Once his nature had been as a lake in midsummer, its surface shimmering in the sunlight, reflecting something of the beauty that came to it. Now, cold, sordid, callous, it lay incased in winter ice and neither could the sunlight go in nor its reflection go out. It slept on in coarse opaqueness, covered with an impenetrable crust which he himself did not understand.

" But," said the old Bishop more than once, " God can touch him and he will thaw like a spring day. There is somethin' great in Richard Travis if he can only be touched."

But vice cannot reason. Immorality cannot deduce. Only the moral ponders deeply and knows both the premises and the conclusions, because only the moral thinks.

Vice, like the poisonous talons of a bird of prey, while it buries its nails in the flesh of its victim, carries also the narcotic which soothes as it kills.

And Richard Travis had arrived at this stage. At first it had been with him any woman, so there was a romance — and hence Maggie. But he had tired of these, and now it was the woman beautiful as Helen, or the woman pure and lovely as Alice Westmore.

What a tribute to purity, that impurity worships it the more as itself sinks lower in the slime of things. It is the poignancy of the meteorite, which, falling from a star, hisses out its life in the mud.

The woman pure — Alice — the very thought of her sent him farther into the mud, knowing she could not be his. She alone whom he had wanted to wed all his life, the goal of his love's ambition, the one woman in the world he had never doubted would one day be his wife.

Her note to him — "*Never* . . . *never* . . . *again*"— he kept reading it over, stunned, and pale with the truth of it. In his blindness it had never occurred to him that Alice Westmore and Maggie would ever meet. In his blindness — for Wrong, daring as a snake, which, however alert and far-seeing it may be in the hey-dey of its spring, sees less clearly as the Summer advances, until, in the August of its infamy, it

ceases to see altogether and becomes an easy victim for
all things with hoofs.

Then, the poignant reawakening. Now he lay in the
mud and above him still shone the star.

The star — his star! And how it hurt him! It was
the breaking of a link in the chain of his life.

Twice had he written to her. But each time his notes
came back unopened. Twice had he gone to Westmoreland to see her. Mrs. Westmore met him at the door,
cordial, sympathetic, but with a nervous jerk in the little metallic laugh. His first glance at her told him she
knew everything — and yet, knew nothing. Alice was
locked in her room and would not see him.

"But, oh, Richard," and again she laughed her little insincere, unstable, society laugh, beginning with
brave frankness in one corner of her mouth and ending
in a hypocritical wave of forgetfulness before it had
time to finish the circle, but fluttering out into a cynical
twitching of a thing which might have been a smile or
a sneer —

"True love — you know — dear Richard — you
must remember the old saying."

She pressed his hand sympathetically. The mouth
said nothing, but the hand said plainly: "Do not
despair — I am working for a home at The Gaffs."

He pitied her, for there was misery in her eyes and
in her laugh and in the very touch of her hand. Misery
and insincerity, and that terrible mental state when
weakness is roped up between the two and knows, for
once in its life, that it has no strength at all.

And she pitied him, for never before on any human

face had she seen the terrible irony of agony. Agony she had often seen — but not this irony of it — this agony that saw all its life's happiness blasted and knew it deserved it.

Richard Travis, when he left Westmoreland, knew that he left it forever.

" The Queen is dead — long live the Queen," he said bitterly.

And then there happened what always happens to the thing in the mud — he sank deeper — desperately deeper.

Now — now he would have Helen Conway. He would have her and own her, body and soul. He would take her away — as he had planned, and keep her away. That was easy, too — too far away for the whisper of it ever to come back. If he failed in that he would marry her. She was beautiful — and with a little more age and education she would grace The Gaffs. So he might marry her and set her up, a queen over their heads.

This was his determination when he went to the mill the first of the week. All the week he watched her, talked with her, was pleasant, gallant and agreeable. But he soon saw that Helen was not the same. There was not the dull wistful resignation in her look, and despair had given way to a cheerfulness he could not understand. There was a brightness in her eyes which made her more beautiful.

The unconscious grip which the shamelessness of it all had over him was evidenced in what he did. He confided his plans to Jud Carpenter, and set him to work to discover the cause.

" See what's wrong," he said significantly. " I am going to take that girl North with me, and away from here. After that it is no affair of yours."

" Anything wrong? " He had reached the point of his moral degradation when right for Helen meant wrong for him.

Jud, with a characteristic shrewdness, put his finger quickly on the spot.

Edward Conway was sober. Clay saw her daily.

" But jes' wait till I see him ag'in — down there. I'll make him drunk enough. Then you'll see a change in the Queen — hey? "

And he laughed knowingly. With a little more bitterness she would go to the end of the world with him.

It was that day he held her hands in the old familiar way, but when he would kiss her at the gate she still fled, crimson, away.

The next morning Clay Westmore walked with her to the mill, and Travis lilted his eyebrows haughtily:

" If anything of that kind happens," he said to himself, " nothing can save me."

He watched her closely — how beautiful she looked that day — how regally beautiful! She had come wearing the blue silk gown, with the lace and beads which had been her mother's. In sheer delight Travis kept slipping to the drawing-in room door to watch her work. Her posture, beautifully Greek, before the machine, so natural that it looked not unlike a harp in her hand; her half-bent head and graceful neck, the flushed face and eyes, the whole picture was like a Titian, rich in color and life.

And she saw him and looked up smiling.

It was not the smile of happiness. He did not know it because, being blind, he could not know. It was the happiness of work — achievement.

He came in smiling. " Why are you so much happier than last week? "

" Would you really like to know? " she said, looking him frankly in the eyes.

He touched her hair playfully. She moved her head and shook it warningly.

" It is because I am at work and father is trying so hard to reform."

" I thought maybe it was because you had found out how much I love you."

It was his old, stereotyped, brazen way, but she did not know it and blushed prettily.

" You are kind, Mr. Travis, but — but that mustn't be thought of. Please, but I wish you wouldn't talk that way."

" Why, it is true, my queen — of The Gaffs? " he said smiling.

She began to work again.

He came over to her and bent low:

" You know I am to take you Monday night "—

Her hands flew very rapidly — her cheeks mantled into a rich glow. One of the threads snapped. She stopped, confused.

Travis glanced around. No one was near. He bent and kissed her hair:

" My queen," he whispered, " my beautiful queen."

Then he walked quickly out. He went to his office,

but he still saw the beautiful picture. It thrilled him
and then there swept up over him another picture, and he
cried savagely to himself:

"I'll make her sorry. She shall bow to that fine
thing yet — my queen."

Nor would it leave him that day, and into the night
he dreamed of her, and it was the same Titian picture
in a background of red sunset. And her machine was
a harp she was playing. He wakened and smiled:

"Am I falling in love with that girl? That will
spoil it all."

He watched her closely the next day, for it puzzled
him to know why she had changed so rapidly in her
manner toward him. He had ridden to Millwood to
bring her to the mill, himself; and he had some exquisite
roses for her — clipped in the hothouse by his own
hands. It was with an unmistakable twitch of jealousy
that he learned that Clay Westmore had already come
by and gone with her.

"I know what it is now," he said to Jud Carpenter
at the mill that morning; "she is half in love with that
slow, studious fellow."

Jud laughed: "Say, excuse me, sah — but hanged
if you ain't got all the symptoms, y'self, boss?"

Travis flushed:

"Oh, when I start out to do a thing I want to do
it — and I'm going to take her with me, or die trying."

Jud laughed again: "Leave it to me — I'll fix the
goggle-eyed fellow."

That night when the door bell rang at Westmoreland,
Jud Carpenter was ushered into Clay's workshop. He

sat down and looked through his shaggy eyebrows at the lint and dust and specimens of ore. Then he spat on the floor disgustedly.

" Sorry to disturb you, but be you a surveyor also? "

The big bowed glasses looked at him quietly and nodded affirmatively.

" Wal, then," went on Jud, " I come to git you to do a job of surveying for the mill. It's a lot of timber land on the other side of the mountain — some twenty miles off. The Company's bought five thousand acres of wood and they want it surveyed. What'll you charge? "

Clay thought a moment: " Going and coming, on horse-back — it will take me a week," said Clay thoughtfully. " I shall charge a hundred dollars."

" An' will you go right away — to-morrow mornin'? "

Clay nodded.

" Here's fifty of it," said Jud —" the Company is in a hurry. We want the survey by this day week. Let me see, this is Sat'dy — I'll come next Sat'dy night."

Clay's face flushed. Never before had he made a hundred dollars in a week.

" I'll go at once."

" To-morrow at daylight? " asked Jud, rising.

Clay looked at him curiously. There was something in the tone of the man that struck him as peculiar, but Jud went on in an easy way.

" You see we must have it quick. All our winter wood to run the mill is there an' we can't start into

cordin' till it's surveyed an' the deed's passed.   Sorry to
hurry you "—

Clay promised to start at daylight and Jud left.

He looked at his watch.   It was late.   He would like
to tell Helen about it — he said aloud: " Making a
hundred dollars a week.   If I could only keep up that
— I'd — I'd —"

He blushed.   And then he turned quietly and went
to bed.   And that was why Helen wondered the next
day and the next, and all the next week why she did not
see Clay, why he did not come, nor write, nor send her a
message.   And wondering the pang of it went into her
hardening heart.

CHAPTER XII

IT was the middle of Saturday afternoon, and all the week Edward Conway had fought against the terrible thirst which was in him. Not since Monday morning had he touched whiskey at all, and now he walked the streets of the little town saying over and over to himself: "I am a Conway again."

He had come to town to see Jud Carpenter about the house which had been promised him — for he could not expect to hold Millwood much longer. With his soberness some of his old dignity and manhood returned, and when Carpenter saw him, the Whipper-in knew instinctively what had happened.

He watched Edward Conway closely — the clear eye, the haughty turn of his head, the quiet, commanding way of the man sober; and the Whipper-in frowned as he said to himself:

"If he keeps this up I'll have it to do all over."

And yet, as he looked at him, Jud Carpenter took it all in — the weakness that was still there, the terrible, restless thirst which now made him nervous, irritable, and turned his soul into a very tumult of dissatisfaction.

Carpenter, even as he talked to him, could see the fight which was going on; and now and then, in spite of it and his determination, he saw that the reformed drunkard was looking wistfully toward the bar-room of Billy Buch.

And so, as Jud talked to Edward Conway about the house, he led him along toward the bar-room. All the time he was complimenting him on his improved health, and telling how, with help from the mill, he would soon be on his feet again.

At the bar door he halted:

" Let us set down here an' res', Majah, sah, it's a good place on this little porch. Have somethin'? Billy's got a mighty fine bran' of old Tennessee whiskey in there."

Jud watched him as he spoke and saw the fire of expectancy burn in his despairing eyes.

" No — no — Carpenter — no — I am obliged to you — but I have sworn never to touch another drop of it. I'll just rest here with you." He threw up his head and Jud Carpenter saw how eagerly he inhaled the odor which came out of the door. He saw the quivering lips, the tense straining of the throat, the wavering eyes which told how sorely he was tempted.

It was cool, but the sweat stood in drops on Edward Conway's temple. He gulped, but swallowed only a dry lump, which immediately sprang back into his throat again and burned as a ball of fire.

" No — no — Carpenter," he kept saying in a dazed, abstracted way —" no — no — not any more for me. I've promised — I've promised."

And yet even while saying it his eyes were saying: " For God's sake — bring it to me — quick — quick."

Jud arose and went into the bar and whispered to

Billy Buch. Then he came back and sat down and talked of other things. But all the time he was watching Edward Conway — the yearning look — turned half pleadingly to the bar — the gulpings which swallowed nothing.

Presently Jud looked up. He heard the tinkle of glasses, and Billy Buch stood before them with two long toddies on a silver waiter. The ice tinkled and glittered in the deep glasses — the cherries and pineapple gleamed amid it and the whiskey — the rich red whiskey!

"My treat — an' no charges, gentlemen! Compliments of Billy Buch."

Conway looked at the tempting glass for a moment in the terrible agony of indecision. Then remorse, fear, shame, frenzy, seized him:

"No — no — I've sworn off, Billy — I'll swear I have. My God, but I'm a Conway again" — and before the words were fairly out of his mouth he had seized the glass and swallowed the contents.

It was nearly dark when Helen, quitting the mill immediately on its closing, slipped out of a side door to escape Richard Travis and almost ran home across the fields. Never had she been so full of her life, her plans for the future, her hopes, her pride to think her father would be himself again.

"For if he will," she whispered, "all else good will follow."

Just at the gate she stopped and almost fell in the agony of it all. Her father lay on the dry grass by the roadside, unable to walk.

She knelt by his side and wept. Her heart then and there gave up — her soul quit in the fight she was making.

With bitterness which was desperate she went to the spring and brought water and bathed his face. Then when he was sufficiently himself to walk, she led him, staggering, in, and up the steps.

Jud Carpenter reached the mill an hour after dark: He sought out Richard Travis and chuckled, saying nothing.

Travis was busy with his books, and when he had finished he turned and smiled at the man.

" Tell me what it is? "

" Oh, I fixed him, that's all."

Then he laughed:

" He was sober this morning an' was in a fair way to knock our plans sky high — as to the gal, you kno'. Reformed this mornin', but you'll find him good and drunk to-night."

" Oh," said Travis, knitting his brows thoughtfully.

" Did you notice how much brighter, an' sech, she's been for a day or two? " asked Jud.

" I notice that she has shunned me all day "— said Travis —" as if I were poison."

" She'll not shun you to-morrow," laughed Jud. " She is your's — for a woman desperate is a woman lost —" and he chuckled again as he went out.

CHAPTER XIII

HIMSELF AGAIN

NEVER had the two old servants been so happy as they were that night after their rescue. At first they looked on it as a miracle, in which the spirits of their young master and his body-servant, their only son, had come back to earth to rescue them, and for a while their prayers and exhortations took on the uncanny tone of superstition. But after they had heard them talk in the old natural way and seen Captain Tom walking in the living flesh, they became satisfied that it was indeed their young master whom they had supposed to be dead.

Jack Bracken, with all the tenderness of one speaking to little children, explained it all to them — how he had himself carried Captain Tom off the battle-field of Franklin; how he had cared for him since — even to the present time; how Ephraim would not desert his young master, but had stayed with them, as cook and house boy. And how Captain Tom had now become well again.

Jack was careful not to go too much into details — especially Ephraim having lived for two years within a few miles of his parents and not making himself known! The truth was, as Jack knew, Ephraim had become in-

fatuated with the free-booting life of Jack Bracken.
He had gone with him on many a raid, and gold came
too easy that way to dig it out of the soil, as in a cotton
field.

The old people supposed all this happened far away,
and in another country, and that they had all come
home as soon as they could.

With this they were happy.

" And now," added Jack, " we are going to hide with
you a week or so, until Captain Tom can lay his plans."

" Thank God — thank God!"— said Uncle Bisco,
and he would feel of his young master and say: " Jes'
lak he allus wus, only his hair is a leetle gray. An'
in the same uniform he rid off in — the same gran'
clothes."

Captain Tom laughed: " No, not the same, but like
them. You see, I reported at Washington and explained it to the Secretary of War, Jack. It seems
that Mr. Lincoln had been kind enough to write a personal letter about me to my grandfather,— they were
old friends. It was a peculiar scene — my interview
with the Secretary. My grandfather had filed this letter at the War Department before he died, and my return to life was a matter of interest and wonder to
them. And so I am still Captain of Artillery," he
smiled.

In the little cabin the old servants gave him the best
room, cleanly and sweet with an old-fashioned feather-
bed and counterpane. Jack Bracken had a cot by his
bed, and on the wall was a picture of Miss Alice.

Long into the night they talked, the young man ask-

ing them many questions and chief of all, of Alice.
They could see that he was thinking of her, and often
he would stop before the picture and look at it and fall
into a reverie.

"It seems to me but yesterday," he said, " since I
left her and went off to the war. She is not to know
that I am here — not yet. You must hide me if she
runs in," he smiled. " I must see her first in my own
way."

He noticed Jack Bracken's cot by his bedside and
smiled.

" You see, I have been takin' keer of you so long,"
said Jack after the old servants had left them to themselves, " that I can't git out of the habit. I thought
you wus never comin' home."

" It's good we came when we did, Jack."

" You ought to have let me shoot."

The young Captain shook his head: " O Jack —
Jack, I've seen murder enough — it seems but yesterday
since I was at Franklin."

" Do you know who's at the head of all this? " asked
Jack. " It's Richard Travis."

" The Bishop told me all, Jack — and about my
grandfather's will. But I shall divide it with him —
it is not fair."

Jack watched the strong, tall man, as he walked to
and fro in the room, and a proud smile spread over the
outlaw's face.

" What a man you are — what a man you are, Cap'n
Tom ! "

" It's good to be one's self again, Jack. How can I
ever repay you for what you have done for me? "

" You've paid it long ago — long ago. Where would
Jack Bracken have been if you hadn't risked yo' life to
cut me down, when the rope "—

Captain Tom put his hand on Jack's shoulder affectionately: " We'll forget all those horrible things
— and that war, which was hell, indeed. Jack — Jack
— there is a new life ahead for us both," he said, smiling happily.

" For you — yes — but not for me "— and he shook
his head.

" Do you remember little Jack, Cap'n Tom — him
that died? I seem to think mo' of him now than
ever —"

" It is strange, Jack — but I do distinctly; an' our
home in the cave, an' the beautiful room we had, an'
the rock portico overlaid with wild honey-suckle and
Jackson vines overlooking the grand river."

" Jack, do you know we must go there this week and
see it again? I have plans to carry out before making
my identity known."

An hour afterwards the old servants heard Captain
Tom step out into the yard. It was then past mid-
night — the most memorable night of all their lives.
Neither of the old servants could sleep, for hearing
Ephraim talk, and that lusty darkey had sadly mixed
his imagination and his facts.

The old man went out: " Don't be uneasy," said
Captain Tom. " I am going to saddle John Paul Jones
and ride over the scenes of my youth. They might see

me by daylight, and the moonlight is so beautiful to-
night. I long to see The Gaffs, and Westmoreland,
my grandfather's grave," and then in a tenderer tone —
"and my father's; he lies buried in the flag I love."

He smiled sadly and went out.

John Paul Jones had been comfortably housed in the
little stable nearby. He nickered affectionately as his
master came up and led him out.

The young officer stood a few moments looking at
the splendid horse, and with the look came a flood of
memories so painful that he bowed his head in the saddle.

When he looked up Jack Bracken stood by his side:
"I don't much like this, Cap'n Tom. Not to-night,
after all we've done to them. They've got out spies
now — I know them; a lot of negroes calling themselves
Union League, but secretly waylaying, burning and killing all who differ with them in politics. They're made
the Klu-Klux a necessity. Now, I don't want you to
turn me into a Klu-Klux to-night."

"Ah, they would not harm me, Jack, not me, after
all I have suffered. It has all been so hazy," he went
on, as if trying to recall it all, "so hazy until now.
Now, how clear it all is! Here is the creek, yonder the
mountain, and over beyond that the village. And yonder is Westmoreland. I remember it all — so distinctly.
And after Franklin, my God, it was so hazy, with something pressing me down as if I were under a house
which had fallen on me and pinned me to the ground.
But now, O God, I thank Thee that I am a man again!"

Jack went back into the cabin.

Captain Tom stood drinking it all in — the moonlight, on the roof of Westmoreland, shining through the trees. Then he thought of what the old Bishop had told him of Alice, the great pressure brought to bear on her to marry Richard Travis, and of her devotion to the memory of her first love.

"And for her love and her constancy, oh, God, I thank Thee most of all," he said, looking upward at the stars.

He mounted his horse and rode slowly out into the night, a commanding figure, for the horse and rider were one, and John Paul Jones tossed his head as if to show his joy, tossed his head proudly and was in for a gallop.

Captain Tom's pistols were buckled to his side, for he had had experience enough in the early part of the night to show him the unsettled state of affairs still existing in the country under negro domination.

There were no lights at Westmoreland, but he knew which was Alice's room, and in the shadow of a tree he stopped and looked long at the window. Oh, to tear down the barriers which separated him from her! To see her once more — she the beautiful and true — her hair — her eyes, and to place again the kiss of a new betrothal on her lips, the memory of which, in all his sorrows and afflictions, had never left him. And now they told him she was more beautiful than ever. Twelve years — twelve years out of his life — years of forget·fulness — and yet it seemed but a few months since he had bade Alice good-bye — here — here under the crepe-myrtle tree where he now stood. He knelt and kissed

the holy sod. A wave of triumphant happiness came
over him. He arose and threw passionate kisses toward
her window. Then he mounted and rode off.

At The Gaffs he looked long and earnestly. He
imagined he saw the old Colonel, his grandfather, sitting
in his accustomed place on the front porch, his feet
propped on the balcony, his favorite hound by his side.
Long he gazed, looking at every familiar place of his
youth. He knew now that every foot of it would be
his. He had no bitterness in his heart. Not he, for
in the love and constancy of Alice Westmore all such
things seemed unspeakable insignificance to the glory of
that.

In the old family cemetery, which lay hid among
the cedars on the hill, he stood bare-headed before the
grave of his grandsire and silently the tears fell:

" My noble old grandsire," he murmured, " if the
spirits of the dead look down on the living, tell me I
have not proved unworthy. It was his flag — my
father's, and he lies by you wrapped in it. Tell me I
have not been unworthy the same, for I have suffered."

And from the silent stars, as he looked up, there fell
on him a benediction of peace.

Then he drew himself up proudly and gave each
grave a military salute, mounted and rode away.

CHAPTER XIV

A LL the week, since the scene at Maggie's death-
bed, Alice Westmore had remained at home,
while strange, bitter feelings, such as she had
never felt before, surged in her heart. Her brother
was away, and this gave her more freedom to do as she
wished — to remain in her room — and her mother's
presence now was not altogether the solace her heart
craved.

Of the utmost purity of thought herself, Alice Westmore had never even permitted herself to harbor anything reflecting on the character of those she trusted;
and in the generosity of her nature, she considered all
her friends trustworthy. Thinking no evil, she knew
none; nor would she permit any idle gossip to be repeated before her. In her case her unsuspecting nature
was strengthened by her environment, living as she was
with her mother and brother only.

It is true that she had heard faint rumors of Richard
Travis's life; but the full impurity of it had never
been realized by her until she saw Maggie die. Then
Richard Travis went, not only out of her life, but out
of her very thoughts. She remembered him only as she
did some evil character read of in fiction or history.
Perhaps in this she was more severe than necessary —

since the pendulum of anger swings always farthest in
the first full stroke of indignation.   And then the surprise of it — the shock of it! Never had she gone
through a week so full of unhappiness, since it had come
to her, years before, that Tom Travis had been killed at
Franklin.

Her   mother's   entreaties — tears,   even — affected
her now no more than the cries of a spoiled child.

" Oh, Alice," she said one night when she had been
explaining and apologizing for Richard Travis —" you
should know now, child, really, you ought to know by
now, that all men may not have been created alike, but
they are all alike."

" I do not believe it," said Alice with feeling —" I
never want to believe it — I never shall believe it."

" My darling," said the mother, laying her face
against Alice's, " I have reared you too far from the
world."

But for once in her life Mrs. Westmore knew that her
daughter, who had heretofore been willing to sacrifice
everything for her mother's comfort, now halted before
such a chasm as this, as stubborn and instinctively as a
wild doe in her flight before a precipice.

Twice Alice knew that Richard Travis had called; and
she went to her room and locked the door.   She did not
wish even to think of him; for when she did it was not
Richard Travis she saw, but Maggie dying, with the
picture of him under her pillow.

She devised many plans for herself, but go away she
must, perhaps to teach.

In the midst of her perplexity there came to her Sat-

urday afternoon a curiously worded note, from the old
Cottontown preacher, telling her not to forget now that
he had returned and that Sunday School lessons at
Uncle Bisco's were in order. He closed with a remark
which, read between the lines, she saw was intended to
warn and prepare her for something unexpected, the
greatest good news, as he said, of her life. Then he
quoted:

" *And Moses stretched forth his hand over the sea,
and the sea returned to his strength when the morning
appeared.*"

There was but one great good news that Alice Westmore cared for, and, strange to say, all the week she had
been thinking of it. It came about involuntarily, as
she compared men with one another.

It came as the tide comes back to the ocean, as the
stars come with the night. She tried to smother it, but
it would not be smothered. At last she resigned herself
to the wretchedness of it — as one when, despairing of
throwing off a mood, gives way to it and lets it eat its
own heart out.

She could scarcely wait until night. Her heart beat
at intervals, in agitated fierceness, and flushes of red
went through her cheek all the afternoon, at the thought
in her heart that at times choked her.

Then came the kindly old man himself, his face radiant with a look she had not seen on a face for many
weeks. After the week she had been through, this itself
was a comfort. She met him with feigned calmness and
a little laugh.

" You promised to tell me where you had been,

Bishop, all these weeks. It must have made you very,
very happy."

"I'll tell you down at the cabin, if you'll dress yo'
very pretties'. There's friends of yo's down there you
ain't seen in a long time — that's mighty anxious to see
you."

"Oh, I do indeed feel ashamed of myself for having
neglected the old servants so long; but you cannot
know what has been on my mind. Yes, I will go with
you directly."

The old man looked at her admiringly when she was
ready to go — at the dainty gown of white, the splendid
hair of dark auburn crowning her head, the big wistful
eyes, the refined face. Upon him had devolved the duty
of preparing Alice Westmore for what she would see in
the cabin, and never did he enter more fully into the
sacredness of such an occasion.

And now, when she was ready and stood before him
in all her superb womanhood, a basket of dainties on
her arm for the old servants, he spoke very solemnly as
he handed her an ambrotype set in a large gold breast-
pin.

"You'll need this to set you off — around yo' neck."

At sight of it all the color left her cheeks.

"Why, it is mine — I gave it to — to — Tom. He
took it to the war with him. Where "— A sob leaped
into her throat and stopped her.

"On my journey," said the old man quickly, "I
heard somethin' of Cap'n Tom. You must prepare yo'-
se'f for good news."

Her heart jumped and the blood surged back again,

and she grew weak, but the old man laughed his cheery laugh, and, pretending to clap her playfully on the shoulder, he held her firmly with his great iron hand, as he saw the blood go out of her cheeks, leaving them as white as white roses:

"Down there," he added, "I'll tell you all. But God is good — God is good."

Bewildered, pale, and with throbbing heart, she let him take her basket and lead her down the well-beaten path. She could not speak, for something, somehow, said to her that Captain Tom Travis was alive and that she would see him — next week perhaps — next month or year — it mattered not so that she would see him. And yet — and yet — O all these years — all these years! She kept saying over the words of the old Bishop, as one numbed, and unable to think, keeps repeating the last thing that enters the mind. Trembling, white, her knees weak beneath her, she followed saying:

"God is good — oh, Bishop — tell me — why — why — why —"

"Because Cap'n Tom is not dead, Miss Alice, he is alive and well."

They had reached the large oak which shadowed the little cabin. She stopped suddenly in the agony of happiness, and the strong old man, who had been watching her, turned and caught her with a firm grasp, while the stars danced frantically above her. And half-unconscious she felt another one come to his aid, one who took her in his arms and kissed her lips and her eyes . . . and carried her into the bright fire-lighted

cabin, . . . carried her in strength and happiness
that made her lay her cheek against his, . . . and
there were tears on it, and somehow she lay as if she
were a child in his arms, . . . a child again and
she was happy, . . . and there were silence and
sweet dreams and the long-dead smell of the crepe-myrtle. . . . She did not remember again until she sat
up on the cot in the clean little cabin, and Tom Travis,
tall and in the splendor of manhood, sat holding her
hands and stroking her hair and whispering: "*Alice,
my darling — it is all well — and I have come back for
you at last!*"

And the old servants stood around smiling and happy,
but so silent and composed that she knew that they had
been schooled to it, and a big man, who seemed to watch
Captain Tom as a big dog would his master, kept
blowing his nose and walking around the room. And
by the fire sat the old Cottontown preacher, his back
turned to them and saying just loud enough to be
heard: "*The Lord is my shepherd, I shall not want.
He maketh me to lie down in green pastures, .* . .
he restoreth my soul — . . . *my cup runneth
over.* . . ."

And then sillily, as Alice thought, she threw her arms
around the neck of the man she loved and burst into
the tears which brought the sweetness of assurance, the
calmness of a reality that meant happiness.

And for an hour she sobbed, her arms there, and he
holding her tight to his breast and talking in the old
way, natural and soothing and reassuring and taking
from her heart all fear and the shock of it, until at last

it all seemed natural and not a dream, . . . and the sweetness of it all was like the light which cometh with the joy of the morning.

CHAPTER XV

THE TOUCH OF GOD

T HE news of Captain Tom's return spread quickly.
By noon it was known throughout the Tennessee
Valley.

The sensational features of it required prompt action
on his and Alice's part, and their decision was quickly
made: they would be married that Sunday afternoon
in the little church on the mountain side and by the old
man who had done so much to make their happiness
possible.

For once in its history the little church could not hold
the people who came to witness this romantic marriage,
and far down the mountain side they stood to see the
bride and groom pass by. Many remembered the
groom, all had heard of him,— his devotion to his country's flag; to the memory of his father; his gallantry,
his heroism, his martyrdom, dying (as they supposed)
rather than turn his guns on his brave old grandsire.
And now to come back to life again — to win the woman
he loved and who had loved him all these years! Besides, there was no one in the Tennessee Valley considered
more beautiful than the bride, and they loved her as if
she had been an angel of light.

And never had she appeared more lovely.

A stillness swept over the crowd when the carriage

drove up to the little church, and when the tall, handsome man in the uniform of a captain of artillery lifted Alice out with the tenderness of all lovers in his touch and the strength of a strong lover, with a lily in his hand, the crowd, knowing his history, could not refrain from cheering. He lifted his cap and threw back his iron-gray hair, showing a head proud and tender and on his face such a smile as lovers only wear. Then he led her in,— pale and tearful.

The little church had been prettily decorated that Sabbath morning, and when the old preacher came forward and called them to him, he said the simple words which made them man and wife, and as he blessed them, praying, a mocking-bird, perched on a limb near the window, sang a soft low melody as if one singer wished to compliment another.

They went out hand in hand, and when they reached the door, the sun which had been hid burst out as a benediction upon them.

Among the guests one man had stepped in unnoticed and unseen. Why he came he could not tell, for never before did he have any desire to go to the little church.

It was midnight when the news came to him that Tom Travis had returned as from the dead. It was Jud Carpenter who had awakened him that Saturday night to whisper at the bedside the startling news.

But Travis only yawned from his sleep and said: " I've been expecting it all the time — go somewhere and go to bed."

After Carpenter had gone, he arose, stricken with a feeling he could not describe, but had often seen in

race horses running desperately until within fifty yards
of the wire, and then suddenly — quitting. He had almost reached his goal — but now one week had done
all this. Alice — gone, and The Gaffs — he must divide that with his cousin — for his grandfather had left
no will.

Divide The Gaffs with Tom Travis? — He would as
soon think of dividing Alice's love with him. In the
soul of Richard Travis there was no such word as division.

In the selfishness of his life, it had ever been all or
nothing.

All night he thought, he walked the halls of the old
house, he ran over a hundred solutions of it in his mind.
And still there was no solution that satisfied him, that
seemed natural. It seemed that his mind, which had
heretofore worked so unerringly, deducing things so
naturally, now balked before an abyss that was bridge-
less. Heretofore he had looked into the future with
the bold, true sweep of an eagle peering from its mountain home above the clouds into the far distance, his
eyes unclouded by the mist, which cut off the vision of
mortals below. But now he was the blindest of the
blind. He seemed to stop as before a wall — a chasm
which ended everything — a chasm, on the opposite wall
of which was printed: Thus far and no farther.

Think as he would, he could not think beyond it. His
life seemed to stop there. After it, he was nothing.

Our minds, our souls — are like the sun, which shines
very plainly as it moves across the sky of our life of
things — showing them in all distinctness and clearness;

so that we see things as they happen to us with our eyes of daylight. But as the sun throws its dim twilight shadows even beyond our earth, so do the souls of men of great mind and imagination see, faintly, beyond their own lives, and into the shadow of things.

To-night that mysterious sight came to Richard Travis, as it comes in the great crises of life and death, to every strong man, and he saw dimly, ghostily, into the shadow; and the shadow stoppèd at the terrible abyss which now barred his ken; and he felt, with the keen insight of the dying eagle on the peak, that the thing was death.

In the first streak of light, he was rudely awakened to it. For there on the rug, as naturally as if asleep, lay the only thing he now loved in the world, the old setter, whose life had passed out in slumber.

All animals have the dying instinct. Man, the highest, has it the clearest. And Travis remembered that the old dog had come to his bed, in the middle of the night, and laid his large beautiful head on his master's breast, and in the dim light of the smouldering fire had said good-bye to Richard Travis as plainly as ever human being said it. And now on the rug, before the dead gray ashes of the night, he had found the old dog forever asleep, naturally and in great peace.

His heart sank as he thought of the farewell of the night before, and bitterness came, and sitting down on the rug by the side of the dead dog he stroked for the last time the grand old silken head, so calm and poised, for the little world it had been bred for, and ran his palm over the long strong nose that had never lied to

34

the scent of the covey.   His lips tightened and he said:
"O God, I am dying myself, and there is not a living
being whom I can crawl up to, and lay my head on its
breast and know it loves and pities me, as I love you, old
friend."

The thought gripped his throat, and as he thought of
the sweetness and nobility of this dumb thing, his gentleness, faithfulness and devotion, the sureness of his life
in filling the mission he came for, he wept tears so
strange to his cheek that they scalded as they flowed, and
he bowed his head and said: "Gladstone, Gladstone,
good-bye — true to your breeding, you were what your
master never was — a gentleman."

And the old housekeeper found this strong man, who
had never wept in his life, crying over the old dead
setter on the rug.

And the same feeling, the second sight — the presentiment — the terrible balking of his mind that had
always seen so clearly, ever into the future, held him
as in a vise all the morning and moved him in a strange
mysterious way to go to the church and see the woman
he had loved all his life, the being whose very look uplifted him, and whose smile could make him a hero or a
martyr, married to the man who came home to take her,
and half of his all.

Numbed, hardened, speechless, and yet with that terrible presentiment of the abyss before him, he had stood
and seen Alice Westmore made the wife of another.

He remembered first how quickly he had caught the
text of the old man; indeed, it seemed to him now that
everything he heard struck into him like a brand of

fire — for never had life appeared to him as it did to-
day.

" *For the hand of God hath touched me* —" he kept
repeating over and over — repeating and then cursing
himself for repeating it — for remembering it.

And still it stayed there all day — the unbidden
ghost-guest of his soul.

And everything the old preacher said went searing
into his quivering soul, and all the time he kept looking
— looking at the woman he loved and seeing her giving
her love, her life, with a happy smile, to another.   And
all the time he stood wondering why he came to see it,
why he felt as he did, why things hurt him that way,
why he acted so weakly, why his conscience had awakened
at last, why life hurt him so — life that he had played
with as an edged tool — why he could not get away
from himself and his memory, but ran always into it,
and why at last with a shudder, why did nothing seem
to be beyond the wall?

He saw her go off, the wife of another.   He saw their
happiness — unconscious even that he lived, and he
cursed himself and kept saying: " *The hand of God
hath touched me.*"

Then he laughed at himself for being silly.

He rode home, but it was not home.   Nothing was
itself — not even he.   In the watches of one night his
life had been changed and the light had gone out.

When night came it was worse.   He mounted his
horse and rode — where?   And he could no more help
it than he could cease to breathe.

He did not guide the saddle mare, she went herself

through wood sombre and dark with shadows, through cedar trees, dwarfed, and making pungent the night air with aromatic breath; through old sedge fields, garish in the faint light; up, up the mountain, over it; and at last the mare stopped and stood silently by a newly made grave, while Richard Travis, with strained hard mouth and wet eyes, knelt and, knowing that no hand in the world cared to feel his repentant face in it, he buried it in the new made sod as he cried: "Maggie — Maggie — forgive me, for the hand of God hath touched me!"

And it soothed him, for he knew that if she were alive he might have lain his head there — on her breast.

CHAPTER XVI

T HAT Monday was a memorable day for Helen
Conway. She went to the mill with less bitterness than ever before — the sting of it all was
gone — for she felt that she was helpless to the fate that
was hers — that she was powerless in the hands of
Richard Travis:

" *I will come for you Monday night. I will take
you away from here. You shall belong to me forever
— My Queen!* "

These words had rung in her ears all Saturday night,
when, after coming home, she had found her father
fallen by the wayside.

In the night she had lain awake and wondered. She
did not know where she was going — she did not care.
She did not even blush at the thought of it. She was
hardened, steeled. She knew not whether it meant wife
or mistress. She knew only that, as she supposed, God
had placed upon her more than she could bear

" If my life is wrecked," she said as she lay awake
that Sunday night — " God himself will do it. Who
took my mother before I knew her influence? Who
made me as I am and gave me poverty with this fatal
beauty — poverty and a drunken father and this terrible temptation? "

"Oh, if I only had her, Mammy — negro that she is."

Lily was asleep with one arm around her sister's neck.

"What will become of Lily, in the mill, too?" She bent and kissed her, and she saw that the little one, though asleep, had tears in her own eyes.

Young as she was, Helen's mind was maturer than might have been supposed. And the problem which confronted her she saw very clearly, although she was unable to solve it. The problem was not new, indeed, it has been Despair's conundrum since the world began: Whose fault that my life has been as it is? In her despair, doubting, she cried:

"Is there really a God, as Mammy Maria told me? Does He interpose in our lives, or are we rushed along by the great moral and physical laws, which govern the universe; and if by chance we fail to harmonize with them, be crushed for our ignorance — our ignorance which is not of our own making?"

"By chance — by chance," she repeated, "but if there be great fixed laws, how can there be any — chance?"

The thought was hopeless. She turned in her despair and hid her face. And then out of the darkness came the strong fine face of Clay Westmore — and his words: "We must all work — it is life's badge of nobility."

How clearly and calmly they came to her. And then her heart fluttered. Suppose Clay loved her — suppose this was her solution? He had never pressed his love on her. Did he think a woman could be loved that way — scientifically — as coal and iron are discovered?

She finally slept, her arms around her little sister. But the last recollection she had was Clay's fine face smiling at her through the darkness and saying: "We must all work — it is life's badge of nobility."

It was Monday morning, and she would take Lily with her to the mill; for the child's work at the spinning frames was to begin that day. There was no alternative. Again the great unknown law rushed her along. Her father had signed them both, and in a few days their home would be sold.

They were late at the mill, but the little one, as she trudged along by the side of her sister, was happier than she had been since her old nurse had left. It was great fun for her, this going to the mill with her big sister.

The mill had been throbbing and humming long before they reached it. Helen turned Lily over to the floor manager, after kissing her good-bye, and bade her do as she was told. Twice again she kissed her, and then with a sob hurried away to her own room.

Travis was awaiting her in the hall. She turned pale and then crimson when she saw him. And yet, when she ventured to look at him as she was passing, she was stopped with the change which lay on his face. It was a sad smile he gave her, sad but determined. And in the courtly bow was such a look of tenderness that with fluttering heart and a strange new feeling of upliftedness — a confidence in him for the first time, she stopped and gave him her hand with a grateful smile. It was a simple act and so pretty that the sadness went from Travis' face as he said:

"I was not going to stop you — this is kind of you. Saturday, I thought you feared me."

"Yes," she smiled, "but not now — not when you look like that."

"Have I changed so much since then?" and he looked at her curiously.

"There is something in your face I never saw before. It made me stop."

"I am glad it was there, then," he said simply, "for I wished you to stop, though I did not want to say so."

"Saturday you would have said so," she replied with simple frankness.

He came closer to her with equal frankness, and yet with a tenderness which thrilled her he said:

"Perhaps I was not so sure Saturday of many things that I am positive of to-day."

"Of what?" she asked flushing.

He smiled again, but it was not the old smile which had set her to trembling with a flurry of doubt and shame. It was the smile of respect. Then it left him, and in its stead flashed instantly the old conquering light when he said:

"To-night, you know, you will be mine!"

The change of it all, the shock of it, numbed her. She tried to smile, but it was the lifeless curl of her lips instead — and the look she gave him — of resignation, of acquiescence, of despair — he had seen it once before, in the beautiful eyes of the first young doe that fell to his rifle. She was not dead when he bounded to the spot where she lay — and she gave him that look.

Edward Conway watched his two daughters go out
of the gate on their way to the mill, sitting with his
feet propped up, and drunker than he had been for
weeks. But indistinct as things were, the poignancy of
it went through him, and he groaned. In a dazed sort
of way he knew it was the last of all his dreams of
respectability, that from now on there was nothing for
him and his but degradation and a lower place in life.
To do him justice, he did not care so much for himself;
already he felt that he himself was doomed, that he could
never expect to shake off the terrible habit which had
grown to be part of his life,— unless, he thought, unless,
as the Bishop had said — by the blow of God. He
paled to think what that might mean. God had so
many ways of striking blows unknown to man. But
for his daughters — he loved them, drunkard though he
was. He was proud of their breeding, their beauty,
their name. If he could only go and give them a
chance — if the blow would only fall and take him!

The sun was warm. He grew sleepy. He remembered afterwards that he fell out of his chair and that
he could not arise. . . . It was a nice place to
sleep anyway. . . . A staggering hound, with
scurviness and sores, came up the steps, then on the
porch, and licked his face. . . .

When he awoke some one was bathing his face with
cold water from the spring. He was perfectly sober
and he knew it was nearly noon. Then he heard the
person say: "I guess you are all right now, Marse
Ned, an' I'm thinkin' its the last drink you'll ever take
outen that jug."

His astonishment in recognizing that the voice was the voice of Mammy Maria did not keep him from looking up regretfully at sight of the precious broken jug and the strong odor of whiskey pervading the air.

How delightful the odor was!

He sat up amazed, blinking stupidly.

" Aunt Maria — in heaven's name — where? "

" Never mind, Marse Ned — jes' you git into the buggy now an' I'll take you home. You see, I've moved everything this mohnin' whilst you slept. The last load is gone to our new home.

" What? " he exclaimed —"where? " He looked around — the home was empty.

" I thort it time to wake you up," she went on, " an' besides I wanter talk to you about my babies.

" You'll onderstan' all that when you see the home I've bought for us "— she said simply. " We're gwine to it now. Git in the buggy "— and she helped him to arise.

Then Edward Conway guessed, and he was silent, and without a word the old woman drove him out of the dilapidated gate of Millwood toward the town.

" Mammy," he began as if he were a boy again — " Mammy," and then he burst into tears.

" Don't cry, chile," said the old woman —" it's all behind us now. I saved the money years ago, when we all wus flush — an' you gave me so much when you had an' wus so kind to me, Marse Ned. I saved it. We're gwine to reform now an' quit drinkin'. We'se gwine to remove to another spot in the garden of the Lord, but the Lord is gwine with us an' He is the tower of strength — the tower of strength to them that trust Him—Amen. But I must have my babies—that's part of the barg'in. No mill for them — oh, Marse Ned, to think that whilst I was off, fixin' our home so nice to s'prize you all—wuckin' my fingers off to git the home ready—you let them devils get my babies! Git up heah"—and she rapped the horse down the back with the lines. "Hurry up—I'm gwine after 'em es soon es I git home."

Conway could only bow his head and weep.

It was nearly noon when a large coal-black woman, her head tied up with an immaculately white handkerchief, with a white apron to match over her new calico gown, walked into the mill door. She passed through Kingsley's office, without giving him the courtesy of a nod, holding her head high and looking straight before her. A black thunder-cloud of indignation sat upon her brow, and her large black eyes were lit up with a sarcastic light.

Before Kingsley could collect his thoughts she had passed into the big door of the main room, amid the whirl and hum of the machinery, and walking straight to one of the spinning frames, she stooped and gathered into her arms the beautiful, fair-skinned little girl who was trying in vain to learn the tiresome lesson of piecing the ever-breaking threads of the bewildering, whirling bobbins.

The child was taken so by surprise that she screamed in fright—not being able to hear the foot-fall or the voice of her who had so suddenly folded her in her arms and showered kisses on her face and hair. Then, seeing the face, she shouted:

" It's Mammy Maria—oh, it's my mammy! " and she threw her arms around the old woman's neck and clung there.

" Mammy's baby—did you think old Mammy dun run off an' lef' her baby ? "

But Lily could only sob for joy.

Then the floor manager came hurriedly over—for the entire force of the mill had ceased to work, gazing at the strange scene. In vain he gesticulated his protests—the big fat colored woman walked proudly past him with Lily in her arms.

In Kingsley's office she stopped to get Lily's bonnet, while the little girl still clung to her neck, sobbing.

Kingsley stood taking in the scene in astonishment. He adjusted his eye-glasses several times, lilting them with the most pronounced sarcastic lilt of which he was capable.

He stepped around and around the desk in agitated briskness.

He cleared his throat and jerked his pant legs up and down. And all the time the fat old woman stood looking at him, with the thunder-cloud on her brow and unexpressed scorn struggling for speech in her eyes.

" Ah-hem — ah-ha — Aunt Maria " for Kingsley had caught on to the better class of Southern ways— " inform me—ah, what does all this mean? "

The old woman drew herself up proudly and replied with freezing politeness:

" I beg yo' pardon, sah—but I was not awares that

I had any nephew in the mill, or was related to anybody in here, sah. I hav'nt my visitin' cyard with me, but if I had 'em heah you'd find my entitlements, on readin', was somethin' lak this: *Miss Maria Conway, of Zion!*"

Kingsley flushed, rebuked. Then he adjusted his glasses again with agitated nervous attempts at a lilt. Then he struck his level and fell back on his natural instinct, unmixed, with attempts at being what he was not :

" I beg your pardon, Mrs. Conway "—

" Git my entitlements right, please sah. I'm the only old maid lady of color you ever seed or ever will see again. Niggahs, these days, lak birds, all git 'em a mate some way—but I'm Miss Conway of Zion."

"Ah, beg pardon, Miss Conway—Miss Conway of Zion. And where, pray, is that city, Miss Conway? I may have to have an officer communicate with you."

" With pleasure, sah—It's a pleasure for me to he'p people find a place dey'd never find without help—no —not whilst they're a-workin' the life out of innocent tots an' babes—"

Kingsley flushed hot, angered :

" What do you mean, old woman ?"

" The ole woman means," she said, looking him steadily in the eye, "that you are dealin' in chile slavery, law or no law ; that you're down heah preachin' one thing for niggahs an' practisin' another for yo' own race; that yo' hair frizzles on yo' head at tho'rt of niggah slavery, whilst all the time you are enslavin' the po' little whites that's got yo' own blood in their veins. An' now you wanter know what I come for ? I come for my chile!"

Kingsley was too dumfounded to speak. In all his
life never had his hypocrisy been knocked to pieces so
completely.

"What does all this mean?" asked Jud Carpenter
rushing hastily into the room.

"Come on baby," said the old woman as she started
toward the door. "I've got a home for us, an' whilst
old mammy can take in washin' you'll not wuck yo' life
out with these people."

Jud broke in harshly: "Come, ole 'oman,—you put
that child down. You've got nothin' to support her
with."

She turned on him quickly: "I've got mo' silver tied
up in ole socks that the Conways give me in slavery
days when they had it by the bushel, than sech as you
ever seed. Got nothin'? Jus' you come over and see
the little home I've got fixed up for Marse Ned an' the
babies. Got nothin'? See these arms? Do you think
they have forgot how to cook an' wash? Come on, baby
— we'll be gwine home — Miss Helen'll come later."

"Put her down, old woman," said Carpenter sternly.
"You can't take her — she's bound to the mill."

"Oh, I can't?" said the old woman as she walked out
with Lily — "Can't take her. Well, jes' look at me an'
see. This is what I calls Zion, an' the Lam' an' the
wolves had better stay right where they are," she remarked dryly, as she walked off carrying Lily in her
arms.

Down through a pretty part of the town, away from
Cottontown, she led the little girl, laughing now and

chatting by the old woman's side, a bird freed from a cage.

"And you'll bring sister Helen, too?" asked Lily.

"That I will, pet,— she'll be home to-night."

"Oh, Mammy, it's so good to have you again — so good, and I thought you never would come."

They walked away from Cottontown and past pretty houses. In a quiet street, with oaks and elms shading it, she entered a yard in which stood a pretty and nicely painted cottage. Lily clapped her hands with laughter when she found all her old things there — even her pet dolls to welcome her — all in the cunningest and quaintest room imaginable. The next room was her father's, and Mammy's room was next to hers and Helen's. She ran out only to run into her father's arms. Small as she was, she saw that he was sober. He took her on his lap and kissed her.

"My little one," he said —"my little one "—

"Mammy," asked the little girl as the old woman came out —"how did you get all this?"

"Been savin' it all my life, chile — all the money yo' blessed mother give me an' all I earned sence I was free. I laid it up for a rainy day an' now, bless God, it's not only rainin' but sleetin' an' cold an' snowin' besides, an' so I went to the old socks. It's you all's, an' all paid fur, an' old mammy to wait on you. I'm gwine to go after Miss Helen before the mill closes, else she'll be gwine back to Millwood, knowin' nothin' of all this surprise for her. No, sah,— nary one of yo' mother's chillun shall ever wuck in a mill."

Conway bowed his head. Then he drew Lily to him

as he knelt and said: "Oh, God help me — make me a man, make me a Conway again."

It was his first prayer in years — the beginning of his reformation. And every reformation began with a prayer.

CHAPTER XVII

THE DOUBLE THAT DIED

TWO hours before the mill closed Richard Travis came hurriedly into the mill office. There had been business engagements to be attended to in the town before leaving that night for the North, and he had been absent from the mill all day. Now everything was ready even to his packed trunk — all except Helen.

"He's come for her," said Jud to himself as he walked over to the superintendent's desk.

Then amid the hum and the roar of the mill he bent his head and the two whispered low and earnestly together. As Jud talked in excited whispers, Travis lit a cigar and listened coolly — to Jud's astonishment — even cynically.

"An' what you reckin' she done — the ole 'oman? Tuck the little gyrl right out of my han's an' kerried her home — marched off as proud as ole Queen Victory."

"Home? What home?" asked Travis.

"An' that's the mischief of it," went on Jud. "I thort she was lyin' about the home, an' I stepped down there at noon an' I hope I may die to-night if she ain't got 'em all fixed up as snug as can be, an' the Major is there as sober es a jedge, an' lookin' like a gentleman an' actin' like a Conway. Say, but you watch yo' han'.

That's blood that won't stan' monkeyin' with when it's
in its right mind. An' the little home the ole 'oman's
got, she bought it with her own money, been savin' it all
her life an' now "—

"What did you say to her this morning?" asked
Travis.

"Oh, I cussed her out good — the old black "—

A peculiar light flashed in Richard Travis' eyes.
Never before had the Whipper-in seen it. It was as if
he had looked up and seen a halo around the moon.

"To do grand things — to do grand things — like
that — negro that she is! No — no — of course you
did not understand. Our moral sense is gone — we mill
people. It is atrophied — yours and mine and all of us
— the soul has gone and mine? My God, why did you
give it back to me now — this ghost soul that has come
to me with burning breath?"

Jud Carpenter listened in amazement and looked at
him suspiciously. He came closer to see if he could
smell whiskey on his breath, but Travis looked at him
calmly as he went on: "Why, yes, of course you cursed
her — how could you understand? How could you
know — you, born soulless, know that you had witnessed
something which, what does the old preacher call him
— the man Jesus Christ — something He would have
stopped and blessed her for. A slave and she saved it
for her master. A negro and she loved little children
where we people of much intellect and a higher civilization and Christianity — eh, Jud, Christians "— and he
laughed so strangely that Jud took a turn around the
room watching Travis out of the corner of his eyes.

" Oh — and you cursed her ! "

Jud nodded. " An' to-morrow I'll go an' fetch the little 'un back. Why she's signed — she's our'n for five years."

Travis turned quickly and Jud dodged under the same strange light that showed again in his eyes. Then he laid his hand on Jud's arm and said simply: " No — no — you will not ! "

Jud looked at him in open astonishment.

Travis puffed at his cigar as he said:

" Don't study me too closely. Things have happened — have happened, I tell you — my God! we are all double — that is if we are anything — two halves to us — and my half —my other half, got lost till the other night and left this aching, pitiful, womanly thing behind, that bleeds to the touch and has tears. Why, man, I am either an angel, a devil, or both. Don't you go there and touch that little child, nor thrust your damned moral Caliban monstrosity into that sweet isle, nor break up with your seared conscience the glory of that unselfish act. If you do I'll kill you, Jud Carpenter — I'll kill you ! "

Jud turned and walked to the water bucket, took a drink and squirted it through his teeth.

He was working for thinking time: " He's crazy — he's sho' crazy —" he said to himself. Coming back, he said:

" Pardon me, Mr. Travis — but the oldes' gyrl — what — what about her, you know ? "

" She's mine, isn't she? I've won her — outgeneraled the others — by brains and courage. She should be-

long to my harem — to my band — as the stallion of
the plains when he beats off with tooth and hoof and
neck of thunder his rival, and takes his mares."

Jud nodded, looking at him quizzically.

"Well, what about it?" asked Travis.

"Nothin' — only this"— then he lowered his voice
as he came nearer —"the ole 'oman will be after her in
an hour — an' she'll take her — tell her all. Maybe
you'll see somethin' to remind you of Jesus Christ in
that."

Travis smiled.

"Well," went on Jud, " you'd better take her now —
while the whole thing has played into yo' hands; but
she — the oldes' gyrl — she don't know the ole 'oman's
come back an' made her a home; that her father is sober
an' there with her little sister, that Clay is away an'
ain't deserted her. She don't know anything, an' when
you set her out in that empty house, deserted, her folks
all deserted her, as she'll think, don't you know she'll
go to the end of the worl' with you?"

"Well?" asked Travis as he smiled calmly.

"Well, take her and thank Jud Carpenter for the
Queen of the Valley — eh?" and he laughed and tried
to nudge Travis familiarly, but the latter moved away.

"I'll take her," at last he said.

"She'll go to The Gaffs with you"— went on Jud.
"There she's safe. Then to-night you can drive her
to the train at Lenox, as we told Biggers."

He came over and whispered in Travis's ear.

"That worked out beautifully," said Travis after
a while, " but I'll not trust her to you or to Charley

Biggers. I'll take her myself — she's mine — Richard
Travis's — mine — mine! I who have been buffeted
and abused by Fate, given all on earth I do not want,
and denied the one thing I'd die for; I'll show them
who they are up against. I'll take her, and they may
talk and rave and shoot and be damned!"

His old bitterness was returning. His face flushed:

" That's the way you love to hear me talk, isn't it —
to go on and say I'll take her and do as I please with
her, and if it pleases me to marry her I'll set her up over
them all — heh?"

Jud nodded.

"That's one of me," said Travis —" the old one.
This is the new." And he opened the back of his watch
where a tiny lock of Alice Westmore's auburn hair lay:
" Oh, if I were only worthy to kiss it!"

He walked into the mill and down to the little room
where Helen sat. He stood a while at the door and
watched her — the poise of the beautiful head, the
cheeks flushed with the good working blood that now
flowed through them, the hair falling with slight disorder, a stray lock of it dashed across her forehead and
setting off the rest of it, darker and deeper, as a cloud-
let, inlaid with gold, the sunset of her cheeks.

His were the eyes of a connoisseur when it came to
women, and as he looked he knew that every line of her
was faultless; the hands slender and beautifully high-
born; the fingers tapering with that artistic slope of the
tips, all so plainly visible now that they were at work.
One foot was thrust out, slender with curved and high
instep. He flushed with pride of her — his eyes bright-

ened and he smiled in the old ironical way, a smile of dare-doing, of victory.

He walked in briskly and with a business-like, forward alertness. She looked up, paled, then flushed.

" Oh, I was hoping so you had forgotten," she said tremblingly.

He smiled kindly: " I never forget."

She put up one hand to her cheek and rested her head on it a moment in thought.

He came up and stood deferentially by her side, looking down on her, on her beautiful head. She half crouched, expecting to hear something banteringly complimentary; bold, commonplace — to feel even the touch of his sensual hand on her hair, on her cheek and *My Queen — my Queen!*

After a while she looked up, surprised. The excitement in her eyes — the half-doubting — half-yielding fight there, of ambition, and doubt, and the stubborn wrong of it all, of her hard lot and bitter life, of the hidden splendor that might lie beyond, and yet the terrible doubt, the fear that it might end in a living death — these, fighting there, lit up her eyes as candles at an altar of love. Then the very difference of his attitude, as he stood there, struck her,— the beautiful dignity of his face, his smile. She saw in an instant that sensualism had vanished — there was something spiritual which she had never seen before. A wave of trust, in her utter helplessness, a feeling of respect, of admiration, swept over her. She arose quickly, wondering at her own decision.

He bowed low, and there was a ringing sweetness in

his voice as he said: "I have come for you, Helen —
if you wish to go."

"I will go, Richard Travis, for I know now you will
do me no harm."

"Do you think you could learn to love me?"

She met his eyes steadily, bravely: "That was never
in the bargain. That is another thing. This is barter
and trade — the last ditch rather than starvation, death.
This is the surrender of the earthen fort, the other the
glory of the ladder leading to the skies. Understand
me, you have not asked for that — it is with me and
God, who made me and gave it. Let it stay there and
go back to him. You offer me bread "—

"But may it not turn into a stone, an exquisite, pure
diamond?" he asked.

She looked at him sadly. She shook her head.

"Diamonds are not made in a day."

The light Jud Carpenter saw flashed in his eyes: "I
have read of one somewhere who turned water into wine
— and that was as difficult."

"If — if —" she said gently —" if you had always
been this — if you would always be this "—

"A woman knows a man as a rose knows light," he
said simply — " as a star knows the sun. But we men
— being the sun and the star, we are blinded by our
own light. Come, you may trust me, Sweet Rose."

She put her hand in his. He took it half way to his
mouth.

"Don't," she said —" please — that is the old way."

He lowered it gently, reverently, and they walked out.

CHAPTER XVIII

THE DYING LION

"LILY has been taken home," he said as she walked out with him. "She is safe and will be cared for — so will be your father. I will explain it to you as we drive to Millwood."

She wondered, but her cheeks now burned so that all her thoughts began to flow back upon herself as a tide, flowing inland, and forgetting the sea of things. Her heart beat faster — she felt guilty — of what, she could not say.

Perhaps the guilt of the sea for being found on the land.

The common mill girls — were they not all looking at her, were they not all wondering, did they not all despise her, her who by birth and breeding should be above them? Her lips tightened at the thought — she who was above them — now — now — they to be above her — poor-born and common as they were — if — if — he betrayed her.

He handed her quietly — reverently even, into the buggy, and the trotters whirled her away; but not before she thought she saw the mill girls peeping at her through the windows, and nodding their heads at each other, and some of them smiling disdainfully. And yet when she looked closely there was no one at the windows.

The wind blew cool.   Travis glanced at her dress, her
poorly protected shoulders.

"I am afraid you will be too cold after coming from
a warm mill and going with the speed we go."

He reached under the seat and drew out a light overcoat. He threw it gently over her shoulders, driving,
in his masterful way, with the reins in one hand.

He did not speak again until he reached Millwood.

The gate was down, bits of strewn paper, straw and
all the debris of things having been moved, were there.
The house was dark and empty, and Helen uttered a surprised cry:

"Why, what does all this mean?   Oh, has anything
happened to them?"

She clung in pallor to Travis's arm.

"Be calm," he said, "I will explain.   They are all
safe.   They have moved.   Let us go in, a moment."

He drew the mares under a shed and hitched them,
throwing blankets over them and unchecking their heads.
Then he lifted her out.   How strong he was, and how
like a limp lily she felt in the grasp of his hands.

The moon flashed out now and then from clouds scur-
rying fast, adding a ghostliness to the fading light, in
which the deserted house stood out amid shadowy trees
and weeds tall and dried.   The rotten steps and balcony, even the broken bottles and pieces of crockery
shone bright in the fading light.   Tears started to her
eyes:

"Nothing is here — nothing!"

Travis caught her hand in the dark and she clung to
him.   A hound stepped out from under the steps and

licked her other hand. She jumped and gave a little
shriek. Then, when she understood, she stroked the
poor thing's head, its eyes staring hungrily in the dim
light.

She followed Travis up the steps. Within, he struck
a match, and she saw the emptiness of it all — the
broken plastering and the paper torn off in spots, a
dirty, littered floor, and an old sofa and a few other
things left, too worthless to be moved.

She held up bravely, but tears were running down her
cheeks. Travis struck another match to light a lamp
which had been forgotten and left on the mantel. He
attempted to light it, but something huge and black
swept by and extinguished it. Helen shrieked again,
and coming up timidly seized his arm in the dark. He
could feel her heart beating excitedly against it.

He struck another match.

" Don't be uneasy, it is nothing but an owl."

The light was turned up and showed an owl sitting on
the top of an old tester that had formerly been the
canopy of her grandmother's bed.

The owl stared stupidly at them — turning its head
solemnly.

Helen laughed hysterically.

" Now, sit down on the old sofa," he said. " There
is much to say to you. We are now on the verge of a
tragedy or a farce, or —"

" Sometimes plays end well, where all are happy, do
they not? " she asked, smiling hysterically and sitting
by him, but looking at the uncanny owl beyond. She
was silent, then:

"Oh, I — I — don't you think I am entitled now — to have something end happily — now — once — in my life?"

He pitied her and was silent.

"Tell me," she said after a while, "you have moved father and Lily to — to — one of the Cottontown cottages?"

He arose: "In a little while I will tell you, but now we must have something to eat first — you see I had this lunch fixed for our journey." He went out, over to his lap-robe and cushion, and brought a basket and placed it on an old table.

"You may begin now and be my housekeeper," he smiled. "Isn't it time you were learning? I daresay I'll not find you a novice, though."

She flushed and smiled. She arose gracefully, and her pretty hands soon had the lunch spread, Travis helping her awkwardly.

It was a pretty picture, he thought — her flushed girlish face, yet matronly ways. He watched her slyly, with a sad joyousness in his eyes, drinking it in, as one who had hungered long for contentment and peace, such as this.

She had forgotten everything else in the housekeeping. She even laughed some at his awkwardness and scolded him playfully, for, man-like, forgetting a knife and fork. It was growing chilly, and while she set the lunch he went out and brought in some wood. Soon a fine oak fire burned in the fireplace.

They sat at the old table at last, side by side, and ate the delightful lunch. Under the influence of the bottle

of claret, from The Gaffs cellar, her courage came and
her animation was beautiful to him — something that
seemed more of girlhood than womanhood.   He drank it
all in — hungry — heart-hungry for comfort and love;
and she saw and understood.

Never had he enjoyed a lunch so much.   Never had
he seen so beautiful a picture!

When it was over he lit a cigar, and the fine odor
filled the old room.

Then very quietly he told her the story of Mammy
Maria's return, of the little home she had prepared for
them; of her coming that day to the mill and taking
Lily, and that even now, doubtless, she was there looking for the elder sister.

She did not show any surprise — only tears came
slowly: "Do you know that I felt that something of
this kind would happen?   Dear Mammy — dear, dear
Mammy Maria!   She will care for Lily and father."

She could stand it no longer.   She burst into childish
tears and, kneeling, she put her beautiful head on
Travis's lap as innocently as if it were her old nurse's,
and she, a child, seeking consolation.

He stroked her hair, her cheek, gently.   He felt his
lids grow moist and a tenderness he never had known
came over him.

"I have told you this for a purpose," he whispered
in her ear —"I will take you to them, now."

She raised her wet eyes — flushed.   He watched her
closely to see signs of any battle there.   And then his
heart gave a great leap and surged madly as she said
calmly: "No — no — it is too late — too late — now.

I — could — never explain. I will go with you, Richard Travis, to the end of the world."

He sat very still and looked at her kneeling there as a child would, both hands clasped around his knee, and looking into his eyes with hers, gray-brown and gloriously bright. They were calm — so calm, and determined and innocent. They thrilled him with their trust and the royal beauty of her faith. There came to him an upliftedness that shook him.

" To the end of the world," he said —" ah, you have said so much — so much more than I could ever deserve."

" I have stood it all as long as I could. My father's drunkenness, I could stand that, and Mammy's forsaking us, as I thought — that, too. When the glory of work, of earning my own living opened itself to me,— Oh, I grasped it and was happy to think that I could support them! That's why your temptation — why — I —"

He winced and was silent.

" They were nothing," she went on, " but to be forgotten, forsaken by — by —" .

" Clay? " he helped her say.

" Oh," she flushed —" yes,— that was part of it, and then to see — to see — you so different — with this strange look on you — something which says so plainly to me that — that — oh, forgive me, but do you know I seem to see you dying — dying all the time, and now you are so changed — indeed — oh please understand me — I feel differently toward you — as I would toward one dying for sympathy and love."

She hid her face again. He felt his face grow hot.
He sat perfectly still, listening. At last she said:

"When I came here to-night and saw it all — empty
— I thought: 'This means I am deserted by all — he
has brought me here to see it — to know it. What can
I do but go with him? It is all that is left. Did I
make myself? Did I give myself this fatal beauty —
for you say I am beautiful. And did I make you with
your strength — your conquering strength, and — Oh,
could I overcome my environment?' But now — now
— it is different — and if I am lost, Richard Travis —
it will be your fault — yours and God's."

He stroked her hair. He was pale and that strange
light which Jud Carpenter had seen in his eyes that
afternoon blazed now with a nervous flash.

"That is my story," she cried. "It is now too late
even for God to come and tell me through you — now
since we — you and I — oh, how can I say it — you
have taken me this way — you, so strong and brave and
— grand —"

He flushed hot with shame. He put his hand gently
over her mouth.

"Hush — hush — child — my God — you hurt me
— shame me — you know not what you say."

"I can understand all — but one thing," she went on
after a while. "Why have you brought me to this —
here — at night alone with you — to tell me this — to
make me — me — oh, change in my feelings — to you?
Oh, must I say it?" she cried —"tell you the truth —
that — that — now since I see you as you are — I — I,
— I am willing to go!"

"Hush, Helen, my child, my God — don't crush me — don't — listen, child — listen! I am a villain — a doubly-dyed, infamous one — when you hear "—

She shook her head and put one of her pretty hands over his mouth.

"Let me tell you all, first. Let me finish. After all this, why have you brought me here to tell me this, when all you had to do was to keep silent a few more hours — take me on to the station, as you said — and — and —"

"I will tell you," he said gently. "Yes, you have asked the question needed to be explained. Now hear from my own lips my infamy — not all of it, God knows — that would take the night; but this peculiar part of it. Do you know why I love to stroke your hair, why I love to touch it, to touch you, to look into your eyes; why I should love, next to one thing of all earth, to take you in my arms and smother you — kill you with kisses — your hair, your eyes, your mouth?"

She hid her face, crimson.

"Did no one tell you, ever tell you — how much you look like your cousin "— he stopped — he could not say the word, but she guessed. White with shame, she sprang up from him, startled, hurt. Her heart tightened into a painful thing which pricked her.

"Then — then — it is not I — but my Cousin Alice — oh — I — yes — I did hear — I should have known "— it came from her slowly and with a quivering tremor.

He seized her hands and drew her back down by him on the sofa.

"When I started into this with you I was dead — dead. My soul was withered within me. All women were my playthings — all but one. She was my Queen — my wife that was to be. I was dead, my God — how dead I was! I now see with a clearness that is killing me; a clearness as of one waking from sleep and feeling, in the first wave of conscience, that inconceivable tenderness which hurts so — hurts because it is tender and before the old hard consciousness of material things come again to toughen. How dead I was, you may know when I say that all this web now around you — from your entrance into the mill till now — here to-night — in my power — body and soul — that it was all to gratify this dead sea fruit of my soul, this thing in me I cannot understand, making me conquer women all my life for — oh, as a lion would, to kill, though not hungry, and then lie by them, dying, and watch them,— dead! Then this same God — if any there be — He who you say put more on you than you could bear — He struck me, as, well — no — He did not strike — but ground me, ground me into dust — took her out of my life and then laid my soul before me so naked that the very sunlight scorches it. What was it the old preacher said — that 'touch of God' business? 'Touch —'" he laughed, "not touch, but blow, I say — a blow that ground me into star-dust and flung me into space, my heart a burning comet and my soul the tail of it, dissolving before my very eyes. What then can I, a lion, dying, care for the doe that crosses my path? The beautiful doe, beautiful even as you are. Do you understand me, child?"

She scarcely knew what she did. She remembered only the terrible empty room. The owl uncannily turning its head here and there and staring at her with its eyes, yellow in the firelight.

She dropped on the floor by him and clung again to his knees, her head in his lap in pity for him.

" That is the story of the dying lion," he said after a while. " The lion who worked all his cunning and skill and courage to get the beautiful doe in his power, only to find he was dying — dying and could not eat. Could you love a dying lion, child?" he asked abruptly — " tell me truly, for as you speak so will I act — would make you queen of all the desert."

She raised her eyes to his. They were wet with tears. He had touched the pity in them. She saw him as she had never seen him before. All her fear of him vanished, and she was held by the cords of a strange fascination. She knew not what she did. The owl looked at her queerly, and she almost sobbed it out, hysterically:

" Oh, I could — love — you — you — who are so strong and who suffer — suffer so "—

" You could love me?" he asked. " Then, then I would marry you to-night — now — if — if — that uncovering — that touch — had not been put upon me to do nobler things than to gratify my own passion, had not shown me the other half which all these years has been dead — my double." He was silent.

" And so I sent to-day," he began after a while, " for a friend of yours, one with whom you can be happier than — the dying lion. He has been out of the county — sent out — it was part of the plan, part of the snare

36

of the lion and his whelp. And so I sent for him this morning, feeling the death blow, you know. I sent him an urgent message, to meet you here at nine." He glanced at his watch. " It is past that now, but he had far to ride. He will come, I hope — ah, listen! "

They heard the steps of a rider coming up the gravel walk.

" It is he," said Travis calmly —" Clay."

She sprang up quickly, half defiantly. The old Conway spirit flashed in her eyes and she came to him tall and splendid and with half a look of protest, half command, and yet in it begging, pleading, yearning for — she knew not what.

" Why — why — did you? Oh, you do not know.! You do not understand — love — love — can it be won this way — apprenticed, bargained — given away? "

" You must go with him, he loves you. He will make you happy. I am dying — is not part of me already dead? "

For answer she came to him, closer, and stood by him as one who in war stands by a comrade shot through and ready to fall.

He put his arms around her and drew her to him closer, and she did not resist — but as a child would, hers also she wound around his neck and whispered:

" My lion! Oh, kill me — kill me — let me die with you! "

" Child — my precious one — my — oh, God, and you — forgive me this. But let me kiss you once and dream — dream it is she "—

She felt his kisses on her hair, her eyes.

"Good-bye — Alice — Alice — good-bye — forever —"

He released her, but she clung to him sobbing. Her head lay on his breast, and she shook in the agony of it all.

"You will forgive me, some day — when you know — how I loved her," he gasped, white and with a bitter light in his face.

She looked up: "I would die," she said simply, "for a love like that."

They heard the steps of a man approaching the house. She sat down on the old sofa pale, trembling and with bitterness in her heart.

Travis walked to the door and opened it:

"Come in, Clay," he said quietly. "I am glad that my man found you. We have been waiting for you."

"I finished that survey and came as fast as I could. Your man rode on to The Gaffs, but I came here as you wrote me to do," and Clay came in quietly, speaking as he walked to the fire.

CHAPTER XIX

FACE TO FACE WITH DEATH

HE CAME in as naturally as if the house were still inhabited, though he saw the emptiness of it all, and guessed the cause. But when he saw Helen, a flushed surprise beamed through his eyes and he gave her his hand.

"Helen! — why, this is unexpected — quite unusual, I must say."

She did not speak, as she gave him her hand, but smiled sadly. It meant: "Mr. Travis will tell you all. I know nothing. It is all his planning."

Clay sat down in an old chair by the fire and warmed his hands, looking thoughtfully at the two, now and then, and wonderingly. He was not surprised when Travis said:

"I sent for you hurriedly, as one who I knew was a friend of Miss Conway. A crisis has arisen in her affairs to-day in which it is necessary for her friends to act."

"Why, yes, I suppose I can guess," said Clay thoughtfully and watching Helen closely all the while as he glanced around the empty room. "I was only waiting. Why, you see —"

Helen flushed scarlet and looked appealingly at Travis. But he broke in on Clay without noticing her.

" Yes, I knew you were only waiting.   I think I understand you, but you know the trouble with nearly every good intention is that it waits too long."

Clay reddened.

Helen arose and, coming over, stood by Travis, her face pale, her eyes shining.   " I beg — I entreat — please, say no more.   Clay," she said turning on him with flushed face, " I did not know you were coming. I did not know where you were.   Like all the others, I supposed you too had — had deserted me."

" Why, I was sent off in a hurry to —" he started.

" Mr. Travis told me to-night," she interrupted.   " I understand now.   But really, it makes no difference to me now.   Since — since —"

" Now look here," broke in Travis with feigned lightness,—" I am not going to let you two lovers misunderstand each other.   I have planned it all out and I want you both to make me happy by listening to one older, one who admires you both and sincerely wishes to see you happy.   Things have happened at your house," he said addressing Clay —" things which will surprise you when you reach home — things that affect you and me and Miss Conway.   Now I know that you love her, and have loved her a long time, and that only —"

" Only our poverty," said Clay thankfully to Travis for breaking the ice for him.

Helen stood up quickly — a smile on her lips: " Don't you both think that before this bargain and sale goes further you had better get the consent of the one to be sold ? "   She turned to Clay.

" Don't you think you have queer ideas of love — of

winning a woman's love — in this way? And you "—
she said turning to Travis —" Oh you *know* better."

Travis arose with a smile half joyous, half serious,
and Clay was so embarrassed that he mopped his brow
as if he were plowing in the sun.

" Why, really, Helen — I — you know — I have
spoken to you — you know, and but for my —"

" Poverty "— said Helen taking up the word —
"And what were poverty to me, if I loved a man? I'd
love him the more for it. If he were dying broken-
hearted, wrecked — even in disgrace,—"

Travis flushed and looked at her admiringly, while the
joyous light flashed yet deeper in his eyes.

" Come," he said. " I have arranged all. I am not
going to give you young people an excuse to defer your
happiness longer." He turned to Clay: " I shall show
you something which you have been on the track of for
some time. I have my lantern in the buggy, and we
will have to walk a mile or more. But it is pleasant to-
night, and the walk will do us all good. Come."

They both arose wonderingly — Helen came over and
put her hand on his arm: " I will go," she whispered,
" if there be no more of that talk."

He smiled. " You must do as I say. Am I not now
your guardian? Bring your leathern sack with your
hammer and geological tools," he remarked to Clay.

Clay arose hastily, and they went out of the old house
and across the fields. Past the boundaries of Millwood they walked, Travis silently leading, and Clay
following with Helen, who could not speak, so mo-
mentous it all seemed. She saw only Travis's fine

square shoulders, and erect, sinewy form, going before them, into the night of shadows, of trees, of rocks, of the great peak of the mountain, silent and dark.

He did not speak. He walked in silent thought. They passed the boundary line of Millwood, and then down a slight ravine he led them to the ragged, flinty hill, on which the old preacher's cabin stood on their right.

"Now," he said stopping —"if I am correct, Clay, this hill is the old Bishop's," pointing to his right where the cabin stood, "and over here is what is left of Westmoreland. This gulch divides them. This range really runs into Westmoreland," he said with a sweep of his hand toward it. "Get your bearings," he smiled to Clay, "for I want you to tell whose fortune this is."

He lit his lantern and walking forward struck away some weeds and vines which partially concealed the mouth of a small opening in the hillside caused by a landslide. It was difficult going at first, but as they went further the opening grew larger, and as the light flashed on its walls, Clay stopped in admiration and shouted:

"Look — look — there it is!"

Before them running right and left — for the cave had split it in two, lay the solid vein of coal, shining in the light, and throwing back splinters of ebony, to Clay more beautiful than gold.

Travis watched him with an amused smile as he hastily took off his satchel and struck a piece off the ledge. Helen stood wondering, looking not at Clay, but at

Travis, and her eyes shone brilliantly and full of proud splendor.

Clay forgot that they were there. He measured the ledge. He chipped off piece after piece and examined it closely. " I never dreamed it would be here, in this shape," he said at last. " Look! — and fully eight feet, solid. This hill is full of it. The old preacher will find it hard to spend his wealth."

" But that is not all," said Travis; " see how the dip runs — see the vein — this way." He pointed to the left.

Clay paled: " That means — it is remarkable — very remarkable. Why, this vein should not have been here. It is too low to be in the Carboniferous." He suddenly stopped: " But here it is — contrary to all my data and — and — why really it takes the low range of the poor land of Westmoreland. It — it — will make me rich."

" You haven't seen all," said Travis —" look!" He turned and walked to another part of the small cave, where the bank had broken, and there gleamed, not the black, but the red— the earth full of rich ore.

Clay picked up one eagerly.

" The finest iron ore! — who — who — ever heard of such a freak of nature?"

" And the lime rock is all over the valley," said Travis, " and that means, coal, iron and lime —"

" Furnaces — why, of course — furnaces and wealth. Helen, I — I — it will make Westmoreland rich. Now, in all earnestness — in all sincerity I can tell you —"

" Do not tell me anything, Clay — please do not.

You do not understand. You can never understand."
Her eyes were following Travis, who had walked off
pretending to be examining the cave. Then she gave
a shriek which sounded frightfully intense as it echoed
around.

Travis turned quickly and saw standing between him
and them a gaunt, savage thing, with froth in its mouth
and saliva-dripping lips. At first he thought it was a
panther, so low it crouched to spring; but almost instantly he recognized Jud Carpenter's dog. Then it
began to creep uncertainly, staggeringly forward, toward Clay and Helen, its neck drawn and contracted
in the paroxysms of rabies; its deadly eyes, staring, un-
earthly yellow in the lantern light. Within two yards of
Clay, who stood helpless with fear and uncertainty, it
crouched to spring, growling and snapping at its own
sides, and Helen screamed again as she saw Travis's
quick, lithe figure spring forward and, grasping the
dog by the throat from behind, fling himself with crushing force on the brute, choking it as he fell.

Total darkness — for in his rush Travis threw aside
his lantern — and it seemed an age to Helen as she heard
the terrible fight for life going on at her feet, the
struggles and howls of the dog, the snapping of the
huge teeth, the stinging sand thrown up into her face.
Then after a while all was still, and then very quietly
from Travis:

" A   match,   Clay — light   the   lantern!   I   have
choked him to death."'

Under the light he arose, his clothes torn with tooth
and fang of the gaunt dog, which lay silent. He stood

up hot and flushed, and then turned pallid, and for a
moment staggered as he saw the blood trickling from his
left arm.

Helen stood by him terror-eyed, trembling, crushed,—
with a terrible sickening fear.

"He was mad," said Travis gently, "and I fear he
has bitten me, though I managed to jump on him before
he bit you two."

He took off his coat — blood was on his shirt sleeve
and had run down his arm. Helen, pale and with a
great sob in her throat, rolled up the sleeve, Travis sub-
mitting, with a strange pallor in his face and the new
light in his eyes.

His bare arm came up strong and white. Above the
elbow, near the shoulder, the blood still flowed where the
fangs had sunk.

"There is only one chance to save me," he said
quietly, "and that, a slim one. It bleeds — if I could
only get my lips to it —"

He tried to expostulate, to push her off, as he felt
her lips against his naked arm. But she clung there
sucking out the virus. He felt her tears fall on his arm.
He heard her murmur:

"My dying lion — my dying lion!"

He bent and whispered: "You are risking your own
life for me, Helen! Life for life — death for death!"

It was too much even for his great strength, and
when he recovered himself he was sitting on the sand of
the little cave. How long she had clung to his arm he
did not know, but it had ceased to pain him and her own
handkerchief was tied around it.

He staggered out, a terrible pallor on his face, as he said: " Not this way — not to go this way. Oh, God, your blow — I care not for death, but, oh, not this death? "

" Clay," he said after a while —" Take her — take her to your mother and sister to-night. I must bid you both good-night, ay, and good-bye. See, you walk only across the field there — that is Westmoreland."

He turned, but he felt some one clinging to his hand, in the dark. He looked down at her, at the white, drawn face, beautiful with a terrible pain: " Take me — take me," she begged —" with you — to the end of the world — oh, I love you and I care not who knows."

" Child — child "— he whispered sadly —" You know not what you say. I am dying. I shall be mad — unless — unless what you have done —"

" Take me," she pleaded —" my lion. I am yours."

He stooped and kissed her and then walked quickly away.

CHAPTER XX

THE ANGEL WITH THE FLAMING SWORD

IT WAS nearly time for the mill to close when Mammy Maria, her big honest face beaming with satisfaction at the surprise she had in store for Helen, began to wind her red silk bandana around her head. She had several bandanas, but when Lily saw her put on the red silk one, the little girl knew she was going out —"dressin' fur prom'nade"— as the old lady termed it.

"You are going after Helen," said the little girl, clapping her hands.

She sat on her father's lap: "And we want you to hurry up, Mammy Maria," he said, "I want all my family here. I am going to work to-morrow. I'll redeem Millwood before my two years expire or I am not a Conway again."

Mammy Maria was agitated enough. She had been so busy that she had failed to notice how late it was. In her efforts to surprise Helen she had forgotten time, and now she feared the mill might close and Helen, not knowing they had moved, would go back to Millwood. This meant a two mile tramp and delay. She had plenty of time, she knew, before the mill closed; but the more she thought of the morning's scene at the mill and of Jud Carpenter, the greater her misgivings. For

Mammy Maria was instinctive — a trait her people have. It is always Nature's substitute when much intellect is wanting.

All afternoon she had chuckled to herself. All afternoon, the three of them,— for even Major Conway joined in, and helped work and arrange things — talked it over as they planned. His face was clear now, and calm, as in the old days. Even the old servant could see he had determined to win in the fight.

" Marse Ned's hisse'f ag'in," she would say to him encouragingly —" Marse Ned's hisse'f — an' Zion's by his side, yea, Lord, the Ark of the Tabbernackle ! "

For the last time she surveyed the little rooms of the cottage. How clean and fresh it all was, and how the old mahogany of Millwood set them off ! And now all was ready.

It was nearly dark when she reached the mill. It had not yet closed down, and lights began to blaze first from one window, then another. She could hear the steam and the coughing of the exhaust pipe.

This was all the old woman had hoped — to be in time for Helen when the mill closed.

But one thing was in her way, or she had taken her as she did Lily : She did not know where Helen's room was in the mill. There was no fear in the old nurse's heart. She had taken Lily, she would take Helen. She would show the whole tribe of them that she would ! But in which room was the elder sister ?

So she walked again into the main office, fearless, and with her head up. For was she not Zion, the Lord's chosen, the sanctified one, and the powers of hell were naught?

No one was in the office but Jud Carpenter, and to her surprise he treated her with the utmost courtesy. Indeed, his courtesy was so intense that any one but Zion, who, being black, knew little of irony and less of sarcasm, might have seen that Jud's courtesy was strongly savored of the two.

" Be seated, Madam," he said with a profound bow. " Be seated, Upholder of Heaven, Chief-cook-an'-bottle-washer in the Kingdom to come! An' what may have sent the angel of the Lord to honor us with another visit? "

The old woman's fighting feathers arose instantly:—

" The same that sent 'em to Sodom an' Gomarrer, suh," she replied.

" Ah," said Jud apologetically, " an' I hope we won't smell any brimstone to-night."

" If you don't smell it to-night, you'll smell it befo' long. And now look aheah, Mister White Man, no use for you an' me to set here a-jawin' an' 'spu'tin'. I've come after my other gyrl an' you know I'm gwine have her ! "

" Oh, she'll be out 'torectly, Mrs. Zion! Jes' keep yo' robes on an' hol' yo' throne down a little while. She'll be out 'torectly."

There was a motive in this lie, as there was in all others Jud Carpenter told.

It was soon apparent. For scarcely had the old woman seated herself with a significant toss of her head when the mill began to cease to hum and roar.

She sat watching the door keenly as they came out. What creatures they were, lint-and-dust-covered to their very eyes. The yellow, hard, emotionless faces of the men, the haggard, weary ones of the girls and women and little children! Never had she seen such white people before, such hollow eyes, with dark, bloodless rings beneath them, sunken cheeks, tanned to the color of oiled hickory, much used. Dazed, listless, they stumbled out past her with relaxed underjaws and faces gloomy, expressionless — so long bent over looms, they had taken on the very looks of them — the shapes of them, moving, walking, working, mechanically. Women, smileless, and so tired and numbed that they had forgotten the strongest instinct of humanity — the romance of sex; for many of them wore the dirty, chopped-off jackets of men, their slouched black hats, their coarse shoes, and talked even in the vulgar, hard irony of the male in despair.

They all passed out — one by one — for in them was not even the instinct of the companionship of misery.

Every moment the old nurse expected Helen to walk out, to walk out in her queenly way, with her beautiful face and manners, so different from those around her.

Jud Carpenter sat at his desk quietly cutting plug tobacco to fill his pipe-bowl, and watching the old woman slyly.

" Oh, she'll be 'long 'torectly — you see the drawer-in bein' in the far room comes out last."

The last one passed out. The mill became silent, and yet Helen did not appear.

The old nurse arose impatiently: " I reck'n I'll go find her," she said to Carpenter.

" I'd better sho' you the way, old 'oman," he said, lazily shuffling off the stool he was sitting on pretending to be reading a paper —" you'll never fin' the room by yo'self."

He led her along through the main room, hot, lint-filled and evil-smelling. It was quite dark. Then to the rear, where the mill jutted on the side of a hill, he stopped in front of a door and said: " This is her room; she's in there, I reckin — she's gen'ly late."

With quickening heart the old woman entered and, almost immediately, she heard the door behind her shut and the key turn in the bolt. The room was empty and she sprang back to the door, only to find it securely locked, and to hear Jud Carpenter's jeers from without. She ran to the two small windows. They were high and looked out over a ravine.

She did not utter a word. Reared as she had been among the Conways, she was too well bred to act the coward, and beg and plead in undignified tones for relief. At first she thought it was only a cruel joke of the Whipper-in, but when he spoke, she saw it was not.

" Got you where I want you, Mother of Zion," he said through the key hole. " I guess you are safe there till mornin' unless the Angel of the Lord opens the do' as they say he has a way of doin' for Saints — ha — ha — ha!"

No word from within.

" Wanter kno' what I shet you up for, Mother of all

Holiness? Well, listen: It's to keep you there till to-morrow — that's good reason, ain't it? You'll find a lot of cotton in the fur corner — a mighty good thing for a bed. Can't you talk? How do you like it? I guess you ain't so independent now."

There was a pause. The old woman sat numbly in Helen's chair. She saw a bunch of violets in her frame, and the odor brought back memories of her old home. A great fear began to creep over her — not for herself, but for Helen, and she fell on her knees by the frame and prayed silently.

Jud's voice came again: "Want to kno' now why you'll stay there till mornin'? Well, I'll tell you—it'll make you pass a com'f'table night — you'll never see Miss Helen ag'in —"

The old nurse sprang to her feet. She lost control of herself, for all day she had felt this queer presentiment, and now was it really true? She blamed herself for not taking Helen that morning.

She threw herself against the door. It was strong and secure.

Jud met it with a jeering laugh.

"Oh, you're safe an' you'll never see her agin. I don't mind tellin' you she has run off with Richard Travis — they'll go North to-night. You'll find other folks can walk off with yo' gals — 'specially the han'sum ones—besides yo'se'f."

The old nurse was stricken with weakness. Her limbs shook so she sat down in a heap at the door and said pleadingly : — " Are you lyin' to me, white man ? Will — will he marry her or —"

37

"Did you ever hear of him marryin' anybody?"
came back with a laugh. "No, he's only took a deserted young 'oman in out of the cold — he'll take care
of her, but he ain't the marryin' kind, is he?"

The reputation of Richard Travis was as well known
to Mammy Maria as it was to anyone. She did not
know whether to believe Jud or not, but one thing she
knew — something — something dreadful was happening to Helen. The old nurse called to mind instantly
things that had happened before she herself had left
Millwood — things Helen had said — her grief, her despair, her horror of the mill, her belief that she was
already disgraced. It all came to the old nurse now so
plainly. Tempted as she was, young as she was, deserted and forsaken as she thought she was, might not
indeed the temptation be too much for her?

She groaned as she heard Jud laugh and walk off.

"O my baby, my beautiful baby!" she wept, falling
on her knees again.

The mill grew strangely silent and dark. On a pile
of loose cotten she fell, praying after the manner of her
race.

An hour passed. The darkness, the loneliness, the
horror of it all crept into her superstitious soul, and she
became frantic with religious fervor and despair.

Pacing the room, she sang and prayed in a frenzy of
emotional tumult. But she heard only the echo of her
own voice, and only the wailings of her own songs
came back. Negro that she was, she was intelligent
enough to know that Jud Carpenter spoke the truth
— that not for his life would he have dared to say this

if it had not had some truth in it. What?— she did not
know — she only knew that harm was coming to Helen.

She called aloud for help — for Edward Conway.
But the mill was closed tight — the windows nailed.

Another hour passed. It began to tell on the old
creature's mind. Negroes are simple, religious, superstitious folks, easily unbalanced by grief or wrong.

She began to see visions in this frenzy of religious
excitement, as so many of her race do under the nervous
strain of religious feeling. She fell into a trance.

It was most real to her. Who that has ever heard
a negro give in his religious experience but recognizes
it? She was carried on the wings of the morning down
to the gates of hell. The Devil himself met her, tempting her always, conducting her through the region of
darkness and showing her the lakes of fire and threat-
ening her with all his punishment if she did not cease
to believe. She overcame him only by constant prayer.
She fled from him, he followed her, but could not approach her while she prayed. . . . She was rescued
by an angel — an angel from heaven . . . an
angel with a flaming sword. Through all the glories of
heaven this angel conducted her, praised her, and bidding her farewell at the gate, told her to go back to
earth and take this: *It was a torch of fire!*

"*Burn! burn!* " said the angel —"*for I shall make
the governors of Judah like an hearth of fire among the
wood, and like a torch of fire on a sheaf. And they
shall devour all the people around about, on the right
hand and the left; and Jerusalem shall be inhabited
again in her own place, even in Jerusalem.*"

She came out of the trance in a glory of religious fervor: "Jerusalem shall be inhabited ag'in! — the Angel has told me — told me — Burn — burn," she cried. "Oh Lord — you have spoken and Zion has ears to hear — Amen."

Quickly she gathered up the loose cotton and placed it at the door, piling it up to the very bolt. She struck a match, swaying and rocking and chanting: "Yea, Lord, thy servant hath heard — thy servant hath heard!"

The flames leaped up quickly enveloping the door. The room began to fill with smoke, but she retreated to a far corner and fell on her knees in prayer. The panels of the door caught first and the flames spreading upward soon heated the lock around which the wood blazed and crackled. It burned through. She sprang up, rushed through the blinding smoke, struck the door as it blazed, in a broken mass, and rushed out. Down the long main room she ran to a low window, burst it, and stepped out on the ground:

"Jerusalem shall be inhabited again," she shouted as she ran breathless toward home.

CHAPTER XXI

THE GREAT FIRE

EDWARD CONWAY sat on the little porch till the stars came out, wondering why the old nurse did not return. Sober as he was and knew he would ever be, it seemed that a keen sensitiveness came with it, and a feeling of impending calamity.

"Oh, it's the cursed whiskey," he said to himself — "it always leaves you keyed up like a fiddle or a woman. I'll get over it after a while or I'll die trying," and he closed his teeth upon each other with a nervous twist that belied his efforts at calmness.

But even Lily grew alarmed, and to quiet her he took her into the house and they ate their supper in silence.

Again he came out on the porch and sat with the little girl in his lap. But Lily gave him no rest, for she kept saying, as the hours passed: "Where is she, father — oh, do go and see!"

"She has gone to Millwood through mistake," he kept telling her, "and Mammy Maria has doubtless gone after her. Mammy will bring her back. We will wait awhile longer — if I had some one to leave you with," he said gently, "I'd go myself. But she will be home directly."

And Lily went to sleep in his lap, waiting.

The moon came up, and Conway wrapped Lily in a shawl, but still held her in his arms. And as he sat holding her and waiting with a fast-beating heart for the old nurse, all his wasted life passed before him.

He saw himself as he had not for years — his life a failure, his fortune gone. He wondered how he had escaped as he had, and as he thought of the old Bishop's words, he wondered why God had been as good to him as He had, and again he uttered a silent prayer of thankfulness and for strength. And with it the strength came, and he knew he could never more be the drunkard he had been. There was something in him stronger than himself.

He was a strong man spiritually — it had been his inheritance, and the very thought of anything happening to Helen blanched his cheek. In spite of the faults of his past, no man loved his children more than he, when he was himself. Like all keen, sensitive natures, his was filled to overflowing with paternal love.

" My God," he thought, " suppose — suppose she has gone back to Millwood, found none of us there, thinks she had been deserted, and — and —"

The thought was unbearable. He slipped in with the sleeping Lily in his arms and began to put her in bed without awakening her, determined to mount his horse and go for Helen himself.

But just then the old nurse, frantic, breathless and in a delirium of religious excitement, came in and fell fainting on the porch.

He revived her with cold water, and when she could

talk she could only pronounce Helen's name, and say they had run off with her.

" Who? "— shouted Conway, his heart stopping in the staggering shock of it.

The old woman tried to tell Jud Carpenter's tale, and Conway heard enough. He did not wait to hear it all — he did not know the mill was now slowly burning.

" Take care of Lily "— he said, as he went into his room and came out with his pistol buckled around his waist.

Then he mounted his horse and rode swiftly to Mill-wood.

He was astonished to find a fire in the hearth, a lamp burning, and one of Helen's gloves lying on the table.

By it was another pair. He picked them up and looked closely. Within, in red ink, were the initials: *R. T.*

He bit his lips till the blood came. He bowed his head in his hands.

Sometimes there comes to us that peculiar mental condition in which we are vaguely conscious that once before we have been in the same place, amid the same conditions and surroundings which now confront us. We seem to be living again a brief moment of our past life, where Time himself has turned back everything. It came that instant to Edward Conway.

" It was here — and what was it? Oh, yes:— 'Some men repent to God's smile, some to His frown, and some to His fist?' "— He groaned:—" This is His fist. Never — never before in all the history of the Conway family has one of its women —"

He sat down on the old sofa and buried, again, his face in his hands.

Edward Conway was sober, but he still had the instincts of the drunkard — it never occurred to him that he had done anything to cause it. Drunkenness was nothing — a weakness — a fault which was now behind him. But this — this — the first of all the Conway women — and his daughter — his child — the *beautiful one.* He sat still, and then he grew very calm. It was the calmness of the old Conway spirit returning. "Richard Travis," he said to himself, "knows as well what this act of his means in the South,— in the unwritten law of our land — as I do. He has taken his chance of life or death. I'll see that it is death. This is the last of me and my house. But in the fall I'll see that this Philistine of Philistines dies under its ruins."

He arose and started out. He saw the lap robe in the hall, and this put him to investigating. The mares and buggy he found under the shed. It was all a mystery to him, but of one thing he was sure: "He will soon come back for them. I can wait."

Choosing a spot in the shadow of a great tree, he sat down with his pistol across his knees. The moon had arisen and cast ghostly shadows over everything. It was a time for repentance, for thoughts of the past with him, and as he sat there, that terrible hour, with murder in his heart, bitterness and repentance were his.

He was a changed man. Never again could he be the old self. "But the blow — the blow," he kept saying, "I thought it would fall on me — not on her —

my beautiful one — not on a Conway woman's chastity — not my wife's daughter —"

He heard steps coming down the path. His heart ceased a moment, it seemed to him, and then beat wildly. He drew a long breath to relieve it — to calm it with cool oxygen, and then he cocked the five chambered pistol and waited as full of the joy of killing as if the man who was now walking down the path was a wolf or a mad dog —down the path and right into the muzzle of the pistol, backed by the arm which could kill.

He saw Richard Travis coming, slowly, painfully, his left arm tied up, and his step, once so quick and active, so full of strength and life, now was as if the blight of old age had come upon it.

In spite of his bitter determination Conway noticed the great change, and instinct, which acts even through anger and hatred and revenge and the maddening fury of murder,— instinct, the ever present — whispered its warning to his innermost ear.

Still, he could not resist. Rising, he threw his pistol up within a few yards of Richard Travis's breast, his hand upon the trigger. But he could not fire, although Travis stood quietly under its muzzle and looked without surprise into his face.

Conway glanced along the barrel of his weapon and into the face of Richard Travis. And then he brought his pistol down with a quick movement.

The face before him was begging him to shoot!

"Why don't you shoot?" said Travis at last, breaking the silence and in a tone of disappointment.

"Because you are not guilty," said Conway —"not with that look in your face."

"I am sorry you saw my face, then," he smiled sadly —"for it had been such a happy solution for it all — if you had only fired."

"Where is my child?"

"Do you think you have any right to ask —having treated her as you have?"

Conway trembled, at first with rage, then in shame:

"No,"— he said finally. "No, you are right — I haven't."

"That is the only reply you could have made me that would make it obligatory on my part to answer your question. In that reply I see there is hope for you. So I will tell you she is safe, unharmed, unhurt."

"I felt it," said Conway, quietly, "for I knew it, Richard Travis, as soon as I saw your face. But tell me all."

"There is little to tell. I had made up my mind to run off with her, marry her, perhaps, since she had neither home nor a father, and was a beautiful young thing which any man might be proud of. But things have come up — no, not come up, fallen, fallen and crushed. It has been a crisis all around — so I sent for Clay — a fine young fellow and he loves her — I had him meet me here and — well, he has taken her to Westmoreland to-night. You know she is safe there. She will come to you to-morrow as pure as she left, though God knows you do not deserve it."

Something sprang into Edward Conway's throat — something kin to a joyous shout. He could not speak.

He could only look at the strange, calm, sad man before him in a gratitude that uplifted him. He stared with eyes that were blinded with tears.

" Dick — Dick," he said, " we have been estranged, since the war. I misjudged you. I see I never knew you. I came to kill, but here —" He thrust the grip of his pistol toward Travis —" here, Dick, kill me — shoot me — I am not fit to live — but, O God, how clearly I see now; and, Dick — Dick — you shall see — the world shall see that from now on, with God's help, as Lily makes me say — Dick, I'll be a Conway again."

The other man pressed his hand: " Ned, I believe it — I believe it. Go back to your little home to-night. Your daughter is safe. To-morrow you may begin all over again. To-morrow —"

" And you, Dick — I have heard — I can guess, but why may not you, to-morrow —"

" There will be no to-morrow for me," he said sadly. " Things stop suddenly before me to-night as before an abyss —"

He turned quickly and looked toward the low lying range of mountains. A great red flush as of a rising sun glowed even beyond the rim of them, and then out of it shot tinges of flame.

Conway saw it at the same instant:

" It's the mill — the mill's afire," he said.

CHAPTER XXII

A CONWAY AGAIN

IT WAS a great fire the mill made, lighting the valley for miles. All Cottontown was there to see it burn, hushed, with set faces, some of anger, some of fear — but all in stricken numbness, knowing that their living was gone.

It was not long before Jud Carpenter was among them, stirring them with the story of how the old negro woman had burned it — for he knew it was she. Indeed, he was soon fully substantiated by others who heard her when she had run home heaping her maledictions on the mill.

Soon among them began the whisper of lynching. As it grew they became bolder and began to shout it: *Lynch her!*

Jud Carpenter, half drunk and wholly reckless, stood on a stump, and after telling his day's experience with Mammy Maria, her defiance of the mill's laws, her arrogance, her burning of the mill, he shouted that he himself would lead them.

"Lynch her!" they shouted. "Lead us, Jud Carpenter! We will lynch her."

Some wanted to wait until daylight, but "Lynch her — lynch her now," was the shout.

The crowd grew denser every moment.

The people of Cottontown, hot and revengeful, now
that their living was burned; hill dwellers who sympa-
thized with them, and coming in, were eager for any
excitement; the unlawful element which infests every
town — all were there, the idle, the ignorant, the
vicious.

And a little viciousness goes a long way.

There had been so many lynchings in the South that
it had ceased to be a crime — for crime, the weed, culti-
vated — grows into a flower to those who do the tending.

Many of the lynchings, it is true, were honest —
the frenzy of outraged humanity to avenge a terrible
crime which the law, in it's delay, often had let go
unpunished. The laxity of the law, the unscrupulous-
ness of its lawyers, their shrewdness in clearing criminals if the fee was forthcoming, the hundreds of technicalities thrown around criminals, the narrowness of supreme courts in reversing on these technicalities. All
these had thrown the law back to its source — the people. And they had taken it in their own hands. In
violent hands, but deadly sure and retributory.

If there was ever an excuse for lynching, the South
was entitled to it. For the crime was the result of
the sudden emancipation of ignorant slaves, who, backed
by the bayonets of their liberators, and attributing a
far greater importance to their elevation than was war-
ranted, perpetuated an unnameable crime as part of their
system of revenge for years of slavery. And the South
arose to the terribleness of the crime and met it with
the rifle, the torch and the rope.

Why should it be wondered at? Why should the

South be singled out for blame? Is it not a fact that
for years in every newly settled western state lynch-
law has been the unchallenged, unanimous verdict for
a horse thief? And is not the honor of a white woman
more than the hide of a broncho?

But from an honest, well intentioned frenzy of justice
outraged to any pretext is an easy step. From the
quick lynching of the rapist and murderer — to be sure
that the lawyers and courts did not acquit them — was
one step. To hang a half crazy old woman for burning a mill was another, and the natural consequence of
the first.

And so these people flocked to the burning — they
who had helped lynch before — the negro-haters, who
had never owned a negro and had no sympathy — no
sentiment for them. It is they who lynch in the South,
who lynch and defy the law.

The great mill was in ruins — it's tall black smoke-
stacks alone stood amid its smoking, twisted mass of
steel and ashes — a rough, blackened, but fitting monument of its own infamy.

They gathered around it — the disorderly, the vicious,
the lynchers of the Tennessee Valley.

Fitful flashes of flame now and then burst out amid
the ruins, silhouetting the shadows of the lynchers into
fierce giant forms with frenzied faces from which came
first murmurs and finally shouts of:

" *Lynch her!   Lynch her!* "

Above, in the still air of the night, yet hung the pall
of the black smoke-cloud, from whose heart had come

the torch which had cost capital its money, and the mill people their living.

They were not long acting. Mammy Maria had flown to the little cottage — a crazy, hysterical creature — a wreck of herself — overworked in body and mind, and frenzied between the deed and the promptings of a blind superstitious religion.

Lily hung to her neck sobbing, and the old woman in her pitiful fright was brought back partly to reason in the great love of her life for the little child. Even in her feebleness she was soothing her pet.

There were oaths, curses and trampling of many feet as they rushed in and seized her. Lily, screaming, was held by rough arms while they dragged the old nurse away.

Into a wood nearby they took her, the rope was thrown over a limb, the noose placed around her neck.

" Pray, you old witch — we will give you five minutes to pray."

The old woman fell on her knees, but instead of praying for herself, she prayed for her executioners.

They jeered — they laughed. One struck her with a stick, but she only prayed for them the more.

" String her up," they shouted — " her time's up!"

" Stand back there!"

The words rang out even above the noise of the crowd. Then a man, with the long blue deadly barrel of the Colt forty-four, pushed his way through them — his face pale, his fine mouth set firm and close, and the splendid courage of many generations of Conways shining in his eyes.

"*Stand back!*—" and he said it in the old commanding way — the old way which courage has ever had
in the crises of the world.

"O Marse Ned! — I knowed you'd come!"

He had cut the rope and the old woman sat on the
ground clasping his feet.

For a moment he stood over her, his pale calm face
showing the splendor of determination in the glory of
his manhood restored.   For a moment the very beauty
of it stopped them — this man, this former sot and
drunkard, this old soldier arising from the ashes of his
buried past, a beautiful statue of courage cut out of
the marble of manhood.   The moral beauty of it —
this man defending with his life the old negro — struck
even through the swine of them.

They ceased, and a silence fell, so painful that it
hurt in its very uncanniness.

Then Edward Conway said very clearly, very slowly,
but with a fitful nervous ring in his voice: "Go back
to your homes!   Would you hang this poor old woman
without a trial?   Can you not see that she has lost her
mind and is not responsible for her acts?   Let the law
decide.   Shall not her life of unselfishness and good
deeds be put against this one insane act of her old age?
Go back to your homes!   Some of you are my friends,
some my neighbors — I ask you for her but a fair trial
before the law."

They listened for a moment and then burst into
jeers, hoots, and hisses:

"Hang her, now!   That's the way all lawyers talk!"

And one shouted above the rest: "He's put up a plea of insanity a-ready. Hang her, now!"

Edward Conway flashed hot through his paleness and he placed himself before the bowed and moaning form while the crowd in front of him surged and shouted and called for a rope.

He felt some one touch his arm and turned to find the sheriff by his side — one of those disreputables who infested the South after the war, holding office by the votes of the negroes.

"Better let 'em have her,— it ain't worth the while. You'll hafter kill, or be killed."

"You scallawag!" said Conway, now purple with anger —" is that the way you respect your sworn oath? And you have been here and seen all this and not raised your hand?"

"Do you think I'm fool enuff to tackle that crowd of hillbillies? They've got the devil in them — fur they've got a devil leadin' 'em — Jud Carpenter. Better let 'em have her — they'll kill you. We've got a good excuse — overpowered — don't you see?"

"Overpowered? That's the way all cowards talk," said Conway. "Do one thing for me," he said quickly —" tell them you have appointed me your deputy. If you do not — I'll fall back on the law of riots and appoint myself."

"Gentlemen," said the sheriff, turning to the crowd, and speaking half-shamedly —" Gentlemen, it's better an' I hopes you all will go home. We don't wanter hurt nobody. I app'ints Major Conway my deputy to take

38

the prisoner to jail. Now the blood be on yo' own heads. I've sed my say."

A perfect storm of jeers met this. They surged forward to seize her, while the sheriff half frightened, half undecided, got behind Conway and said:—" It's up to you — I've done all I cu'd."

" Go back to your homes, men "— shouted Conway —" I am the sheriff here now, and I swear to you by the living God it means I am a Conway again, and the man who lays a hand on this old woman is as good as dead in his tracks ! "

For an instant they surged around him cursing and shouting; but he stood up straight and terribly silent; only his keen grey eyes glanced down to the barrel of his pistol and he stood nervously fingering the small blue hammer with his thumb and measuring the distance between himself and the nearest ruffian who stood on the outskirts of the mob shaking a pistol in Conway's face and shouting: " Come on, men, we'll lynch her anyway ! "

Then Conway acted quickly. He spoke a few words to the old nurse, and as she backed off into the nearby wood, he covered the retreat. To his relief he saw that the sheriff, now thoroughly ashamed, had hold of the prisoner and was helping her along.

In the edge of the wood he felt safe — with the trees at his back. And he took courage as he heard the sheriff say:

" If you kin hold 'em a little longer I'll soon have my buggy here and we'll beat 'em to the jail."

But the mob guessed his plans, and the man who had

been most insolent in the front of the mob — a long-haired, narrow-chested mountaineer — rushed up viciously.

Conway saw the gleam of his pistol as the man aimed and fired at the prisoner. Instinctively he struck at the weapon and the ball intended for the prisoner crushed spitefully into his left shoulder. He reeled and the grim light of an aroused Conway flashed in his eyes as he recovered himself, for a moment, shocked, blinded. Then he heard some one say, as he felt the blood trickling down his arm and hand:

"Marse Ned! Oh, an' for po' ole Zion! Don't risk yo' life — let 'em take me!"

Dimly he saw the mob rushing up; vaguely it came to him that it was kill or be killed. Vaguely, too, that it was the law — his law — and every other man's law — against lawlessness. Hazily, that he was the law — its representative, its defender, and then clear as the blue barrel in his hand,— all the dimness and uncertainty gone,— it came to him, that thing that made him say: "I am a Conway again!"

Then his pistol leaped from the shadow by his side to the gray light in front, and the man who had fired and was again taking aim at the old woman died in his tracks with his mouth twisted forever into the shape of an unspoken curse.

It was enough. Stricken, paralyzed, they fell back before such courage — and Conway found himself backing off into the woods, covering the retreat of the prisoner. Then afterward he felt the motion of buggy wheels, and of a galloping drive, and the jail, and he in the sheriff's room, the old prisoner safe for the time.

CHAPTER XXIII

DIED FOR THE LAW

A ND thus was begun that historical lynching in the
Tennessee Valley — a tragedy which well might
have remained unwritten had it not fallen into
the woof of this story.

A white man had been killed for a negro — that was
enough.

It is true the man was attempting to commit murder
in the face of the law of the land; and in attempting it
had shot the representative of the law. It is true, also,
that he had no grievance, being one of several hundred
law-breakers bent on murder. This, too, made no difference; they neither thought nor cared; — for mobs,
being headless, do not think; and being soulless, do not
suffer.

They had failed only for lack of a leader.

But now they had a leader, and a mob with a leader
is a dangerous thing.

That leader was Richard Travis.

It was after midnight when he rode up on the scene.
Before he arrived, Jud Carpenter had aroused the mob
to do its first fury, and still held them, now doubly
vengeful and shouting to be led against the jail. But
to storm a jail they needed a braver man than Jud
Carpenter. And they found him in Richard Travis —

596

especially Richard Travis in the terrible mood, the black despair which had come upon him that night.

Why did he come? He could not say. In him had surged two great forces that night — the force of evil and the force of good. Twice had the good overcome — now it was the evil's turn, and like one hypnotized, he was led on.

He sat his horse among them, pale and calm, but with a cruel instinct flashing in his eyes. At least, so Jud Carpenter interpreted the mood which lay upon him; but no one knew the secret workings of this man's heart, save God.

He had come to them haggard and blanched and with a nameless dread, his arm tied up where the dog's fang had been buried in his flesh, his heart bitter in the thought of the death that was his   Already he felt the deadly virus pulsing through his veins. A hundred times in the short hour that had passed he suffered death — death beginning with the gripping throat, the short-ened breath, the foaming mouth, the spasm!

He jerked in the saddle — that spasmodic chill of the nerves,— and he grew white and terribly silent at the thought of it — the death that was his!

Was his! And then he thought: " No, there shall be another and quicker way to die. A braver way — like a Travis — with my boots on — my boots on — and not like a mad-dog tied to a stake.

" Besides — Alice — Alice! "

She had gone out of his life. Could such a thing be and he live to tell it? Alice — love — ambition — the future — life! Alice, hazle-eyed and glorious, with hair the smell of which filled his soul with perfume as from the stars. She who alone uplifted him — she another's, and that other Tom Travis!

Tom Travis — returned and idealized — with him, the joint heir of The Gaffs.

And that mad-dog — that damned mad-dog! And if perchance he was saved — if that virus was sucked out of his veins, it was she — Helen!

"This is the place to die," he said grimly —" here with my boots on. To die like a Travis and unravel this thing called life. Unravel it to the end of the thread and know if it ends there, is snapped, is broken or —

" Or — my God," he cried aloud, " I never knew what those two little letters meant before — not till I face them this way, on the Edge of Things!"

He gathered the mob together and led them against the jail — with hoots and shouts and curses; with flaming torches, and crow-bars, with axes and old guns.

" Lynch her — lynch the old witch! and hang that devil Conway with her!" was the shout.

In front of the jail they stopped, for a man stood at the door. His left arm was in a sling, but in his right hand gleamed something that had proved very deadly before. And he stood there as he had stood in the edge of the wood, and the bonfires and torches of the mob lit up more clearly the deadly pale face, set and more determined than before.

For as he stood, pale and silent, the shaft of a terrible pain,— of broken bone and lacerated muscle — twinged and twitched his arm, and to smother it and keep from crying out he gripped bloodlessly — nervously — the stock of his pistol saying over and over:

"I am a Conway again — a man again!"

And so standing he defied them and they halted, like sheep at the door of the shambles. The sheriff had flown, and Conway alone stood between the frenzied mob and the old woman who had given her all for him.

He could hear her praying within — an uncanny mixture of faith and miracle — of faith which saw as Paul saw, and which expected angels to come and break down her prison doors. And after praying she would break out into a song, the words of which nerved the lone man who stood between her and death:

"'I'm a pilgrim, and I'm a stranger,
I can tarry, I can tarry but a night.
Do not detain me, for I am going
To where the streamlets are ever flowing.
I'm a pilgrim — and I'm a stranger
I can tarry — I can tarry but a night.'"

And now the bonfire burned brighter, lighting up the scene — the shambling stores around the jail on the public square, the better citizens making appeals in vain for law and order, the shouting, fool-hardy mob, waiting for Richard Travis to say the word, and he sitting among them pale, and terribly silent with something in his face they had never seen there before.

Nor would he give the command. He had nothing against Edward Conway — he did not wish to see him killed.

And the mob did not attack, although they cursed and bluffed, because each one of them knew it meant death — death to some one of them, and that one might be — I!

Between life and death " I " is a bridge that means it all.

A stone wall ran around the front of the jail. A small gate opened into the jail-yard. At the jail door, covering that opening, stood Edward Conway.

They tried parleying with him, but he would have none of it.

" Go back —" he said, " I am the sheriff here — I am the law. The man who comes first into that gate will be the first to die."

In ten minutes they made their attack despite the commands of their leader, who still sat his horse on the public square, pale and with a bitter conflict raging in his breast.

With shouts and curses and a headlong rush they went. Pistol bullets flew around Conway's head and scattered brick dust and mortar over him. Torches gleamed through the dark crowd as stars amid fast flying clouds in a March night. But through it all every man of them heard the ringing warning words:

" Stop at the gateway — stop at the dead line! "

Right at it they rushed and crowded into it like cattle — shooting, cursing, throwing stones.

Then two fell dead, blocking the gateway. Two more, wounded, with screams of pain which threw the others into that indescribable panic which comes to all

mobs in the death-pinch, staggered back carrying the
mob with them.

Safe from the bullets, they became frenzied.

The town trembled with their fury.

All order was at an end.

And Edward Conway stood, behind a row of cotton
bales, in the jail-yard, covering still the little gateway,
and the biting pain in his shoulder had a companion pain
in his side, where a pistol ball had ploughed through,
but he forgot it as he slipped fresh cartridges into the
chambers of his pistol and heard again the chant which
came from out the jail window, like a ghost-voice from
the clouds:

> " Of that City, to which I journey,
> My Redeemer, my Redeemer is the light.
> There is no sorrow, nor any sighing,
> Nor any tears there, nor any dying. . . ,
> I'm a pilgrim, and I'm a stranger,
> I can tarry — I can tarry but a night."

At a long distance they shot at Conway,— they hoot-
ed, jeered, cursed him, but dared not come closer, for
he had breast-worked himself behind some cotton-bales
in the yard, and they knew he could still shoot.

Then they decided to batter down the stone wall first
— to make an opening they could rush through, and not
be blocked in the deadly gateway.

An hour passed, and torches gleamed everywhere.
Attacking the wall farther down, they soon had it torn
away. They could now get to him. It was a perilous

position, and Conway knew it. Help — he must have it — help to protect his flank while he shot in front. If not, he would die soon, and the law with him.

He looked around him — but there was no solution. Then he felt that death was near, for the mob now hated him more than they did the prisoner. They seemed to have forgotten her, for all their cry now was:

"*Kill Conway!   Kill the man who murdered our people!*"

In ten minutes they were ready to attack again, but looking up they saw a strange sight.

Help had come to Conway. On one side of him stood the old Cottontown preacher, his white hair reflecting back the light from the bonfires and torches in front — lighting up a face which now seemed to have lost all of its kindly humor in the crisis that was there. He was unarmed, but he stood calm and with a courage that was more of sorrow than of anger.

By him stood the village blacksmith, a man with the wild light of an old, untamed joy gleaming in his eyes — a cruel, dangerous light — the eyes of a caged tiger turned loose at last, and yearning for the blood of the thing which had caged him.

And by him in quiet bravery, commanding, directing, stood the tall figure of the Captain of Artillery.

When Richard Travis saw him, a cruel smile deepened in his eyes. "I am dying myself," it said —"why not kill him?"

Then he shuddered with the hatred of the terrible thing that had come into his heart — the thing that made him do its bidding, as if he were a puppet, and overthrew all the good he had gathered there, that terrible night, as the angels were driven from Paradise. And yet, how it ruled him, how it drove him on!

" Jim — Jim," he whispered as he bent over his horse's neck —" Jim — my repeating rifle over the library door — quick — it carries true and far! "

As Jim sped away his master was silent again. He thought of the nobility of the things he had done that night — the touch of God that had come over him in making him save Helen — the beautiful dreams he had had. He thought of it all — and then — here — now — murdering the man whose life carried with it the life, the love of —

He looked up at the stars, and the old wonder and doubt came back to him — the old doubt which made him say to himself: " It is nothing — it is the end. Dust thou art, and unto dust — dust — dust — dust —" he bit his tongue to keep from saying it again —" Dust — to be blown away and mingle with the elements — dust! And yet, I stand here — now — blood — flesh — a thinking man — tempted — terribly — cruelly — poignantly — dying — of a poison in my veins — of sorrow in my heart — sorrow and death. Who would not take the dust — gladly take it — the dust and the — forgetting."

He remembered and repeated:

> " Our birth is but a sleep and a forgetting,
> The soul that rises with us, our life's star,

Hath had elsewhere its setting
And cometh from afar —"

" ' And cometh from afar,' " he whispered —" My
God — suppose it does — and that I am mistaken in it
all? —Dust — and then maybe something after dust."

With his rifle in his hand, it all vanished and he began
to train it on the tall figure while the mob prepared to
storm the jail again — and his shot would be the signal
— this time in desperate determination to take it or die.

In the mob near Richard Travis stood a boy, careless
and cool, and holding in his hand an old pistol. Richard
Travis noticed the boy because he felt that the boy's eyes
were always on him — always. When he looked down
into them he was touched and sighed, and a dream of the
long-ago swept over him — of a mountain cabin and a
maiden fair to look upon. He bit his lip to keep back
the tenderness — bit his lip and rode away — out of
reach of the boy's eyes.

But the boy, watching him, knew, and he said in his
quiet, revengeful way: " Twice have I failed to kill you
— but to-night — my Honorable father — to-night in
the death that will be here, I shall put this bullet through
your heart."

Travis turned to the mob: " Men, when I fire this
rifle — it will mean for you to charge!"

A hush fell over the crowd as they watched him. He
looked at his rifle closely. He sprang the breech and
threw out a shell or two to see that it worked properly.

" Stay where you are, men," came that same voice they
had heard so plainly before that night. " We are now

four and well armed and sworn to uphold the law and protect the prisoner, and if you cross the dead line you will die."

There was a silence, and then that old voice again, the voice that roused the mob to fury:

" I'm a pilgrim, and I'm a stranger,
    I can tarry — I can tarry but a night —"

" Lead us on — give the signal, Richard Travis," they shouted.

Again the silence fell as Richard Travis raised his rifle and aimed at the tall figure outlined closely and with magnified distinctness in the glare of bonfire and torch. How splendidy cool and brave he looked — that tall figure standing there, giving orders as calmly as he gave them at Shiloh and Franklin, and so forgetful of himself and his own safety!

Richard Travis brought his rifle down — it shook so — brought it down saying to himself with a nervous laugh: " It is not Tom — not Tom Travis I am going to kill — it's — it's Alice's husband of only two days — her lover—"

" Shoot! Why don't you shoot?" they shouted. " We are waiting to rush —"

Even where he stood, Richard Travis could see the old calm, quiet and now triumphant smile lighting up Tom Travis's face, and he knew he was thinking of Alice — Alice, his bride.

And then that same nervous, uncanny chill ran into the very marrow of Richard Travis and brought his gun down with an oath on his lips as he said pitifully —" I am poisoned — it is that!"

The crowd shouted and urged him to shoot, but he sat shaking to his very soul. And when it passed there came the old half humorous, half bitter, cynical laugh as he said: "Alice — Alice a widow—"

It passed, and again there leaped into his eyes the great light Jud Carpenter had seen there that morning, and slipping the cartridges out of the barrel's breech, he looked up peacefully with the halo of a holy light around his eyes as he said: "Oh, God, and I thank Thee — for this — this touch again! Hold the little spark in my heart — hold it, oh, God, but for a little while till the temptation is gone, and I shall rest — I shall rest."

"Shoot — Richard Travis — why the devil don't you shoot?" they shouted.

He raised his rifle again, this time with a flourish which made some of the mob think he was taking unnecessary risk to attract the attention of the grim blacksmith who stood, pistol in hand, his piercing eyes scanning the crowd. He stood by the side of Tom Travis, his bodyguard to the last.

"Jack — Jack —" kept whispering to him the old preacher, "don't shoot till you're obleeged to,— maybe God'll open a way, maybe you won't have to spill blood. 'Vengeance is mine,' saith the Lord."

Jack smiled. It was a strange smile — of joy, in the risking glory of the old life — the glory of blood-letting, of killing, of death. And sorrow — sorrow in the new.

"Stand pat, stand pat, Bishop," he said; "you all know the trade. Let me who have defied the law so long, let me now stand for it — die for it. It's my atonement — ain't that the word? Ain't that what you said about that there Jesus Christ, the man you said wouldn't flicker even on the Cross, an' wouldn't let us flicker if we loved Him — Hol' him to His promise, now, Bishop. It's time for us to stand pat. No — I'll not shoot unless I see some on 'em makin' a too hasty movement of gun-arm toward Cap'n —"

Had Richard Travis looked from his horse down into the crowd he had seen another sight. Man can think and do but one thing at a time, but oh, the myrmidons of God's legions of Cause and Effect!

Below him stood a boy, his face white in the terrible tragedy of his determination. And as Richard Travis threw up his empty rifle, the octagonal barrel of the pistol in the boy's hand leaped up and came straight to the line of Richard Travis's heart. But before the boy could fire Travis saw the hawk-like flutter of the blacksmith's pistol arm, as it measured the distance with the old quick training of a bloody experience, and Richard Travis smiled, as he saw the flash from the outlaw's pistol and felt that uncanny chill starting in his marrow again, leap into a white heat to the shock of the ball, and he pitched limply forward, slipped from his horse and went down on the ground murmuring, " Tom — Tom — safe, and Alice — he shot at last — and — thank God for the touch again! "

He lay quiet, feeling the life blood go out of him. But with it came an exhalation he had never felt before — a glory that, instead of taking, seemed to give him life.

The mob rushed wildly at the jail at the flash of Jack

Bracken's pistol, all but one, a boy — whose old dueling pistol still pointed at the space in the air, where Richard Travis had sat a moment before — its holder nerveless — rigid — as if turned into stone.

He saw Richard Travis pitch forward off his horse and slide limply to the ground. He saw him totter and waver and then sit down in a helpless, pitiful way,— then lie down as if it were sweet to rest.

And still the boy stood holding his pistol, stunned, frigid, numbed — pointing at the stars.

Silently he brought his arm and weapon down. He heard only shouts of the mob as they rushed against the jail, and then, high above it, the words of the blacksmith, whom he loved so well: " Stand back — all ; Me — me alone, shoot — me! I who have so often killed the law, let me die for it."

And then came to the boy's ears the terrible staccato cough of the two Colts pistols whose very fire he had learned to know so well. And he knew that the black-smith alone was shooting — the blacksmith he loved so — the marksman he worshipped — the man who had saved his life — the man who had just shot his father.

Richard Travis sat up with an effort and looked at the boy standing by him — looked at him with frank, kindly eyes,— eyes which begged forgiveness, and the boy saw himself there — in Richard Travis, and felt a hurtful, pitying sorrow for him, and then an uncontrolled, hot anger at the man who had shot him out of the saddle. His eyes twitched wildly, his heart jumped in smothering

beats, a dry sob choked him, and he sprang forward crying: "My father — oh, God — my poor father!"

Richard Travis looked up and smiled at him.

"You shoot well, my son," he said, "but not quick
enough."

The boy, weeping, saw. Shamed, — burning — he
knelt and tried to staunch the wound with a handkerchief. Travis shook his head: "Let it out, my son —
let it out — it is poison! Let it out!"

Then he lay down again on the ground. It felt sweet
to rest.

The boy saw his blood on the ground and he shouted:
"Blood,— my father — blood is thicker than water."

Then the hatred that had burned in his heart for his
father, the father who had begot him into the world, disgraced, forsaken — the father who had ruined and aban-
doned his mother, was turned into a blaze of fury against
the blacksmith, the blacksmith whom he had loved.

Wheeling, he rushed toward the jail, but met the mob
pouring panic-stricken back with white faces, blanched
with fear.

Jack Bracken stood alone on the barricade, shoving
more cartridges into his pistol chambers.

The boy, blinded, weeping, hot with a burning revenge, stumbled and fell twice over dead men lying near
the gate-way. Then he crawled along over them under
cover of the fence, and kneeling within twenty feet of the
gate, fired at the great calm figure who had driven the
mob back, and now stood reloading.

Jack did not see the boy till he felt the ball crush
into his side. Then all the old, desperate, revengeful

39

instinct of the outlaw leaped into his eyes as he quickly turned his unerring pistol on the object from whence the flash came. Never had he aimed so accurately, so carefully, for he felt his own life going out, and this — this was his last shot — to kill.

But the object kneeling among the dead arose with a smile of revengeful triumph and stood up calmly under the aim of the great pistol, his fair hair flung back, his face lit up with the bravery of all the Travises as he shouted:

"Take that — damn you — from a Travis!"

And when Jack saw and understood, a smile broke through his bloodshot, vengeful eyes as starlight falls on muddy waters, and he turned away his death-seeking aim, and his mouth trembled as he said:

"Why — it's — it's the Little 'Un! I cudn't kill him —" and he clutched at the cotton-bale as he went down, falling — and Captain Tom grasped him, letting him down gently.

CHAPTER XXIV

A ND now no one stood between the prisoner and
death but the old preacher and the tall man
in the uniform of a Captain of Artillery. And
death it meant to all of them, defenders as well as
prisoners, for the mob had increased in numbers as in
fury. Friends, kindred, brothers, fathers — even
mothers and sisters of the dead were there, bitter in the
thought that their dead had been murdered — white men,
for one old negress.

In their fury they did not think it was the law they
themselves were murdering. The very name of the law
was now hateful to them — the law that had killed their
people.

Slowly, surely, but with grim deadliness they laid their
plans — this time to run no risk of failure.

There was a stillness solemn and all-pervading. And
from the window of the jail came again in wailing uncanny notes: —

" I'm a pilgrim and I'm a stranger,
I can tarry, I can tarry but a night —"

It swept over the mob, frenzied now to the stillness of
a white heat, like a challenge to battle, like the flaunt of

a red flag. Their dead lay all about the gate of the rock
fence, stark and still. Their wounded were few — for
Jack Bracken did not wound. They saw them all —
dead — lying out there dead — and they were willing to
die themselves for the blood of the old woman — a negro
for whom white men had been killed.

But their wrath now took another form. It was the
wrath of coolness. They had had enough of the other
kind. To rush again on those bales of cotton doubly
protected behind a rock fence, through one small gate,
commanded by the fire of such marksmen as lay there,
was not to be thought of.

They would burn the jail over the heads of its defenders and kill them as they were uncovered. A hundred men would fire the jail from the rear, a hundred
more with guns would shoot in front.

It was Jud Carpenter who planned it, and soon oil and
saturated paper and torches were prepared.

" We are in for it, Bishop," said Captain Tom, as he
saw the preparation; " this is worse than Franklin, because there we could protect our rear."

He leaped up on his barricade, tall and splendid, and
called to them quietly and with deadly calm:

" Go to your homes, men — go! But if you will come,
know that I fought for my country's laws from Shiloh
to Franklin, and I can die for them here! "

Then he took from over his heart a small silken flag,
spangled with stars and the blood-splotches of his father
who fell in Mexico, and he shook it out and flung it
over his barricade, saying cheerily: " I am all right
for a fight now, Bishop. But oh, for just one of my

guns — just one of my old Parrots that I had last week at Franklin!"

The old man, praying on his knees behind his barricade, said:

"Twelve years ago, Cap'n Tom, twelve years. Not last week."

The mob had left Richard Travis for dead, and in the fury of their defeat had thought no more of him. But now, the loss of blood, the cool night air revived him. He sat up, weak, and looked around. Everywhere bonfires burned. Men were running about. He heard their talk and he knew all. He was shot through the left lung, so near to his heart that, as he felt it, he wondered how he had escaped.

He knew it by the labored breathing, by the blood that ran down and half filled his left boot. But his was a constitution of steel — an athlete, a hunter, a horseman, a man of the open. The bitterness of it all came back to him when he found he was not dead as he had hoped — as he had made Jack Bracken shoot to do.

"To die in bed at last," he said, "like a monk with liver complaint — or worse still — my God, like a mad dog, unless — unless — her lips — Helen!"

He lay quite still on the soft grass and looked up at the stars. How comfortable he was! He felt around.

A boy's overcoat was under him — a little roundabout, wadded up, was his pillow.

He smiled — touched: "What a man he will make — the brave little devil! Oh, if I can live to tell him he is mine, that I married his mother secretly — that I broke her heart with my faithlessness — that she died and the other is — is her sister."

He heard the clamor and the talk behind him. The mob, cool now, were laying their plans only on revenge, — revenge with the torch and the bullet.

Jud Carpenter was the leader, and Travis could hear him giving his orders. How he now loathed the man — for somehow, as he thought, Jud Carpenter stood for all the seared, blighted, dead life behind him — all the old disbelief, all the old infamy, all the old doubt and shame. But now, dying, he saw things differently. Yonder above him shone the stars and in his heart the glory of that touch of God — the thing that made him wish rather to die than have it leave him again to live in his old way.

He heard the mob talking. He heard their plans. He knew that Jud Carpenter, hating the old preacher as he did, would rather kill him than any wolf of the forest. He knew that neither Tom Travis nor the old preacher could ever hope to come out alive.

The torches were ready — the men were aligned in front with deadly shotguns.

"When the fire gets hot," he heard Jud Carpenter say, "they'll hafter come out — then shoot — shoot an' shoot to kill. See our own dead!"

They answered him with groans, with curses, with shouts of " *Lead us on, Jud Carpenter!* "

"When the jail is fired from the rear," shouted Carpenter, "stay where you are and shoot; they've no chance at all. It's fire or bullet."

Richard Travis heard it and his heart leaped — but

only for one tempting moment, when a vision of loveliness in widow's weeds swept through that soul of his inner sight, which sees into the future. Then the new light came back uplifting him with a wave of joyous strength that was sweetly calm in its destiny — glad that he had lived, glad that this test had come, glad for the death that was coming.

It was all well with him.

He forgot himself, he forgot his deadly wound, the bitterness of his life, the dog's bite — all — in the glory of this feeling, the new feeling which now would go with him into eternity.

For, as he lay there, he had seen the bell's turret above the jail and his mind was quick to act.

He smiled faintly — a happy smile — the smile of the old Roman ere he leaped into the chasm before the walls of Rome — leaped and saved his countrymen. He loved to do difficult things — to conquer and overcome where others would quit. This always had been his glory — he understood that. But this new thing — this wanting to save men who were doomed behind their barricade — this wanting to give what was left of his life for them — his enemies — this was the thing he could not understand. He only knew it was the call of something within him, stronger than himself and kin to the stars, which, clear and sweet above his head, seemed to be all that stood between him and that clear Sweet Thing out, far out, in the pale blue Silence of Things.

He reached out and found his rifle. In his coat pocket were cartridges. His arms were still strong — he sprang the magazine and filled it.

Then slowly, painfully, he began to crawl off toward the jail, pulling his rifle along. No one saw him but, God! how it hurt! . . . that star falling . . . . scattering splinters of light everywhere . . . . so he lay on his face and slept awhile. . . . .

When he awoke he flushed with the shame of it: "Fainted — me — like a girl!" And he spat out the blood that boiled out of his lips.

Crawling — crawling — and dragging the heavy rifle. It seemed he would never strike the rock fence. Once — twice, and yet a third time he had to sink flat on the grass and spit out the troublesome blood . . . .

The fence at last, and following it he was soon in the rear of the jail. He knew where the back stair was and crawled to it. Slowly, step by step, and every step splotched with his blood, he went up. At the top he pushed up the trap-door with his head and, crawling through, fell fainting.

But, oh, the glory of that feeling that was his now! That feeling that now — now he would atone for it all — now he would be brother to the stars and that Sweeter Thing out, far out, in the pale blue Silence of Things.

Then the old Travis spirit came to him and he smiled: "*Dominecker — oh, my old grandsire, will you think I am a Dominecker now? I found your will — in the old life — and tore it up. But it's Tom's now — Tom's anyway — Dominecker! Wipe it out — wipe it out! If I do not this night honor your blood, strike me from the roll of Travis.*"

Around him was the belfry railing, waist high and

sheeted with metal save four holes, for air, at the base, where he could thrust his rifle through as he lay flat.

He was in a bullet proof turret, and he smiled: " I. hold the fort!"

Slowly he pulled himself up, painfully he stood erect and looked down. Just below him was the barricade of cotton bales, its two defenders, grim and silent behind them — the two wounded ones lying still and so quiet — so quiet it looked like death, and Richard Travis prayed that it was not.

One of them had given him his death wound, but he held no bitterness for him — only that upliftedness, only the glory of that feeling within him he knew not what.

He called gently to them. In astonishment they looked up. Thirty feet above their heads they saw him and heard him say painfully, slowly, but oh, so bravely: " *I am Richard Travis; Tom, and I'll back you to the death. . . . . They are to burn you out . . . but I command the jail, both front and rear. Stay where you both are . . . be careful . . . do not expose yourselves, for while I live you are safe . . . and the law is safe.*"

And then came back to him clear and with all sweetness the earnest words of the old preacher:

" God bless you, Richard Travis, for He has sent you jus' in time. I knew that He would, that He'd touch yo' heart, that there was greatness in you — all in His own time, an' His own good way. Praise God!"

Travis wished to warn the mob, but his voice was nearly gone. He could only sink down and wait.

He heard shouts. They had formed in the rear, and

now men with torches came to fire the jail. Their companions in front, hearing them, shouted back their approval.

Richard Travis thrust his rifle barrel through the air hole and aimed carefully. The torches they carried made it all so plain and so easy.

Then two long, spiteful flashes of flame leaped out of the belfry tower and the arm of the first incendiary, shot through and through — holding his blazing torch, leaped like a rabbit in a sack, and the torch went down and out. The torch of the second one was shot out of its bearer's hand.

Panic-stricken, they looked up, saw, and fled. Those in front also saw and bombarded the belfry with shot and pistol ball. And then, on their side of the belfry, the same downward, spiteful flashes leaped out, and two men, shot through the shoulder and the arm, cried out in dismay, and they all fell back, stampeded, at the deadliness of the spiteful thing in the tower, the gun that carried so true and so far — so much farther than their own cheap guns.

They rushed out of its range, gathered in knots and cursed and wondered who it was. But they dared not come nearer. Travis lay still. He could not speak now, for the blood choked him when he opened his mouth, and the stars which had once been above him now wheeled and floated below, and around him. And that Sweeter Thing that had been behind the stars now seemed to surround him as a halo, a halo of silence which seemed to fit the silence of his own soul and become part of him forever. It was all around him, as he had often seen it around the summer moon; only now he felt it where he only saw it before. And now, too, it was in his heart and filled it with a sweet sadness, a sadness that hurt, it was so sweet, and which came with an odor, the smell of the warm rain falling on the dust of a summer of long ago.

And all his life passed before him — he lived it again — even more than he had remembered before — even the memory of his mother whom he never knew; but now he knew her and he reached up his arms — for he was in a cradle and she bent over him — he reached up his arms and said: " *Oh, mother, now I know what eternity is — it's remembering before and after!* "

Visions, too — and Alice Westmore — Alice, pitying and smiling approval — smiling,— and then a burning passionate kiss, and when he would kiss again it was Helen's lips he met.

And through it all the great uplifting joy, and something which made him try to shout and say: " The atonement — the atonement —"

Clear now and things around him seemed miles away.

He knew he was sinking and he kicked one foot savagely against the turret to feel again the sensation of life in his limb. Then he struck himself in his breast with his right fist to feel it there. But in spite of all he saw a cloud of darkness form beyond the rim of the starlit horizon and come sweeping over him, coming in black waves that would rush forward and then stop — forward, and stop — forward and stop. . . . And the stops kept time exactly with his heart, and he knew the last stop of the wave meant the last beat of his heart — then for-

ward . . . for the last time. . . . "Oh, God,
not yet! . . . Look!"

His heart rallied at the sight and beat faster, making
the black waves pulse, in the flow and ebb of it . . .
The thing was below him . . . a man . . .
a ghostly, vengeful thing, whose face was fierce in hatred
. . . crawling, crawling, up to the rock fence — a
snake with the face . . . the eyes of Jud Carpenter . . .

And the black wave coming in . . . and he did
so want to live . . . just a little . . . just
a while longer . . .

He pushed the wave back, as he gripped for the last
time his rifle's stock, and he knew not whether it was only
visions such as he had been seeing . . . or Jud Carpenter really crouching low behind the rock fence, his
double-barrel shotgun aimed . . . drawing so fine
a bead on both the unconscious defenders . . . going to shoot, and only twenty paces, and now it rose up,
aiming: "*God, it is — it is Jud Carpenter* . . .
back — back — black wave!" he cried, "*and God have
mercy on your soul, Jud Carpenter* . . ."

And, oh, the nightmare of it! — trying to pull the
trigger that would not be pulled, trying to grip a stock
that had grown so large it was now a tree — a huge tree
— flowing red blood instead of sap, red blood over
things, . . . and then at last . . . thank God
. . . the trigger . . . and the flash and report . . . the flash so far off . . . and the report that was like thunder among the stars . . . the
stars. . . . Among the stars . . . all around

him . . . and Alice on one star throwing him a
kiss . . . and saying: " *You saved his life, oh,
Richard, and I love you for it!* " A kiss and forgiveness . . . and the two walking out with him
. . . out into the dim, blue, Sweet Silence of Things,
hand in hand with him, beyond even the black wave, beyond even the rim of the rainbow that came down over
all . . . out — out with music, quaint, sweet, weird
music — that filled his soul so, fitted him . . . was
he . . .

> " *I'm . . . a pilgrim . . . I'm a stranger,
> I can tarry — I can tarry but a night.*"

In the early dawn, a local company of State troops,
called out by the governor, had the jail safe.

It was a gruesome sight in front of the stone wall
where the deadly fire from Jack Bracken's pistols had
swept. Thirteen dead men lay, and the back-bone of
lynching had been broken forever in Alabama.

It was the governor himself, bluff and rugged, who
grasped Jack Bracken's hand as he lay dying, wrapped
up, on a bale of cotton, and Margaret Adams, pale,
weeping beside him: " Live for me, Jack — I love you.
I have always loved you! "

" And for me, Jack," said the old governor, touched
at the scene —" for the state, to teach mobs how to respect the law. In the glory of what you've done, I
pardon you for all the past."

" It is fitten," said Jack, simply; " fitten that I should
die for the law — I who have been so lawless."

He turned to Margaret Adams: "You are lookin' somethin' you want to say — I can tell by yo' eyes."

She faltered, then slowly: "Jack, he was not my son — my poor sister — I could not see her die disgraced."

Jack drew her down and kissed her.

And as his eyes grew dim, a figure, tall and in military clothes, stood before him, shaken with grief and saying, "Jack — Jack, my poor friend —"

Jack's mind was wandering, but a great smile lit up his face as he said: "*Bishop — Bishop — is — is — it Cap'n Tom, or — or — Jesus Christ?*" And so he passed out.

And up above them all in the belfry, lying prone, but still gripping his rifle's stock which, sweeping the jail with its deadly protruding barrel, had held back hundreds of men, they found Richard Travis, a softened smile on his lips as if he had just entered into the glory of the great Sweet Silence of Things. And by him sat the old preacher, where he had sat since Richard Travis's last shot had saved the jail and the defenders; sat and bound up his wound and gave him the last of his old whiskey out of the little flask, and stopped the flow of blood and saved the life which had nearly bubbled out.

And as they brought the desperately wounded man down to the surgeon and to life, the old governor raised his hat and said: "The Travis blood — the Irish Gray — when it's wrong it is hell — when it's right it is heaven."

But the old preacher smiled as he helped carry him tenderly down and said: "He is right, forever right, now, Gov'nor. God has made him so. See that smile on his lips! He has laughed before — that was from the body. He is smiling now — that is from the soul. His soul is born again."

The old governor smiled and turned. 'Edward Conway, wounded, was sitting up. The governor grasped his hand: "Ned, my boy, I've appointed you sheriff of this county in place of that scallawag who deserted his post. Stand pat, for you're a Conway — no doubt about that. Stand pat."

Under the rock wall, they found a man, dead on his knees, leaning against the wall; his gun, still cocked and deadly, was resting against his shoulder and needing only the movement of a finger to sweep with deadly hail the cotton-bales. His scraggy hair topped the rock fence and his staring eyes peeped over, each its own way. And one of them looked forward into a future which was Silence, and the other looked backward into a past which was Sin.

CHAPTER XXV

THE SHADOWS AND THE CLOUDS

WHEN Richard Travis came to himself after that terrible night, they told him that for weeks he had lain with only a breath between him and death.

"It was not my skill that has saved you," said the old surgeon who had been through two wars and who knew wounds as he did maps of battlefields he had fought on. "No," he said, shaking his head, "no, it was not I — it was something beyond me. That you miraculously live is proof of it."

He was in his room at The Gaffs, and everything looked so natural. It was sweet to live again, for he was yet young and life now meant so much more than it ever had. Then his eyes fell on the rug, wearily, and he remembered the old setter.

"The dog — and that other one?"

He sat up nervously in bed, trembling with the thought. The old surgeon guessed and bade him be quiet.

"You need not fear that," he said, touching his arm. "The time has passed for fear. You were saved by the shadow of death and — the blood letting you had — and, well, a woman's lips, as many a man has been saved before you. You'd better sleep again now. . . ."

624

He slept, but there were visions as there had been all along. And two persons came in now and then. One was Tom Travis, serious and quiet and very much in earnest that the patient might get well.

Another was Tom's wife, Alice, who arranged the wounded man's pillows with a gentleness and deftness as only she could, and who gave quiet orders to the old cook in a way that made Richard Travis feel that things were all right, though he could not speak, nor even open his eyes long enough to see distinctly.

A month afterward Richard Travis was sitting up. His strength came very fast. For a week he had sat by the fire and thought — thought. But no man knew what was in his mind until one day, after he had been able to walk over the place, he said:

" Tom, you and Alice have been kinder to me — far kinder — than I have deserved. I am going away forever, next week — to the Northwest — and begin life over. But there is something I wish to say to you first."

" Dick," said his cousin, and he arose, tall and splendid, before the firelight —" there is something I wish to say to you first. Our lives have been far apart and very different, but blood is blood and you have proved it, else I had not been here to-night to tell it."

He came over and put his hand affectionately on the other's shoulder. At its touch Richard Travis softened almost to tears.

" Dick, we two are the only grandsons that bear his name, and we divide this between us. Alice and I have planned it. You are to retain the house and half the

40

land. We have our own and more than enough. You will do it, Dick? "

Richard Travis arose, strangely moved. He grasped his cousin's hand. " No, no, Tom, it is not fair. No Travis was ever a welcher. It is all yours — you do not understand — I saw the will — I do not want it. I am going away forever. My life must lead now in other paths. But—"

The other turned quickly and looked deep into Richard Travis's eyes. " I can see there is no use of my trying to change your mind, Dick, though I had hoped—"

The other shook his head. It meant a Travis decision, and his cousin knew it.

" But as I started to say, Tom, and there is no need of my mincing words, if you'll raise that boy of mine—" he was silent awhile, then smiling: " He is mine and more of a Travis to-day than his father ever was. If you can help him and his aunt—"

" He shall have the half of it, Dick, and an education, under our care. We will make a man of him, Alice and I."

Richard Travis said no more.

The week before he left, one beautiful afternoon, he walked over to Millwood for the last time. For Edward Conway was now sheriff of the county, and with the assistance of the old bishop, whose fortune now was secured, he had redeemed his home and was in a fair way to pay back every dollar of it.

A new servant ushered Travis in, for the good old nurse had passed away, the strain of that terrible night being too much, first, for her reason, and afterwards, her life.

Edward Conway was away, but Helen came in presently, and greeted him with such a splendid high-born way, so simple and so unaffected that he marveled at her self-control, feeling his own heart pulsing strangely at sight of her. In the few months that had elapsed how changed she was and how beautiful! This was not the romantic, yet buffetted, beautiful girl who had come so near being the tragedy of his old life? How womanly she now was, and how calm and at her ease! Could independence and the change from poverty and worry, the strong, free feeling of being one's self again and in one's sphere, make so great a difference in so short a while? He wondered at himself for not seeing farther ahead. He had come to bid her good-bye and offer again — this time in all earnestness and sincerity, to take her with him — to share his life — but the words died in his mouth.

He could no more have said them than he could have profanely touched her.

When he left she walked with him to the parting of the ways.

The blue line of tremulous mountain was scrolled along a horizon that flamed crimson in the setting sun. A flock of twilight clouds — flamingoes of the sky — floated toward the sunset as if going to roost. Beyond was the great river, its bosom as wan, where it lay in the shadow of the mountain, as Richard Travis's own cheek; but where the sunset fell on it the reflected light turned it to pink which to him looked like Helen's.

The wind came down cool from the frost-tinctured

mountain side, and the fine sweet odor of life everlasting
floated in it — frost-bitten — and bringing a wave of
youth and rabbit hunts and of a life of dreams and the
sweet unclouded far-off hope of things beautiful and immortal.   And the flow of it hurt Richard Travis — hurt
him with a tenderness that bled.

The girl stopped and drank in the beauty of it all, and
he stood looking at her, " the picture for the frame "—
as he said to himself.

It had rained and the clouds were scattered, yet so
full that they caught entirely the sunset rays and held
them as he would that moment have loved to hold her.
Something in her — something about her thrilled him
strangely, as he had often been thrilled when looking
at the great pictures in the galleries of the old world.
He repeated softly to her, as she stood looking forward
— to him — into the future:

" What thou art we know not,
    What is most like thee?
From rainbow clouds there flow not
    Drops so bright to see,
As from thy presence showers a rain of melody."

She turned and held out her hand.

" I must bid you good-bye now and I wish you all
happiness — so much more than you have ever had in
all your life."

He took it, but he could not speak.   Something shook
him strangely.   He knew nothing to say.   Had he spoken,
he knew he had stammered and blundered.

Never had the Richard Travis of old done such a thing.

"Helen — Helen — if — if — you know once I asked you to go with me — once — in the old, awful life. Now, in the new — the new life which you can make sweet —"

She came up close to him. The sun had set and the valley lay in silence. When he saw her eyes there were tears in them — tears so full and deep that they hurt him when she said:

"It can never — never be — now. You made me love you when you could not love; and love born of despair is mateless ever; it would die in its realization. Mine, for you, was that —" She pointed to the sunset. "It breathed and burned. I saw it only because of clouds, of shadow. But were the clouds, the shadows, gone —"

"There would be no life, no burning, no love," he said. "Ah, I think I understand," and his heart sank with pain. What — why — he could not say, only he knew it hurt him, and he began to wonder.

"You do not blame me," she said as she still held his hand and looked up into his eyes in the old way he had seen, that terrible night at Millwood.

For reply he held her hand in both of his and then laid it over his heart. She felt his tears fall on it, tears, which even death could not bring, had come to Richard Travis at last, and he wondered. In the old life he never wondered — he always knew; but in this — this new life — it was all so strange, so new that he feared even himself. Like a sailor lost, he could only look up, by day, helplessly at the sun, and, by night, helplessly at the stars.

" Helen — Helen," he said at last, strangely shaken in it all,— " if I could tell you now that I do — that I could love —"

She put her hand over his mouth in the old playful way and shook her head, smiling through her tears: " Do not try to mate my love with a thing that balks."

It was simply said, and forceful. It was enough. Richard Travis blushed for very shame.

" Do you not see," she said, " how hopeless it is? Do you not know that I was terribly tempted — weak — maddened — deserted that night? That now I know what Clay's love has been? Oh, why do we not learn early in life that fire will burn, that death will kill, that we are the deed of all we think and feel — the wish of all we will to be? "

Travis turned quickly: " Is that true? Then let me wish — as I do, Helen ; let me wish that I might love you as you deserve."

She saddened: " Oh, but you have wished — you have willed — too often — too differently. It can never be now."

" I understand you," he said. " It is natural — I should say it is nature — nature, the never-lying. I but reap my own folly, and now good-bye forever, Helen, and may God bless you and bring you that happiness you have deserved."

" Do you know," she said calmly, " that I have thought of all that, too. There are so many of us in the world, and so little happiness that like flowers it cannot go around — some must go without."

She held his hand tightly as if she did not want him
to go.

"My child, I must go out of your life — go — and
stay. I see — I see — and I only make you wretched.
And I have no right to. It is ignoble. It is I who should
bear this burden of sorrow — not you. You who have
never sinned, who are so young and so beautiful. In
time you will love a nobler man — Clay —"

She looked at him, but said nothing. She knew for
the first time the solution of her love's problem. She
was silent, holding his hand.

"Child," he said again. "Helen, you must do as I
say. There is happiness for you yet when I am gone —
when I am out of your life and the memory and the pain
of it cease. Then you will marry Clay —"

"Do you really think so? Oh, and he has loved me so
and is so splendid and true."

Travis was silent, waiting.

"Now let me go," she said —" let me forget all my
madness and folly in learning to love one whose love was
made for mine. In time I shall love him as he deserves.
Good-bye."

Then she broke impulsively away, and he watched her
walk back through the shadows and under the clouds.

At the turning of the path across the meadow, he saw
another shadow join her. It was Clay, and the two went
through the twilight together.

Travis turned. "It is right — it is the solution —
he alone deserves her. I must reap my past, reap it and
see my harvest blighted and bound with rotten twine.
But, oh, to know it when it is too late — to know that I

might love her and could be happy — then to have to give it up — now — now — when I need it most. The Deed," he said —" we are the deed of all we think and feel."

CHAPTER XXVI

THE discovery of coal and iron made both the old Bishop and Westmoreland rich. Captain Tom sent James Travis to West Point and Archie B. to Annapolis, and their records were worthy of their names.

And now, five years after the great fire, there might be seen in Cottontown, besides two furnaces, whose blazing turrets lighted the valley with Prosperity's torch — another cotton mill, erected by the old Bishop.

Long and earnestly he thought on the subject before building the mill. Indeed, he first prayed over it and then preached on the subject, and this is the sermon he preached to his people the Sunday before he began the erection of The Model Cotton Mill:

" Now, it's this way, my brethren: God made cotton for a mill. You can't get aroun' that; and the mill is to give people wuck an' this wuck is to clothe the worl'. That's all plain an' all good, because it's from God. Man made the bad of it — child labor, and overwuck and poor pay and the terrible everlastin' grind and foul air an' dirt an' squaller an' death.

" The trouble with the worl' to-day is that it don't carry God into business. Why should we not be kinder an' mo' liberal with each other in business matters? We

are unselfish in everything but business. All social life
is based on unselfishness. To charity we give of our
tears an' our money. For the welfare of mankind an'
the advancement of humanity you can always count us on
the right side. Even to those whose characters are rotten
an' whose very shadows leave dark places in life, we pass
the courtesies of the hour or the palaverin' compliments
of the day. But let the struggler for the bread of life
come along and ask us to share our profits with him, let
the dollar be the thing involved an' business shrewdness
the principle at stake, an' then all charity is forgotten,
every man for himse'f, an' the chief aim of man seems to
be to get mo' out of the trade than his brother.

" Now the soul of trade is Selfishness, an' Charity
never is invited over her doorway.

" I have known men with tears in their eyes to give
to the poor one day an' rob them the nex' in usurious interest an' rent, as cheerful as they gave the day befo'. I
have known men to open their purses as wide as the gates
of hades for some church charity, an' then close them the
nex' day, in a business transaction, as they called it —
with some helpless debtor or unexperienced widder. The
graveyard is full of unselfish, devoted fathers an' husbands who worked themselves to death for the comfort
an' support of their own families, yet spendin' their days
on earth tryin' to beat their neighbors in the same game.

" It's funny how we're livin'. It's amusin', it is —
our ethics of Christianity. We've baptised everything
but business. We give to the church an' rob the poor.
We weep over misfortune an' steal from the unfortunate.
We give a robe to Charity one day and filch it the nex'.

We lay gifts at the altar of the Temple of Kindness for the Virgin therein, but if we caught her out on the highways of trade an' commerce we'd steal her an' sell her into slavery. An' after she was dead we'd go deep into our pockets to put up a monument over her!

"We weep an' rob, an' smile an' steal, an' laugh an' knife, an' wring the hand of friendship while we step on her toes with our brogans of business. Can't we be hones' without bein' selfish, fair without graspin', make a profit without wantin' it all? Is it possible that Christ's religion has gone into every nook an' corner of the worl' an' yet missed the great highway of business, the everyday road of dollars an' cents, profit an' loss!

"So I am goin' to build the mill an' run it like God intended it should be run, an' I am goin' to put, for once, the plan of salvation into business, if it busts me an' the plan too! For if it can't stand a business test it ought to bust!"

He planned it all himself, and, aided by Captain Tom, and Alice, the beautiful structure went up. Strong and airy and with every comfort for the workers. "For it strikes me," said the old man, "that the people who wuck need mo' comforts than them that don't — at least the comforts of bein' clean. The fust thing I learned in geography was that God made three times as much water on the sufface of the earth as he did dirt. But you wouldn't think so to look at the human race. It takes us a long time to take a hint."

The big mountain spring settled the point, and when the mill was finished there were hot and cold baths in it for the tired workers. "For there's nothin' so good," said the old man, " for a hot man or a hot hoss as a warm body-wash. It relaxes the muscles an' makes them come ag'in. An' the man that comes ag'in is the man the worl' wants."

In the homes of the workers, too, he had baths placed, until it grew to be a saying of the good old man " that it was easier to take a bath in Cottontown than to take a drink."

The main building was lofty between floor and ceiling, letting in all the light and air possible, and the floors were of hard-wood and clean. As the greatest curse of the cotton lint was dust, atomizers for spraying the air were invented by Captain Tom. These were attached to the machinery and could be turned off or on as the operators desired. It was most comfortable now to work in the mill, and tired and hot employees, instead of lounging through their noon, bathed in the cool spring water which came down from the mountain side and flowed into the baths, not only in the mill, but through every cottage owned by the mill. And as the bath is the greatest civilizer known to man, a marked difference was soon noticed in every inhabitant of Cottontown. They were cleanly, and cleanliness begets a long list of other virtues, beginning with cleaner and better clothes and ending with ambition and godliness.

But it was the old Bishop's policy for the wage-earners, which put the ambition there — a system never heard of before in the ranks of capital, and first tested and proved in his Model Cotton Mill.

" There are two things in the worl'," said the Bishop, " that is as plain as God could write them without tellin' it Himself from the clouds. The first is that the money of the worl' was intended for all the worl' that reaches out a hand an' works for it.

" The other is that every man who works is entitled to a home.

" It was never intended for one man, or one corporation or one trust or one king or one anything else, to own more than his share of the money of the worl', no matter how they get it. Every man who piles up mo' money than he needs — actually needs — in life, robs every other man or woman or child in the worl' that pinches and slaves and starves for it in vain. Every man who makes a big fortune leaves just that many wrecked homes in his path."

In carrying out this idea the old bishop had the mill incorporated at one hundred thousand dollars, which included all his fortune, except enough to live on and educate his grandchildren; for he never changed his home, and the only luxury he indulged in was a stable for Ben Butler.

The stock was divided into shares of ten dollars each, which could be acquired only by those who worked in the mill, to be held only during life-time, and earned only in part payment for labor, given according to proficiency and work done, and credited on wages. In this way every employee of the mill became a stockholder — a partner in the mill, receiving dividends on his stock in addition to his regular wages, and every year he worked in the mill added both to his stock and dividends. At death it reverted again to The Model Cotton Mill Company, to be obtained again, in turn, by other mill workers

coming on up the line. This made every mill worker a
partner in the mill and spurred them on to do their best.

But the home idea of the bishop was the more original
one, and a far greater boon to the people. Instead of
paying rent to the mill for their homes, as they had before, every married mill worker was deeded a home in the
beginning, a certain per cent. of his wages being appropriated each month in part payment; in addition, ten
per cent. of the stock acquired, as above, by each indivi-
dual home owner, went to the payment of the home, and
the whole was so worked out and adjusted that by the
time a faithful worker had arrived at middle age, the
home, as paid for, was absolutely his and his children's,
and when he arrived at old age the dividends of the stock
acquired were sufficient to support him the balance of his
life.

In this way the mill was virtually resolved into a corporation or community of interests, running perpetually
for the maintenance and support of those who worked in
it. The only property actually acquired by the indivi-
dual was a home, his savings in wages, and the dividends
on his stock acquired by long service and work.

Some wanted the old man to run a general store on
the same plan of community of interest, the goods and
necessities of life to be bought at first cost and only the
actual expenses of keeping the store added. But he
wisely shook his head, saying: "No, that will not do;
that's forming a trust ag'in the tillers of the earth an'
the workers in every other occupation. That's cuttin' in
on hones' competition, an' if carried out everywhere

would shut off the rest of the worl' from a livin'. We're makin' our livin'— let them make theirs."

The old bishop was proud of the men he selected to carry out his plans. Captain Tom was manager of the Model Mill.

" Now," said the old man, after the mill had run two years and declared a semi-annual dividend, both years, of eight per cent. each, " now you all see what it means to run even business by the Golden Rule. Here is this big fortune that I accidentally stumbled on, as everybody does who makes one — put out like God intended it sh'ud, belonging to nobody and standing there, year after year, makin' a livin' an' a home an' life an' happiness for over fo' hundred people, year in an' year out, an' let us pray God, forever. It was not mine to begin with — it belonged to the worl'. God put the coal and iron in the ground, not for me, but for everybody. An' so I've given it to everybody. Because I happened to own the lan' didn't make the treasure God put there mine, any mo' than the same land will be mine after I've passed away. We're only trustees for humanity for all we make mo' than we need, jus' as we're only tenants of God while we live on the earth."

As for children, the bishop settled that quickly and effectively. His rule was that no boy or girl under sixteen should be permitted to work in the mill, and to save any parents, weakly inclined, from the temptation, he established a physical standard in weight, height and health.

He found afterwards there was really small need of

his stringent rule, for under this system of management the temptations of child labor were removed.

Among the good features of the mill, established by Alice Travis, was a library, a pretty little building in the heart of Cottontown. It was maintained yearly by the mill, together with donations, and proved to be the greatest educational and refining influence of the mill. It was kept, for one week at a time, by each girl in the mill over twenty, the privilege always being given by the mill's physician to the girl who seemed most in need of a week's rest. It came to be a great social feature also, and any pretty afternoon, and all Saturday afternoon,— for the mill never ran then — could be seen there the young girls and boys of Cottontown.

To this was afterwards added a Cottontown school for the younger children, who before had been slaves to the spinner and doffer carts.

And so it ran on several years, but still the Bishop could see that something was lacking — that there was too much sickness, that in spite of only eight hours his people, year in and year out, grew tired and weak and disheartened, and with his great good sense he put his finger on it.

" Now, it's this a-way," he said to his directors, " God never intended for any people to work all the time between walls an' floors. Tilling the soil is the natural work of man, an' there is somethin' in the very touch of the ground to our feet that puts new life in our bodies.

" The farmin' instinct is so natural in us that you can't stop it by flood or drought or failure. Year in an' year out the farmer will plant an' work his crop in spite

of failure, hopin' every year to hit it the nex' time.
Would a merchant or manufacturer or anybody else do
that? No, they'd make an assignment the second year
of failure. But not so with the farmer, and it shows
God intended he shu'd keep at it.

"Now, I'm goin' to give this mill a chance to raise
its own cotton, besides everything else its people needs to
eat. I figger we can raise cotton cheaper than we can
buy it, an' keep our folks healthy, too."

Near Cottontown was an old cotton plantation of four
thousand acres. It had been sadly neglected and run
down. This the bishop purchased for the company for
only ten dollars an acre, and divided it into tracts of
twenty acres each, building a neat cottage, dairy and
barn, and other outhouses on each tract — but all arranged for a family of four or five, and thus sprang up
in a year a new settlement of two hundred families around
Cottontown. It was no trouble to get them, for the
fame of The Model Mill had spread, and far more applied yearly for employment than could be accommo-
dated. This large farm, when equipped fully, represented fifty thousand dollars more, or an investment of
ninety thousand dollars, and immediately became a valuable asset of the mill.

It was divided into four parts, each under the super-
vision of a manager, a practical and experienced cotton
farmer of the valley, and the tenants were selected every
year from among all the workers of the mill, preference
always being given to the families who needed the out-
door work most, and those physically weak from long
work in the mill. It was so arranged that only fifty

41

families, or one-fourth of the mill, went out each year, staying four years each on the farm. And thus every four years were two hundred families given the chance in the open to get in touch with nature, the great physician, and come again. After four years they went back to the mill, sunburnt, swarthy, and full of health, and what is greater than health,— cheerfulness — the cheerfulness that comes with change.

On the farm they received the same wages as when in the mill, and each family was furnished with a mule, a cow, and poultry, and with a good garden.

To reclaim this land and build up the soil was now the chief work of the old man; but having been overseer on a large cotton plantation, he knew his business, and set to work at it with all the zeal and good sense of his nature.

He knew that cotton was one of the least exhaustive crops of the world, taking nearly all its sustenance from the air, and that it was also one of the most easily raised, requiring none of the complicated and expensive machinery necessary for wheat and other smaller grains. He knew, too, that under the thorough preparation of the soil necessary for cotton, wheat did best after it, and with clover sown on the wheat, he would soon have nature's remedy for reclaiming the soil. He also knew that the most expensive feature of cotton raising was the picking — the gathering of the crop — and in the children of Cottontown, he saw at once that he had a quick solution — one which solved the picking problem and yet gave to each growing boy and girl three months, in the cool, delightful fall, of healthful work, with pay more than equal to a year of the old cheap labor behind the spinners. For,— as it proved, at seventy-five cents per hundred pounds for the seed cotton picked,— these children earned from seventy-five cents to a dollar and a half a day. The first year, only half of the land was put in cotton, attention being given to reclaiming the other half. But even this proved a surprise for all, for nearly one thousand bales of cotton were ginned, at a total cost to the mill of only four cents per pound, while Cottontown had been fed during summer with all the vegetables and melons needed — all raised on the farm.

That fall, the land, under the clean and constant plowing necessary to raise the cotton, was ready to sow in wheat, which in February was followed with clover — nature's great fertilizer — the clover being sown broadcast on the wheat, behind a light harrow run over the wheat. The wheat crop was small, averaging less than ten bushels to the acre, but it was enough to keep all Cottontown in bread for a year, or until the next harvest time, and some, even, to sell. Behind the wheat, after it was mowed, came the clover, bringing in good dividends. After two years, it was turned under, and then it was that the two thousand acres of land produced fifteen hundred bales of cotton at a total cost of four cents per pound, or twenty dollars per bale. And this included everything, even the interest on the money and the paying of seventy-five cents per hundred pounds to the Cottontown children for picking and storing the crop.

In a few years, under this rotation, the farm produced all the cotton necessary to run The Model Mill, besides raising all its vegetables, fruit, and bread for all the families of Cottontown.

But the most beautiful sight to the old man was to see the children every fall picking the cotton. Little boys and girls, who before had worked twelve hours a day in the old, hot, stifling, ill-smelling mill, now stood out in the sunshine and in the frosty air of the mornings, each with sack to side, waist deep in pure white cotton, flooded in sunshine and health and sweetness.

They were deft with their fingers — the old mill had taught many of them that — and their pay, daily, ran from seventy-five cents to a dollar and a half — as much as some of them had earned in a week of the old way. And, oh, the health of it, the glory of air and sky and sunshine, the smell of dew on the bruised cotton-heads, the rustle of the mountain breeze cooling the heated cheeks; the healthy hunger, and the lunches in the shade by the cool spring; the shadows of evening creeping down from the mountains, the healthy fatigue — and the sweet home-going in the twilight, riding beneath the silent stars on wagons of snowy seed cotton, burrowing in bed of down and purest white — this snow of a Southern summer — with the happy laughter of childhood and the hunger of home-coming, and the glory and freedom of it all!

THE END.